THIS
BRIGHT
RIVER

ALSO BY PATRICK SOMERVILLE

The Universe in Miniature in Miniature

The Cradle: A Novel

Trouble: Stories

THIS
BRIGHT
RIVER

A NOVEL

PATRICK SOMERVILLE

A REAGAN ARTHUR BOOK
LITTLE, BROWN AND COMPANY
NEW YORK   BOSTON   LONDON

Copyright © 2012 by Patrick Somerville

Reagan Arthur Books / Little, Brown and Company
Hachette Book Group
237 Park Avenue, New York, NY 10017
www.hachettebookgroup.com

First Edition: June 2012

Reagan Arthur Books is an imprint of Little, Brown and Company, a division of Hachette Book Group, Inc. The Reagan Arthur Books name and logo are trademarks of Hachette Book Group, Inc.

The publisher is not responsible for websites (or their content) that are not owned by the publisher.

The Hachette Speakers Bureau provides a wide range of authors for speaking events. To find out more, go to www.hachettespeakersbureau.com or call (866) 376-6591.

Library of Congress Cataloging-in-Publication Data
Somerville, Patrick.
    This bright river : a novel / Patrick Somerville. — 1st ed.
        p. cm.
    Summary: "Lauren Sheehan's career in medicine came to a halt after a sequence of violent events abroad. Now she's back in the safest place she knows — St. Helens, Wisconsin — cut off from career, friendship, and romance. Ben Hanson's aimless life bottomed out when he went to prison. But after his release, a surprising offer from his father draws him home. In Wisconsin, he finds his family fractured, still unable to face the truth behind his troubled cousin's death a decade earlier. As Lauren cautiously expands her world and Ben tries to unravel the mysteries of his family and himself, their paths intersect. Could each be exactly what the other needs? A compelling family drama and a surprising love story, THIS BRIGHT RIVER confirms Patrick Somerville's status as one of the most exciting young writers at work today." — Provided by publisher.
    ISBN 978-0-316-12931-2 (hardback)
    1. Single women — Fiction. 2. Ex-convicts — Fiction. 3. Wisconsin — Fiction.
4. Domestic fiction. I. Title.
    PS3619.O45T48 2012
    813'.6 — dc23   2011046159

10 9 8 7 6 5 4 3 2 1

RRD-C

Printed in the United States of America

For AJ and LS

4213126

The language of the river was scarcely less enchanting than that of the wind and rain; the sublime overboom of the main bouncing, exulting current, the swash and gurgle of the eddies, the keen dash and clash of heavy waves breaking against rocks, and the smooth, downy hush of shallow currents feeling their way through the willow thickets of the margin. And amid all this varied throng of sounds I heard the smothered bumping and rumbling of boulders on the bottom as they were shoving and rolling forward against one another in a wild rush, after having lain still for probably 100 years or more.

— JOHN MUIR

Find the cost of freedom buried in the ground.

— STEPHEN STILLS

THIS
BRIGHT
RIVER

January

Some Frozen Night
Madison, Wisconsin

He's been drinking with this guy for a long time.
It's good.
It was a rough day and this just sort of happened. The guy sat down and ordered a bourbon, neat, and after ten minutes of silence, the two of them saying nothing and drinking their drinks, looking up at the TV, they started to chat. First about the basketball game, then about campus, then about classes, then about the cold. Then women.
"There are amazing women in this town," he says. "You know? It's crazy."
"College towns."
"That could be it."
He's completely drunk now, and he can't see very well, but he's been talking a lot, he's sort of opened up to this guy, and the guy has continued to listen. He likes him. He's a listener. He likes anyone who will listen to him when he gets going on a rant, but he likes this guy specifically because he's tuned in. Listening in that good way. Bars are funny and it's tough for two strangers to start talking because everybody's got a thousand friends and everything is a party and everyone's always on the way somewhere, and somehow he doesn't have any friends anymore. But apparently this guy

came here to do the same thing: sit down alone and drink out the gremlins.

"We make a good pair," he says. "You know? We're like Pancho and Lefty."

The guy nods. "Yes. Totally."

Gremlins is the word he uses when he thinks about everything bad within himself.

"I'm completely feeling it right now."

The guy says he is too.

They're both quiet for a bit.

The guy asks him if he wants to go get high.

He considers.

Then: "Yes," he says, nodding at his drink, furrowing his brow, very serious about it, because sometimes he has panic attacks and he doesn't want that to happen this time. "I think I do. Let's keep it going."

"Okay," says the guy. "Let's go."

They both put on their jackets, get up, and walk out of the smoky bar.

Outside it's freezing, but it's a nice relief from all the cigarette smoke.

The guy says, "I'm parked down here. Around the corner."

"This'll be interesting," he says, raising his eyebrows, following the guy.

He doesn't really know what he means, he thinks, looking down at his feet, watching them walk him. Everyone in Madison's a pothead, though. It's a real thing.

They turn off State Street, cross Johnson, and walk down Henry.

He's sort of sick of it. He's sick of a lot of things. It's dark here. Pretty much everyone is a pothead.

"That's an awesome jacket," says the guy.

"Yeah?" he says, looking down at his own sleeve. "I never thought about it." In truth he has not.

"It's just so cold. That looks warm."

"It is."

"I have this thing, but it's never as warm as it seems like it should be, you know? I mean, for the money I paid. It eats it."

"I actually like it."

"What?"

"I like yours. You like mine. We should switch."

"But people never actually do things like that, you know."

"That's accurate."

"Did you say you lived here? Or you're visiting?"

"I live here."

"Me too."

"I'm not sure how I feel about it."

"Okay, right here," the guy says, nodding at a car. They both stop by the door.

"Cool."

"Here we are."

"Cool."

"Cool," the guy says back.

The guy unlocks the door, leans in, reaches across to the glove compartment, and rustles around.

Now the guy's got something in his hand.

"You wanna just smoke on the street?" he says, squinting at the thing in his hand. "Or what? Maybe we should just sit in your car? It is cold. I knew it was cold, but I didn't know it was this cold." And it's an amazing thing, he thinks, how cold it gets, and how nevertheless we usually do okay. He has something of a moment while pondering this.

Take hypothermia. Take, for instance, the stories of the lost men who wander away from their trapped vehicles in search of roads, in search of cars, in search of help. Even as a child, he was terrified by these stories. Usually there is a family left behind. Maybe a mother and an infant. There's no more gas and they've been there for days and they've finally run out of crackers. The father decides he has to go for help. He's tried to be reasonable up to this point, but it's now or never. He leaves the car and goes out in a blizzard. He walks around in circles and almost always dies frozen, alone, and excruciatingly close to his starting point.

As a child, he would hear these stories and think to himself: How could this be possible? How could something so terrible and cruel even be possible? But this is what nature does to people.

"No," says the guy. "I don't want to smoke on the street."

The tone of the guy's voice awakens him from his brief, mediocre reverie. "Where, then?" he says.

"It's not that," says the guy. "I'm sorry about this. I really am, dude. I'm actually going to kill you now."

He looks.

"What did you say?"

"It's the principle," the guy says.

Then the guy hits him over the head with whatever he's got in his hand.

~~~~~

When he comes to, he's confused, and what he worries about first, for some reason, is the smell. It smells like wet towels. Musty. Moldy. It's terrifying to smell it. Then he worries because he doesn't know how much time has passed, then he worries because he starts to remember.

It's pitch-black now, not just dark, and he can hear the sounds of the road.

It's cold.

It takes him a few minutes of careful thinking to remember the bar in detail, to remember the guy, to remember that they left the bar, and to make sense of the pain in his skull. He hit him. The guy hit him in the head.

Eventually, the pieces all tumble together.

He's contorted in here.

He scrapes around in the dark, remembering what the guy said at the end.

He said it was the principle.

He scrapes around some more, tries to push.

He starts to pound.

At some point he starts to scream.

I

THE WANDERERS

First learn the meaning of what you say, and then speak.

—Epictetus

1

Regarding the Unreliable Jesuit Explorer Pierre Bettencourt

Sleep on the plane.

Dream of the ancient ocean I am leaving and a farewell glance at the tops of mountains I have not climbed.

O'Hare, then, changed in an unsayable way, but changed alongside the grays and whites and moving walkways, people drifting with their rolling bags, the smell of the Cinnabon, and the wedge-shaped line at the corner McDonald's.

A disembodied voice compels the sea of walkers to part from behind; we watch as his beeping white cart crawls through the gap we've created, and he nods his chill thanks, chewing his gum and wearing his three-piece United Airlines suit like a tuxedo. An elderly couple is aboard his vessel, seated on the back puff seats, facing stern, facing us, eyes sleepy as heads rock left, right, absorbing buffets. They get to ride because they are so old.

Bubblers.

Children run the wrong way on the moving walkway and therefore have no motion.

A girl asleep with her back against a white pillar in an empty gate, and she's in her pajamas, as though she knew that it would come to this.

Planes like toys I used to fly with arm-power, drifting down to land, parking on the tarmac. I see them through the windows.

Shoeshine guys have a station against the wall.

And then the Quiznos, and I know that I am closer.

〰〰

We'd heard about the vandalism from the cops, but even so, neither of my parents had been able to drive up to see the fallout for themselves. Since Denny was the last of our relatives to be living in Wisconsin, no one else had been up to see either, and all we knew about the Fourth of July party came down to a phone call, a county sheriff's PDF, and the phrase *significant damage* scribbled in a few pieces of mail. You never knew what a cop might label as significant, though; it could be understatement or overstatement. Most cops I'd known saw the world through the wrong end of a broken telescope.

On the way into St. Helens proper I considered stopping at Golden's to pick up cleaning supplies, but I hesitated at the turn-off, then drifted by the entrance to the store, foot up over the brake. Too soon for any of that, I decided. I figured I'd survey the damage first and see what needed to be done. I was tired and not used to driving, and I wanted to take a shower. At this point I was also three steps past disgusting.

I went by, kept straight, and a few minutes later I was halfway up the hill, and a few minutes after that, I was there. The turn into Denny's driveway came back to me like I'd done it the week before.

Looking at the garage door, I killed the engine and rolled my neck in a stretch, marveled (as far as I could marvel) at how far a person could go in one day, especially if he put his mind to it and was wired enough dollars from his parents.

I'd flown from Seattle to Chicago on an early flight and taken a cab out to Peregrine Park, where I'd had to stop to pick up the car — which, according to my father, was now my car, registered in my name. It was a Nissan Maxima with a sewing machine for an engine. I had ignored my parents' request that I spend a night at their place and instead headed directly to Denny's, fearing that an evening in their home would begin with an unrelenting assault on my decision-making skills and conclude with the usual half-drunk sales pitch about permanently moving back to the Midwest. I did not want to hear it.

I played with the moon roof. I looked at the clouds. I looked back at the house.

I was thirty-two now, absurdly, and as far as I could remember, the last time I had been here was twelve years ago, when I was half-way through college and drove out from Madison for a weekend visit. It was a two-story cottage-style home made of what I thought might be limestone; I'd never really noticed how nice — how strong? sturdy? — it was when I was a kid. Now it struck me as a small keep, really. Not in perfect shape by any means, but a keep nonetheless.

I glanced over my shoulder at Jeremy's computer, still snug down behind the passenger seat. I needed a monitor to do anything with it. I probably needed to talk to Jeremy too, as I had stolen it on my way out of Washington.

I started the engine again, turned up the air conditioner, and called my sister.

"I'm here," I said. "I've made it to Constantinople."

"Welcome home," she said. "I'm there." Which meant Boston. "Does St. Helens look the same?" she asked. "I always wonder. Are there Moors?"

"Wonder when?"

"When I think about St. Helens."

"I don't know," I said. "Yes? I didn't actually go into town. I did just go past Golden's, though. Totally weird."

She had worked at the grocery store too, but she and I intersected as employees for only a couple of months. She was the object of desire for many of the other bagboys, who never did much to hide their attraction to her when I was around. One kid, with whom I often faced the shelves at night, once turned to me to whisper, with grave seriousness, that he would give me upwards of fifty dollars if I brought him a pair of my sister's panties. This kid was named Will Normal. One hundred if they were used, he said, which to me, at that age — and still, actually — made no erotic sense.

Back then there was a rumor circulating — these were the last months Haley lived in town, before she left to go to Choate — that she'd gotten involved with one of the managers, a man named Rick Hagan, who was married and in his early forties. People gave me shit about Haley and her looks all the time. I hated it. Will Normal, who I think ended up a semitruck driver in Canada, was the worst of them. His teeth had been like almonds.

When I confronted her about the Rick rumor a few nights before she left town, Haley laughed and said, "Um, no."

"So it's not true," I said, watching her pack, because I wanted to know, and a part of me felt as though my sister was capable of it. I had already slashed Will Normal's tires, but that hadn't been about revenge so much as it was just to feel better.

"You're asking me if I'm banging Rick, the four-hundred-year-old night manager at Golden's, the grocery store where we work? Because some bagboy said so?"

"Yes."

"No, Ben. I'm not having sex with Rick." She dropped an

INXS T-shirt into the suitcase. "And this is why I am leaving," she said. "Exactly this."

"What?"

"*This*," she said, making two circles with her hands, Miyagi-like, I suppose to indicate the whole world around us and everything that was wrong with it.

Remembering this, thirty-two-year-old me leaned back into the seat and laid a hand on the wheel. "I'm sure the town is the same," I said. "Time stands still here, like it does in a postcard. Or something. Right?"

"Or in hell."

I guessed Haley would add some withering condemnation of the people here next, something along the lines of St. Helens being populated by the modern cultural equivalent of fourteenth-century peasantry, her usual attitude about Wisconsin, but she said nothing. I looked at a cloud of bugs floating in front of Denny's garage, and then to the right, at the frame of an unfinished fence. It occurred to me that Denny had been the one who'd been working on it. And I knew my uncle. I knew how annoyed he would have been, had he still existed, that he'd left something partially finished.

We lingered in the silence.

"So?" I said eventually. "Anything new?"

"With John?"

"Yeah."

"He's back in Winchester at his parents' house, living in the room where he grew up, masturbating into his socks."

"That's nice."

"The maid's doing his laundry and he's golfing with his father in the afternoons. He's finally figured out how to crawl back into his own adolescence. It turned out to be easy."

"John masturbates into his socks?" I asked. I frowned at the garage door. It seemed so uncomfortable.

"That's his way."

The situation regarding John Carraway, my sister's husband, was simple on the surface, but the whole thing became a little more complicated if you'd spent any time with him and knew him, as I did, as a pretty decent fellow. Beyond the adultery. He was a soft-spoken, sensitive, balding Episcopalian from Connecticut who enjoyed birding and had studied classics at Yale, where he and Haley first met. (He liked watching squirrels too, although it's possible this was just a deeply weird joke Haley liked to tell that I'd never understood.) He was an industrial-machinery executive — sinecure — who traveled a great deal, and a few months before, on some Tuesday night in St. Louis, idling in his rental car on a street corner in the Landing, he had managed to get himself arrested by a police officer who was posing as a hooker.

This had happened on a bleak night in March, and for weeks afterward John tried to conceal his arrest from my sister and from his employers. I found there to be great disharmony to it all. I didn't know what to think and I was doing my best to stay out of it. Maybe it was a one-time thing. Maybe not. It was very hard to tell. For all I knew John had been doing this for years and years, possibly even running around with his penis out while chasing unsuspecting female bird enthusiasts through the woods of New England. The point is that it's hard to know a person.

In the end it was just a piece of mail about his trial date that came while he was out of town that got him caught. Haley opened it; that's it. She found his mug shot online and e-mailed me the link a few days after she kicked him out of the house, but his company still didn't know, and so far my sister had stopped herself from telling John's bosses, who were all a part of their social circle.

She'd admitted to me that she'd been tempted more than once. Our parents didn't know. They just knew about the separation.

John and Haley had three kids, two girls and a boy, and that made things, according to Haley, complicated.

I was trying to have no opinion.

"Things will be better when school starts again and it's just me and the baby," Haley said. "I'll have more time to kill myself."

"I think you should come up here for a visit."

I did want to see her. How had she aged; how did it seem in the flesh? What had the middle of her thirties done to her? What might Haley look like walking through the downtown streets of St. Helens, where she hadn't been in almost twenty years? Where she had once been a kind of queen? Time-related questions abounded. I had not seen her in almost five years. There were different explanations for this, but most of it was my fault.

"We'll see."

Denny had a couple of flower beds dappled across the front yard, and I couldn't remember whether they'd been there before. They were just the kinds of things Denny would have insisted on putting in himself, and I imagined him at work, hauling rocks in a wheelbarrow on a Sunday morning.

From the look of the woods at the end of the yard and Denny's brown lawn, it had been a dry summer here. I would need to put sprinklers out for the grass. Nothing alive in the flower beds anymore — instead of color, just patches of vertical twigs.

"So how are you?" said my sister.

Which meant: Now let's talk about your fucked-up life instead.

"Good," I said. "I made it. I guess that's it."

"Is it feeling like the right decision?"

"I don't know yet."

Which was totally true, I wasn't just avoiding. There was more to the story than my sister needed to know, though; a lot of it had to do with Jeremy and Allie, and the game, and not feeling comfortable in my own skin out west since my release, where I had been walking the streets of Southeast like a zombie, doing very little. How do I say it without putting people off? We've only just met. For some time I'd been feeling as though my whole self were coated in Novocain.

In the silence, I could hear her trying to figure out what could have gone so wrong for me in Portland, post-Chestik, that I would actually agree to my father's recent proposal. Then I heard the clinks of her pouring wine.

Haley and John lived in some part of Boston the name of which I could never recall — something that sounded like an English fiefdom — and from what I could gather, the place was large, expensive, and sterile. John's family was already rich, and Haley still had her trust fund, and between the two of them and all that wealth, they'd made themselves even wealthier. Unlike me, my sister inherited our father's gift for understanding the flow of money in the river of the American economy, and I suspected she and he engaged in late-night chats, both of them drinking sixteen-year Glenlivet, discussing aspects of the day's stock exchange action that made little sense to anyone but the 1 percent. The 1 percent of the 1 percent.

On top of this intuitive savvy, Haley worked too — she did IT consulting, usually from home, under the aegis of a company she'd created. Her clients were multinational corporations I had never heard of. Sinetco, based in Singapore. Lorent. One-word corporations, the kind with no function in the eyes of a regular person, the kind that did not pay taxes, the kind that spent money bulldozing the bodies of indigenous peoples into tremendous holes in order to make room for resource exploitation. (Or so I cynically imagined. In truth, I just knew nothing. At this moment in my life, my only real areas of expertise concerned ultra-obscure strains of genetically enhanced marijuana and backgammon strategy; it made me defensive to think that my sister knew so much more than I did about the world.) What I did know: her hourly consulting rate was more than I had ever legitimately earned in a week.

"Have you found a meeting yet?" she asked.

"I got here ten minutes ago," I said.

"And?"

"And leave me alone."

"Why?"

"Do you think Denny has internet?"

"I think so," she said. "We used to e-mail. Has anyone been paying his bills?"

"Mom has."

"You have it then."

"You and Denny used to e-mail?"

"Why do you say it like that?"

"I didn't know he even had an e-mail address."

"Of course he did," she said. "It's not 1996, Benjy."

"I thought he only used Pony Express."

"I think we've moved into a time in history when all people have e-mail addresses."

"You actually think that?"

"The Luddite thing is not as compelling as you think it is."

"As though most of the world isn't poor and without plumbing, let alone internet?"

"Oh my God," she said. "I mean among people who matter."

"Do you know how much you sometimes sound like our father?"

"Often."

"It's gross."

"It's totally on purpose."

"You should not be proud of that."

"Denny had a Facebook account too," she said, ignoring this. "Didn't you know that? When he died I put something up on his wall, just a little RIP note. It turned into a memorial. People all posted things, remembrances. You know. E-funeral. That's what happens now. We may as well not even have bodies. We are the cloud."

"I've never understood Facebook," I said.

"I've been trying to e-mail them about Denny's account. And tell them that he's, you know...not alive."

"What a bizarre thing to have to do."

"But yesterday I was thinking — don't you think it would make sense for them to give us his password and just let us into his account?"

"How come?"

"I think it would be nice to set up a kind of permanent memorial. Or so we can take the page down, eventually. Otherwise he's going to be up there forever. It creeps me out."

"I have no idea what that even means," I said.

"Of course you don't."

"You can handle all of that. I'll handle his house."

I looked at his fence.

"I'll finish the fence."

〰〰

The good news was that it turned out *significant damage* was not that significant. The house was not trashed — not according to my understanding of trashed, anyway, which was essentially unlimited. Yes, there were small signs. There was a coffee can full of cigarettes sitting on the kitchen table (I found that to be thoughtful, actually), a couple of broken glasses in the sink, lots of bottles, and the smell of stagnant alcohol about the place. However, but for a half-empty bottle of Colt 45 on the coffee table, on a coaster, Denny's living room had been untouched. It really wasn't so bad. The kids who'd had the party had kept themselves confined to the kitchen and the back porch, and I spent a few moments imagining the scene, imagining all of them around the table, laughing and drinking, not in the least bit disturbed by their surroundings, a dead man's home, just glad to have found a place where they were safe — or so they thought. An insomniac jogger had been the one to do them in; at 3:00 a.m., he'd seen the cars in the driveway. And that's all it ever takes, isn't it? An intercepted e-mail, an unexpected jogger. A lost number. A rock in the wrong place. A man who can't sleep who happens to be somewhere he usually isn't.

I found that the sheets were a little messed up in Denny's bedroom, but who knew whether that had been the work of the kids or just the remnants of Denny's last morning on Earth. There could very well have been teenager sex here, I thought, surveying. Some lines I would not cross. I couldn't decide, though, thinking about my uncle, whether he was the type to make the bed right away.

In the end I stripped it and took the heap of sheets downstairs and stuffed everything into the washing machine.

Upstairs, in the living room, I sat on the couch for a few minutes, sniffing at the air, trying to judge whether I was going to have to steam-clean the carpet, then just trying not to nod off. If I did now, there would be no chance of sleep tonight. So, lids heavy, I spied Denny's record player in the built-in bookshelf across the room and got up to browse.

I found the CSNY right away.

I got some water, sat back down.

Stared at the wall.

"Suite: Judy Blue Eyes."

〜〜〜〜

A little background as the song plays:

My sinecure was to guard the house. It was my job to clean it up, fix it up, and do whatever needed to be done in order to usher it onto the market and get it sold. For my services as flipper and resident, per insane agreement with my father, I was to receive 25 percent on the sale, which was a stupid percentage for the work I would be doing, but my father was aware that my whole trust was shot, and he had to have suspicions about the extent of my debt too. He knew for sure that I had nothing, is what I'm saying, and he had found a way to give me, at the very least, ground upon which I might potentially stand. Again.

They'd inherited Denny's house, but my parents wanted nothing to do with the place. My dad thought it was haunted by his brother's ghost; I think the whole thing just made my mother sad beyond words and that she couldn't bear to think of Denny dying alone in the basement sanding a table, like he had. She never wanted to see the house again, she said.

That was all well and good and would have been no trouble in 2002, but now, because the real estate market had tanked — especially for old, unusual homes in little Wisconsin towns, and ones that needed work, to boot — there was no telling how long it would take to sell. After the Independence Day fiesta, the pressure had gone up. Now my parents thought of the house as more of a liability than an asset. What if those kids had burned it down and fried themselves during their party? What if snakes took over the basement? You know all the nightmares. What if "hoboes" began to squat? The risks were intolerable.

My dad called Portland in July.

"I have an alternative to your reprehensible plan to travel around the world, Ben. You might call it a favor."

I had happened upon a copy of *Eat, Pray, Love* at the bookstore and had sent my parents a postcard telling them that I was going to do it too.

"I'm not traveling around the world," I said. "That was a joke."

"We have an alternative."

He explained his fears about Denny's house.

"Why don't you just sell it for half of what it's worth," I said, "and just be done with it? It's not like you need the money. And there's no mortgage anymore."

He laughed.

This was a nice July day out west. I was sitting on my front porch in Portland with a cup of coffee resting on my stomach, my feet up, crossed over the white paint chips of my railing, book (Vonnegut, *Galápagos*) hugging the arm of the chair, glad we had the sun. It was July 13, I think, a Sunday, and I hadn't seen my mother or father since May, when they'd come to visit after my release and we'd spent three uncomfortable days going out to meal after meal in the nicest Portland restaurants, only to sit in an awkward triangle around the different tables as I said nothing about my time in Chestik and my mother attempted to keep things lively by flirting with the sommeliers. We'd talked when Denny died too, but I hadn't come home for the funeral, nor had I wanted to — not because I didn't think what had happened to him was sad, but because I guessed it would have been impossible for me to stay sober at the wake, and I had been doing well. Word to the wise and to those who will one day follow in my footsteps: it's a hell of a lot easier to reinvent yourself when your family's not there.

I explained my nonappearance away — they seemed to accept it. I'd gotten a new copywriting job in June, even after checking the I AM A FELON box on the application (hilarious), and I told my parents that my employer, a pharmaceutical company called Krieg Industries, wouldn't give me the days off. In truth, I didn't even ask. The day after Denny had his heart attack and died, I got laid off anyway, right along with every other employee at Krieg. They'd tanked — the FDA had pulled the plug during the phase II trials of what the company had hoped would be its flagship drug. It was called Hezonica, and it was supposed to help men stop snoring. Which it did. But it also decreased the circumference of their testicles.

"That sort of solution," said my father, responding to my idea of selling Denny's house cheap, "is how you started with money and now have nothing. And why your sister started with the same amount and now has quite a lot."

"Isn't it all profit anyway?" I said. "And besides," I added, "isn't there a value to having the inconvenience gone?"

"There is, yes," he said, "but just because that's the case, it doesn't mean you have to immediately make a rash decision. I have a different idea. Let me run it by you."

"Okay."

"What exactly is your current employment situation? Are they still wearing you out at the drug shop? Krieg?"

"No."

"Oh, no?"

"The snore pills shrunk everyone's balls."

"What?" he said.

"It turned out that the drug, along with being the cure for snoring, shrunk everyone's testicles."

"By how much?"

"The company's dead, Dad. I got laid off last week. That's the whole story."

"Entirely dead?"

"Dead. Gone."

"It's an amazing time in the American economy," he mused, and I imagined him grin-squinting like Theodore Roosevelt, shaking his head, because of course he was insulated from it all; as an executive at Hedley, he would continue to get richer as the realities of our failing economy became more and more apparent in the coming years. As payback for moments of smugness such as this one, for a long time it had given me great satisfaction to imply to members of my family, by way of well-placed hints here and there, that I believed in Soviet-style communism. The simple truth, though, was that I didn't understand money. I just didn't. I didn't want to. I still don't want to. And while I was aware, then, that this was a paradoxical privilege of the wealthy, to be able to choose to *not* understand it, I hadn't yet come close to realizing how cowardly it was to detach oneself completely from the past.

"Have you heard about the current state of Lehman?" my father continued. "I suppose you don't follow that kind of thing. But more important. This means you're currently unemployed?"

"Yes."

That was what he needed.

~~~~~

I unpacked in Denny's room. I hesitated in the hallway, wondering if it might be better to sleep in the living room on the couch, or in Wayne's room, but Denny's bed was the best, and I didn't want to start my exile on a superstitious note. For all my father's and sister's realpolitiking about money and life and their cynicism about people and the way things were, for all their *realism*, the belief in ghosts and spirits was part of their shared ethos, another way in which they were the same. How does that happen? It's as though all worldviews need escape valves of insanity. My mother — who was the principal of an elementary school and who spent a large part of her days talking to people who could barely count or tie their shoes, let alone tell the difference between fantasy and reality — found anything supernatural, whether it was God, pixies, vampires, zombies, werewolves, ghosts, or krakens, silly. So did I.

I went out to the garage and got Denny's empty blue recycling bin and started cleaning the kitchen, which stank of alcohol. The linoleum underfoot was sticky with spilled beer, but I discovered a half a bottle of Mr. Clean under the sink and mopped the floor. Then I gathered up the bottles and the cans. I found Denny's liquor cabinet and poured everything he had down the sink.

After four or five bottles, the smell was strong enough to push me into the other room. I took a break and put on side two of the CSNY and then went and looked at the photos on the mantel — there were some pictures of Denny and my father as boys; a few of the whole family; and single shots of me, Haley, and Wayne, all from our high school years. We were the three of this generation. My picture was one I had seen a thousand times in my parents' house. My hair was longer then, my face skinnier, but I had the same raised-eyebrow dipshit smirk I always wore when someone told me to smile.

I looked at Wayne. He was smiling a big-toothed smile, as though the person taking the picture had caught him in the act of laughing a genuine laugh, the opposite of mine. The guy had probably only said, "Say cheese," in a lifeless monotone. I remembered that about my cousin. As long as he detected a try at humor, he would give up a good yelp. His hair was bushy and curly, and in the picture he wore a white button-down and a tie even though he'd gone to St. Helens High, just like me, and we had no uniforms. There was something about Wayne, though, in that era of his life — informal, but I could see him dressing up on picture day on principle, when most of his peers would have been wearing the same T-shirts they always wore. He cared about stuff like that; he always had. He looked neither dark nor depressed. He looked happy. This was taken before college.

It was past eight o'clock, deep into dusk, when I finally hauled the full recycling bin to the end of the driveway. There were too many bottles for the one bin, so I ended up using Denny's wheelbarrow for the second load. I had worked up a sweat cleaning, and my white T-shirt was wet at the chest and under my arms.

Out at the end of the driveway, I saw some headlights. Unlike the county highways that crisscrossed Wisconsin and made the state into a grid of boxes, Beau Pointe Road, Denny's road, wound up through the woods and the hills like a deer path, connecting maybe twenty homes to Highway 121, which led to St. Helens's downtown and eventually became Main Street. Denny's house wasn't really in a neighborhood, and there wasn't all that much traffic on the road.

I stood and watched, one hand on the wheelbarrow and one hand on my hip. I watched as a pickup truck towing a horse trailer wound up the hill.

The truck eased around the bend. I don't think the driver looked at me, and the light was not good at all, but as it passed I was surprised to realize that the woman driving looked familiar.

〜〜〜〜

My parents waited until I graduated high school before they moved to Chicago and left St. Helens, my father's hometown, behind. For all those years in St. Helens, my father slowly climbed into and then upward through the ranks at Astronautics Corporation of America, a large company outside Milwaukee that for decades had been making technical instruments for the aeronautics field. His own father had worked there as an engineer for forty years, designing the gyroscopic gizmos that went into the cockpits of fighter jets.

My father did well. But the money — the big money — was all on my mother's side. Her family name was Weltz, and the fortune was linked to a chemical company called Hedley. The money was old, diverse, and enormous. Even so, my father, after meeting my mother in Hyde Park at U of C in the late sixties, had insisted on coming back to St. Helens to work in his own way and raise his family like he'd been raised. Not in New York, where her parents were. Not "aristocratic." Rather, with family nearby. With real people nearby. To prevent his children from "becoming psychopaths." He and Denny had been closer in the seventies, right after the war, and St. Helens was a safer place to be than Chicago. The schools were good. It was his home, he'd grown up there, and he could vouch for the quality of life. So the complex argument went. My mother, who — to him, then — seemed to have grown up drinking tea in various Connecticut gazebos, surprised him by liking the idea.

Twenty years later, fully aware of my father's weakness for the wholesome, or at least the appearance of the wholesome, my sister came up with the ingenious idea of working at Golden's Grocery and Supply, something my mother didn't understand — it meant the end of both of Haley's careers, as ballerina and opera singer — but that my father loved, as he had been a bagboy there back in his school days. Bagboys: true labor. He liked to talk about good character and work ethic, how minimum wage could teach you some things about life. How customer service at that intimate a level would put good business sense in your bones. In other words: my sister worked my father's class guilt until he let her apply for the job. He was a fundamentalist when it came to the narrative of the Midwest, and in this way he was vulnerable. Add to that that he could never say no to my sister, and the lessons in ruling-class activities were dropped; Haley learned to work the cash register instead.

I started working there when I was old enough, but only because Haley told me it was an unguarded portal to cigarettes, alcohol, and any drug I could possibly need.

It was 9:30 p.m., a half hour before closing time, and the store was now lit up like a Christmas tree. I'd come down because there was no food in the house.

After a moment of simply looking, remembering, I walked through the sliding doors.

The first thing I noticed was that they'd expanded and moved the checkout lanes. But the smell from the bakery was the same, and so were the yellow T-shirts of the girls working the registers. Only two right now, the hour being what it was. Mr. Golden had a strict policy: girls at the registers, boys at the bags.

I saw an old man bent over some ledgers at the customer-service kiosk. Muzak overhead. Not many customers around. Over at the end of the produce aisle, a skinny kid lazily pushed a gray parallelogram-shaped floor cleaner.

I filled a handbasket with some staples — for me, this meant saltine crackers and smooth peanut butter, two products of the modern era that can sustain the life of a vegetarian indefinitely and with great efficiency — and then wandered the aisles until I found the tea. I was impressed; the selection was more substantial than it had been in my time. I was reading the back of a box of something fancy when I felt somebody amble up to me on my left.

I stepped to the side to let the other shopper pass, not looking up, and heard a man's voice say, "That's not Benjy Hanson, is it?"

I glanced over. It was the same old man who'd been at the ledgers. He smiled, hands in pockets. He looked embarrassed.

"It is," I said, trying to put face to name, still holding the box of tea near my eyes. I was about to say Do I know you? when I saw his name tag.

His face manufactured a new smile, some relief at being recognized, as I held out my hand, and we shook. It was Rick Hagan, the same manager I'd long ago asked Haley about and who'd come to mind when I'd driven by the first time. He looked like he'd aged 3,750 years.

"What's it been?" he said. "Fifteen years?"

"At least that," I said.

"Listen, I'm down a guy tonight," he said. He cocked his thumb. "What say you throw on an apron and go face up aisle three for me?"

"I'm still wearing my apron under these clothes."

This, for a moment, stopped Rick's jokey smile in its tracks as he recomputed the new vector of humor, and his eyes ticked down to my chest for a moment as he solved the equation, then hammed up some fake investigating, squinting and looking closely at my T-shirt. Not the greatest timing in the world.

"I'm not seeing an apron under there," he said. "Whoa!"

He laughed loudly now.

"It's really good to see you," I said.

"What gives us the pleasure?"

"I'm staying up at my uncle's place," I said, thumb over my shoulder in what I thought might be the right direction. "It's empty now. There was a break-in, so I'm back to watch over it for a little bit. Just kind of passing through and helping out my parents. You know."

"Oh, sure, sure," he said. "Dennis." He shook his head. "That was sad news," he said. "Dennis. Always the nicest guy. Back then and now. He was always in here chatting up the girls."

"What? The high school girls?"

"Oh God, no, not like that," Rick said, performing a small, crisp version of an umpire's safe signal with hands and forearms, shaking his head at the same time. *Safe*...from small-town pedophilia! "Harmless, harmless. Denny was just a big showoff. They all loved him. You know how he was."

"I do."

"He really was a character."

"He was."

"Really too bad."

"It is."

"It really is."

"And you?" I said. "How are you?"

"Fine, good, yup," he said, nodding deeply. "May's doing well. Still at Prevea. The girls both went to Milwaukee for school and they're still over there."

"Remind me of their names?"

"Christy and Jennifer. You probably remember them, I bet. Am I right? We had 'em down here all the time."

I did remember them, actually. They'd been tiny then, both under ten. In the summers they would come for ice cream from the dairy cooler and ride their scooters in the parking lot. You would sometimes see them shoot past the front windows. Wheeled nymphs.

"How long you staying around?" he asked. "This'll just be a

temporary thing, then, I'm guessing? Have you got a permanent setup somewhere else? Somewhere out west, is it?"

"I'll probably just stick around until we can get Denny's house sold."

"You have a family with you?"

"No."

"You have a career out there?"

"Nope."

"You been doing anything interesting?"

"Not at all."

"But you'll head back after this, then."

"Probably," I said. "Either that or travel around the world. Like in *Eat, Pray, Love*."

Rick nodded at this as though I had told him I had throat cancer.

It occurred to me that he was being kind by not asking about it, though, and that he probably knew that I'd gone to pansy prison and didn't have much to show for myself as an adult, that I was a fairly pathetic case and that there was very little explanation, and that it was right for him to be showing me great pity, all things considered. And he knew that I was as reliably full of shit as I had been years ago. And that it was a stupid joke, actually, this joke of mine which I'd now double-used, and that it didn't really mean anything and was even a little condescending. But I didn't see anything like judgment in his eyes. Just that I was not anonymous, that he felt I was probably lost and, because of this, an object of curiosity.

"Well," he said. "Okay then. I'll let you get your shopping done. Just wanted to say hello." He held out a hand to shake again. "If you don't have too much stuff, come by customer service and I'll check you out with the discount."

He turned and walked away down the aisle.

He didn't look that old, actually, now that I saw him walking. He looked healthy. It was only that now, today, I was nearly as old as he'd been back then. At least that's how it felt.

〜〜〜

I was outside putting my groceries in the trunk when I glanced over toward the dumpsters and saw another specter. This one was sitting on the concrete stoop smoking a cigarette.

I closed the trunk and wandered over in that direction, hands in my pockets.

"Do you have any extra meat you could spare?" I said. "Sir?"

He barely looked over.

When I took a few more steps, he finally glanced up to appraise me sidelong, but after a few seconds his expression changed, and he snorted and smiled and said, "Jesus. Fucking Benjamin. The prodigal son. What's up, dude? Welcome back to the S-H."

"Hey," I said, walking over to him as he stood. We hugged. Grant was bigger than me, height and girth both. "You smell like pork chops," I said. "Let go of me."

He was smiling wide when he leaned away to take me in. His hair was long, like it had been years ago, but it was pulled back in a little knot and tucked up under a hairnet. He'd put on a little weight but he actually looked pretty good, I thought. Pretty close to how I remembered him. He'd never been my closest friend, but we'd always had a thing, me and him. (Besides, I thought right then, had I even had a closest friend?) We'd always connected well, and back when I first started at Golden's, he'd taken me under his wing, taught me how to steal beer by putting it in the dumpster.

He'd been a good football player, I recalled, but not quite good enough for college. He'd stuck around in town after he graduated, and he had an apartment where I often went to drink, play video games, hang around when I was skipping school or didn't feel like being at home. His apartment was where I stayed, too, those times I would come back to St. Helens during college. He never went.

We drifted apart, though, and I came back less often my junior and senior years, then never. I guess Grant was the kind of friend with whom you always had fun but with whom you did not keep in touch.

"I gotta say it, dude," he said. "What happened to you out there?"

"What?" I said. "In Oregon?"

"Uh, yeah, out in Oregon. Prison? Were you not in prison?"

"I got out a few months ago."

"How much time'd you do?"

"Fourteen months," I said. "Most of it was in minimum security."

"That's intense."

"You'd be surprised." I considered my groceries. Chestik was the prison for people who ate baby arugula when they weren't in prison.

"And what'd you do again? Burn something down?"

"Not really," I said. Then: "Kind of. It's really very boring."

He let it go after a few more vague questions. After, Grant and I sat for a while. I told him what I was doing back, told him some of my stories from Denver, told him about blowing out my ankle at Breckenridge. I didn't tell him about the arson and he didn't ask again. He told me how he'd gotten married to a girl from Mishicot and had a kid, but they were divorced now, and he only ever saw his daughter on the weekends.

"Which is the worst, man. I had a couple OWIs and that was it. Hell no, custody. It took me two years just to get a few days." He took a drag from his cigarette. "If you don't want pain, don't have kids."

"I'm not planning on it."

We chatted for a little while longer, then I gave him my cell and stood up.

"I gotta go eat," I said. "But, hey, before I go, let me ask you something."

"What's up?"

"So tonight I was there at my uncle's place and I swear, I swear, that I saw Lauren Sheehan drive by in a pickup truck. Is that possible? Is she around? Do you remember her?"

"Yeah, she's around. I think she does drive a truck. For work."

"Why's she here?"

"What, in town?"

"Yeah."

"She came back maybe three or four years ago," he said. "I honestly don't even know why. Her brother says she had some crazy husband go psycho on her."

"Psycho how?"

"I don't know. Just snapped, I guess? I don't know," he said. "But that whole family's all secretive about it. And Bobby's so fucked up I don't trust anything he says anyway."

"So she's not married?"

"Look at you," he said, smiling.

"Answer the question."

~~~~~

I woke up at around two thirty. Insomnia since Chestik. Something to do with the size of the world.

I got out of bed and got dressed, went downstairs, and looked for a moment at Jeremy's computer, still not hooked up to anything. Instead of booting it up, I rooted around in Denny's kitchen drawers until I found a flashlight and then I got my keys.

Outside, the stars were bright, the houses on either side were dark. I went down the middle of the road, and after ten minutes of walking I came to the T I remembered from the times I'd walked this way in search of my cousin. Go right, pass the quarry and a half a mile of cornfields, and you could wind your way back down into town; go left and you could ascend the steeper part of Beau Pointe Hill. It was no more than five hundred feet high, but it was a mountain when I was young.

I went left, up. I walked past a half dozen driveways, the nearby houses hidden by the woods, the road still empty, silent. Being up here reminded me of Wayne. He used to make me answer riddles each time I came to see him. His riddles weren't very good — they were just the ones you always heard, the who-am-Is. You've heard them. I think he had a book. But back then, I found them to be a kind of magic, and I have to say that looking at them again now, it's difficult not to see them as inadvertently profound, no matter the answers. *I make you weak at the worst of all times, I keep you safe, I keep you fine. I make your hands sweat and your heart grow cold, I visit the weak but seldom the bold. Who am I?* You are fear. *I am like day, you can find me near the river any day, and you can make almost anything out of me. Who am I?* You are clay. *The rich eat me, the poor have me, if you eat me you will die. Who am I?* You are nothing.

This was Wayne, though, and so, mixed in with questions from his book, every fourth or fifth, there would also come from the Keeper of the Tree House — he yelled them down in a spooky voice — totally practical questions: *How do you remember how to tighten and untighten screws, Benjamin?* Lefty loosey, righty tighty. *And what's* the *best way to ensure that your car battery won't die in cold weather, Benjamin? I mean, if you're really serious about it not dying?* You have to take the battery out. *What is the exact temperature right now?* Seventy-two. *That is incorrect, according to my thermometer. What do you say to that?* You don't have a thermometer. *You are banished!*

Those times were all gone.

I came to the place I'd been looking for, a path that led off from the road, marked by a brown wooden sign, small-cap letters engraved and painted gold. I hadn't turned on the flashlight and I didn't need to do it now. I knew what the sign said. BEAU POINTE OVERLOOK. Discovered (white-man discovered) and named by a Jesuit explorer, Pierre Bettencourt, who'd come south from the river system in the Fox Valley at the end of the 1600s, making a slow trip inland while the more pragmatic of his fellow explorers stuck to Lake Michigan or the Fox or the Wisconsin, many of them still in search of a Northwest Passage. I liked to think of old Pierre as the black sheep of the Jesuits, either lost here in this place or completely impractical — or maybe just a wanderer — because there was no good reason to come here, fifty-five miles west of the big lake, or to climb a hill that overlooked nothing. Other than just to come.

I strolled across the empty parking lot and looked down at St. Helens.

The streetlights made a yellow grid, and the black line meandering through the center was the river, dark enough to be the river Styx. A few homes were lit up, a few spirits squaring off against the vacuum, like me. I watched toy-size cars crawl down Main. But there was no sound coming up. No sound of the city. Just what I could see. Just my breath. Just the trees. Just me, and beside me, the ghost of old Pierre.

I tried to guess what might have gone through his mind when he first looked down in this manner. What does a Jesuit consider? Most likely he was exhausted, starving. There was no town. His feet hurt. I have no idea if it was night.

I thought: *All that we are given shall be taken in the end.*

And I don't know why these particular words came into my head, as they don't strike me as appropriate even now, but those were the words I heard.

I took them as a greeting.

2

My Father Has a Ridiculous Request

Here is something.

From first grade on, after the SRAs, Haley and I were "gifted," which meant we buzzed along the advanced track of the public school system.

This was right for Haley; my sister's mind was a supercomputer. She thought through problems deliberately, slowly, carefully. She took excellent notes. She went back and checked her work. She was anal; she was a perfectionist. She was uncompromising but also good at everything.

I was not like Haley.

I hated details. I was sloppy; I often didn't care about being right or wrong. I never talked to my teachers. I showed no interest beyond the interest I was supposed to show. I barely read. I thought about nothing. I forgot everything four days after learning it. I enjoyed playing Zork. I learned how to read playing King's Quest.

But I was on the advanced track too, all the better classes, all the APs, all the telling signs of the future leaders of the world. And the only reason I got on that track, and later managed to get myself into Madison — though barely, as my GPA had gone from the high 3s to the low 2s by my senior year — was one simple, crucial characteristic that harmonized with our quantitative world: I was, and am, an amazing test taker.

This is different than understanding the world.

How do I say it? I listen. If you approach a situation in the right way — if you don't care much but still listen — you can perceive what a poorly devised question's getting at: you can hear the truth in the background. And most questions on standardized tests are poorly devised.

I needed to work for two years when I got to Denver after I graduated college — this calculation was based, simply, on knowing that I was going to gain control of my trust when I was twenty-four, so long as my parents believed I was responsible enough to handle it. They'd built it that way on purpose and had made it clear, all our lives, that during the two years after graduation, they would not support either of us. (As though floating for two years, single and with no children, resembled anything like making it in the real world.) But whatever. That was the task. I picked Denver because I wanted to ski.

For a few months I was a waiter. A bad waiter. (I was eventually fired for not knowing the difference between lobster and red snapper.)

But then one day, broke, having almost failed the test that had been manufactured by my mother and father, the test of simple self-sufficiency (especially humiliating because I was, as I've just said, a good test taker, but I think what I mean refers to paper, not life), I was walking home down Sixteenth Street and saw the storefront of a place where they taught classes on all the big standardized exams.

Kaplan, it was called.

I realized, watching a couple kids go through the glass doors, that there was an entire industry based on bullshitting.

I became a bullshitting tutor.

And I helped them.

I just helped them hear.

So, listen, person, because all of this matters.

~~~~~

Sleep came that first night eventually — sleep and dreams I could not remember. I woke earlier than I wanted, then ran, eyes greedy, pulling at the new greens and yellows of the farms, the stone and wood and sheet metal of the houses, sheds, silos, and warehouses of this place.

After I showered and ate my cereal, I hooked Jeremy's computer to Denny's monitor and connected the Ethernet to the back.

Haley was right — Denny's internet still worked. When I logged in I saw there was an e-mail from my father with a subject line that read *Extremely Important, Ben, Read Immediately*, which I ignored, and an e-mail from our real estate agent welcoming me to town and telling me to let her know when I wanted to start showing the house. Her name was Theresa Orgogliosi. She used an emoticon.

In the chat box there were two green dots that showed who among my modestly populated address book was online: Haley and Jeremy.

I clicked Jeremy's name and the chat window opened up.

I thought for a moment that it might be wiser to create some kind of fake address and try to disguise where I was (this was the extent of what I knew about internet espionage), but I figured that (a) this was Jeremy, and he'd be able to find me, regardless, by using dork internet magic, and (b) it didn't matter, because I wasn't hiding anyway. I chose aggressive honesty.

Me: As you probably know, J, I stole your computer.
Me: Sorry.
Me: That's sincere.
Me: Really.

It took him about a minute to respond. I imagined him sitting at his desk in some vibrant loft office outside of Seattle, surrounded by two or three dozen twenty-somethings coding away, speaking Klingon to one another, riding unicycles to and from the bathroom. Jeremy, silent, staring at my words, considering. Jeremy: not joking around or even noticing the background because he was more serious than his employees. More calculating. Pencil in mouth. Wondering about my angle, or if I had an angle, or if I was only being impulsive and rash.

He had to know already that it was me who'd broken into his house, but since I'd taken the computer, I'd heard nothing from him, no e-mail or phone calls demanding it back.

Maybe he wanted me to see the complete version of the game. I hadn't looked for it yet, but I thought there was a good chance it was on the drive. It's possible he liked the idea.

Finally:

Jeremy: why?
Me: I think you know.
Jeremy: i'm sure i do not know, benjy
Me: Think harder.

Jeremy: ok. i'll play. you broke into my house and stole my
computer for reverse-revenge because you inexplicably
also DESTROYED OUR COMPANY FOR NO REASON
RIGHT WHEN WE WERE ABOUT TO ACTUALLY MAKE
SOMETHING AMAZING AND GOT CAUGHT BECAUSE
YOU'RE STUPID

Me: Caps means you're yelling?

Jeremy: its emphasis

Me: There are lots of interesting things on your computer.

Like the picture of him and Allie on some beach, but not a
beach in the Northwest, which I was now staring at in another
open window. It looked like Hawaii; the water was Photoshop
aqua. Jeremy looked healthier than he used to look — he had a tan
and definitely had started going to the gym; the softness I associ-
ated with his body, the patina of blubber that is the inheritance of
all nerds who spend their days entranced by computer monitors,
leaning into them, drinking soda, psychically caressing pixels, was
gone. Maybe yoga, considering Allie. (She looked painfully lean
and amazing.) He was leaning back on a towel, waving a meek
casual wave from the wrist, stupid grin on his face as though
uncomfortable in this new body, uncomfortable in this new place
with this new, too beautiful woman beside him. (Uncomfortable
also because he now had no functioning soul.)

Allie was kneeling on her towel, caught in the act of getting up
on her way to the water, smiling a big smile. Displaying her usual
unself-consciousness, wearing a red and yellow bikini I had never
seen. Her hair was still dyed black — she'd always hated her natural blond — but she'd grown it longer and the bangs were gone.
She looked happy. Happier.

No message then, and so I stared at the picture for a little longer, felt myself getting sad and turned on at the same time. It wasn't a great combination.

I clicked the little *x* and made Hawaii disappear.

Jeremy: theres nothing interesting — like damaging, i mean — on that hard drive, ben. you can keep it, i don't care. and i get that you were sending a message about the game, but honestly, i moved on when you got arrested. i'm pretty sure you understood that then. we don't have a contract because you don't sign things. i appreciate all of your contributions but we don't have a contract. and you and i both know that our friendship was fucked up beyond allie. way before.

Jeremy: three things, ok? i'm just pissed. let me say these.

Me: Go for it.

Jeremy: 1. wtf are you doing in wisconsin? i can see your ip. aren't you on parole? can you really go wherever? or, hm, come to think of it, do you really think it's smart to document in writing that you stole property from my house? invaded OUR house? why am I not just going to the police rt now? again? tell me.

Jeremy: 2. I think you knew, probably expected, when you were mailing me all those puzzles from chestik that I was gonna use some of it in the game, that I was still working on everything, that it was all gonna be real, and I think you felt desperate and stupid about throwing yr life away and all yr money away on nothing, so far as i can tell, and you were trying in some fucked-up way to apologize to me and stay connected to allie and still pass it off like it was no big deal and you were all mr. breezy about everything still, oh hey here's another totally f'ing ingenious puzzle for you, sent to you from inside of my white-collar prison because i just happened to write it, oh, hey, i just make these up to entertain the other guys in here, oh, no big deal, which is something you love, and that you didn't care about anything, your favorite pose in the world…

Jeremy: …that you didn't care one way or another just like everything you ever do. but you do care, b. you care about everything. a lot. i know you. i know that u fucking desperately care abt the world and everything and u have no idea how to talk abt it or connect to it and that that's what makes you how you r.

Me: Are you going to need a copay for this?

Jeremy: so pretending you're somehow outraged that i actually MADE the fucking game despite what you did and used some — SOME — of your stuff is passive-aggressive nonsense, esp. considering we ALWAYS agreed that your role was going to be generate the content. and because you were really good at it!!!! u r trickier than jareth the goblin king!!!

Jeremy: 3. that said, why not just come up and talk to me about it and work something out? allie and i are both sitting up here waiting to hear from you since the day you got out. excited to show u what we did. hoping we can all find a way to have a friendship again. technology is changing, the way people use technology is changing. apps make everything different. hardware is going to be built around them, not vice versa. that's what's going to make us rich and make this all work. it's not like i'm pretending that i thought up everything or that allie's art isn't hugely important to it or that you don't deserve a windfall or part ownership or credit too…you do, you'll get it, we're working things out still, we're gonna have an ipo eventually... you can have credit, whatever, did you even look through the credits on the site, btw? HAVE YOU PLAYED IT? you're in there already. if breaking into my house is supposed to be some symbol of me stealing from you, either allie or anything else, it just doesn't make sense because i'm not stealing anything from you and i think you'd get that if you thought about it more. you're smart. i wanted to be your friend. you were nice to me. so let me be yr friend now. we're not children and in life there are complicated fucked-up emotional situations and the way people get through those is by communicating. not weird symbolic tricks and un-decodable secret messages.

Me: I stuck your toothbrush in my anus when I was in there.

Jeremy: great

Me: I did.

Me: You guys don't need to worry about me. (I can't believe I just wrote that sentence, but I know you think you are being sincere right now.) What's your home address?

Jeremy: you mean the house you just burgled?

Me: Yes.

Jeremy: really?

Me: I lost the scrap of paper.

Jeremy: REALLY????

Jeremy: 2673 tower dr., nola, wa, 68913. why?

Me: I'll send you back your computer.

Me: Good luck with the game. I guess. I gotta go. And I don't want your money, btw. I don't care about the company or an IPO. Please. I also don't care about you or Allie. In fact I fucking hate you. Please lose this e-mail address. The game's yours.

Jeremy: well. we'll talk. when I know more.

Me: There's no need.

Jeremy: i know you think that

Me: I'm serious.

Jeremy: i know that but i don't believe u, u always say shit
like that.

〰〰

There was a meeting in downtown St. Helens at 3:00, and so
after lunch and after I mowed the lawn (not too short, summer
sun, rain's been light) and set out some sprinklers, I drove to town
and parked in front of the library. I was early, so I walked past it
and went along the river to John Muir Park and sat on one of the
benches that ringed the statue.

I looked up at the statue.

It had always been here, right in the middle of this park. I
didn't know the first thing about the man.

I looked to the right, at a bird.

I had no idea what kind of bird it was.

I knew nothing.

The meeting: same circle and the same tired faces I had seen
out west.

〰〰

When I got back to the house there was a cleanly taped brown
package on the doorstep, addressed to me in my mother's meticulous handwriting.

I brought it inside, opened it up, and looked at the contents.

I called my father.

"Are you kidding?" I said.

"Did you read the e-mail, Ben?" He sounded like he was yelling at me from a helicopter.

"No."

"Why didn't you read the e-mail? I don't understand. Did you receive the e-mail?"

"I didn't read it."

"I marked it as priority," he said. "Did you not see that?"

"No one uses that. Where are you?"

"I do. I certainly do, son. If it's a priority, I do."

"I haven't checked my e-mail."

"Well," he said after an exaggerated, yelled sigh. "It's all there." He yell-sighed again. "Read it and call me back if you've got questions. I'm in the middle of something."

"Are you in Atlantis?"

"Atlanta? What?"

"The lost city of Atlantis."

"I can't hear you."

"Is this what I think it is?"

"Is *what* what you think it is, Ben?"

"What you sent."

"I'm very stressed right now for multiple reasons," he yelled. "I lost my telephone and had to get a new one. I'm speaking to you on an entirely different telephone setup right now, if you can believe that. But the number is the same. It's all in the letter."

"Is it not illegal to ship . . . organic matter through the mail?"

"I don't know, son!" he yelled. "Probably. I don't know. It's Denny, though. There's your uncle! Surely you can ship a man back to his own home. Where else does he belong? There's nothing illegal about *that!* Not on my watch!"

From: j.hanson@hedleylabs.com
To: hansonben3@gmail.com
Date: 8/10/2008

Subject: Sadness and Cell Phone on the Shores of the Bright River

My Dearest Ben, Light of My Life, Residue of My Loins,

I hope you're settling in well at the house and that you haven't come across Denny's disembodied and moaning ghoulish presence or been disturbed by more teenagers, the true ghouls of our modern times. You've had a tough couple of days, son, what with the move, and I should start out not by joshing you around but by reiterating just how glad your mother and I are to have you back in our neck of the woods, your troubles from the past now fully behind you. You're very smart and still very young — the substance-abuse issues were always difficult for us to understand, always extremely troubling and complex for us, and I imagine for you, and I'm happy that you've got them under control. I've always been impressed by the intelligence of both of my children, and although your sister has gone on to build a more stable and traditional existence and lifestyle, we respect your adventurous rogue spirit, your (we presume) knowledge of the underside of humanity, and your ability to help us with Sudoku. You're fully on the road to recovery. We can see that. Your mother and I believe in you and look forward to watching as you forge new paths of success. That last sentence was not a joke. We know it hasn't been easy getting it together. We are proud of your strength and proud that you're our son.

Now. The matter at hand, which is not so much a priority, now that I think of it, but more of an important matter with a somewhat flexible timeline. A notable distinction. When something is a priority it means that it's at the top of the list, and that it most likely requires IMMEDIATE attention. Priority is preeminence. I would call this important. It will require some attention on your part, but not immediate, and the task is somewhat laborious. What it amounts to is a small rider with regards to our agreement concerning Denny's house and this excellent business arrangement you seem to have lucked into.

Your mother and I have, between the two of us, committed something of an administrative error, Ben. We've argued about its physical, metaphysical, and karmic implications for the past few weeks, your mother being of the mind that we simply tell no one, as is her chosen method of handling all conflict and unpleasantness, myself being of the mind that, out of respect for my brother and his wishes and a larger, more general respect for the dead and the various nearby planes the recently dead very well may continue to inhabit, as well as my own personal, tangential fear of my brother's ghost one day rising up out of the sand trap on the local club's sixteenth hole and burying a set of phantasmagorical fangs in my neck, or at least chastising me and interfering with my sand shot, or entering my dreams to talk to me about my faults, etc., as well as my own additional personal desire to either eventually retrieve my cell phone or be certain it's no longer functional—it's a little confusing to me which thing is most worrisome, in all honesty—we'll need to make this right. You'll need to make this right, I should say. Ben: you are the only one who can make this right. Help me, Obi-Ben Kenobi! You're my only hope!

It looks like we've had a little mix-up with the ashes.

Let me explain. Do you happen to remember Billingsworth, the fabulously expensive show dog we had for a little more than a year before your mother backed over him in the driveway?

A beautiful animal. It's possible you never heard the story, as it happened in the era when we weren't doing much communicating. Sad stuff. I believe you were some combination of high and snowboarding for roughly a decade and you rarely answered your phone—otherwise we would have told you all about it. Billingsworth, God rest his soul, was not smart and not likable, not to mention ugly, placing nineteenth out of twenty-two dogs at the only show your mother and I managed to take him to. (Upon realizing the general degree of insanity required to participate in that subculture, we opted out in favor of drinking in our living room, as we often do, and watching him sleep as a kind of perverse entertainment. This had no effect on Billingsworth's self-esteem, I don't think, although they say show dogs—good ones, at least—do have hangups with vanity that require servicing if they're taken away from the pageantry lifestyle. Your mother and I discussed purchasing some kind of audio CD with recorded applause that we could play for him from time to time, not to mention play for ourselves, as we were given this advice, but for his brief time on the planet, with or without the thrill of competition, he seemed content to sleep under the ottoman and fart his way through the evenings. The veterinarian suspected he suffered from narcolepsy, but I remain convinced that it is not possible for a dog to have narcolepsy. That is another issue, and I am no veterinarian. It just feels wrong.)

Billingsworth, overall, was a very difficult dog to care *about*. This is what I am saying. He had no traits outside of his defi-ciencies, no real personality to speak of, and on top of that, walking him was an incredible chore, as it was always pos-sible that you might look down and find him unconscious at the other end of the leash. If you did, you most likely would then have to carry him the rest of the way home. He was not small. And he was asleep, incidentally, when your mother killed him. He was very catlike in the way he used to seek out the shade. Another disconcerting characteristic, as all cats are untrustworthy, haughty, and evil.

Your uncle Denny's will directed that he (Denny, not Billingsworth) be cremated, which, I am happy to report, went off without a hitch. (!) Fire. The memorial service also went well although we missed you. In his will, though, Denny requested — somewhat sentimentally, I think, but that is neither here nor there — that his ashes be scattered in the Bright River, just where it passes through his property in the UP. Do you remember Denny's cabin up north? You must, considering Wayne's death in 1994. You went once or twice when you were young but we never went back after Wayne. It was too awful a thing. And I know Denny tried to continue using the cabin and making trips, but I'm fairly certain he stopped spending time there in the last few years.

Nevertheless, he wouldn't sell it. Which is understandable, I suppose. I therefore now own the property and am unsure what to do with it. Eventually I may seek your counsel on what might be done, as I'm truly at a loss, but that's for later. Either way, here's the point, son: Dennis wanted to be scattered in the river, Dennis was my brother, and it naturally fell on me to take him up there, which I did two weeks ago, not long before your arrival. I left at 5:00 a.m., as there was no way in hell I was going to actually spend the night there, and I got to his property a little past 1:00 p.m. I made good time. I sped wildly. I ate in the car. And after a few wrong turns and a few consultations of the map, I finally got to where I was supposed to be, unlocked the chain, drove up the long dirt driveway, parked, went past the cabin and straight to the river, sat down on the bank, said a few perfunctory words, ate a banana, scattered the ashes, wept uncontrollably for longer than I thought I had it in me to weep, had trouble standing due to some mud, and drove the eight hours home, stopping once for gas and more food. I didn't want to get too caught up in mourning for Dennis all over again, as the memorial itself, back in St. Helens, had just about completely done me in. But seeing the property and being there added Wayne back into the equation, and added many very old memories of my brother and me spending time up there together alone, and drew into focus how tragic, really, my brother's life was. How unfair and tragic. Almost through and through. One horror after the next, all of it random. He went to war, a choice that lost him the respect of our father for the remainder of his life, and while at war he lost his friends and was backed into unacceptable moral situations. He largely failed as a businessman, then lost his wife, then lost his son. At least he's at peace now. But what I thought, as I stood looking at the river after having a little trouble standing up, mud covering the ass area of my most comfortable pair of khakis, etc., was this: Denny had the misfortune of bearing witness to the natural tragedies of life unfurling before him in a well-spaced, chronological fashion. As though it had been arranged for him beforehand. We do all die, yes. Our loved ones do all die, but it's unfair to be asked to watch such things happen and experience them as though they're chapters in a book. At least he's now at peace.

Well, *nearly* at peace. You see, here's the first problem, and the point of this message. When I got home that night, exhausted, emotionally drained, I found your mother in the kitchen. She pointed at a small brown box near the telephone and said, "You forgot Dennis. Did you drive all the way up there and realize you didn't have him?" I said, "I had the red urn from the mantel. You told me that was Denny." "No," your mother told me. "That was Billingsworth. Billy, I said." "Billingsworth?" I said. "The f**king dog? We had the *dog* cremated?" "Of course we did," your mother said. "I did, at least. You know how horrible I felt about that." "Billingsworth the terrible dog?" I said. She laughed at me then. I stood staring. "You just drove nine hundred miles to scatter Billingsworth on your brother's property," she said. "I tried to call you."

I patted my pocket to verify this. I said, "I don't seem to have my phone." I squinted at the wall, recalled the bank and the mud. Your mother, in her typical fashion, walked out of the room.

As you know, Ben, I am a very busy man.

Very busy.

And I have tangled with death enough.

Therefore, at your earliest convenience and, at the latest, before winter comes, please make the trip and scatter Dennis's ashes in the Bright River. Right where the river runs through his property. Soon the urn, which is stainless steel (don't confuse it with your travel coffee thermos!), will arrive at the house, sealed and — this time — clearly labeled.

A second issue, then: As I say, I believe my phone may have fallen from my pocket while I sat beside the river. I've already replaced it, but there are some documents and somewhat sensitive passwords on it, those sorts of things. Passwords that pertain to my business and my personal finances that

I wouldn't want anyone else to have in his possession. My guess is that the weather and the elements will destroy the phone—certainly in the winter—but I've been waking up with identity-theft nightmares for the past week, and I don't think I'll be able to rest easy until I know it's no longer out there. Please try to find it, and if you do, throw the thing in the river.

All right, there you are. Go take care of these things when you can. It might be beautiful up there. Maybe you can find a girl and take her along. Our financial arrangement is absolutely and irrevocably contingent upon this additional duty.

Thank you!
Your Father

~~~~~

Here is something else.

See it in the frame: a lime-green pickup truck, Denny's '66 F-150, and in front of it, my sister and I stand smiling, but the smiles are different.

I am twelve, wearing yellow swim trunks and making the shit-eating face again.

She is fourteen, wearing jean shorts and an orange bikini top, squinting at the person holding the camera, unprepared for the timing of the click.

Wayne, our cousin, is the one holding the camera. I remember him making us stop and pose. I remember him saying, "Ben, please. Chill with the stupid faces."

I don't know that I am making one. It is a hot August day. I am glad to be going along, glad that I am here.

We are up north, as we usually are for a week in the summer. This is the first year, though, that Wayne has his driver's license, and he has just convinced my parents and his parents to let him drive us to the other side of the peninsula, past Gladstone and past the Little Bay de Noc to the Big Bay de Noc, at the border of the Hiawatha, where the Niagara Escarpment breaks up from the crust at the shore and shows itself for what it is: the edge of an ancient limestone and dolomite dish that is four hundred and fifty million years old and used to be the coast of a sea the size of Texas.

I am having trouble believing this is true, that *this* used to be a sea. That anything could have previously been a sea. But Wayne says so, and the adults seem to agree.

This morning, at the cabin, Wayne sold the experience as educational. Now, twenty minutes after the picture, we are doing sixty-eight down Highway 2, which is empty, and my legs are sweating and sticking to the F-150's seat, and my cousin is driving, lighting his one-hitter, and trying to tell us about geologic time.

I am at the window.

My sister's in the middle.

"Slow down," Haley says, and I'm relieved.

But then she says, "Here. I'll hold the wheel. You light the thing."

"Thank you, darling," Wayne says.

I smell the tangy weed when my cousin exhales a cloud of smoke. He then (shockingly, to me) hands the dugout and the lighter to my sister, coughs once, and says, "Take the Bright River. It's nothing compared to the escarpment. Fuck. In terms of age. Or even the lakes? Michigan? It's like a . . . it's a puddle compared to what the sea was. Four hundred and fifty million years. Can you guys even *imagine* four hundred and fifty million? Even the number? Try to put that bitch in your head."

"I can't," I say, because I can't.

Haley is coughing now, having tried to smoke the thing.

"But that's great, it's beautiful," Wayne says. "All of this. Up here, wherever. The Michigan Sea used to be here; now it's not. The Bright River shouldn't even be called *the* Bright River, you know? Because that's not even how rivers work. It should be *this* one. And then you go up to it the next day and it's *this* one."

"You are," Haley says, "super-deep."

She is making fun of him but only teasing. I can tell. She is holding the dugout toward him and has not offered it to me, which is okay because it terrifies me and this entire outing terrifies me and I am wishing I stayed back at the cabin. They ignore me when it's the three of us.

Wayne chuckles at Haley's teasing in a way that reminds me of my uncle Denny. "Fine, I'll shut up," he says. "Just don't make fun of rocks." It sounds sad to me, like rocks have been getting made fun of for a long time and there's now a self-esteem crisis. Haley says nothing. Wayne turns on the radio and starts scrolling through the static, looking for a song. Or anything.

We get to where we're going.

It's more than an hour. I don't know where we are and Wayne hasn't used a map, but he seems to know everything there is to know about the peninsula, a place that has always frightened me a little, frightened me for its differences, frightened me because it is wild. So big and so unknown. And yet Wayne knows its empty roads by heart. And I don't even know if where we are now is a real park, though there's a dirt parking lot, at least. We drove ten minutes through pines down a dirt road to get here.

Wayne is quiet and confident, leading us through the woods to the water. He sings a song called "Go Away, Bear." He is shirtless. Tall and wiry. He has worked construction this summer and has become muscular. His skin is brown, not pasty white like mine.

He has crossed the line and become a man. I don't know him in the same way now. Haley walks in the middle. I walk at the back, listening to the *flip-flops* of our three sets of flip-flops, wondering if my sister is stoned, and what that even feels like. I am annoyed. She's trying to act cool.

There's a sandy beach at the shore, and Wayne stops at the water, hands on his hips, and looks out at the bay.

To the right, Lake Michigan opens up like an ocean and seems to go forever. Directly ahead of us, across the bay, a long rocky finger of land extends out, and it's as though it's pointing toward the same infinity I've just considered.

"That's it," Wayne says. "That whole thing's fucking dolomite. And half a billion years old. Right there."

I stare at it.

"How old are dinosaurs?" I say.

"Not that old."

I imagine a brontosaurus out on the rocks.

Haley has taken a few more steps out into the water, hands on her hips just like my cousin.

"That's so cool," she says. "It's so old."

Wayne nods.

"How's the water?" he says.

"Kinda cold," she says. "It feels nice."

Wayne glances at me, then back at the escarpment.

"I feel like swimming out there," he says. "I did it last time I was here. It's about a quarter mile, I think."

"We can just walk around," I say.

"Not really," Wayne says, turning left, appraising the shore. "The woods are terrible all through there. See?" He points. "Dragons."

"No."

"Well. Shitty walking, anyway."

"Let's swim out there."

Haley has turned, her face bright at the idea. She looks at me. "You're probably too little though, Benjy."

I am furious that she has said this and terrified by the idea of swimming to the ancient rocks, and so I'm also glad that she's said it.

"I can guard here," I say. "I can guard the truck."

Wayne looks back at the woods, then at me. "Yeah, okay," he says. "We need a guard."

He comes over to me, puts a hand on my shoulder, and squats down, pulling me to squat too.

"Here, though," he says. "Check this out."

He sweeps his fingers through the sand. Eventually, he pulls up a perfectly smooth, oval-shaped stone.

"There might be fossils here," he says, turning it over so we can both look. But there's nothing.

He drops it in the sand. "Trilobites."

"What's that?"

"Weird little ancient sea creatures."

"What?"

Wayne stands up, looks at Haley, nods. "Okay?"

"Yeah," she says. "Totally."

She comes out of the water and unbuttons her shorts. As she starts pulling them down, revealing the other half of her suit, she hands me her sunglasses with her other hand. "These are for you, Dr. Watson," she says, and I have no idea what she means. I take them; she smiles. I see that she is intimidated by the swim. I wonder if I should say something, because it seems too far to swim, but instead I put on the sunglasses.

"Find us one trilobite by the time we're back, dude," Wayne says to me, "and you are then the champion."

I watch them from the sand, Haley's sunglasses on my face, for fifteen minutes. At first I can hear them talking, but as they get smaller and smaller, their noises fade into the sound of Lake Michigan's waves lapping the shore all around me and soon I can see only Wayne's hair and the orange of Haley's suit when she bobs up and down. When they are far enough away to be only dots, I sit down, take off Haley's glasses. I look at her shorts, stand up, and start hunting for trilobites. At first I stay up on the sand, but there are fewer rocks here, and so I move to the water and wade up to my calves, looking up at them every couple of minutes, then going back to my search. I think about how weird the word *trilobite* is and I say it out loud to myself a few times. A horsefly lands on the back of my neck, but I feel it land, and slap backward right away, and it drops down into the water, its small body dead and floating next to my calf. I pick it up, hold it close to my face. It's dead there in my hand. I wonder about how this horsefly could get squashed into a rock and preserved for another five hundred million years. If someone could make a fossil. I look back at the woods, then out toward the escarpment.

I see them soon. They are already up on the shore.

I see that they're waving.

I wave back.

They're tiny.

"You're trilobites," I say. "Both of you are trilobites."

It was a funny joke to me, then.

3

Space Station

In 1987, my mother, Miriam Sheehan, finally got up the courage to run away from my father, David Ryan Sheehan, who had moved the family to Montreal the year before and who would sometimes punch my mother in the face at the dinner table. My brother, Bobby, says he remembers this happening each night, remembers the crack of the impact and the blood, the Kleenex, the cut-short cries, the sound of the silverware on the floor, the drag of the wooden chair leg in the scramble afterward, the earnest explanations once the emergencies were through, long talks from our father, sitting on our beds, telling us in a patient voice that it had been an accident, unintentional, that he was sorry, that he was only glad that our mother was okay and had not been hurt — all of the things. But I think Bobby has embellished what was real in order to fill the gaps of what he doesn't know and what he can't remember. As we are all wont to do.

(This is Lauren.)

What I mean is that I don't think it happened every night. Just some nights. Back then, her — my mother's — only skills were gardening and child rearing, and it's best to think of that second skill in the loosest way possible, if you'd like to imagine her with any accuracy. I don't say that because I want to ignore everything she did for my brother and me or to be dismissive about how courageous she was to run away with us or to minimize how hard it must have been for her, those first years especially. I say it to emphasize how vulnerable she was, economically, once we were on our own, and how much that matters when you're in a bad situation. Even more when you're a woman. The same thing happened to me — I had not seen it coming. I hadn't learned anything, and it's disturbing to me that I could have been so blind, even after I'd learned the lesson once.

(And also, finally, I say it just to acknowledge that hard truth about people, how you can be a brave person in the world and make sacrifices and do a number of good things but still not exactly *be* good.)

(Sorry.)

She was born in Atlanta but had lost her accent by the time I met her, which was when I began to exist, which was technically in October of 1977, although my consciousness didn't perceive her as a person to meet until somewhere around 1978 or 1979, when I knew that she was not myself. She was third-generation Hungarian American. She liked beets. Until a few years ago, her hair was brown and had a curl to it and she kept it shoulder length, but when it started to go gray she switched colors to something I would call almost black. She wasn't pretty, my mother, but I realize now that she had sex appeal, maybe a lot of sex appeal. She had a way about her that fascinated men. Verve. I feel stiff when I think of myself in relation to her, and I think I even did when I was small — the way she walked, the way she spoke, the way she laughed. The color of her lips, or perhaps the way she bent them around certain words. I couldn't do any of it. And I was jealous of all those things she knew how to do, and even though she also used to tell me how I was prettier than she'd ever been, and even though she used to brush my hair for hours at a time and tell me that it would always be something special that I had and that most women would kill for the hair that I had, which was probably from my father's side, my mother made me angry. Just generally. And it was bound up in not being able to be what she was.

I think it took her as long as it did to pack us up and leave Montreal because she was practical; she imagined herself alone with two young children with nothing whatsoever and realized it would be only a matter of time before social services, either Canadian or American, wherever she took us, would find her unfit and incapable — because of the money — and either send us back to Montreal and our father, who had money *then*, or put us under government care, and from that point, who knew what could happen? That's a mother's worst nightmare and she could see a simple chain of events that would get us there. So she was very careful. Neither of her parents was alive by the time we made our big escape, but she did have a half sister who lived in Santa Fe, and through some long-developed system of codes — codes built right into the letters they sent to each other (and yes, our father really was the kind of man, at that time at least, who would get jealous if he saw his wife had received a letter from somebody, man or woman, and he would read whatever he found) — the two women organized my mother's departure from hell, and from Canada, and from him, which happened under the guise of a vacation to Niagara Falls. The three of us were U.S. citizens already, and it was our father who was Canadian; it wasn't hard for us to get across the border. And it's not as though we had to request asylum or do anything dramatic. They don't do that for domestic abuse. We were just running.

Once we were there, and by *there*, I mean anywhere away, I

hear that my father was informed of what had happened but he expressed little interest in bringing us back.

(We did get to know him a little better later on. Once Bobby and I were older, once he'd made a number of huge gestures to apologize about the past even though he probably could have just not done it. But he did do it.)

The escape. I remember it. I knew that something was strange when we passed the signs for the falls and my mother didn't so much as tap the brakes; instead, she intently smoked cigarettes, window hardly cracked, both hands on the wheel, no talking. And I knew something extraordinary was happening when, after another two hours, we pulled into the parking lot of a roadside restaurant and watched through the window as my mother hugged, for a very long time, a woman we had never seen. There was a man, too, and the three of them talked for what felt like an hour.

After the first ten minutes of the three of them talking, and my brother and me completely in the dark, watching, sitting in the backseat, Bobby started to cry.

I turned to look at him, and he turned from the window and looked at me and said, totally terrified, "Who are *they*, now?" He was seven and I was ten. I sensed that it was now my job to help take care of him.

I said, "Those are the people who are going to eat you for dinner."

I got out and stood on the other side of the gravel parking lot and picked up rocks and studied them for however long it took my mother to calm Bobby down. He had a way of getting hysterical and I knew how to do it to him. This was fun for me. Obvs. I expected either my mother or the man or the other woman to eventually come over and slap me for it, as my mother sometimes did, at which point I was going to run across the highway and time it in such a way that it would be impossible for anyone to pursue me. I felt as though I could find my way in America. I could be Fievel. But nobody stormed over. Eventually, they all just went to the restaurant door, and before going inside my mother turned and smiled in my direction and waved at me and signaled for me to come too. She wasn't mad, not at all, and so I did a skipping run toward her and went inside as well.

From that point on — for a couple of days, at least — it was an adventure. Everything was different. The man transferred our luggage from our car to another car (it seemed like a miracle to me that my things, virtually *all* of my things, had been in the trunk all along), shook my hand and Bobby's hand as though we were adults, hugged my mother and the woman, and drove away in the white station wagon that had driven our family around Montreal since we'd been there. I never saw this man again. I still don't know who he was, exactly. Later that night, when we were driving west in the other car, I asked my mother who he was and she turned and put her hand on my arm and said, "That was a lawyer taking Daddy's car back to him." In the rearview mirror, I saw the eyes of the other woman, whom I'd been told was my aunt, which I was very skeptical of, tick to the side to watch my reaction to what my mother said, and I understood that it was lie. I knew what they were. I was not as stupid as my brother.

"Okay," I said, leaning back.

I looked out the window, then asked my mother for the brush so I could brush my hair.

~~~~

We moved from Santa Fe to St. Helens before I started the ninth grade and after my mother had earned her master's degree in library science and been told about a job there by one of her professors, but it wasn't until three years later, at the start of my senior year, that I had any significant interaction with Ben Hanson.

Throughout most of high school, I didn't know anyone, let alone him. I had *seen* him, yes. I knew *of* him, in that way you know *of* every person at your school. I spent most of my time at St. Helens High not talking at all, though, just sitting wherever a teacher told me to sit and taking comprehensive, amazing notes in every single class. I didn't play sports and I didn't have a group of friends — both of which came easily for Bobby. I was half-friends with one girl in my neighborhood, and even though she was nice to me, she frightened me. In Santa Fe, half of my school (I suppose a quarter, actually) had been Latina, but here, there was only one Latina in the whole school — this girl named Rhona. There was also one black boy. But I didn't know anybody. Sometimes my brother tried to tease me about not having a life, but I didn't care about it, I truly didn't. Someone, you see, had told me that I was a genius, and I was therefore busy being one.

The genius thing.

It's not as though I didn't talk to anyone. I wasn't toxic in any way, I wasn't someone who people hated, and actually, I think if I'd had different ideas about what was good, I might have been able to shift things and slide over and join a group of popular girls. Or just have friends. Not the ultra-popular girls, most of whom were on either the dance team, the volleyball team, or both (that's just what it was at our school, I don't know) and most of whom I doubted I had very much in common with anyway. But there was another group, a clique of a half dozen or so pretty girls who were also good students and who you got the feeling would be happy to talk to you if you approached them and asked them a question or if something came up where you had to interact. They were the nice/smart/decent sort of populars. I was partners with one of them in my English class junior year, a girl named Nicole Tolestra, and I actually even felt like now and again she was inviting me to do that, to cross over in that way and not be a quiet loner girl floating down the halls and drifting left to avoid the skaters and then drifting right to avoid the wrestlers, my posture bad because I was self-conscious about my boobs and being tall. I feel like I probably passed some kind of key test in Nicole's head about being pretty enough and smart enough to be in their group, but every time she made an overture I figured out a way to turn her down. After a semester she asked me one more time to do something, I think to go Rollerblading with her and her friend Erika, this other girl, and I turned her down again and she gave me a smile and was almost nodding and smiling in disappointment, as if to say *The offer will continue to stand, but I see that you are actually rejecting me now, so I'm going to stop asking.* The truth was I didn't want to be in any group. I was too afraid and I thought that would automatically have too many consequences. I didn't want to drink and I didn't want to be involved with any boys. I didn't want to think about sex until I was in my twenties. That seemed reasonable.

I know that my mother was never quite sure that she hadn't made the wrong choice in running away and leaving our father, and her not realizing that she had done the right thing seemed to make no sense, looking at her imprisonment in Montreal for what it was. It made me hate her during high school when she would out of nowhere make some sentimental comment about their wedding, or a party they'd gone to, or some noble characteristic of her husband, and I would think to myself: Wasn't that awesome when he kicked you too?

But I understand it a little better now. She was so hurt. I was so young. What happened to my childhood? How could I have been *that* angry as a child? I was so, so angry for all of those years. I would look at my mother and just think: You are a fool. How can you not see it about yourself? How can anyone's blind spot be this big? You are an absolute fool. I think I actually did hate her, I'm sad to say.

And it wasn't only these free-floating, abstract, and ultimately self-created emotions that all teenage girls end up directing at their mothers for some time. There were particular reasons I'd built up so much animosity toward her by the time we got to St. Helens. I'm sorry — there should be some specifics. She was often inappropriate, for example. One way she acted on her guilt, early on, was to take us, a lot, to different psychologists and psychotherapists. This was Santa Fe, I mean. Bobby hated going to therapy, but I liked it, I liked it right away.

My first therapist was a man named George Dumbler, who had a stark, unusually warm, almost entirely white office and whom I felt a connection with right away. (That was surprising, because I was *so* angry with my mother when I first realized where I was and what I was doing because I thought it meant she thought I was crazy, and I thought it might mean that at any moment, men could burst into Dr. Dumbler's office and put me into a straitjacket, depending on what I said to him. I didn't think that I was crazy; I thought that I was very sane, but I knew that my mother was always looking for power advantages and ways she could make the outside world appear to be in agreement with her about my insufficiencies.) But actually, on that first day, it was like Dr. Dumbler knew that *that's* what I was thinking, and so he started right into explaining, very clearly, that the only reason I was there was that I had seen a lot of pretty bad things happen between my mother and father when I was very young, and that — just based on how people are, and what usually happens when children see this — probably meant that I had a lot of emotions built up about it and to take care of that, I was just going to have to talk my way through some of it, and that there was nothing wrong with that. I felt deep joy hearing that. For real. He talked to me like I was an adult, actually, just like the man at the restaurant, and I appreciated it again, and so right away I started to listen to him, because it felt different. And then — this still on the first day — he told me that he'd looked over a few things, a few records of my schoolwork and tests, and that from his perspective, I was a gifted child and that it was especially important to deal with these things early on because I had such potential and that getting interrupted could prevent me from going a long way with whatever it was I wanted to do. So of course I responded to that too, because — just like every single person in the world — I'd always thought something like this might be true and here was a man talking to me like an adult and telling me that it was. So it was.

I don't know why he started down that track, started telling that story so early on, because I think if you were to dig up any actual report cards I had back in Montreal or find any standardized tests I'd taken, you would probably find that I was maybe *slightly* on the right side of the bell curve but that I wasn't in any kind of elite territory of intelligence according to the tests. But from that point on, we would always go back to that idea, and it became, actually, the guiding principle behind much of what we discussed. How I was uniquely talented. And the strange thing was I suddenly started doing well in school once we started talking this way. I started getting As on everything and studying in all my free time, and I hadn't cared much about school up until that point. So it might have been just an ingenious motivational technique. Maybe somebody should study that. (Although it has its downside, which is quarter-life psychological collapse.)

I met with Dr. Dumbler for about six months, but then during one of our meetings, right at the end, after we'd pretty much talked our way through the session and it was those last minutes when you feel like the therapist and you are both aware of it almost being over but you're still wondering if you might have one more flurry of productive talk, he said, "I need to talk to you about something else now, regarding our arrangement and our work together." He told me then that there was another therapist, a woman whose office was in the same building, and that he wanted to refer me to her in order for me to continue — productively — my work and move on to the next steps of self-knowledge and the next steps of dealing with the different traumas that had happened to me back in Canada. Of course this made me incredibly angry, right away, because now I had a crush on him, I suppose, and I asked him why we couldn't just keep working together, and why some other therapist would somehow be better for me, and he told me that he'd become worried about the state of our countertransference — after he said this he launched into an aside and told me that he usually didn't use words like this but that the concept really *actually* made up the backbone of a lot of his ideas in therapy and it really *was* a real thing — having to do with me being a young girl with an absent father and him being an older man around the age of my father who also had a daughter (even though she was older now, and this completely surprised me because I had no idea he had a daughter), and that the situation itself, nothing we did about it, might be "blocking" the next steps forward, and that he felt as though his colleague Jane, who, unlike him, focused on children, would probably be better equipped to take our work forward.

I wasn't devastated by this, that's not what I'm saying, and in advance of your concerns: no, it didn't have anything to do with

Dr. Dumbler being somehow attracted to me or him being a secret monster. He was actually a good therapist (essentially, minus this maneuver) and I still think back to some of the things we talked about. He was kind, intelligent, and a little bit bumbling — he once knocked over the plant next to his chair when he swiveled as he was trying to make a point, then became unbelievably flustered as he tried to scoop up the dirt and continue to be *engaged* with me and what we were talking about. I found that endearing. And on top of all this, the woman down the hall — Jane — turned out to be amazing too, and in many ways much better than he was, and it took me switching to realize that there could be even better therapists. He was right, maybe. His point about us not being a good match might have been right. One thing that was probably good, even though I immediately resented it: she picked up on the genius thing and seemed skeptical about it — at the very least, she challenged me all the time, even though at that point, I wasn't just getting As in every class but turning into the kind of student-vacuum-cleaner person who asked a thousand extra questions and signed up for every single academic-related after-school activity. Part of the reason for this was that it meant I never had to be home. Part of it was, I think, that I wanted to be the opposite of my mother, and not just self-sufficient but able to *do things* for other people. *That* self-sufficient. Before high school, even, I started looking at medical schools. That's what I wanted to be. A doctor. There was no doubt. I had taken to planning everything. And so naturally a part of this was based on my believing that I was special, intellectually, although now that I knew that I just needed good grades and a good transcript and good extracurriculars, I was starting to get a little more realistic. Still, for a long time, I didn't get why Jane always seemed to be trying to undermine this way I had of thinking about myself. I thought: What does she want?

For me to feel like I'm average? But then she sensed my irritation about it all, I think, because she stopped asking about it and we talked about different things.

Two things happened when I was in eighth grade, though. Some time in September, my mother asked if she could speak with me about having someone over for dinner the coming Saturday. She asked me this from the door of my bedroom. I was lying in bed, reading a book, reading *Superfudge*, even though I thought it was stupid and unsophisticated, but I liked it, I don't know. I was already in my pajamas, and I just looked at her, because I could hear already something in the tone of her voice that I didn't like, and she stayed in the doorway, hanging there on the doorknob. I told her fine. She came in a little bit and then told me that it was embarrassing but that she thought she needed to talk to me about it, and then she told me that she and Dr. Dumbler — George now, actually — had run into each other at the mall about a month before and had been seeing each other — only a few times since then, but they'd been seeing each other — and she wanted to know whether I would feel okay about him coming over for dinner?

"Not as a doctor," she said. "Just as a friend."

I didn't know *exactly* what *seeing each other* meant, but I could tell that whatever it was, it was something she was expecting me to be upset about, so I said something sarcastic and went back to reading my book.

So there was that, and they dated for about six months, and for all that time I hated both of them.

The second thing that happened was that in May, right when I was finishing eighth grade, my mother told me that she'd found a job and that we were going to have to move to Wisconsin, a little town there called St. Helens, and I told her great, that was just absolutely thrilling to me.

The only real time Ben Hanson and I spent together during high school came in my senior year, when I was forced against my will to be his lab partner in AP physics. There was a project. I was certain that it would be a disaster when I heard Mr. Entwild call our names, it was obvious there were problems with the pairing, and it was (therefore) also obvious that my 4.3 was going to be endangered because of the random-selection process performed by a teacher who didn't care anymore. After he read the names, I clenched up, sitting there, thinking of the arbitrariness. I couldn't bring myself to look back in the direction of my new "partner." Ben Hanson was a rich, scraggly, silent pothead who shouldn't even have been in the class; he had just gotten onto the AP track because he was a good tester and his sister had been smart. But he was not a good student. Not by my definition, anyway. So that brought up two things I hated. First: I hated people who were good at tests and didn't actually have to try very hard, because that's not what I was like, even though I wanted to be like that, and it didn't seem fair in the least. I believed then that there should be a meritocracy built around how much energy people put into something, how much they tried. (I held on to this for a long time, through most of college, somehow, but I had to just grow up and finally let go of that completely during medical school, where I met, time and time again, people who did far better than me on every test and studied much, much less. There's no justice when it comes to those things. That's okay too. It's not even a question of justice. It's just life, it's just people. And really, if I'm going to be adult about it myself now: there's just no justice. I don't know why people expect there to be. Animals don't.) And second: I hated *group* work — I hated it for justice reasons as well, the idea that you could end up paired with someone who didn't care and you therefore would have to do all these things just to come out even, and meanwhile, the other person would have to do less and would come out better than he would have on his own. It took your autonomy away from you and made you reliant on fate. So I obviously hated that, and add to that how much I hated other people's mediocrity, and how much I just hated physics, and I had a lot of hate.

This day, as soon as class was over, I went to Mr. Entwild to complain.

"What's his grade point right now, even?" I said. "Isn't he like a C student? He only shows up like every other class. Is he flunking?" I was lining up more arguments. There were plenty of non-academic arguments.

"It's not because he's not intelligent," said Mr. Entwild, who was clearing an acceleration equation — $a = dv/dt = (dv/dx)v = v(dv/dx)$ — from the dry-erase board. I watched his red chicken scratch disappear. "More like unmotivated." Mr. Entwild was an acceptable teacher, maybe somewhat old and somewhat on cruise control, just a year or two away from his retirement and his pension. I knew about these types. It was the younger teachers who usually put up with me the best. To them, a student showing up after class for extra help or a student signing up for every offered extra opportunity was a reason for optimism about education in general. People cared. They were the easiest kind for me to handle. Teachers like Mr. Entwild, realizing I was going to be "energetic," greeted me with something else, something I would maybe call weary fondness but also maybe call exhausted annoyance.

"Our grade is weighted really heavily on this project, though," I said. "You said in the syllabus —"

"Do a good job then."

"But it doesn't matter if I do a good job, necessarily."

"Lauren, come on."

"I'm going to have to check over all of his work."

"You have heard of science, haven't you?" he said. "You know we do a lot of checking over other people's work?"

"I know, but isn't it about being fair too? I mean in class? Shouldn't grades be fair?"

"It will be fair. Because first, Ben Hanson is a lot smarter than you're giving him credit for, I know that for a fact, and second, I understand the situation. You won't necessarily get the same grade as your partner. Now, which project are you choosing? Did you decide?"

"Yes."

"Which?"

"Space station."

"Good," he said. "You'll do well."

We lived in a house on Jackson Street on the east side of the river. It was a nice house but it was an older house, as were all the houses around it. Our neighborhood looked a lot like the suburban-neighborhood template you might call up in your head, but the one from the 1960s, not the one from the 1990s. The houses had yards but they weren't gigantic. They were smaller. All of the houses were about the same size. Some were bungalows, some were ranch style, some were just typical two-story homes.

Ben lived over on the west side of town, and technically I think his house — the whole development where his house was — was a little outside of St. Helens proper. Not by a lot, but by enough that on the drive there for our first outside-of-school meeting about our project, I spent a minute or two on a county highway, bleak and empty farm fields on my left and my right, feeling irritated that (a) someone would think it was a good idea to build a pod of huge, expensive houses so far away from everything, because that seemed so elitist, (b) people would want to buy houses so far away from everything, and (c) he had somehow convinced me that I was the one who should travel to *his* house to work on our project. When I agreed, I'd felt like it would be a show of strength to be the one to *go*, like he would understand this to mean that I was irritated that I was going to have to do more than him for us to do a good job and so I might as well do more all-around. But now, driving, it seemed as though he'd somehow won. I imagined him sitting in his parents' kitchen, waiting for me, eating chips and salsa. I had that exact vision and it infuriated me. It was freezing, and of course there was about a foot of snow covering everything. My mom's car was a complete-piece-of-junk Chevrolet Corsica and I was embarrassed, in advance, about pulling into an expensive house's driveway and leaving it there like a big turd I had brought along with me.

The first thing that happened was that Ben's mom offered us chips and salsa.

She really did. That set the tone. I said no and Ben said yes, and so the whole time we outlined the project at their kitchen table and divvied up the work, I had to listen to him chomping on tortilla chips. And under most circumstances, I would have been awful to him and barely even spoken and left after about twenty minutes. The feeling in their house, though — I'm not sure. It wasn't because it was big and they were rich. And no one was around but Ben and his mom. But the feeling in the house was different than the feeling in my house, very different, and I just felt sort of *good* in a way that wasn't normal for me. Ben, too, wasn't acting as badly as I'd expected him to act, and he actually seemed interested in the problems and what we were doing. I didn't think that he was high or anything. And like I said, I didn't know him at all. I had barely ever talked to him. I think I probably expected him to have awful breath and snicker at idiotic comments he made to himself and not know how to add 3 and 8. But the first thing he did, even before we started talking about the problem set, was ask me about what I was going to do for college and what I had thought of the application process and which of the AP tests I was going to take and whether I was studying for all of them. By the time we actually started doing the work I was in a different mood.

The basic idea of the project was that we were two researchers aboard a space station positioned somewhere past the asteroid belt and we had to make maybe twenty different calculations to describe some of the research we were doing. (I didn't understand, really, why there was such a big conceit, but Mr. Entwild was famous for his story problems and how he integrated the physics concepts into ways of understanding that weren't just the equations and the numbers, not just the "quantifiable bombast," and he said that was very important. He was famous at St. Helens High; I mean, in that way that high school teachers sometimes get famous when you and the other students are stuck back in eighth grade, waiting to move up, and the whole place gets romanticized until you realize a few years later that all along, it's been this awful modernist concrete building with terrible lighting and exhausted, flawed, underpaid people showing you around some ideas. Like you heard gooey whispers about that one *magic* teacher, even, and you made special requests to get into his class because of these famous *story problems*, even though actually, if you thought about it, I mean, if you really looked at them, there wasn't anything profound about them, and he had probably thought them all up thirty years before and had just Xeroxed them over and over again and changed some of the variables because it had always worked in the past and it chewed up a solid three weeks of the semester. I remember one time my sophomore year, someone, another nerd girl, telling me, "You get to learn about Einstein's theories in his class," and I thought that was romantic and exciting too, and in preparation read a number of texts on relativity, but in the end it just turned out that we got through Newtonian physics, and, after that, we did like two days of relativity, and he directed us to a big study packet we could do on our *own* if we wanted to be ready for any of the relativity problems on the AP test. He also said he had a videotaped episode of *Nova* he would lend us if we were interested that could also potentially be helpful. A videotape. [Because there usually was at least one of those problems, and more often than not, something on Bohr-Einstein too. I got a Bohr-Einstein problem but I was ready for it. I received a 5 on the AP physics test. That's not something you can fake, whatever Ben says.]) So there was a problem about the mass of the space station, then another one about the orbit of the station around the sun, then another problem about the impact *our* space station's mass had on a small asteroid particle that was near us. Beyond the mass problems there were problems about how well our telescope could see Earth, a Doppler-shift problem, a starlight-bending problem, an oxygen-consumption problem. Then there were a couple more steps, and this is when Mr. Entwild seemed to take everything *way* too far with the narrative aspects; apparently, according to the story of the story problem, we then had mechanical failure aboard our space station after a year of research, and I'm saying it was phrased like that, like we were asked to think about it as if *Ben and I* had been alone together in a space station for a year, really in outer space, and then our station started coming apart at the seams, and it was now an *emergency situation*, and so after that there were three or four problems that didn't even seem like physics, honestly, they were more like: Here's the situation. Here's the dilemma. Your partner's dying over there; you're over here. This and this and this and this and this and therefore this and then this. What do you do to get out of it? You didn't use math at all. And so of course Ben picked those ones to do first.

"So you're going to do the easy ones, and I'll do the hard ones," I said.

"These aren't easy," he said. "These are the hardest ones. Look at them. Did you even read number seventeen?"

"It makes no sense. I mean, there's like this magic space suit waiting in a special closet on the other side of the space station? And how do you get there with just the bad space suit if you have the two people? It's totally — it's, like, arbitrary. Why don't you just say, 'Oh, to get there, I pull out the *other* magic space suit I've been keeping in my space suitcase and we both go over to it and get it.'" I probably said the word *arbitrary* ten times a day.

"Because that's not the problem. Really, it's a logic problem. What *you're* saying is arbitrary."

"It is not."

"Do you know what *arbitrary* means?"

"But don't you see what I'm saying?"

"You're not really —" he said, and yes, okay: I understood what he was saying. But I didn't want him to be right.

"It's fine, actually," I said. "You can do those ones, it's fine. I'll just do — why don't I just do the first ten and you do the second ten? That way you get all the easy ones too."

He raised his eyebrows, pen in hand, looked down at his notebook, then up at me. He smiled. "Okay," he said. "Sounds fine."

"What?" I said. "Is that not okay?"

"No, it's good, it's okay," he said. "That's fine. And I can type all our stuff up for us too."

"Oh," I said. "You don't have to. I can type it. I can type it at the library."

"We have a computer," he said. "I can just do it after we meet next time."

According to Mr. Entwild's instructions, we had to meet at least twice out of school.

"We have a computer too," I lied.

"That's not what I meant."

"No," I said. "I'll type it. It's fine. It's really fine."

He laughed a little. He looked amused. "I feel like you think you have to do more because I'm dumb," he said. "Don't worry. I'm not gonna screw up your GPA. I like this project."

"It's not about my GPA. I don't —"

I could feel my cheeks immediately heat up and after five seconds I knew that they were scarlet. This is what happens to Irish skin. One among many other problems I had when I was a teenager was that I never thought that people could hear my irritation with them. I thought I was somehow expertly sneaky about it. Totally undetectable. But I had no ability to mask my emotions, really, and it was obvious. And so whenever anyone — anyone not my mother — pointed out that I seemed upset, or worked up, or anything, the first thing that happened was that I right away got embarrassed.

"I don't think you're dumb," I said. I tried, and failed, to smile at him, because now I really did feel like an awful person and he wasn't even that bad. "I'm a total control freak. It's fine. You're really smart."

"Thanks," he said. "Thanks, Lauren."

"You don't have to get mad about it," I said, but now he was just sitting there looking at me with a smirk on his face. Now he was acting more like I'd thought he would act when I first got there. But I had been the one to cause it. I crossed my arms, then uncrossed them and started going through my papers and organizing things without actually looking at them. I looked up at him again after a minute and he was still sitting in the same position.

"I guess I don't have my calculator," I said, because that's just what came out.

"I'm not mad," he said. "I'm totally not mad. I'm sorry. Seriously. This'll be good." He nodded. "I'm glad that we're partners. We'll do good."

I was uncomfortable for the whole ride home. Uncomfortable because I didn't really understand what had happened, and because of this, I was furious with him. Because somehow again it seemed like he had won and I had lost, or that he had somehow tricked me when I was first there, or at least he was acting like he had, but actually we'd only divided up our problems, had that conversation, had another conversation about cats, and had one conversation before that (with Ben's mother there, when she was giving him the chips and salsa) about how I'd applied early admission to Michigan and was definitely going there. When I said that she nodded toward Ben and said, "That's what I told him to do too. And instead he just barely got his one application to one school in on time." Ben didn't look embarrassed or irritated by this, though. He just sat there, then shrugged. He said: "I like Madison."

So anyway, that was the mood I was in — uncomfortable and mad at the same time — when I got to my house and my mom met me at the door, in tears, and told me that my father had been in some kind of car accident and was in the hospital in Pittsburgh, Pennsylvania.

"What?" I said.

She was in a hyperactive state and had already rushed away from me, back toward the stairs. Over her shoulder she said, "I don't know, I don't know the details. I'm packing right now." She continued up the stairs and disappeared, and I was left standing there in the foyer, bundled up in my huge coat and hat, backpack over my shoulder. It was freezing out. Really freezing.

"Why are you packing?" I said at the stairs. But she didn't hear me. "Mom?"

I dropped my backpack, took off my coat and hat, hung both up, and started up the stairs. Whenever my mom got (or gets — this is still true) crazy like this, I got (get) calmer and calmer. We're an inverse system. It's just sort of hardwired into us. If you gave her methamphetamines, I would probably go into a coma.

In her bedroom, I found her packing a suitcase that was open on the bed. She didn't look back at me in the doorway, even though I stood silently with my arms crossed for at least a minute, trying to reprimand her with my eyeballs.

"What are you doing?" I said. "I don't understand."

"I'm packing," she said. "I'm going to have to go over there and help him."

"What do you mean?" I said. "You have kids. You have — you can't just *go*. You have — you don't even talk to him. Why would you go help him?"

"Lauren."

"What? It's a totally normal question."

"Because he doesn't *have* anyone there to help him," she said. "He was on a business trip. He doesn't know a soul in Pittsburgh."

"So what?"

"So what? So what so what?"

"So what if he doesn't know anyone? How about how he doesn't know me? Or Bobby? How about that? Does that make you want to *help* him?"

"You'll understand," she said. "Eventually you'll understand."

My arms were still crossed. "That is such a cheap thing to say to someone younger than you."

My mother placed a folded sweater in the suitcase and then delicately crossed the arms of it across the chest. "Then you won't," she said.

"And what?" I said. "I'm just supposed to babysit Bobby the whole time you're gone? How long are you going to be gone? I have homework. I have this big project I'm doing."

"The tone of your voice suggests you would rather your father had *died*, Lauren. My goodness. Just calm down."

"How long are you going to be gone?"

She finally stopped packing, turned to me, twisted her palms so they faced the ceiling, shrugged in irritation, and said, "I don't know, Lauren. I do not know. A couple of days. It's not the end of the world. Things happen. People react. It's all complicated."

"No," I said. "It's not."

She left the next morning — I drove her to General Mitchell in Milwaukee and didn't say anything else to her about how strange I thought it was that she was traveling a thousand miles to nurse a wounded man who had once broken her scapula by pushing her into a bookshelf. She supposedly hadn't spoken to him in five years. Now I didn't believe that. She supposedly hated him. I hated him.

"You'll be okay for a couple of days," she said after I'd stopped in the loading zone. "You don't need to pout. You're old enough to — you're old enough now to understand how complicated these things are."

"Whatever," I said. "It's not complicated, but fine. Have fun."

"You have the money?"

"Yes."

"I'm going to call you right away," she said. "Tonight."

"Fine."

"Lauren," she said. "I mean this. Thank you. Thank you for being such an adult about this. I appreciate it. I do. I don't think Bobby could really understand, but I think you can."

I kept staring straight ahead, my hands on the wheel, and I could feel her staring at the side of my face. I was not capable of turning my head ninety degrees to look at her; I would not have been able to bear the expression on her face.

She didn't call for two days. She was gone for a total of eight. I don't know what happened while she was gone, nor do I know how much she and my father talked. I assume she sat with him in the hospital, but nothing came of it. It's not like they got back together. And actually, once she got home, she barely talked about the trip. She just told us that Dad said hello.

I admit that I got dressed up to meet Ben that night, and I went there planning — I don't know. This is too embarrassing. I have to go now; that is enough w/r/t what Ben asked me to provide. To sum up: What I remember from that time, my childhood and adolescence, was being furious. That's when I met Ben, that's the gap of time in which I knew him, which I think was the point. Sometimes two people just — sometimes there is no explanation. That could be another thesis. We got an A. Hooray! As far as I could tell, he made no mistakes on his part of the project. I was furious with him anyway, though, because he came to our second meeting, at the library, high, he was completely high, and this was only after I decided that maybe I did like him. That is what I'm saying. It was nothing, it was just — it was high school. It was a week of knowing someone. At the library I was wearing clothes that I would never usually wear, borrowed from my neighbor Rhona, who I had talked to about what I should do, what I could do, as in *what are the ways you can do things*, and so I was sitting there stinking of her perfume, and I had all these plans of things to talk about and I knew where I was going to sit at the table, even, and Bobby was being awful and he'd been lighting M-80s in the backyard for days, and so I don't know, I just got all dressed *up* and I was going to see, and he came late and he didn't even sit down or take off his coat. He just stared glassy-eyed at the wall after saying "Hey."

I said, "Come on. Take off your coat." I pulled the chair out and showed it to him.

He looked at me, then looked at the chair, then put his hands in his pockets.

"You look different," he said.

"No," I said. "It's just — it's just clothes."

He nodded.

"My cousin's dead," he said. "I just found out."

"What?"

He looked at me.

"He froze," he said. "I guess he's frozen."

"I don't understand," I said. "Your cousin?"

"Yes."

"Oh my God, Ben."

"I know."

"He's frozen?"

"Yes."

"I don't understand."

"I know."

He said he had to go.

Anyway.

Now so do I.

4

I Talk to Lauren and Realize I Know Nothing about Anything

The real estate lady came by later that week.

The first thing she said when I opened the door: "Isn't Ben Hanson a difficult person to get on the phone?"

To which I replied: "I don't know. Is he?"

To which she replied. "Yes."

She was on the stoop, and I stood inside, hand on the doorknob. She looked me up and down, seemingly disappointed already, then handed me her enormous paper coffee cup and started digging through her silver purse.

"Okay then. Here we are."

"I've been settling in."

Theresa Orgogliosi glanced up at that, then looked back down to her purse. "It's fine, Ben, actually," she said, waving a hand. "I was a little concerned you were in there dead too." She laughed at her own joke. "Can you imagine me trying to sell the house then?"

"That would be awkward."

"Hopefully we'll get an out-of-towner and we can just ignore your uncle. Sometimes they ask, unfortunately."

She was an attractive woman. The amount of *g*'s and *o*'s in her name had made me expect her to be a frumpy demon of some kind, but she was in fact a pretty, petite, olive-skinned, non-demonic, almond-eyed forty-something who smelled of Suave deodorant and had an amazing body.

"I'm not *totally* joking, though," she said, looking up again from her search. "Just so you know, I know about — I know about your struggles."

"You'll have to be more specific."

"You doing okay? Sort of nesting in here?"

"Sure," I said. "It's a big nest. I'm used to crappy little garbage homes."

She pulled a disposable camera from her purse and held it up.

"Come in," I said, stepping back and putting down her cup. "I was just going to make some coffee."

"My older brother had a whole thing with crystal meth, by the way," she said once she was inside, speaking loudly as she looked around the living room. "It was *terrible*," she continued, drifting over toward the fireplace. "I mean, the sheer amount of *bullshit* was unbearable, to start with, not to mention everything with the money — I need money, Mom, I need to borrow some money; Theresa, I need to borrow some money, no, I'm clean now, no, I stopped, no, that's done now. It took us *years* to figure out it was all bullshit. *All* of it. I still sometimes go back to Al-Anon just to remember. And then how much it aged him, how he acted to my sister-in-law that whole time. He used to be so *handsome* and he turned into a skeleton. It was a sad thing." She nodded as though she'd made the final point on the matter. "Drugs. But he did get clean," she said. "He did eventually completely clean up. So that was good. He's in Eau Claire now."

"I'm not really — I'm not really in that state. I never was."

"No, I know," she said. "You're more of a flub."

"What's a flub?"

"Hm? Oh, I don't know," she said, shrugging. "Just sort of a...pfft." Mouth sounds of failure. "When you're playing golf. When you hit the ground in front of the ball. You know. Do you bowl? A gutter ball. Whatever."

Theresa said then that she was on her way to work in Milwaukee and needed a set of pictures for the online listing. She apologized about the time, but I assured her it didn't matter and that I had been up baking bread since 4:00 a.m. anyway.

"I'm surprised you don't use a digital camera," I said, moving us along. "It seems like everyone else does." I thought of my sister telling me that my Ludditeism was lame. And yet here it was being awesome.

"Oh, I know, isn't that funny?" she said, looking derisively at the little yellow box in her hand. "Everyone says that when I pull these suckers out. You just get used to something, I guess. And besides, all I do is drop this at the drugstore next to my office and they e-mail me a link where I can get all the pictures. It's the same. It's magic either way."

"I can't remember. How exactly is it that you know my mother?"

"I was her real estate agent," she said after she'd snapped a few more pictures of the living room, her face still scrunched up in concentration. "Then too. Do you not remember me? We met once. I sold your old house for you then. You were — well, you were a typical teenager, actually. I don't even think you looked me in the eye. I understand now, trust me! But I was also around a little bit in your mom's book club." She looked at me as though she were seeing my face for the first time. "That only started after you were gone to college, I think. So, no. You wouldn't. And, my

God, can I just say that you look *exactly* like your uncle, Ben? It's *uncanny*."

"You think so?"

"Jesus," she said, coming closer. "It's a little scary, actually."

"My dad says I look like my grandpa."

"Genes," she said. She went back to her pictures. "Also, and I'm just saying this: Did you ever think about shaving once in a while? Or possibly getting a haircut?"

"I sometimes do those things."

"And you went to Wisconsin? For college?"

"Yes."

"My son — my son is thirteen. Maybe it's a little early to plan his college career, but I hope that he goes there, I really do. I always wanted to go there. It seemed so *fun*. I ended up at Carroll. Which was fine, but it wasn't Madison, you know? I went once for Halloween. *Amazing* experience. I woke up lying with my feet in the lake, dressed in a different costume than the one I'd gone out wearing."

"I liked it there."

"Mm," she said, looking at the fridge. "Do you mind if I just get the upstairs? The living room's really the selling point, but I just want to be sure I have everything."

She didn't wait for me to answer and soon disappeared up the stairs.

I didn't follow her. Instead I went into Denny's small office and sat down at the desk, passing through the invisible clouds of her perfume. I put my head on my hand for a moment, letting the smell linger, trying to decide if she was the type of woman who liked to discuss mortgage payments during sex. I looked at the computer. I had placed Jeremy's tower — which was silver, and sleek, and *brushed*, and probably custom-made, as I could see no decals or branding anywhere — beside Denny's more modest gray Dell. I stared at it for a good five minutes.

After prison I spent a lot of time at my old diner. I went every day near the end. There was a girl. I didn't know her name, but she knew me, this waitress, or she knew my face at least, and it had now been a solid two years since I'd come in with Allie for pancakes. (How was it that she was still here, this waitress? I wondered it all the time. Still the same? How was it that she hadn't seemed to change after I'd spent all those nights in the darkness?) So the last visit to the diner before leaving for Wisconsin, via Seattle. After I'd decided what I was going to do. It was in the afternoon. It was two thirty; the place wasn't very full. There were a few women with babies near the front window, an older couple two tables down, a handful of singles scattered about. It felt good to be near people. I didn't get conversations out of solitary meals at the diner, but at least I was required to talk and could be reminded that other lives were out there. Prison — even white-collar prison — is a weird place. You see people and talk to people all the time, but after a while, you start to imagine that you are the only one actually incarcerated. That your prison is a ghost town and you're the only one in it. Of course there's no sex. Not for me, at least, as I had nobody to visit me for conjugals. Right here among these people in the diner, though, you could almost force yourself into imagined relationships, and I had become good at it. My waitress was my wife, the women with the babies were my sisters, and those babies were my nieces and nephews. Amazingly, they were all born only four months apart, and now my sisters would have this bond for the rest of their lives. I would be the uncle who would not forget birthdays, because they all came in the same season. They'd be able to discuss the terrible twos as they came, they'd be able to discuss the pros and cons of different preschools and kindergartens and whatnot. Occasionally I would join them for their weekly baby lunches, depending on whether I was busy that day, and all of us could discuss how strange it was that we were no longer part of the youngest generation or (for that matter) the generation of the main people on TV, that marketing didn't seem directed at us anymore, how we didn't quite know what to make of the early days of this new status as adults but that it did seem to have its benefits, like a remarkable unbounded free-dom, despite the stresses and responsibilities, which seemed to want to take that same freedom right back. Their husbands, my three brothers-in-law? It was a shame they didn't all get along per-fectly, but at least no one had married anyone unbearable, there wasn't a toxic member of the family; at least everything felt stable, despite that land deal gone bad and despite the unfortunate argu-ment about God and politics that one night three years ago when we were all in Phoenix and when (we can now admit) we'd all had too much to drink. My sisters would chide me for my immaturity, but only a little, and warmly. I loved them. For the most part we'd always have a good time. We would never mention that life, our one life, was slipping away.

It would be different with Theresa. I would get fat immedi-ately, I thought. I would covet the fatness. She would let it happen and it would make her happy. But only after a decade. I'd stay in shape for one decade. Being as I was the younger one — the young trophy husband, if you will — she would spend the first few years showing me off around town, and I would therefore need to stay in shape so as to *not* humiliate her. But there would come a point when the passions cooled and I began to use half-and-half in my cereal. That point would come. What's interesting is that it would not matter so much. Because by then we'd have our chil-dren, and we'd be preoccupied with preparing them for the world.

One of them, Betty, would be interested in creating houses out of large cardboard boxes. She'd be so interested that we'd clear out an entire room for her creations and begin crawling through them before they were finished. My obesity would become a problem when she decided to create an eco-friendly home out of the boxes, as I would become trapped amid the cardboard water-recycling tanks and would have to call for help and then eventually tear my way out like Godzilla. Our son, though, would be interested in centaurs...

"Ben?" called Theresa. "Where'd you go?"

"I'm here," I called. "In the office."

"All done."

I got up and walked with her to the door. I asked her — for no better reason than to prove to myself after my extensive daydream that I was not insane — I asked her if the economy being as bad as it was and all the doom-talk about real estate had been trouble for her business.

"Oh God. You have no idea," she said. "I haven't sold a house in six months."

"Well," I said. "I hope you sell this one."

"That's right," she said. "The faster I sell it, the faster you can go home. Is that what you mean?"

To which I did not know quite what to say.

~~~~~

I took an unexpectedly dramatic shower and went back to the computer. Grant had called, and I called him back. He said there was something happening in town. Did I remember Bobby Sheehan? Lauren Sheehan's little brother? He was an artist now, or at least was calling himself one, and he was having an opening at the gallery downtown. Grant said I should go.

"What art gallery?"

"I don't know," he said. "We've got one now."

"Are you going?"

"Me?" he said. "Of course not. I don't like art."

"Everyone likes art."

"I don't."

"You're calling me to ask me to go to an art show you don't want to go to?"

"That's right."

"What kind of art is it?"

"Paintings, I think. I saw on the flyer that the show's called Painting My Feather."

"I'm picking you up. I have to get out of here anyway."

"I got my kid tonight, man," he said. "I can't go."

"Bring her along," I said. I tried to say it like a jolly, grizzled old man.

"What was that?"

"What?"

"The voice?"

"That was a voice I was doing," I said. "A guy. An old guy."

"I didn't find it convincing."

"I'd like you to come."

It took about ten minutes of this before I got him to say yes. But I suddenly did not want to stay there; I hadn't just been saying that. Not another night doing nothing.

It had been a week and the only journeys I'd made were to the grocery store and back up to the top of Beau Pointe to idiotically look down on my town, with less and less peaceful thoughts. So far, I was nowhere near the epiphanic newness I'd dreamed about on the plane. My anxiety levels were at record-breaking heights. I'd spent time in all the different rooms, studying the fossilized remnants of my uncle's life, thinking back, thinking forward. But the truth was, the feeling of not knowing what I was doing here or why I was doing it had hardened in my gut and turned into a dense little diamond. I had already begun to think about going back west. I had started over before. I could start over again somewhere else.

I put down the phone, then double-clicked the icon in the middle of the desktop. I had placed it there after finding it in the Downloads folder. It was called THERIVERSGAME_beta_v3.2.

They'd actually made the thing.

Jeremy and I were in Denver when we were both around twenty-four. He'd come to Denver from Phoenix and I had come from Madison, and our mutual friend was our mutual dealer, a kid named Derek Something whose last name I never knew and who disappeared into thin air in the summer of 2000. This was not all that unusual a thing for drug dealers to do, mind you, and I didn't think too much about it, as I had plenty of other people I could call, but for a few weeks all of Denver felt cashed, and one day I walked into a coffee shop, recognized Jeremy from a party, and sat down to talk to him. Soon the topic of Derek came up, and he asked me if I had any idea where he'd gone.

"No idea," I said.

"I hope he's okay," Jeremy said.

"I'm sure he's fine."

(I would later find out that he was not and that he had fled to Phoenix to avoid arrest. Which did not work.)

Jeremy nodded at this thoughtfully; he looked like he really did care, I will say that. He was well put together, clean-shaven, and wearing an orange polo shirt, and this made him different than almost anyone I knew. For this reason he seemed interesting.

He had a laptop with him, closed and beside him on the couch he'd taken over. He had papers, books, and notebooks scattered to his left and to his right, as well as on the table between us.

"Do you need me to get you anything?" I said.

"Do you mean coffee?"

"Drugs."

"Oh," he said. "No. It takes me six months to get through one bag of pot. I was just calling him about his bike. He was going to sell it to me."

"You're buying Derek Something's bicycle?"

"I was going to, yes. Do you think there's a problem with that?"

"No."

Jeremy, I was noticing, was the kind of person who always looked distracted. The one or two times we'd talked in the past, I'd been certain he was deeply bored by what I had to say, but now, looking at him, I realized that it was just that his affect was a little off, and that he was painfully shy. His legs were crossed and he had turned to stare out the window at Sixteenth Street. Outside, it was raining. I was about to ask him what he was working on when he turned back and said, "Do you play chess?"

"I do."

"Do you feel like playing?" he asked. "There's a board." He nodded at a shelf to his right.

"Sure."

He beat me twice and I beat him once. The first game was the one I won, and I could tell that it irritated him tremendously. He hadn't expected it to be close, let alone an actual challenge. But I also sensed, when I saw how he opened for the second game — this time he offered a queen's gambit, which I declined — that he was changing his strategy based on how I'd played the previous game, which in turn spelled certain doom for me. I have a weird style of playing, which I'd learned from my cousin Wayne, that had more to do with confusing the shit out of your opponent than it did with mounting a harmonious assault or creating a unified defense. In that way it was superficial. But I could do nothing else, which Jeremy intuited. He beat me handily in the second game and destroyed me in the third. Such is the danger of improvisation when you're outmatched by someone who really knows how to play.

"You're good," he said as he put the pieces back in the box.

"Ah," I said. "Now that you beat me, you can say that."

A quick smile flashed across his mouth — the first one I'd seen since I sat down. His face, though, soon dissolved back into its focused seriousness. "I had lessons," he said. "My parents used to make me go to tournaments."

"I can tell you know what you're doing in a way I don't know what I'm doing."

"Where did you learn to play?"

"My family," I said. "Growing up."

"I'm actually not that competitive a person," he said, to which I thought: Of course not. "I hated those things."

"Stressful."

"They were," he said. "It's bullshit. I had an ulcer by the time I was twelve." He took a sip of his coffee, which had to have been cold. "I really did. It had a big impact on me. But I do like games."

I told him I did too.

Eight years later, here I was looking at the title page of the game Jeremy had made, which was set to launch, according to his company's website, on the first of January. The Rivers. It existed.

A beta version of it, anyway. What the site called a soft launch. The real thing would come out next summer. And it wasn't as though I had stumbled upon some secret copy of the game — there were probably hundreds of copies out there being tested before the launch, and I'm sure Jeremy had just installed a version of it on their computer at home so he and Allie could play around with it. But Jeremy had lied about at least one thing during our chat: my name was not listed anywhere on the credits page. It had taken me a few days to beat the game to get to the credits, and it wasn't fair, since I had written the majority of the puzzles. The others, those that I hadn't written, were weak. I'm not being a dick. They were bad. They weren't easy but they weren't very elegant. And any asshole can make something complicated, difficult, and tedious. Anyone can make something impenetrable. What's interesting is the delight someone feels when it becomes clear that it's all made sense from the start.

It somehow worked with the Rivers, despite the baggy mess of it all. The game's design, the overall visual experience of the game — it was fucking gorgeous. There is no other way to say it. (Most of the twenty million people who've played it by now tend to say the same thing.)

And that was the original plan. That was the whole idea. To make something beautiful and disguise it as something entertaining.

So first things first: For the idea to work, the actual game had to be good. Fair enough. And this is why I had felt a growing sense of real excitement that day as Jeremy and I sat there and talked — real excitement for something, real enthusiasm, which I hadn't felt in years. It had been clear to me that I was good for almost nothing beyond tutoring rich kids for their tests, which I didn't even like doing, but during the conversation I started to think: You know what? I could make a game. That is something that I could do. In fact, that is something I *want* to do.

I don't know any real game designers, but I've always assumed

each has his or her own way of categorizing games, and I've sometimes wondered whether my system resembles any of theirs. For
me, what makes sense most is to think about games based on
the central emotion they summon. And by this I don't mean
tension — all good games should summon tension. I just mean
there's usually a central emotion around which specific games
are built, and the details of the experience, if it's a good game,
should emerge based on that feeling and beholden to that feeling, to that dominant note. I think about it this way because I
can't stand it when I hear this or that "adult" explain to me why
games are foolish, children's things, because they amount to nothing, mean nothing. Whichever games. People say it about sports;
people used to say it about novels; now people say it about video
games. Why would you get so upset? you might hear one of these
imaginationless people mutter as you, for example, I don't know,
throw down the plastic gun attached to a video game at the mall
you've been playing for six hours, pumping quarter after quarter
into the machine because you only want to get to the end, to have
the final battle, to finish it, to know what happens, to feel that
sense of accomplishment, even though yes, you are in your late
twenties, and the gun, which is attached to a metal cord, ricochets
off the machine when you throw it and there is a loud bang and
you think it might be broken. Perhaps you swear. Perhaps you are
asked to leave the arcade. Perhaps there are teenagers looking at
you, unsure what to make of you. So I think about it in this way,
for all the people who don't understand moments like this.

Here's an example: Space Invaders is an anxiety game. So is
Tetris. Another way to think about these: the Apollonian games.
You use a skill you develop during the game — a skill you wouldn't
otherwise have or ever need, like judging which iteration of a
shape will help you most or developing a good touch on a pizza-

grease-stained joystick, tap tap left or one more little tap right, then fire — and you use that skill to dispel anxiety, which accrues like rainwater in a bucket. And it's wish fulfillment, really — we wish we had such a joystick and such a button for life. We play out that fantasy of order. We wish we had the skill of life and the good sense to do what is in our best interests, to not sabotage ourselves because some unstated compulsion tells us that we must. We wish we could do that. We wish we were that good at living. Most anxiety games up the anxiety as you go: more invaders, faster-falling blocks, and so on. Like life. The result is that you need to get better as time goes on just to keep your head above water. The skill is relatively simple but precision is crucial. The pleasure of a game like this is the pleasure of cleanliness, the pleasure of comprehensive control. Imagine, deep into a game, a perfectly clean Tetris field, not a block to be seen after you clear out a quad stack. True freedom.

Then there are frustration games, which are in the same family. Games like darts. Like bowling. Like golf. Frustration games keep the skill but take the time crunch out of the equation completely — you just have to be *good*, on command, at a multistep skill. You are your only antagonist. Frustration builds up because there are no impediments beyond your own limitations; the pleasure comes from intentionality, from trying to do things and succeeding, from doing deliberately.

I've never liked these games.

Then, after those, a whole world of games I like but have always feared: the Dionysian games. Games of utter destruction. First-person shooters, third-person shooters. Doom, Contra. I think the feeling is catharsis. But I wouldn't know where to start.

The previous morning, I had made the very unhealthy decision to play the Rivers through a second time, and now I resisted the urge to load my saved game — I was at the waterfall — and instead shut down the computer. They'd pulled the story out of an elaborate puzzle about rivers I'd come up with at about my halfway point at Chestik, and I was surprised how well it translated into a whole self-contained story, as I had only really written it as a frame for a particular encryption thing and hadn't spent much time on the story. But that's what they used. They'd blown it up, turned it into something much bigger. They'd ignored the puzzle, taken the tale.

I went out to the living room, planning to get a little more coffee before I ran. I stopped on my way to the kitchen and looked at the steel container of Denny's ashes. It was strange to see it there. I thought of what Theresa had said about our resemblance.

And yet now he was this.

"I know," I said. "I know."

~~~~~

Grant called late that afternoon and said it would be better if he drove to the gallery. "Jamie doesn't like other people's cars," he said. "It's not negotiable."

I was surprised to see a minivan pull into the driveway at quarter to five — through the glare of the windshield I saw Grant's somewhat serious driving face, and I stood up from the stoop and came over and got in. I had seen that same face behind the windshield of his car fifteen years before, pulling up to get me before we went out into the country and smoked bowls. Things were different now.

It was a warm night, which meant I could wear the one nice shirt I had, a short-sleeved gray button-down that had been a Christmas present from my parents six years before.

I had also finally shaved and washed my hair.

"You went from the Unabomber to Tucker Carlson," said Grant. "Dude."

"Who's Tucker Carlson?" asked a giggling voice from the backseat, and I turned to see a kitten princess sitting in the back of the van, eyeing me mischievously. She had on a poufy, iridescent white dress and was holding a wand. She also had whiskers and triangular ears.

"He's a douchebag, honey," said Grant.

He glanced at me as he put the minivan into gear. "We were getting a little stoked for Halloween back home. Two months early. That's why the double costume."

Jamie pointed her wand at my head and said, "Who are you, though?"

"I'm Ben."

"My name is Lula, not Jamie."

"Hi, Lula."

"Poof. *Shoop.* Vanish." She said the three words as though she were counting.

"How is it up here?" Grant asked. We'd pulled out of the driveway and were curving back down Beau Pointe, toward town. "You're trying to sell it then, right? Did you clean it up?"

"The real estate agent was over this morning," I said. "It's just getting listed again."

"What's the real estate agent's name?"

"Theresa Orgogliosi."

"Oh, man. I know her," he said. "She doesn't live too far from me. I always see her mowing her lawn. Super-hot lawn-mowing, you know? I wouldn't have ever thought to — well. You get it. She's also in my bowling league. She's kinda nuts, I think. In that sort of hot-crazy way."

"How's she nuts?"

"She's just eccentric, I think, you know? Outspoken. She's on the only all-women team in the league, right, and before, when they were trying to get in, the women threatened to sue the bowling alley unless they dropped the men's-teams-only policy. It was funny as shit. All these old dudes up in arms. The guys all quit to go be in the league at the other alley but came back like a week later because all the lanes are warped over there and it's constantly midnight bowling and there's teenagers hanging out everywhere, drinking vodka and Sprite and hooking up in the bathrooms. So all the old-timers come back, all grumbly, but then they realize these ladies are fantastic and totally lively and funny and it's like, 'Whoops, we're dumb-asses.' Not to mention they all get to stare at Theresa's ass when she's bowling."

"Is their team good?"

"No, dude," said Grant. "They're last place every year. They've got one woman who rolls like a two fifty every game and everyone else rolls sixties. Those chicks can party, though. They come in and they've got their matching pink shirts all embroidered up and nice. They've all got their own balls. They come in and there's just gimlets flowing down to them from the start. Gimlets. That's how they do it. You have to respect that."

"What's their team called?"

"They used to be called the Divorcées, because they're all divorced except one of them, the big roller, she was still married at first. But then eventually she got divorced too, which I find hilarious, because her husband is also in the league and the whole thing played out during the run-up to the play-offs, and you could just see this guy losing it, looking over to her lane like a lost puppy dog. But I think the women changed their team name and now they're called the No-Ballers."

"I'm not sure if I feel more or less confident about selling the house now."

"I'm sure you'll sell it," Grant said with optimism. "It's nice up here. Look around. Look at this rural, pristine beauty." He held out a single open hand like a beauty queen and motioned to the woods.

"Very nice," I said.

"Theresa'll sell it. For all the talk of the market having gone to complete shit, these places still sell. It's not like Miami. I would buy it if I had the money. I would love to come up the hill. Oh, also? I forgot this. The best part. Theresa? She packs heat. Always."

"Yeah?"

"Yeah."

I imagined Theresa O. shooting wildly at a firing range.

"I'm glad you called. I haven't really left the house since I saw you at Golden's."

"Yeah, man," Grant said. "You were sounding like a caged animal."

"Weird feelings."

"You haven't even been down to town?"

I shook my head. The feeling in my gut. And there was more, none of which I felt like explaining to Grant. I had felt, since I got to Denny's, an opposing force coming from St. Helens, as though it might not want me in it, or might not want me back. Reverse tractor beam. Very reasonable, this. I had been wary of all the old signifiers and markers and had not wanted to stroll the downtown streets and feel all those things old places make you feel. Going into Golden's was enough.

We came to the bottom of the hill and turned left, went past Golden's, then continued west, toward St. Helens proper. There were other reasons I had stayed put, it wasn't just an aversion to entering into this life; I had been preoccupied playing the game, getting the house in order, but as I watched through the window as 121 slowly transformed into Main Street, I felt a new and more focused wave of some wariness I didn't understand: the tree-lined streets and the perfect sidewalks and the streetlights of my home-town, U-shaped and black, the faux gas lamps hanging from them like flower buds. The past felt awkward and weighty. I felt like I was circling back, but with less than I'd had the first time around. There was something so depressing about that.

"So as I said, I'm not a big art person," Grant said, slowing now to twenty-five as we came to the dead center of town. There were crosswalks here, where pedestrians had the right-of-way, cross-walks I remembered blowing through haphazardly at sixteen. "I don't know what this is going to be like," Grant continued. "All of Bobby's friends are class of '98. I don't really know them. It'll probably be a coke-fest. I mean Coca-Cola, honey."

"I used to have a girlfriend who was a painter," I said. "I had to go to these all the time. Just find one part of the painting that makes you think something, then talk about that. Just keep hitting it." I looked at a new Walgreen's at the corner of Bishop and Shaker. "Whatever. Try to use the word *quadrant* whenever you can."

〰〰〰

The gallery was on Second Street, which ran along the east side of the river; it was in a stone building I thought I remembered as hav-ing been the post office, and when we sifted through the crowd of smokers mingling on the steps and got inside, I saw that I was right. Things looked different — the walls on the first floor were all now clean, white drywall, lit by spotlights and adorned with Bobby's canvases (although I noted that the sign at the entrance called him ROBERT M. SHEEHAN, MFA, not BOBBY, HYPERACTIVE STONER, which was my memory of him). The place was packed. At the edges of the room, guests made their way among the paint-ings, but there was a dense crowd of intense, well-dressed people toward the middle, chatting and laughing in pods of twos and threes. Something jazzy was echoing through the room. I could have been in Portland.

"This is my worst nightmare," Grant said.

He was holding Jamie's hand. Unlike her father, she seemed happy to be here, judging by the way she was casting spells on the people up on the second-floor balcony, which ringed the room about twenty feet above the floor. I wondered if the hand-holding wasn't more for Grant.

"It's good," I said. "It's okay. It'll be good. Who paid for this place?"

"Some woman who moved here a little while ago," he said. "She and her husband built this huge mansion out in the woods and the dude crashed his car and died about six months after they got here."

"That's terrible."

"She's right there," Grant said, and pointed to a silver-haired woman, elegantly dressed, speaking to a small crowd on the other side of the room. "Silver fox," he said. "I hear she was glad he died. Do you want a drink?" He had spied a table with glasses of wine.

"Just some water."

"Watch her, will ya?" he said, nodding to Jamie.

"Sure. We'll go look at some pictures."

"Go with Benjy, baby," Grant said. "Daddy'll be right back."

Upon releasing Grant's hand, she immediately took mine, as though she'd known me her whole life. I didn't understand kids at all.

"You like it so far?" I said.

"Yes."

"What grade are you in anyway?"

We walked together around the wall on the first floor, looking at some of the paintings. I asked her about Jamie's school, which she refused to discuss. But she did tell me a story about her breakfast. We talked about it and both agreed that Life cereal was amazing.

Grant found us a few minutes later, standing in front of one of the bigger canvases in the gallery. Jamie went and stood behind her father's leg. He gave me my water, took a sip of his wine, and said, nodding at a canvas, "That reminds me of the time I took seventeen hits of acid."

"It's a little out-there."

"What am I looking at? Am I looking at Africa?"

"I couldn't tell you. Although actually —" I turned my head. "Maybe."

"I think I'm looking at a big fucked-up map of Africa."

"Daddy!" Jamie said.

"I think it's Africa."

"Hard to tell."

But I meant that in a good way, if such a thing was possible. (Africa. Was there anything I knew less about than *Africa?* What was Africa to me but a place I would never go that was full of people I would never know? I knew virtually nothing.) It had always seemed to me that once an artist chose to create something as abstract as the painting Grant and I were dumbly staring at, you could either find or not find an instruction manual in it. Somewhere. Right now, though, I couldn't see one.

"Are you on the wagon?" Grant asked.

"Yeah."

"I mean, I heard that. I knew that, kinda. But I am asking for a reason," he said. "Not to be nosy."

"What's that?"

"I hate to be the one to tell you this," he said, "but the lady you shaved for is working the wine table."

I looked in the direction Grant had come from. Lauren Shee-han, in a white, collared shirt, was pouring wine for an elderly couple at a table across the room.

Her face was how I remembered it, and the particular darkness of her hair, even her expression as she said something to the woman at the table, but when she spoke, she smiled in a way that was unfamiliar, and did not fit into my memory. Not unlike my reaction to the town on the ride down. Both what I knew and what I didn't, or never did. And yet it all seemed familiar.

"Why is she the caterer?"

"She's probably saving money for Bobby," he said. "I dunno."

The woman she was serving walked away. Lauren straightened her shirt and looked out across the room — and that thing that I had seen was gone. I turned back to Grant before she saw me looking.

"I didn't shave for her," I said.

Grant raised his eyebrows, nodded, and finished his wine all at the same time. He reached down for Jamie's hand. "Come on, sweetheart," he said. "Let's go look at the pictures upstairs. Ben has to go stalk a lady."

"What's *stalk*?"

"I'll tell you up there. It's like love but creepy."

I contemplated the canvas for a few more minutes, sipping my water and visualizing myself walking directly out of the gallery and diving into the river. There was no dignity in this, he was right. There was no dignity in anything I was doing. My presence at this gallery was sheer desperation.

Confidence built back up, I went toward the table. When I got there, I set down my empty plastic cup and she looked at me and smiled a thin, neutral smile and said, "Hello. White or red?"

"Neither, actually," I said.

"Welcome to the wine table."

"I just came over to say hello," I said, holding out a hand. "It's Ben," I said. I brought the hand back — she had not even looked at it — and tapped my own chest. "Ben Hanson. From high school."

"I recognize you."

Her expression was pretty far from joyful, but she did now stick out her hand. Her expression: the look of a driver realizing the air in the right front tire is low.

We shook.

"Hi," I said. "We had that — we did that one project together. Senior year."

I couldn't tell if she expected me to say more or if she was just being polite and waiting for me to leave her alone.

"Anyway. You're busy."

"You don't actually want any wine?"

"No."

"Okay," she said. "It was nice to see you again, Ben Hanson." She looked over my shoulder at a woman behind me and smiled for the first time. "White or red, Mrs. Dobber?"

〰〰〰

"She's like that with everyone, don't worry," Grant said after I found him upstairs on a sofa. "Be cool." Jamie had summoned up a doll from somewhere and was sitting nearby, her skirts in a heap around her. "It's not you," he continued. "She's just got this —" He moved his hands around his face, creating an invisible sphere. "She's got this wall. Maybe created by like eight different kinds of antidepressants."

"I don't remember her being like that," I said. "I remember her as shy. But not cold?"

"Yeah, well. She's different. She's prettier and meaner."

"She was nice to Mrs. Dobber."

"She's different, dude. She showed up in town like three or four years ago and pretty much every single guy in the county went crazy," he said. "Because first, just look at her. But beyond that, she's a doctor. Or now I guess a vet? And the dating pool in St. Helens for people over the age of eighteen and under the age of a hundred is rough. Rough. It was like Marilyn Monroe got a divorce and moved here from New York. There was this huge flurry. But then it became pretty obvious that there was a little — there were damage issues."

"What does that mean?"

"Fucked-up pretty girl," Grant said, shrugging. "I dunno."

"How fucked up are you talking about?" I said. "What are you even meaning when you say that?" Grant was talking in a way that was a little irritating to me. He didn't mean anything by it, I knew that, but it reminded me of something I didn't like about myself. Something glib.

"How's this: She tried to kill herself right after she came back. Pills. Out on the baseball diamond."

I looked down at her over the rail. "Jesus."

"Yeah."

"Well," I said, turning back. "She seems okay now. Sort of. She's not *that* pretty."

"Okay."

"Marilyn Monroe is blond," I said. "And dead."

"Exactly," Grant said. "So she was alive when she came back, which was fantastic, then it was touch-and-go there when she was almost dead. But she doesn't date. She doesn't go out at all, as far as I know. I mean, it's not like I'm all plugged into the social circle or anything, and yeah, actually I spend most of my time with meat, dude, so the only time I ever see her is when she buys cold cuts from me, but I'm just saying that —"

"Whoa whoa whoa whoa whoa!" said someone, a man, and I felt a hand on my arm. "I'm sorry to interrupt, gentlemen. But is that Ben Hanson? *The* Ben Hanson?"

I turned and saw Bobby Sheehan there, bearded and dressed in a three-piece suit.

He had a pair of bright red sunglasses perched on his head. He was smiling like a goon. "Fucking Ben Hanson, right?" he said. "That *is* you!" He slapped me on the shoulder.

"Hey, Bobby."

"Yes!" he cried, and he pulled me into a hug that nearly lifted me off the ground, just as Grant had done the week before. The difference was that Bobby was about six inches shorter than me and I barely knew him.

I bore it with an awkward grin until he put me down.

I was surprised Bobby was so happy to see me — I hadn't known him half as well as I'd known Grant. But then again, he had fit a lot better into my world than Lauren ever had, and so at least I had hung out with him a few times outside of school. I had also sold to him.

"What're you doing here?" he asked happily, stepping back.

"I'm taking care of my uncle's place up on Beau Pointe Road," I said. "But hey, man, congratulations. Congratulations on all of this...work." I looked at Grant, who nodded at me. "Everything looks amazing," I said. "And there are a ton of people here. You're the Jackson Pollock of the Midwest."

"You like these?" he said, motioning in a general way to the nearby canvases. "Hey, which ones do you like? Do you like this?" He pointed to the nearest painting, which was some kind of orange tower against a smoky background.

"I do like that, actually," I said. "I like most of them."

"Here," he said, stepping over to the painting. He reached up and lifted it off the wall. "Take it," he said. "I want you to have it. I'm giving it to you right now."

He brought it over to me and held up the painting between us.

I laughed uncomfortably as he stood there holding it out to me, waving it a little to encourage me to take it. A few people nearby had stopped talking and were watching.

"You'll sell this. I can't afford it."

"I want you to have it, Ben," he said, now very serious. "Really. It's a housewarming gift. I want this to serve as a welcome back to St. Helens. Coming home is a hard thing to do. Especially when you don't know what it's like."

I thought it was an odd comment. I looked over at Grant, who was watching with a little smile. Jamie had the exact same expression on her face.

"Okay," I said, and took the painting.

Bobby nodded proudly, sagely.

"Thank you, Bobby," I said. "I really appreciate it."

"Of course," he said, and he patted me on the shoulder. "Be well. You're back, you're in a good space here. This is me welcoming you, bro. This is me telling you to be well." He nodded again, as though he'd completed a task, then moved on through the crowd.

I went over to the couch with the painting and sat down next to Grant.

"Score," he said.

"What was that?"

"I guess he likes you."

I leaned back, closer to Grant, letting the painting rest on me like a shield. "Was he completely ripped?"

I looked over toward Bobby, who was now glad-handing with the Silver Fox.

"Yes," Grant said. "I believe he was."

～～～～

Bobby came back around a little while later to say that people were going up the street to Roy's after the opening and that Grant and I should come. When he saw that Jamie was there beside Grant, he said, "I'm sure it's okay for her to come too. It's Wisconsin. They'll serve her."

"She's five."

Outside, at the minivan, Grant was helping Jamie into the backseat when I saw a troop of about a dozen people, including both Bobby and Lauren, leave the gallery and head down the road toward Roy's. Lauren was walking beside some guy I didn't know, strolling and talking, one hand gripping the strap of her purse.

"You comin' or goin'?" asked Grant, watching me look. "'Cause this train's leavin'. Little girl's up *way* too late." He must have tickled her as he said it; I heard a sleepy giggle emerge from the van.

"I'm just going to go over there for a little while."

"Ah, I see. You're going to lurk."

"I'm going to sit and look at the river."

"All right," he said. He gave me a hug. "Stay safe. Gimme that." He took the painting from me. "I'll drop it off."

Grant pulled away and I walked south along the river, hands in my pockets, then crossed the street and walked up toward Roy's. It was a St. Helens mainstay; its green awning stretched out over the sidewalk, and its sign, a wide rectangle, displayed the illuminated, caricatured face of a smiling man holding a mug of beer. There were a few smokers in quiet circles around me, and rock and roll from inside the bar drifted out through the propped door. It was a nice night.

I stared at the door for a minute or so, then turned and went back across the street. The benches were a part of the river walk, and I sat down at one and got out my phone and called Pete, my old sponsor from Portland. He'd said I could call if I needed to call but that that wasn't an excuse to quit meetings or to not find someone new. Whatever.

He didn't answer.

I crossed my legs, played around with my phone, wondered if there was a way to get it to check my e-mail. I would ask Haley the next time I talked to her.

The river and the river walk both looked nicer than they had when I was a teenager. St. Helens had always been a middle-class town, but there was more money here now; you could feel it in the art gallery, you could feel it in the new shops I'd seen on Main Street. You could see it in how nice the benches were. I had missed not only the beginning of the economic downturn but also the earlier decade of wealth that had bubbled up through the cracks of the state. The upturn that caused the downturn. *For I can raise no money by vile means.*

I glanced over my shoulder, back toward Roy's. Smokers, still. The door was still propped open.

I could make out, to my left, a little to the south, the dark line of the railroad bridge that went over the river and I remembered jumping off it with my friends. It wasn't too high and it wasn't as though this were the Mississippi, but the jump had always seemed impossible once you were up there. Do you know this? Do you know this feeling? The feeling of looking down, aware you are going to do it. The desire to, also. And it had been fun, it had been easy. Like everything. I wondered where all those people I'd jumped off with were. I wondered about my old girlfriend Dana, who'd moved down south to Austin for college and hadn't come back and whom I hadn't seen in a decade. I saw her jump down into the water wearing the navy blue bikini she always wore, saw her hair whipping up over her head before the splash, heard the scream. I'd seen her wink at me from down the bridge and hand a joint to someone else just before she jumped — wink because sometime earlier, maybe earlier that day, we'd taken each other's virginity in the back of her father's Jeep, parked by the quarry on a hot afternoon. Afterward we played checkers, sitting on a blanket, and then she went out into a field to see if she still remembered how to do handsprings. I laughed. I watched. I clapped. I saw her friend Carrie, who'd been with my friend Eli, who was brothers with my friend Sam. I had no clue where Carrie had gone. Sam and Eli I thought might be in Chicago.

I got up and began walking toward Main Street to start the two-mile trek back to Denny's and looked one last time at the entrance to Roy's, where I heard some laughter from the smokers. I stopped. Lauren was maybe twenty feet away from the door, talking on the phone. Her back was to me, and she was pacing slowly, looking at the ground. It looked like she was listening.

The smokers laughed at something again, and I looked at them. Bobby was in the middle of a circle, entertaining everyone. But I could see him glancing over and watching his sister, and after a moment, he went over to her, took the phone from her, and handed her his cigarette. He nodded at her like *No, it's okay, I got it.*

He looked right at me, pointed, and his voice carried toward me. I heard him say, "Ben's over there. Go talk to him. Look at that lonely man."

She looked at me, and I felt like a fool standing there, hands in pockets.

"Hey, Ben!" Bobby screamed. "Where's your painting, man? Did you throw it into the river? I wouldn't be pissed!"

"Grant took it for me!" I yelled. "I'm putting it up tomorrow."

"Damn straight!" he yelled. "It's okay if you don't!" He waved then and went back to the phone.

In the meantime, Lauren had been strolling up.

"Hey there," I said. "Your brother's hilarious. Sort of."

"I know," she said. "He's animated tonight." She turned away when she was close and drifted over to the railing. She took a drag of the cigarette, and the smoke came out of her mouth too fast for her to have inhaled. Then she said, "I can tell by the way you're looking at me that I look like I don't know how to smoke, Ben Hanson."

"Not at all."

"What are you doing out here? Are you going into the bar?" she asked, nodding back toward Roy's. "Have you turned into a creepy lurker dude?"

I realized that she had become very drunk in the time she'd been in the bar.

"I'm looking at the river."

"You're not coming in?"

"No, probably not," I said. "Do they have Ovaltine chocolate mix in that bar?"

"You don't drink, I take it?"

"I don't."

"AA don't drink or just-don't-like-to-drink don't drink?"

"NA don't drink," I said. "Very-bad-shit don't drink."

She looked out at the water. "That's nice. And yet you're my brother's hero, for some reason," she said.

"We used to hang out. Your brother and I. A little, I mean."

"What?"

"Your brother and me used to hang out."

"Good," she said.

"Aren't you a doctor?" I asked. "By the way?"

"Why?"

I pointed. "You're smoking."

"Doctors smoke. But also," she said, "I'm not a doctor anymore." She ashed the cigarette over the side of the rail.

"You went from being a doctor to not being a doctor?"

She tilted her head. "Why exactly do you care about all of these things? About me? Ben Hanson? I'm curious. I feel like it's just a coincidence we're standing next to each other right now."

"It's small talk," I said, "and you came over here."

"I feel like this is more the Spanish Inquisition."

"Did I see you with a horse the other day?"

"You might have. I was with a horse the other day."

"What were you doing?"

"I was taking her back to the Peterson ranch," she said. "I've been working for the vet in town. Do you know Dr. Hendrix? I work for him. Would you like my Social Security number? Can I fill out a W-nine for you? How else can I assist you in understanding my situation?"

"Okay then."

"I didn't mean for the tone to be exactly like that. Sorry."

"It's fine."

"Tonal error."

"You were saying. You're switching to being a vet."

"I don't know. Maybe. I do like animals," she said. "Why are we talking about this?"

"I don't know," I said. "It's painful."

She looked at the bar, then back at me.

"So," she said, squinting at me as though she'd just seen me for the first time. "Listen. Are you desperate? Or something? Is that what this is?"

"What?"

"Desperation," she said. "This. Is that you now?"

"I don't know how you're meaning that."

"Why are you here again?"

"The art show?"

"Yeah."

"I don't know."

"No," she said. "That's okay. I know you don't."

We stared at each other.

"It's been a long time, right?" she said. "I think it's been, what? Over one million years?"

"Eons."

"Well."

"Well. Years."

She looked over her shoulder, then back at me. "I'm going to go in. Now. Because this is very weird. I have to take over the phone call with our dad anyway. Are you staying? Here? Out? Even though you're not coming in?"

"Do you actually care?"

"I don't know," she said. "No."

I pointed my thumb over my shoulder. "I have to get home so I can have insomnia."

"You're an insomniac?" she asked, apparently delighted. "Oh." She smiled.

"Why is that funny?"

"Because I have night terrors," she said. "Night sucks for both of us. A pox on night, right? We found one thing. One thing in common. The night is saved. All is not lost."

I smiled.

She smiled.

"Bye," she said. She threw the word at me like it was a dart.

She turned.

I turned.

I walked about ten feet before I stopped, turned back, and called her name.

She turned.

I said: "I forgot to ask you the one thing I wanted to ask you. When I brought up the vet thing and all. I mean, there was a reason. Beyond the Spanish Inquisition."

She said: "Oh. Well, that's good. Maybe we'll end up with two things in common?"

"I forgot."

"Okay," she said. "Ask it."

"Do you know," I said, "if dogs can have narcolepsy?"

She stared.

"What?" she said.

"Can dogs have narcolepsy?" I repeated.

She thought about it.

"Why would you want to know that?" she said.

"I don't know," I said. "I have no idea why I want to know that."

II

THE PASTS

What concerns me is not the way things are,
but rather the way people think things are.

—EPICTETUS

5

My Twisty Little Broken Sense of Time

In January of 1994, my cousin Wayne froze to death in the woods of the Upper Peninsula of Michigan. He died less than a hundred feet from Denny's cabin. He died of hypothermia.

This happened about a month after the usual Hanson family Christmas celebration, when Wayne told me, sipping eggnog and wearing a white cardigan that seemed more suited to a space emperor than a burnout UW senior majoring in geology, that college had sucked his soul out through his mouth with its obsession with "words."

"It's over, man," he said. "Thank God. I had some nice times there. But I gotta get outta that place. College breaks your head open if you actually listen to it. You know? The humanities shit? Like too much. Too many words. You know what my favorite thing used to be?"

"What?"

"Conversations. You know what my favorite thing in the world is now?"

"What?"

"Rocks. Rocks, dude. Rocks."

I looked at him. Even I could tell that something had

changed — not based on what he was saying, exactly, but on the tired smile he gave me, the redness of his eyes, the general look of exhaustion on his face; he was no longer the same person who'd driven Haley and me out to the Big Bay de Noc. He wasn't even the person who I'd talked to forever when I'd visited Madison earlier, in the fall. He was — again — something new. I was not yet old enough to give it a name. Now, thinking back, I might call it desperate. Exactly what Lauren had called me.

He nodded.

"You see?"

"No. I don't."

"Well, just wait, then," he said. "You will."

It was the last time I saw him.

Wayne's death was somewhere within the triangle of suicide, overdose, and schizophrenic break. Maybe an accident, but maybe not. Maybe drugs, maybe not. (His body was out there for almost a week; the autopsy was inconclusive.) Ultimately impossible to understand. There it was: a puzzle, no solution. And yes, sometimes at Chestik I would lie on my cot and try to imagine the different reasons for Wayne's trip up to the Bright River at that time of winter, a great source of mystery and frustration for the whole family. *What happened?* That question replaced Wayne as a member of the family.

I remember how cold it was that week we found out he was dead, how the temperature just kept going down, unrelenting, an epic front from the Arctic, how the school board didn't want us leaving school for lunch or the young kids standing at the bus stop; those who chose to do so needed many layers — skin could not be exposed. I accepted my mother's rides to school that week, grim car treks through the dark mornings, weather intimidating, lunar. She'd drop me off before the other students got there because she had to be at work early as well. The janitor would unlock the door for me at 6:30 and I would make unheroic efforts to do my homework alone in the commons, sipping Mountain Dew, nodding off, now and then glancing up at the windows to watch the useless sun come up and see the white drifts of concretized snow appear. Word had gotten around about Wayne. People knew. People kept their distance. The principal made an announcement that I slept through. I failed to thank Lauren for organizing our answers to the project, checking the work, handing it in. The whole thing drifted off. What I thought about most that week was my cousin sitting upright and dead beneath a tree, his body at a right angle, both parts of him stiff as a board. Do you know this feeling? Tragedy, but not so close it shatters you. Just enough to be unnerving, and for the feeling to never go away. Close enough to feel it, far enough to stay safe. Were his legs crossed? It made me think of Rip van Winkle, and then, a few years later, after I saw *The Shining*, of Jack Nicholson's dead blue body, lost in that maze, ax in lap. The static picture of Wayne under a tree, branches leafless, middle of the night. I hated that this happened.

The cold for the two-week period, the cold that killed him, was worse up in Michigan where the Bright River ran through Uncle Denny's property. I remember hearing forty-five below.

Most people have some deaths; few have inexplicable deaths. It's its own thing. Crystal and Denny eventually got a divorce. Denny never talked about Wayne and neither did my father, who seemed to think that a schizophrenic mental event, drug-induced or otherwise, was an example of a person not trying hard enough to stay sane.

We moved on.

But I'd always felt close to Wayne and thought of him as an older brother growing up, and in the years following his death I continued to think of him and wonder about him as everyone in my family tried to forget. His absence meant something unsayable about life. I knew that. I sensed that. His absence made what had been a simple formula break down. Easy division with no remainders — 16 divided by 4 — was clean. But the family shifted then, slightly. We drifted into the realm of the infinite decimal, because the introduction of unexpected horror made all things possible, clean and unclean both. I thought of him often during my last year of college when I got depressed, got detached from my friends, stopped talking to everyone I knew, made my plans to go. I lived alone that year and I stopped going out. I went to class, did my work. I would say odd things to strangers in that time. Sometimes, walking down State Street on my way to class, getting my hair cut in the barbershop I knew he used to use, entering old university buildings, holding doors and pulling and smelling the trapped air as it rushed out over my face and chest, I would wonder if my cousin had done these same things, touched these very brass handles, smelled the same molecules of air, which had been circulating through the old ducts on a loop since he had exhaled them five years before. I recalled too what now occurred to me as even stranger — I recalled that once I went to a bar and I introduced myself to the bartender as Wayne Hanson. I found it amazing that he believed me as I said this.

I missed him. It's not that complicated. Wayne seemed the better person, and I missed him.

~~~~~

St. Helens, the boat upon which I rode, sailed through August. The town prepared to mourn the death of summer. And I was reminded of a small thing I loved: In the Midwest when the leading edge of fall is near, there is a day when you're walking and the sky looks the same and the temperature is the same and you look up and see that there's one leaf amid a thousand on a tree that's no longer quite the same. It hasn't yet turned but it bears the mark and something in you tightens up. It's the reconnaissance scout of autumn, the test dye of the weaker sun, the onset of the sea change, you're still a good ways out but there won't be any hiding. Which means: It's coming, and we — the trees — we wish you the best, my friends. But you're screwed. We'll be back when it's nice, go the trees. And this year, that day came at the beginning of September, the morning after my parents had left, as I walked back up toward the overlook doing my best to identify the whispering trees with the field guide I'd pulled from Denny's shelf. Because I really did want to know. The feeling of ignorance my return to St. Helens had stoked fully fused with the dense lump of diamond-dread, and the two feelings now seemed to be working in ghastly harmony, and I did not know what to make of it. I felt as though I knew too little about the physical world, that knowing more might help me but that coming home had made the feeling so acute that it was perhaps better to just run the other way. In the west, no one knew what you knew about the world. Here I sensed a different system, and it made me uncomfortable as hell.

And soon afterward there was a day in the fifties, then a day back up in the seventies. Not long after the art show, the football season threatened, and the front pages of the papers began to cover the preseason Packers games alongside the doomed economy and the election, everybody talking about the president. Obama or McCain. Is Sarah Palin nuts? Is Joe Biden too slick for words? If I had been a successful person, I would have been worried about these matters, worried about the money in the world, what people were saying about the housing market, what people said about jobs, all of that. I wasn't a successful person. I had nothing, so I was okay.

But I am getting ahead of myself.

I went to one more meeting, then stopped going.

I sent an e-mail to Ellen Barnum, a poet at Wisconsin, and asked her if she might be able to meet for a coffee and whether she had any memory of my cousin — the thought of driving to Madison and looking around was pleasing to me, if for no better reason than to remember what those years had been like and see the campus again. I finished sanding the table Denny had been working on downstairs. I finished the fence. I talked to my sister on the phone now and then. Nothing seemed resolved between her and John. I tried to be supportive. I went bowling twice: once with Grant, once by myself. I slept with Theresa Orgogliosi one night, both of us a little tipsy.

(I will tell that story too. Bear with me, I am winding.)

But I had time. I had time to sit and read in the den. I reread the Epictetus I'd found in Denny's office and felt the strangeness of his teachings, which felt at once both true and much too easy. I read a Muir biography I'd found on Denny's shelf and enjoyed it. John Muir's life made me love him in a distant way, like a great-uncle you've only heard about, and I started to wish I had known more about him when I was finishing college; I thought it could have helped me with my problems and would have perhaps been a better identity to emulate than Wayne's, of which I had only fantasies. John Muir scoffed at the Christian God and went through life as a wild and unbounded soul; it didn't make much sense, how different his ideas were from the basic beliefs of his day, but more than that, he seemed a lost person too, desperate to build a way of being that suited him and fit his own disposition, not letting himself be told which yoke to bear. There was the view of him as a hero, wandering Canada and the swamps of the Gulf, wandering out west in awe of redwoods, bringing the news to the rest of the world. If I knew anything about him it was that version, and that's why I had never cared, honestly: the Johnny Appleseed, the hero, the public intellectual, the starry-eyed man at rest in nature. Was that not bullshit? Some American propaganda about the woods? Yes. But what I noted in the book, and why I cared now, was the desperation in his life, the way he seemed to both flee and return to his greatest fears. Had he been less confused in his youth, or even as a grown man, we wouldn't know John Muir at all. He would have been too normal. There was a kind of ignominy in the way he ran away from the Civil War, I thought; there was something stupid about how he caught malaria in Florida, as no local with any sense would have walked through the swamps where he walked; and most important, there was the implication that the man had been horribly, pathologically depressed and lonesome as he made his famous jaunts into the woods and up the mountains to locate rare birds and experience earthquakes on the forest floor. Listen too hard to the tone of his writing and you won't see the contentment, hidden as it is in all the joy and all the praise of the landscape. It changes things, though — he was trying too hard to convince me. What I couldn't help but hear was the sadness beneath the things John Muir said, as though it wasn't quite the whole truth, this glory, but would that it were. The man lived alone in the woods for three years. What was that but unhappiness? So I also thought of his wife and his daughters and the odd days they must have had, sitting at their kitchen table and knowing that the missing member of their family had decided he would rather press his cheek against the bark of a tree than spend the afternoons with them, loving them.

I've mentioned Ellen Barnum, and you don't know who she is. I know less how to tell this part of the story. What I'm saying with this ramble is that I started going through Wayne's boxes in the basement as I became more settled in the house, boxes that Denny had labeled and stacked against a wall and that the reclamation project that was my return to this place required me to learn more. It was my duty. What I'm saying is that returning, in this manner, had perhaps been interesting to me because my family was broken, and I wanted to know real things, and with the amount of free time I now had, with the emptiness, there was no reason not to look for facts instead of theories. Amid what I found there was nothing very personal, so what little I learned was based on guesses you can make when you see somebody's things. Simple deductions, although there's a skill to reading the subtext of a young man's possessions. What was here seemed to be the crap that had littered Wayne's last apartment in Madison, none of it unified and none of it very telling. There was no secret hidden note that explained what had happened on the afternoon (of Thursday, January 20, 1994) that he'd packed up and driven to the UP. There was a book of photos of him and his friends throughout his years of college, and they looked like every other set of college pictures I'd ever seen. Wayne looked like I remembered him — hair curly and longer than in the picture in the den, stubble on his chin from time to time, the looseness and roughness of blossoming college masculinity, just found, just embraced. He usually leaned toward the person he was with in photos, whoever it was. I always stood upright, stiff as a board. Little things. There was a picture of him and his parents standing at the top of Bascom Hill, all comically looking up at the statue of Abraham Lincoln with their hands behind their backs and querulous expressions on their faces. Denny looked young. Notebooks and papers. Wayne had studied geology — a fact I thought of now with new appreciation because of all I'd read of Muir's obsession with the same science. Muir was also something of a renegade scientist and thought about things in his own way — Muir matriculated at but never graduated from Madison. He was a man with his own epistemology.

I found a number of applications to graduate school, some half filled out, some not started. Lists of schools and lists of pros and cons, all in Wayne's sloppy handwriting, so jagged and chaotic it seemed more like the writing of an angry fourth-grader than of an ambitious scientist or the logical thinker that he was. There were official transcripts too, and I opened one and looked at what classes Wayne had taken.

There were personal things — a photo of Wayne and his dad fishing, a video of Wayne doing a project for an English class, a small wooden box that contained Wayne's rock collection (I thought). Lots of books, lots of papers. The video was short, a dramatization of "The Purloined Letter," the Poe story. Wayne played the detective Dupin, and a pretty girl (a girlfriend? Who was she? Someone Wayne had loved?) played Dupin's sidekick. The two of them strolled together along the lakeshore path, and Wayne, in a comically bad French accent, wearing a droopy fake mustache, discussed how he had managed to guess exactly the chain of thoughts that had led the girl to ask an initial question, a plot point I only barely recalled from the story. I didn't remember the rest well and their interpretation of it was hard to follow. It was strange to see Wayne moving and existing on the old, low-quality video — I hadn't heard his voice, I don't think, since he'd died. In the video he seemed like his old self. Nothing in the least to suggest what was to come for him, or what would enter *into* him, or how he would appear to me on that last Christmas I saw him. Hollow. The time stamp on the bottom of the video was October 1992.

Wayne kept his graded essays, organized in dated folders stacked at the bottom of one of the boxes. When I saw them I went to the back of the pile and looked at the things he'd written during his last semesters; he had twice taken an introduction to creative writing class (the same one twice — he got an A the first time and an F the second time) his junior year, both with a poet named Ellen Barnum, one class in the American Indian studies program, and an advanced geosciences class called Interfacial Bio-geochemistry, listed as graduate level. Seeing the Indian studies class, I recalled the conversation he and I had had at Nick's when I drove out to visit him and ask about college; he'd taken me all around and introduced me to his friends and fed me generous hits from the cigarette-style one-hitter he frequently produced from his pocket, and then, after dinner, he fed me mushrooms and talked to me for hours. That conversation — that epic conversation — had started with him telling me about a book he'd read for a class, I remembered, a book written by a Spanish monk who had done his best to record the worst atrocities of the conquistadores. I couldn't remember the name of the book. But how many hours had we sat there talking? And then walked, talking more?

There was a paper from the class. It was about the 1960s impris-onment of a group of Indian mystics called the Wabano, and Wayne wrote about the government's conflating religious tradition and "psychedelic xenophobia" to gain control of the widespread dissent in the culture at that time. The Wabano, the paper explained, came from the Algonquin tradition and were thought of — historically, at least — as magicians and healers. They did their work at night and ended their ceremonies at dawn. They found knowledge through hallucination. Fine. But Wayne's focus was more on the details of the government's action than anything else, and he seemed unin-terested in the specifics of the Wabano's practices. There were no notes from the teacher to go along with the A. Just the bold letter on its own, down at the bottom of the last page. It was a good paper.

I also found a poem Wayne had written for his creative writing class. The one he failed. It was in a folder labeled PORTFOLIO, but it was the only thing in there. Handed in in May of 1993. At the bottom of the page there was a large red F.

Here is the poem:

SONG

OR

THE SUM OF ALL HUMANKIND

WAYNE HANSON

Glah glo gla glah

De dlo gloo gla

Ker naken be der lee dah

Asquinton be dean

Requal be sequin

Sharandel.

Perhapa neta.

(Repeat forever.)

〜〜〜

I forgot. Here is this.

To: hansonben3@gmail.com
From: Haley@LicosConsulting.com
Subject: Labor Day
Date: 8/17/2008

Dearest Brother,

As you have apparently decided to FAIL w/r/t your communication duties toward your sad sister, or perhaps because
you have been devoured by the zombie body of Wayne,

your sister, who is in the midst of a personal shitstorm w/r/t husband and St. Louis tranny situation, etc., has made an executive decision to come to investigate your new home and make sure you aren't blowing coke all night every night.

The real story is that John asked to have the kids over Labor Day and I relented because he is pathetic. And now I'm feeling awful. And I'm sorry I just joked about drugs because I'm feeling awful.

I don't want to stay here alone. I'm coming to the haunted house. You said I could! I'm coming home! Is that okay? Please. No kids.

No, really: please. I need to come.

Love,
Haley

PS. Warning: I made a slight mistake and mentioned this to Mom and now it sounds like they're coming up for some kind of barbecue. You know how much they like to celebrate their children's lives and the unshackling of the proletariat.

PPS. Sooorrrrrrrryyyyyy. Your island of tranquillity is going to be invaded. Enjoy the quiet while you can, sucker.

〜〜〜〜

Really, it was nothing with Theresa. The explanation is simple: One day I called her and asked her to dinner — against my better judgment. I thought Theresa'd say no, at which point I planned to retreat and tell her that it had been about business anyhow, but then again I thought there was a chance she'd say yes. I couldn't bear it anymore. I hadn't touched a woman in almost two years.

Two years! And to my surprise, she agreed to dinner right away and seemed — based upon the curl of her voice — to understand the invitation for what it was.

We met the next night at a sushi restaurant in Thiensville, which was not too far from her office. Very early — I think before we'd even gotten our miso soup — she told me that her son was spending the night at her mother's. She said this leaning forward, both elbows on the table, cleavage more visible than could have possibly been permissible at work. My brain flooded with a neurotransmitter the name of which I do not know.

She seemed a different woman than the woman who'd snapped the pictures in my living room — still talkative, yes, but now sexualized, free. She stared at me intently. It occurred to me that there was a simplicity to life for people over the age of forty that I'd never really known about. That's when I ordered a drink. Everything seemed so simple.

I half expected Theresa to reprimand me, or to pull out her phone and call my parents. But she just smiled again and leaned back in her chair and took a sip of her wine.

"So," she said. "All settled in?"

"I am," I said, looking at the beer, looking at the condensation on the outside of the green bottle. I had forgotten all the little things. "I've been doing projects."

"Like what?"

"I finished the fence Denny was working on."

"Are you handy like he was?"

"Did you know him well?" I said. "From what you said before, I'm realizing maybe you did."

"I knew him a little bit," she said. "Sure. Everyone knew Denny." She smiled. "And I'm sorry to say it again, but I can't get over the resemblance."

"I never really thought about it until you said it," I said. "I looked at his picture after you left. I see what you mean."

"You're built like him, that's the most striking thing. You walk like him. You've got your father's face, more, but there's something there about you that's just like Denny."

"I asked my mother if he was actually my father."

"Intriguing as that idea may be," she said, "your mom isn't a cheater; she just doesn't have it in her. And I can think of some more reasons why that theory's so far-fetched. She and Denny didn't get along. At all."

"They completely got along."

"Everyone was *civil*," she said. "That's not what I mean. I don't think she liked the effect Denny had on your father. I always thought — and this is just me, and if you tell your mother I said this I will kill you — but I always thought she was jealous of their friendship."

"I never thought they were that close. Especially not after my parents moved away."

"Well, exactly," she said. "But they used to be inseparable. And Denny was — well, you know. He was a bad influence. Your dad drank more around him. And I wasn't there when you and your sister were babies, but that's when they would have their parties, that's when your mother said the drugs got out of hand."

"Excuse me one moment," I said. "You're talking about my father?"

"That's what your mother always said," she said. "I didn't move to town until 1990. I think by then whatever it was was pretty much over."

"You're blowing my mind right now."

"Oh," she said. "You're welcome."

(Somewhere in here I had taken a long, anticlimactic drink

from the beer and had been letting the taste settle in my mouth and enjoying the slow creep of the alcohol into my bloodstream.)

After we ordered, Theresa said, "So, as for the house, we haven't had any interest so far, I'm sorry to say," she said. "But we'll get something. The open house will be helpful. It's such a terrible time."

"I'll make do."

"And are you — are you planning on getting a job? What are you going to do? I'm not sure your mother told me if there was a ... bigger plan. Around all of this."

"My cost of living is low right now. So that's good."

"But that's not sustainable," she said.

"What isn't?"

"You're living like you're twenty-two."

"That's one way to say it."

"And you're — how old are you?"

"Thirty-two."

"Good God. That makes me feel old. But do you see my point?"

"You're not old at all," I said. "What are you? Are you forty-four?"

"Forty-three."

"You look amazing."

"Thank you, Ben," she said. "It's not exactly true, but thank you."

"You do. You really do."

She held up a hand. "I'm not rejecting the compliment. If you had any idea how much goddamned yoga I do just to keep my body from turning into my mother's body, you'd know that I can't afford to reject the compliment."

"I wouldn't have pegged you for a yoga person."

"But you'll see when you get about ten years older. It's not even fun to look in the mirror once you're about thirty-nine or so. I mean, you actually *avoid* the mirror, I'm saying. You take mirrors *down*. However vain you are when you're young, that's how powerfully it turns against you. And I used to spend hours at the mirror. So now I'm screwed."

"I can't exactly build a life out of living in Denny's house, no, if that's what you mean," I said. "I guess I have to start thinking."

"That's good. Fun. Let's think. What do you *do?*" she said. "What are you good at? Other than finishing fences? Or . . . do you have anything else?"

"I did liberal studies in college and I remember essentially nothing from college," I said. "I used to be an okay skier but I tore my Achilles skiing and quit. I can write okay. I'm good at writing little puzzles, little riddles. I had a copywriting job before I came back."

"What for?"

"A drug company," I said.

"Ah, *now* I see," she said. "You're subconsciously preparing to enter the family business."

"What? You mean Hedley?"

"Sure."

"They're more chemicals and R and D."

"Oh, please. You know what I mean."

"I don't."

"That's what your parents want you to do, isn't it? Come back? Settle in? Get it together, eventually go work for the company they own?" She finished her wine. "Is that not what this is all about? First get you back to the region, then make you respectable. Maybe find a wife. In thirty years you'll be the CEO."

"That would be a total disaster."

"It would be nice and secure, though," she said. "You can't deny that."

"Except I'd be suicidal because I worked for a Fortune five hundred chemical manufacturer."

"How *awful*, yes. How *terrible* to be wealthy."

"Absolutely not what I'm saying."

"Fine, you get a pass because you're a head case. But I find this funny, I've been thinking about this. Listen to this. Don't react badly to the head case comment. Listen to me. You majored in liberal studies and here you are telling me you have no skills," she said. "I" — hand on her chest; my eyes lingered, new injection of unnamed neurotransmitter, now mixed with alcohol — "majored in women's studies. I enjoyed college and I loved my classes. I loved everything about that time in my life. But you'd think *one* professor would have taken me aside and said, 'Pardon me, Theresa. I'm glad you're in my class. But you should think about studying to be a mason also, because when your husband leaves you at twenty-nine — and by the way, no, nothing we talk about in here will prevent you from ending up with a man you should *not* end up with; women's studies can't help you in *that* regard — and you get the kid and it turns out your husband is close to actually *worthless* and you don't have any way of making money, Virginia Woolf, who was rich her entire life, by the way, is not going to be able to help you from the grave. So be a mason also. Or learn to design websites.'"

Our soup came and I looked at it and wondered whether I could pick up the bowl and drink from it like it was a cup.

I glanced up at her to see what she was doing and saw that she'd been watching me stare at my soup.

"You know what I mean?"

"My college degree basically made me just aware enough of the world to be depressed about the world," I said, staring at the soup again. "Is that what you mean?"

"Listen to you," she said. "Poor Benjamin. How difficult for you."

"I thought we were agreeing," I said.

"I have to ask, Ben. I don't think I can avoid asking. I told myself I wouldn't, but now we're here and I just feel like I have to ask because otherwise I'm going to think about it constantly and it's going to end up preventing us from — well, you know. Having fun."

"We are having a good time."

"So far."

"Okay?"

"That's the idea, isn't it?"

"I'm not sure," I said, "that I know what you're saying."

"Don't you think that's why you called me? For fucking?"

"You're pretty much the only person in town that I know."

"That's flattering."

"I'm not — what are you saying right now?"

"Oh, please, don't worry," she said. "You look like I'm accusing you of murder. I'm sorry. It's fine. It's really fine. Sometimes people aren't — I'm sorry. This is a little bit me, now. I do this, I have a bit of an — well, I think these things should just be out on the table, that's all. I'm too old for any games, all of that. I'm aggressive. You and I won't be getting married, you're a totally inappropriate partner. *Obviously.* Right?"

(Pause for laughter. I did not laugh.)

"But you're cute. You *are* cute. You're young. You're *new.* I knew Denny only when he was in his fifties and sixties. You're like the newer version of a man I used to be attracted to, only just out of the packaging. It's like — it's like some fucking joke or something, you know? You're available, you're here. I dunno. It's fun."

"Uproariously, so far."

She leaned forward. "When was the last time you had sex with anyone? You were in *prison*, right?"

I just laughed.

"Am I totally insane right now? Ben? Tell me. I'm not the town whore. I should say that. I know that it makes me sound like the town whore if I say I'm not the town whore. But I'm not."

"I don't think that."

"So let me ask my question. Come on, don't look like that. It's fun. Isn't it fun? Just to be open?"

"It is, actually."

"This is one of the advantages of being an adult."

"I dispute that I'm a totally inappropriate partner."

"Let me ask my question."

"Okay." I held up my empty beer and caught the eye of the waiter, who nodded. Totally fine and not a problem at all. I twisted in my chair. I twisted again in my chair.

"What exactly happened to you?" she said. "With jail. And with the money. Just give me the basics. The *absolute* basics. I don't want or need details."

"Do you mean how did I end up going to jail?"

"You didn't hurt anybody, did you?" she asked. "Just clarify that for me, because that would be completely unacceptable. Your mother said it was some kind of arson. I'm okay with arson. Victimless arson, particularly."

"It was," I said. "It wasn't — no, it didn't hurt anybody. It was an accident. It was just a bad situation." She looked at me, waiting, and so I decided to tell her: "I was close to being totally broke. I had a . . . business dispute. With a friend. So this one night I got drunk, broke in. I didn't plan on doing anything, really. I just wanted to sit at his desk and brood. And I was sitting there, brooding, and I passed out with a cigarette in my mouth."

I shrugged.

"And then it fell out of my mouth."

"Wow."

"Fire," I said, eyebrows up. "It's hot."

"But you got out. Obviously."

"I did."

"But got caught."

"There was video," I said. "The only reason I didn't end up in real prison was my mother pulling strings. With her senator friend."

"Who? Victor Garland?"

I nodded.

"This is unreal."

I scratched my head and saw the waiter approaching with another beer. "Listen, are you sure you want to know about this? I mean, I'll tell you. Like about the dude stealing my girlfriend and all of the unseemly stuff. But it paints me as an amazingly stupid asshole, even though it's not that bad in the end, so I'd just as soon say 'I was an asshole and screwed up.' You know? And then we can talk about other things."

She let her hand drop onto my forearm and said, "You can guess that everyone in town has always been a little confused about why you would have even — I don't know. Been involved in something like that? You're a much-discussed topic. You're something of an enigma."

"More moron."

"And yet you don't seem stupid."

"I was broke. And really mad."

"But your parents are rich."

"I wasn't talking to them."

"But didn't you have money from them? Didn't you have a trust, or —"

"I blew a million-dollar trust," I said. "Yes. In six years. It was gone by then. So I —"

"Get *out* of here," she said, leaning forward, eyes wide. Her hand was still on my arm. "A *million* fucking dollars? *How?*"

"That's what my sister and I each got," I said. "When we turned twenty-four. And she's probably sextupled hers by now."

"Jesus *Christ*, Ben. What did you *do?*"

"With the money?"

"Yes."

"I don't even know," I said.

"How can you not know?"

"That's what's so bad about it. I honestly have no idea. I just bought whatever I wanted. I fired the financial adviser one day when he was telling me about what my father thought I should do. I tried to invest some of it but lost it all in the stock market. I barely worked. I went on trips sometimes. I went to Hawaii once for like a month. Just kinda...burned it. And then by the time I needed a lawyer — well, the last of it went to lawyers."

"And now you literally have nothing left?"

"I have less than nothing left," I said.

"Well, I'm glad to hear you didn't blow anybody's brains out," she said. "This seems a little more...manageable." She smiled. "You're just...wayfaring." She nodded to herself. "I can do wayfaring."

I had a total of five beers, I'm not sure how much wine she had, and we ordered a wide variety of maki. We kissed sloppily in the parking lot and she told me to follow her to her house, which I did, trying my best not to weave and impressed by how perfectly she drove. I thought of her breasts as I drove. It occurred to me that I was the only one who was actually drunk. Just as we got on the highway to leave Thiensville, my headlights caught the gleaming eyes of a deer standing in the woods, staring at me, and I felt judged. Never trust a deer. The sex was amazing.

〰〰〰

The radius of my runs expanded, and near the end of the month, I started going north, away from the overlook and back down Beau Pointe Road, all the way across 121. Beau Pointe in that direction took me — once I was past Golden's, a car wash, and a Menards — right alongside a series of dairy farms. If I ran far enough in that direction I would eventually hit Franklin, an unincorporated town of only two hundred and fifty people with one old restaurant, one gas station, and a collection of broken-down houses lining the tiny strip of road within its town limits. I rarely made it this far, and if I did, I never kept going. At that point I would turn around and run back toward Denny's.

I made it to Franklin the first time I ran after the Theresa date, and I made it there pretty fast. Self-flagellation. Pain on purpose. And I continued this every day for the next week, trying to better my time each day, just to see. And also just to make it even less comfortable.

I did not call Pete about the beers. I had decided to say nothing. I knew what he would say and I had said it all to myself anyway, right there at the table in real time. I think that a part of me had just wanted to see what would happen. Run a test. Play a twisted game against myself. See if all the worst-case versions you imagine actually do come true, see if you spiral, see if you become a monster within forty-eight hours. Invoke the nightmare — I assume to make it go away.

I hadn't turned into a monster, though. I was fine; I was just a guy running around in Wisconsin irritated with himself for doing any of it. In that way. The way I was justifying it to myself was by thinking that you have to feel as though you've chosen your path, not been forced onto it. Not been told what to do. You always have to feel as though you've chosen. And it doesn't do anybody any good to feel as though he lives one misstep from the apocalypse, even if it is another secret truth. Especially for dogs.

Let me explain.

One afternoon I had just made the turn at the edge of Franklin when I saw, along the crest of a meek hill about a quarter mile in the distance, the silhouette of a good-size dog standing near the center line of the road. Just as I was furrowing my brow and think- ing that it was a bad place for a dog to be, considering it was a road and so on, a car came over the ridge and absolutely crushed it.

I did a full-body cringe. The dog went airborne and took what seemed to be an impossible path, helicoptering to the side of the road, the side I was on, and landing with a sickening, weedy thud somewhere down in the ditch.

The car that hit the dog was a blue Volkswagen, and I was jog- ging up as it pulled over on the opposite side of the road. I looked down into the high grass, then over at the driver. He was a stocky young man in a suit and a tie, and he climbed out of the vehicle and stood very still, his door open, looking toward the ditch as though he'd just run over Saul of Tarsus.

He eventually looked at me. He put his hands over his face and crouched down.

"I hit a dog," he called across the street, through his hands. "What the fuck is going on right now?"

"I saw," I said. "You don't have to yell."

"What did I do?"

"You hit a dog."

"I did hit a dog. Is that dog down there?"

"I think so."

"Is that a dog down there, though?"

"Yes."

"I'm not sure what I'm supposed to do in this situation," he called, having turned his hands into a megaphone now. "I'm not even from here," he added. "I'm from Waukegan. Will I be arrested for this?"

We both looked toward the ditch.

"You'd think we would hear something," he said contemplatively, talking now, no longer yelling. "Or something. You know? What's that little rascal up to down there?"

"It's probably dead," I said.

"It's probably okay."

"It's probably dead."

"Right now I'm having a fantasy of the dog just sort of bursting up out of the brush and running over to me," he said. "And jumping into my arms. I could even take it home with me, you know? Sort of adopt it?"

I turned to look at him. "Dude. Are you drunk?"

"What?"

"Are you drunk right now?"

"No," he said. "It's the morning."

"Do you have a phone?" I said. "And also, it's early evening."

"Of course I have a phone."

"Call information and get the number for a Dr. Hendrix's office," I said. "In St. Helens."

"I don't need a doctor," he said. "I'm fine."

"It's a vet," I said. "For the dog."

"Ah," he said, nodding to himself.

He didn't move, though, and instead looked at his fender for a moment, then back toward me. "So are you out here jogging?" he said.

I just looked at him.

"I'm on things," he said, nodding. "Yes, okay. Coming clean. I am on a few things."

I walked to the side of the road another thirty feet or so, looking down into the ditch. Now I could see the depression in the weeds where the dog must have landed, but the grass was so high that it had gobbled up the animal and hidden it from sight. There was a little motion, though, and after glancing back toward the guy and seeing that he was on the phone, I turned and climbed down the steep incline.

I found the dog, an old golden retriever, lying still. I thought it was dead until I saw that its eyes were open. Watching me.

I squatted down and scratched behind the ear I could see, then I checked the tags.

"Molly," I said. "Hey, girl."

She moved her head a bit when I said her name and she reached one of her paws toward me.

"Easy, easy," I said. "Doctor is coming."

"Did you find it?" I heard from above. "Is it dead?"

I looked up. The guy was standing on the gravel emergency lane, watching me and leaning, eyes owl-like. He was eating a granola bar.

"Did you call the vet?"

"He said someone was coming out. I told him where we are. But I can't — I can't really *see*. Is that the dog right there? Is that it? Are you with it?"

"No," I said. "This is a teddy bear I found down here."

"Why would you sit with a teddy bear?"

"It's the dog. It's the fucking dog."

"I don't understand."

"Listen, dude," I said. "Just wait over by your car or something? Sir? And just stop talking to me? You're not helpful. Not at all."

"Oh, excuse me," he said. "I'm sorry, asshole. I'm very sorry to be bothering you, man who runs, which is itself like a totally passive-aggressive, pretentious thing that people do."

"You're calling *me* an asshole?"

"I can't hear you," he said. "I'm standing over by my car."

But he kept standing right there.

We stared at each other for about ten seconds.

He turned and walked away.

I waited there with the dog then, scratching her under the ear. I found it disconcerting that she wasn't making any noise. No whimper, no whines. Just perfectly still and quiet, oddly at peace about what had happened. But alive nonetheless.

I sighed, leaned back, sat in the grass, ready to wait. Control what you can, accept everything. I suppose this was the kind of thing that Epictetus was good for, even though the cleanliness of all his pronouncements hadn't sat too well with me when I read Wayne's copy of the *Enchiridion*. I know that a big part of my problem, when I was reading it, was that it reminded me so much of the AA ethos, but even beyond that, everything he said about how to live well came off as too easy. Control what you control; those things you can't, let them go, because there's nothing you can do, and they're more like misperceptions than upsetting things. A guy like the guy up on the ridge — yes, you could choose whether or not to get angry about a man you didn't know. *I* could, anyway. But here was a dog in my arms, about to die, down here for reasons that were definitely beyond her control, and it didn't seem as though it would have been all that comforting for her to know that the world beyond what she could control was not any of her concern. She'd been standing looking down at a rock. A blue metallic object going sixty miles an hour had materialized from nowhere and thrown her into a ditch. She never had a chance. And she wasn't supposed to care?

Eventually, maybe after about fifteen minutes of sitting there, petting her, getting more and more angry with Epictetus, who I had decided really did not deserve to be a famous philosopher, I heard from above: "Is that Ben?"

I looked up and saw Lauren standing on the side of the road holding a black bag and looking very surprised to see me.

"That is you," she said. "What are you doing here?"

"Hey," I said. "The dog's down here. That guy up there hit her." She looked over her shoulder.

"What guy?" she said.

"It's fine," I said, standing. "It's probably better he left. The driver was up there for a while."

Lauren picked her way down the slope into the ditch and knelt down beside the dog. "Oh," she said. "Molly. Hello, baby. What happened to you?"

"You know her?"

"She lives right here," Lauren said, nodding toward the nearest farm. "The Munsons." She opened up her bag and started looking around. "She's deaf. And pretty much blind. This was going to happen eventually."

I thought it was an odd thing to say. I thought, too, of Molly seeming to respond to my voice when I first came down. Lauren looked up at me for a moment, but I realized she was looking past me, up toward the road. I turned, expecting to see that the asshole had come back, but instead I saw a man in overalls standing with his hands in his pockets.

"Hi, Jim," Lauren said.

"Saw your truck," said the man. "Is that Molly?"

"It is," Lauren said. "She got hit."

The man nodded, now hooking his thumbs around the straps of his overalls. "How is it?"

"It's not good."

"You should probably put her down then," said the man.

Lauren moved her hair out of her eyes and squinted up at him. "I can if you want," she said.

"All right," he said.

He stood for a moment more, looking down at the weeds and the grass, then turned and walked away.

"You can go if you want," she said to me. "Thank you. Thank you for at least having him call."

"Do you want help carrying her?" I said. "Or something?"

"No. I've got it."

About ten minutes later, I was standing by the side of the road, next to Lauren's truck, watching her climb up out of the ditch, awkwardly carrying the big dog's body, which must have weighed eighty pounds.

She carried it down the road toward the farm.

〰〰〰

I didn't feel like running anymore, so instead I walked, thinking about the dog flying sideways through the air. What, exactly, goes on in a dog's head right then? *Good-bye.* I could see 121 about three-quarters of a mile in the distance when Lauren's black truck pulled up beside me.

"What, you run only one way?" she asked through the open window, crawling along at my speed.

"Was that not depressing to you?"

"You're a softie?" she said, smiling. "Who would have thought?"

"I guess I am."

"You want a ride home?" she said. "It's gonna rain. Look at the sky."

I did. Black clouds were coming in on the southwest horizon, right over town. She was right. So I said okay, and she turned the radio down as I climbed in, and as I clicked in my seat belt, she said, "I actually also wanted to tell you that I was sorry for that back there, by the way." She frowned, shook her head. "I'm trying to be better about that."

"For what?" I was confused. I had expected her to apologize for the disjointed conversation we'd had beside the river. And for calling me desperate.

"Telling you I didn't need any help," she said, accelerating.

"I didn't even notice. I don't think you did."

"I did."

"Okay." I shrugged. "It doesn't matter."

"I get into a certain mode when I'm working, you know? With things like that, especially."

"Help, you mean?"

"Yes," she said. "Offers of help. I hate them."

"It's fine," I said. "You didn't need help anyway. You were all over it. You were like Dr. Dolittle in there."

"No, I know."

"It's fine."

"I know it is."

I heard irritation in her voice again, so I looked back out at the clouds.

"So how are things up at your uncle's?" Lauren asked. "I am pressing the conversation reset button. Like you did?" She glanced my way, little sideways smile on her lips. "Any offers?"

"No," I said. "Are you trying to get me out of St. Helens?"

"Yes," she said. "We'd all love for you to leave."

"The agent's going to start showing it soon. So I dunno. Nothing yet."

"But you've also prevented countless teenage parties."

"Yes."

"And the value of that can't be underestimated."

"My uncle would be proud."

"Denny had a heart attack, right?"

"Down in the basement."

"He was how old?"

"Pretty young," I said. "Sixty-five, I think."

"I was sad to hear about it when I found out," she said.

"Did you used to date him too?"

She laughed. "No. Although I knew him because of my mom, and right when I came back here, a few years ago, I'm pretty sure *they* went on some dates."

"You're not serious."

"I think so, yeah," she said, nodding. We were stopped now at the corner of Beau Pointe and 121, waiting for the light. Lauren seemed to know where she was going without any directions, so I didn't give her any.

"That's the second time I've heard that about him," I said. "Was he the town tomcat?"

She laughed again. "I don't think so. I can't say for sure. My mom went to his funeral," Lauren continued. "I couldn't go. But she and I wondered if you would be there."

"Me? You looked at me like you'd never seen me before," I said. "At Bobby's thing."

She shrugged.

"I was surprised to see you," she said.

I watched the side of the road as we wound up toward Beau

Pointe, trying to recall that time in high school, which was so hazy to me. I couldn't remember the details of what had happened with the project itself, at least beyond the basics of calculating orbits for our space station and then the time in the library when I'd just gone to give her my work. I recalled a strange feeling about the interaction in the library. But it was gone.

"Can I ask something I've been wondering about?" I said.

"Yes."

"Are you the vet or are you not the vet? Because it seems like you're the vet."

"I'm *kind of* the vet," she said. "The paperwork is not in order."

"You're not allowed to put dogs to sleep on the side of the road, for instance?"

"Not at all, nope. I can't use pentobarbital. But Dr. Hendrix has been sick," she said. "Right now I'm basically running his whole practice. So I do use it. It's completely against the rules. It's completely unlike me. There needs to be a real vet there. But what do you do?"

"An actual doctor should get a free pass."

"It's not the same, though," she said, flicking on the signal as we approached Denny's house. "It's really not."

"So he wants you to go to vet school," I said, "instead of bringing someone else in."

"Yes."

"Because he thinks you're great and wants the new town vet to be you."

"Yes."

We turned into the driveway. Denny's house looked nice in the evening sun, and I'd managed to bring the lawn back to life. It wasn't a bad place at all.

"It's a big, complicated situation," she said. "It's a huge mess.

I don't know what I'm going to do. That's sort of what's . . . on my mind these days."

"I know the feeling."

"Do you?"

"I do. Thanks for the ride. Sorry about Molly."

"Oh, no, don't be," she said. "It's fine. They've been thinking about putting her down for six months. That made it simple."

"I was back there getting all righteous on Molly's behalf."

"I'm sure Molly appreciated it."

I nodded.

"See you, then?" she said.

"Yeah, thank you. And — you know, actually, maybe this is a bad time to ask," I said, looking at the tarp in the bed of the truck, "considering there's a . . . dead-dog incident in the air." I looked back at her. "But can I call you sometime?"

"Call me?"

"Yeah."

"What for?"

"To go out."

"Oh," she said, looking at the steering wheel. "Oh." At first I thought she was embarrassed, but she looked back at me with what I saw was an amused expression. "Really?" Head tilted forward, eyebrows up. "*Out* out?"

"Out out."

"Did you not just sleep with Theresa Orgogliosi? Your real estate agent?"

"Ummmm."

"Didn't you?"

"You *heard* about that?"

"Uh, yes, Ben," she said. "One piece of advice for you is never, ever entrust Theresa Orgogliosi with any secrets."

"Maybe I should have seen that coming."

"My mom's on her bowling team. She was bragging about banging the mysterious stranger the day after it happened."

"You're making that up."

"I'm not."

"Okay," I said. "Well. That makes me look awful. Have a good rest of your life."

"I realize that you're not actually dating her," Lauren said. "I realize that. I'm just saying." She shrugged. "I mean, you can call me at the office, I guess," she said. "If you really want to. I'm pretty much always there."

"You want me to call you at work?"

"If you need anything." She put the truck into gear. "Regarding pets."

〰〰〰

That night, I went down to Denny's workshop and dug around his wood scraps until I found two pieces of fence post. Sanding them down, I thought again of the beers I'd had with Theresa and decided to tell Pete after all. There was something glib about the way I'd been thinking about it since then, something too easy about saying to myself, "This has only been a test." (When I eventually called Pete and described this to him, he just said, "Well, no shit, Sherlock.") More than what had happened that night at the sushi restaurant, what I really didn't like was this habit I had of being dismissive, this habit of disregarding what I was always quick to call the ephemera, the incidental details.

It took only about thirty minutes to finish my little project, which I decided to put down in that grassy ditch in the morning. It was all very unlike me, but, in my defense, I'd been looking for an excuse to use Denny's wood-burning Dremel, which

I'd found at the back of one of his storage shelves. This was the perfect time.

I plugged it in and waited for the copper tip to heat up. I had made a small, simple cross with the leftover posts, and once the Dremel was ready, I bent over the cross and wrote my message in the wood.

Big letters: R.I.P. MOLLY

Little letters, underneath: A GOOD LIFE: SHE SNIFFED THE ROAD, NO TIME TO COMPLAIN.

6

Haley Blows into Town

My sister, weighed down by a very reasonable amount of luggage, landed at General Mitchell three days later.

In the terminal, I stood among the drivers and held up a sign that said CALAMITY JANE.

"Funny," she said as we hugged. "But not funny."

I hadn't seen her in almost five years. Such an extremely sad number, thinking it, and there was a time when such gaps within the family would have been impossible. Yet it happened, and I imagine it happens to a lot of families. You look up and a half a decade is gone. These people you loved — not just that, but the people who were the first objects of your love, the people through whom you *learned* love — are no longer a part of your life. In that gap she'd had two more children, neither of whom I had met. She had three kids altogether, but looking at her sleek and narrow body, you wouldn't know she'd even had one. Even as a teenager, Haley had been a workout freak, and once she'd gone to the East Coast to scrub clean the remnants of the Midwest, her obsession with being in shape found its natural home on the rowing team, first at Choate, then at Yale. Looking at her, I figured she had a personal trainer. Fuck — she may as well have *been* a personal trainer. Feeling the sinews of her back as we hugged, I wondered how many hours she spent in the gym each day. It turned out we were both compulsive people.

"How was the flight?" I said after we'd collected her things and loaded them into the Nissan.

"Fine, normal," she said. I put my hand on the open trunk, making ready to close it. "You look so *skinny*, Benjy!" she said, eyeing my torso. "What do you eat? Anything?" She looked at the car. "And what the fuck is this *car?*"

"Dad gave it to me." I slammed the trunk. "Nice, right?"

"So nice," Haley said, "to get a car from someone."

As much as I would have liked to pretend there were only vague reasons why Haley and I had drifted so far apart — it's easier that way, to forget the specifics of the past, isn't it? And it was easier to take the blame myself — there had been some incidents in the first years of the decade that caused enough friction to bump us, bit by bit, not just to other ends of the country but to what felt like entirely unrelated realms of reality. She loved making money; I didn't. She loved economics; I didn't. She had a family; I didn't. She had impossibly complex opinions on subjects like immigration; I didn't. In the years after 9/11 and the years leading up to the invasion of Iraq, whenever I came back for Christmas or Thanksgiving, I had to listen to hours of discussion as to why Islam was inherently at odds with Western ideals, or why military intervention, in this particular case, was absolutely justified, or why John Kerry was failing to perceive the *basic* problem with the foreign affairs situation. Hedley, the family company, signed more and more contracts with the government as the war effort gained momentum, and Haley and my father both thought that was unambiguously good for the family; I didn't. I was not very well informed, but still, I didn't. I admit that I had a bad habit of blindly arguing in the other direction when the two of them got worked up and when I sensed smugness in the air, and we had some conflicts, and afterward it was as though Haley and I were two pucks on an air-hockey table, floating in silence, but with no paddle or wall to stop the drift.

"Do I really look skinny?" I said, once we were driving.

"Vegetarians are insane."

"I'm not anemic. And I think you people are insane."

"Who? Us people who eat meat?"

"Yes."

"Yes, how ridiculous. These incisors in my mouth feel so *superfluous*."

"So does this nub of a tail on my spine."

"I just read a study about how bad it is for you to be a vegetarian," she said. "Your health. I'll send you the link."

"Don't send me any links."

"I'll just send you a little linky."

"Are you being Mom?"

"I'm Dad. You're Mom."

"You're both of them and I'm neither of them."

"What, is that your fantasy?"

"I was joking."

"Oh, no, wait. I know. You're now making yourself into Denny. You've found the loophole, right? You're an easygoing, fun-loving contractor of modest means. You're *not* actually rich."

"There's no loophole."

"God knows you've tried to find one."

"What?"

"I said God knows you've tried to find a loophole."

"I'm going to work really hard over here on driving. I'm looking at the road and driving carefully."

Thirty seconds of silence.

"I'm sorry," she said. "I'm sorry. I'm out of control. I'm sorry. I haven't seen you in five hundred years. Something is wrong with me."

I glanced over at her, and when I did, she mustered a little smile, then looked ahead.

"You're being an asshole," I said.

"This is my way of telling you I need food."

"I know."

"Badly. Don't you know who you're talking to?"

"I know exactly who I'm talking to," I said, "and that is why there is a sandwich in the glove compartment with your name on it."

Haley looked at the glove compartment.

"I'm going to be so sad if I open that and there's no sandwich."

When I said nothing, she reached forward and opened the glove box. She saw the sandwich. It was wrapped in wax paper and it had her name on it.

"My God," she said.

"I can't talk to you until you eat it."

"Is it a sprout sandwich? Like your kind eats? Is it going to be . . . sprouts?"

"Eat the sandwich."

She unwrapped the wax paper and looked between the slices of bread.

"Is this roast beef from Golden's?"

"It is."

Haley looked at the meat. Very slowly, then, she brought the sandwich to her lips and kissed it.

〰〰〰

It took about a half hour to get to St. Helens from the airport in Milwaukee, and after Haley ate, she seemed to settle into a friendlier mood. She had just begun to talk about John and where things were with the divorce when she saw that we were close to town and said, "Oh, pause. I take it you don't have any wine at Denny's."

"I don't."

"Does Golden's have wine?"

"Do you not remember stealing wine from the shelf and chugging it in the dairy cooler?"

"I never did that."

"I have a very clear memory of that happening."

"Do you think they'll have any '82 Château Lagrange malbec?"

"I think they'll have something purple and alcoholic."

"Do you mind if people drink around you? I don't know how it works."

"It's fine."

"Would you rather I didn't?"

"Not at all," I said. "Stop it. Let's go."

A few minutes later we pulled into the almost-empty lot, and after I cut the engine, I looked over and saw my sister staring at the old store's bright façade, her eyes catching the yellow light of the Golden's sign.

I smiled. "When was the last time you were actually in St. Helens?"

"Eighteen years ago," she said. "The day I moved to Connecticut."

"You haven't been back here once?"

She turned. "Why would I have been back here?"

~~~~~

My sister was like a kid walking into Disney World when we went into the store, eyes still gleaming as she looked around at everything she remembered. It was past nine o'clock and not many people were in the aisles. The same kid I had seen struggling with the floor-cleaning machine was at it again, and he nodded at me as we strolled past, used to seeing me here at this hour. I was starting to feel sorry for him. He was probably starting to feel sorry for me.

"Are you a regular?" Haley asked after seeing the nod.

"This is where I get my groceries."

"There is something so fantastic about your new life," she said. "It's like you're playing a game."

"It's just Golden's."

"Yes," she said. "That's what I mean."

We turned the corner at the end of the produce aisle and walked along the deli counter. Grant, who worked nights on Mondays and Tuesdays only, was not here, and instead a woman I didn't know was hunched over a table weighing stacks of ham like a moneychanger.

"Do you remember that one girl?" Haley asked. "That girl who worked like forty hours a week even though she was in school and only like fourteen years old? Do you know who I'm talking about?"

"Vaguely."

"Black hair, kind of crazy? She hated me?"

"Nobody hated you."

"She did," Haley said. "She could hardly even look at me. Marissa. Marissa something."

It was entirely possible. Even though I'd just denied it to her, there had been a sizable slice of the St. Helens High School population who'd found my sister unbearable. You could take your pick of reasons — she was beautiful, she was rich, she was smart, she was aware of all these things, and she had no trouble behaving as though she were superior to you, especially if you had ever done something to irritate her. She was a cheerleader, for Christ's sake. And she sometimes got drunk and said odd things to people. But more than anything, what had won my sister her fair share of enemies was the simple fact that she truly did not seem to care, at all, what other people thought of her. And that was still true. And I know, I know: some people project that kind of attitude, then go home and cry in the bathtub. Haley, though...Haley, so far as I could tell, did not spend time thinking about other people's reactions to her. It just wasn't in her.

"Wine time," Haley said.

I waited nearby as my sister browsed at the modest shelf of wine, happy that she was here and that we were at Golden's together. She was her same sturdy self, even after finding out that her husband was a lying twerp, and I appreciated being around someone who was not at all like me.

Haley picked out her two bottles of wine — a pinot noir and a malbec, which Golden's did in fact stock, even though it wasn't exactly a rare vintage — handed them to me, and we made our way back toward the checkout aisles.

"Part of me wants to be buying bourbon," Haley said. "Out of decency toward you, though, I will hold off on the binge drinking. Tonight."

She put her hand on my arm.

"Oh my," she said.

I looked up and saw that Rick was again at the service desk doing the books, glasses perched on his nose.

"What?"

He hadn't seen us.

"He still works here?"

"Rick?" I said, looking at him. "Yeah. Who cares?"

"Nobody," Haley said, taking the bottles from me. "Nobody cares."

She strode past the girls at the regular checkout aisles. I stopped walking. But even from where I stood, a good thirty feet away, I could see Rick's face go from a healthy pink to green to white when he looked up and saw Haley standing in front of him.

They started to talk; Haley began to dig in her purse. I went over. By the time I got there, Rick had changed colors again and was now purple.

"Oh, hey, Benjy too now!" he said to me, nodding, smiling. "It's the Hansons!" He was also punching at buttons on the register, which wasn't responding in the way he wanted it to respond.

Haley smiled.

"I'm sure you remember Haley, Rick," I said.

"Oh, sure, sure," Rick said, nodding enthusiastically as he punched more buttons and futzed with his glasses. I thought his head might just straight up explode.

"I was one of Rick's best employees," Haley said. "Right, Rick?"

Rick was now apparently unable to speak, so instead of responding verbally, he tilted his head and raised his eyebrows in what I assumed was some kind of agreement.

Finally, mercifully, the register chimed and the drawer popped open.

"*There* we go!" Rick exclaimed, counting out the change.

He looked up and emitted a staccato burst of laughter that caught us all off guard. I tried to smile kindly at him, but I don't think he noticed. It was the laugh of a man who had just barely not crashed an airplane into a mountain.

"You did fuck Rick," I said to her once we were sitting in the car. "Jesus."

Haley fastened her seat belt.

"Do you have any idea how much energy I put into squelching

that rumor once you were gone? I was like your own personal publicist here."

"I never had sex with him," she said.

"I don't believe you."

She looked at me.

"I blew him a couple of times, fine."

She was holding two dollar bills toward me, which she flapped dismissively.

I ignored the bills and said, "Rick the manager."

"Take these." She waved the singles again. "Take them."

"Why are you giving me your change?"

"Just take them. I hate singles. Take them." She waved them with each sentence. "*Take.* Takey."

"You're so rich that you don't need singles?"

"Take the singles and I'll tell you about Rick."

I took the singles. "All right then."

"Thank you," Haley said. "I just hate them. It's an OCD thing, I don't know."

She slowly and deliberately put a piece of gum in her mouth, then handed me the wrapper, which I also took.

"Please explain."

"What?"

"Rick, Haley."

"Will you just get over it? It was twice. Two blows." She held her fingers up in a peace sign, then shrugged. "I thought you knew. Everyone knew."

"I asked you. Specifically. Back then. And you lied to my face and then got mad at me for asking you."

"Like I'm going to tell my little brother about my sex life when we're teenagers?" she said, looking back at the storefront.

"There could have been a way," I said, "to communicate it."

"Like a flag signal or something? Yes, Ben. You know what? Yes. A semaphore. I could have raised up a green flag from the other side of the room when his cock was in my mouth."

"Not actually a flag."

"Rick looks pretty good still. Doesn't he? For an old guy?"

"He's in there wondering if he's about to be charged with statutory rape."

"Oh, please. It was completely consensual. You're being way too...militant about this."

"Why would you possibly have consented to doing that?"

"Stop."

"No."

"Oh, Jesus, Benjy, I don't know," she said. "I thought it was funny, okay? It was a long time ago. It was fun and funny."

"Do you still think it's funny?"

"A *little*, yes," she said. "Did you see him in there? Jesus," she said, twisting, and she hit me on the shoulder. "When did you get so self-righteous?"

"You're no longer my sister."

"I can *blow* people, okay? Who do you think —"

"I'm not trying to control your blow jobs," I said. "Let's be clear."

"So what's the point? That you can go out to Denver or Oregon or whatever to be a *ski bum* twenty-something *dude* and, oh, I don't know, turn into a *drug addict* and then *burn down some buildings*, but when one tiny and meaningless sexual indiscretion from my past comes up, which is harmless, which is probably one of Rick the manager's fondest memories, honestly, which will probably help him make passionate love to his wife tonight, you turn into Mother Teresa? You are ridiculous. You don't want to start this with me. Admit that you're a ridiculous person before you turn on the engine and maybe I'll forgive you for being a dick to me so we can sit down at Denny's and I can drink my shitty wine and I can tell you about how my husband is a small man and ask you for your advice, which is the whole reason I came here to see you."

She leaned back into her seat, arms crossed, and chewed her gum angrily.

I looked at the key, which I'd already inserted into the ignition.

"Admit it. Don't turn it. Fight the urge. Admit it. Look at me. Look at me when you say it. Admit it."

I looked at her.

"Don't be a dick. You have a habit. It ruins things."

"I know."

"Say it."

"I am a ridiculous person."

"Good. Good boy."

"And I'm sorry for being judgmental."

"Good," she said, turning forward and nodding at the windshield's glass. "Done. Go. Let's go."

I turned the key; the engine flared to life.

"It is kinda funny," I said.

"I know it is," she said, nodding. Still exasperated, but now grinning. She looked at me sidelong. "Rick, right? Is that not amazing?"

～～～

"Do you not find it amazing," Haley said, "that an entire quadrant of our family is dead?"

It was an hour later. We were sitting on Denny's back porch, looking out at the dark tree line past the lawn. It was cool enough now that the mosquitoes were gone, but it was a nice night, and Haley was apparently back to smoking menthol cigarettes, at least when she was in the middle of a family crisis and out of her children's sight.

A few weeks before, I'd gone down to the RadioShack and bought some cheap speaker wire so I could string a line from the living room and hook up another pair of old speakers to Denny's stereo and run them outside. They were out here with us now. I'd put on Crosby, Stills, and Nash. (Yes, I was out of control.) This time a CD, not a record, so I wouldn't have to get up. The self-titled album; no Young. We'd only gotten to "Marrakesh Express."

"Quadrant?"

"That's what it is, right? Dad has one brother, Mom has a sister and a brother. All four sets have or had their own little clans. We're one. Denny, Crystal, and Wayne were another one. And they're *all* dead. That whole part of the family. Dead. Boom boom boom."

"Heart attack, cancer, accident," I said.

"See?"

"I guess that quadrant was cursed."

"It's like they got all the bad luck," she said. "For everyone. No one else is sick, not one other *tragedy* tragedy. I don't even think they get colds on Mom's side of the family. Our *grandparents* are still alive and healthy on that side."

"You're right," I said. "I hadn't thought about it."

"I just mean there's usually a more reasonable distribution of ill fortune. It's as though Denny's family was a magnet pulling it all over to their side."

"Maybe they protected us."

"Maybe."

"This whole quadrant thing," I said. "It really only works from our perspective. Yours and mine."

"What other perspective would you like me to speak from?" she said. "Mahatma Gandhi's?"

"Denny," I said, "kept a bunch of Wayne's stuff around. I've been looking at some of his college stuff. It makes me think Denny was looking, trying to figure out what happened to him. Or once was."

"Wouldn't you?" she said. "It made no sense." She took a drink of wine, then reached for her Marlboros. "If one of my kids got hit by a bus right in front of me I'd probably spend the rest of my life trying to crack the case and solve the murder." She lit the cigarette. "I know it's irritating when people say this, but it's actually true: you really can't understand what it feels like to be a parent until you're a parent."

"What does it feel like?"

"It feels like..." She trailed off, thinking, then said: "It feels like it's actually *you* in the other little body. I mean, it's not like you can really see the world through your child's eyes or that it even *is* you. It's just — I feel like it's just nature's very simple, elegant plan to align your average human being's narcissism with being a good parent. It really does feel like there are splinters of yourself walking around your feet and asking you questions and holding on to your legs." She smiled at the thought. "I suppose if you think about it like that, it's totally surreal."

I thought of Denny and my own quest to know more about Wayne in these doppelgänger terms. What do you do when word comes that your own young self has been found frozen to death on your property up north?

"So what's going on with John?" I asked.

"Shit, man."

"Only if you want."

"I want," she said. "I do. It's just, just so — it's just so *embarrassing.*"

He had somehow — *somehow* meaning, of course, by unleashing a cavalcade of tremendously expensive lawyers on the St. Louis court system — pleaded down to a simple misdemeanor charge that had enabled him to pay a fine in lieu of doing jail time or community service, so he was clear of any legal troubles. Haley also told me that his mug shot was no longer to be found anywhere on the internet; the *Post-Dispatch*, which usually kept an archive available, showed no signs of ever having hosted it, even though Haley had sent me the link a few months before. "So what it comes down to is this," she explained, "I know what happened. Some cop or a couple cops know what happened, or at least did know, because surely they've forgotten. John knows. And I know. That's it. The kids have no idea what's going on and neither do John's parents, who are probably at this very moment insinuating to my children that whatever is wrong between Mommy and Daddy, it's Mommy who is the problem. Viv is probably old enough to understand that something is very wrong, but what am I supposed to do? Tell her? Make John tell her? Make John tell his parents? Tell *our* parents? Basically, as it stands, there are essentially no consequences for what he's done."

"Other than the fact that you're divorcing him."

Haley looked at me sidelong.

"Right?"

"Well."

"*Right?*"

"I am perched on the edge of filing."

"Jesus Christ, Haley."

"He didn't actually have *intercourse* with a prostitute."

"Who is he, Bill Clinton? The whole point is that he intended to. And how often does he travel for business? Every other week? Don't you think it's safe to assume he's often paying women to fuck him? And that he has been? And will continue to do so?"

"Not if you don't insist on being *that* deductive about it."

"How else are you supposed to be? You don't have all the information."

"I don't know," she said. "Nuanced?"

"Do you hear yourself saying that?"

"Things were particularly bad right at that moment," she said, after a long pause. "And John has maintained, from the day I found the letter, and, honestly, very convincingly, and I don't say that lightly because I am a master of knowing when he's lying, that whatever that night in St. Louis *was*, it was anomalous. He was drunk, he was in a weird part of town. He made a *very* bad choice. And acted so poorly and so clumsily that he immediately got arrested."

"That's not a feather in his cap."

"What's the other alternative, though?" she asked. "That John is a deeply disturbed pathological liar, and that he somehow managed to conceal his actual identity from me for twelve years? *Twelve* years? I am basically his mother and his wife at the same time. The man can't prepare cereal for himself."

"You make it sound like it's endearing that he ended up with a hooker in his car."

"That's not what I'm saying. It is, and will always be, disgusting. Yes. And I know what you're doing and I appreciate it from the bottom of my heart, I see that you're thinking about it from a stark, righteous, totally straightforward pro-Haley position, which I can't even really see anymore. But I have been thinking about this. A lot, Ben. I have charts. I have goddamned cost-benefit analyses about my life scattered throughout my office. I just need you to stop for a second, take a breath, temporarily suspend the idea that John is a sex-monster sociopath, and tell me whether the other version, the John-as-bumbling-idiot-using-extremely-poor-judgment version, doesn't seem possible to you as well? Just knowing — just knowing how men are. You know?"

"I don't really understand what you're asking," I said. "It seems like you're asking me to endorse one fantasy over another one. John is the only person who actually knows, and if he's good enough at lying, then it's going to be a leap of faith in either direction." Haley was quiet after I said this, so I continued, the idea seeming more and more ludicrous the more I thought about it: "But if you're asking me if I think John is capable of constructing complicated, elaborate, disturbingly sophisticated lies that go way, way beyond what you've ever imagined him or anyone actually constructing, then my answer is yes, that's totally possible. I mean, I feel like I know and have known people whose whole lives are focused on lying, like the *actual* meaning of their lives, and it's by far their greatest skill, you know? People who've worked at it for thirty years. And then there's a whole class of people who can't really control it, and past them, there's a whole class of people who don't even know that they're doing it as they do it. And I mean, Jesus, have you ever known a hard-core addict? Have you ever known a heroin addict?"

"Do you count?"

"Most addicts? They're like fucking Lex Luthor, Haley. Only it's worse because they're also just totally unaware of what they're lying about. They don't live in our — they don't share a reality with us, if that makes sense. I know that makes it sound like I'm saying they're psychotic, but it really is — it really is that big of a deal."

"I'm not sure," Haley said, "how we got here. To drugs."

"My point is that the lying John is just a *possibility* that might easily be him. Have you gotten tested?"

"Tested for what?"

"STDs? AIDS? Everything."

"I don't have any STDs."

"Did you get tested?"

"Okay," Haley said. "Fine. That's fine. But add to all of this that John is an amazing father."

"I'm sure he would continue to be an amazing father after you left him."

Haley lit another cigarette.

"I fucking hate this," she said. "Fuck. Fuck you. I mean not fuck *you*, you. But fuck. Everything. Fuck. Fuck fuck fuck."

I had surprised myself with my rant about lying, but it was true, when it came down to it: I had known some amazing liars. Jeremy and Allie came to mind. Myself. But I was not so self-righteous that I couldn't see there was more to it, and that at some level, if you went down deep enough, the whole speech probably sprang from self-loathing. Lying in its ultimate and essential sense: knowing nothing about yourself.

I snorted at the thought.

"What?" Haley said.

"Nothing," I said. "Reflecting on my own hypocrisy."

"Aw, you're not that bad, kid," Haley said. "You're maybe one of the only people in the world I like."

"John's out?"

"John's out right now," she said. "I love him, unfortunately. But I also dislike him immensely. Is there a song like that?"

"Yes."

"I should sing that song."

"You do love him?"

"Yeah," she said. "I do. And do you know what's fucked up? If we're talking about the evil tricks nature plays on us to ensure some kind of genetic continuity? The feeling didn't even waver. I mean, not even a *ripple*, even when I was in the house with the letter, totally in the dark, thinking he actually had been with a prostitute, absolutely screaming at him over the phone. None of it had any effect."

I laughed at that. "Love," I said. "Implacable."

"It's not implacable," she said. "It's just so *strange*. You know? It's like there's no way to say what it is. You can just be in it. Upside down and choking. But then when you have to say what it is, you can't."

I looked out at the trees as she said this, guessing about what she meant. "Lady of the Island" ended right then, and in the silence I had that strange experience of hearing in my head the beginning of the next song before it actually started. That's when you know you've listened to an album a lot.

After a second of my brain's intro, "Helplessly Hoping" actually did start. Haley was sitting with her feet up on the chair now, her knees tucked under her chin, listening, so I listened with her.

"This song is so sad," she said eventually.

"I know."

"Why do you like them so much?"

"I don't really know," I said. "I just always have."

We listened some more.

"What does 'They are three together' possibly mean?" she said. "In that context?"

"I don't know," I said. "Maybe nothing."

She stretched, then took a last sip of wine. "Oh well," she said. "I like the harmonies."

I gave Haley the option of Wayne's or Denny's room, but she

declined both, saying that they were obviously haunted, so we pulled out the sofa bed in the living room and I brought down a stack of clean sheets, which Haley was impressed with me for having.

"You do know that all men are not retarded eleven-year-olds, right?" I said.

"Don't say *retarded* like that," she said. "It's awful." She took one side of the bedding and we spread it out. "It's easy."

"I think one thing women don't ever quite believe," I said, "but that nevertheless is true is that men very often don't care at all about things. That they just — that really, men don't care about many things."

"Things like wives?"

"I meant sheets."

"Oh, oh," she said, taking the end of the next sheet. "Okay. I'm sorry. I can hardly think straight after that much insight."

"I'm telling you," I said. "Listen to me."

"Have you heard of Cashmina sheets?"

"No."

"They are these amazing sheets," she said. "I feel like a kitten when I'm under them."

"Right there, exactly that."

"What?"

"That is exactly something I don't care about."

Haley got into the bed and we said our good nights, but when I was upstairs and brushing my teeth, I heard her call, "Hey, Benjy," and I went back down, brush still in my mouth.

She was veiled in the darkness; all I could see was a blur of blond where her head was.

"What's up?"

"Since we are talking about very serious and real emotional

matters," she said, "and this trip is very adult, I have to ask you something. It's awful."

"I did not get raped in prison."

She didn't say anything.

"Really," I said.

"Oh my God," she said finally. "Thank God."

"You can report that back to Mom and Dad for me too. I could feel Mom wanting to ask me when they were in Portland."

"Let me text them right now."

"I was only in maximum security for like three weeks," I said, "and I was in isolation for most of that. Minimum security's not really like that. It's different. I was fine."

"Did you get into fights?"

"Some," I said. "Small fights. But I was younger than most people. And they liked me because I ran the game night. I was fine."

"Game night?"

"Yes."

"You seem the same," she said. "Except slightly smarter."

"Oh," I said. "Thank you."

"I was so worried you were going to be like the Incredible Hulk. And a Nazi. You can't even imagine prison, it turns out. When you sit down and try to imagine it. And you're not someone who would know what it is. I just kept thinking about the one episode of *Oz* I saw like ten years ago that traumatized me."

"No," I said. "It was not like that. I'm okay."

"Ben?"

"Yes."

"I'm so glad you're doing good. I'm so glad you don't drink."

"Thank you."

"I think I'm even glad you're a vegetarian, for some reason I don't understand."

"Thanks."

"It just seems like you're doing things on purpose now. Somewhat deliberately. That's the distinction. That's what seems smarter. You never used to seem to do anything intentionally."

"I want that on my gravestone."

"Ben Hanson: He did nothing on purpose."

"Perfect."

"Mostly I'm glad because it means we can talk again, though."

"Yeah. I know."

"You know? I feel like I haven't talked to you like that in five years at *all*."

"I'm sorry. It was me. It was my fault."

"I would have come to see you. You told me not to come."

"No. I didn't want you to. It was embarrassing."

"I don't understand what happened. I don't understand what went wrong."

"I know," I said. "But it's really very boring."

7

Very Boring Story I Can't Quite Bring Myself to Tell Because of How Boring It Is; Labor Day

I met Allie in Denver in 2004, and in early 2005, she and I decided to move to Portland. Denver had become burdened with too much history and too many faces I did not want to see anymore, and she had a whole set of friends in Portland — she'd gone to Reed. And what did I care where we went, so long as it was farther west? I would have moved to Hong Kong had she suggested it. Anything to be farther away. We moved into a little dilapidated white bungalow, we both got jobs, I quit right away, and I did my best to stay relatively clean, which was not hard at first because I didn't know anyone. Part of the reason we had left Denver, even though I didn't think it was ever quite stated out loud, was that she and I had both gotten into heroin there, as had a few other friends in our circle. I liked it more than she did, but I'll just say this: I don't think either of our ideas about what we wanted our lives to look like included images of ourselves snorting lines of pure heroin off a kitchen table at a hastily-thrown-together Wednesday-evening party. Heroin is heroin because there's no way to explain why you would ever do heroin. That's really all I'm going to say on the subject.

Portland was better for a while, even though that's where I

started to drink too much and where I really started shutting off to everything again. When Jeremy moved to town there was a new flurry of excitement and energy — he had gone off and gotten a master's degree and had started a company and seemed to have actual ins with some people; he had attracted the interest of a venture capitalist who was willing to fund him as he developed his first game, which was then really just an idea about a few simple puzzles. Jeremy's talents were more in coding and refining, not actually coming up with ideas. He was also one of the few people I had ever met who had true initiative. He *did* things, always. He acted on thoughts. He was not one to let opportunities go by. Nothing better demonstrated this characteristic than his stealing Allie from me, actually. Which was an upsetting thing.

That's around the time things got real dark.

In the morning, I stopped at the Amoco station at the halfway point of my run. There was another purpose for the run: I wanted to call Lauren before too much time went by after our drive, and I did not want my sister there for the conversation.

I had saved the number from Dr. Hendrix's office into my phone right after Lauren had dropped me off. It was Sunday morning at 8:30. I thought: Ben, you are a moron. But I tried it. And she picked up after two rings.

"Hi, Ben. Are you calling about an animal emergency?"

"No. As much as I would like to have one to offer you."

"What's up?"

"I wanted to let you know that my sister's in town and that my parents are going to be here tomorrow, so I've been a little busy."

"That's fine," she said. "You don't have to apologize. Or keep me abreast of your calendar."

"How are you?"

"I learned how to castrate bulls on Thursday."

"That sounds good."

"It was."

"Well, look," I said. "Moving on. Not that I don't want to talk about castration. But I wanted to say that I'll be busy for a little, but I was still wondering if you wanted to go out sometime? Maybe dinner later in the week?"

"Hm," she said. "No. I don't think so."

"Maybe," I said.

"Ben, look," she said. "Can I ask you a question?"

"Please."

"What is it that you want exactly? From me? Specifically?"

"To take you out to dinner."

"A date?"

"Sure," I said. "Yes."

"And how long are you going to be here?" she asked. "In St. Helens? A month?"

"It depends on the house."

"But do you see what I'm saying?"

"No."

"There's not much of a point," she said. "I mean, you're very nice. But honestly, you probably won't be here for very long and on top of that, you and I really don't have anything in common. That was the whole problem before too."

"What do you mean? What before?"

"Do you want to know how it seems to me?"

"Was what you just said not how it seems to you?"

"It just seems to me that you got back, locked onto the first woman who was around, slept with her, then found another person to lock onto, and now you're going to do your best to sleep with her in the short amount of time before you return to wherever it is you came from. You kinda just seem like a player."

"That's not at all true. I asked you on a date."

"I know you probably don't *think* it's true," she said. "I mean, I know. You're funny. You seem like a good person. You're trying to put your life back together, which I understand completely. But I feel like you could just as easily have run into some other girl you used to know, at the library or somewhere, and you would be calling her right now and saying the same thing. Do you know what I mean?"

"Can I just say that this is a very intense conversation for two people who hardly know each other?"

"It's not that intense."

"The only reason I came to your brother's opening is that Grant implied you might be there."

"Who's Grant?"

"My friend," I said. "The big burly guy with the kid."

"Grant MacDowell?"

"Yes," I said. "And I did see you drive by the house the first day I was here, and yes, that reminded me of you and it got me wondering what you were doing here, but I eventually would have heard about you being here or seen you and the same thing would have happened. No, you have not been on my mind for the last fourteen years, and I'm sure I haven't been on yours. At all. I do not have any illusions about that. Don't worry."

"I haven't thought about you once, I don't think."

"But also, no, that doesn't mean that I'm, like, Dudley Moore, here to seduce you before I move to Thailand."

"You're using references I don't understand."

"You get my point though," I said. "Right? The thing with Theresa was just a weird surprise, incidental."

"But it's still the same, either way. You're not going to be here. So I don't want to even go down that road. It just wouldn't make sense."

"What if it takes my uncle's house a year to sell? It easily could."

"It probably won't."

"Are you working all day?"

"No," she said. "I'm doing paperwork here. I'm almost done."

"What are you doing this afternoon?"

"I was going to go to the library," she said. "I'm studying."

"For what?"

"The GRE."

"Aren't you already a doctor?"

"Why are you asking me why I'm taking the GRE?"

"I used to tutor it."

"If you offer to help me study for the GRE I'm going to puke all over myself, Ben."

"No, no," I said. "No. I'm just thinking that maybe the whole idea of a date, sitting there at dinner, chatting, all of that — maybe that's just way too intimate and awkward and seems horrible to you. But it's not actually that you don't, you know — want to hang out."

"It sounds like it seems horrible to you, hearing you say it like that."

"It doesn't at all," I said. "I do not presume to know what the world seems like from your point of view."

"Because you don't."

"It's the same for both of us."

She was silent.

"So I have a proposal."

"That was a trick of logic," she said.

"I have a proposal."

"What."

"Today, later," I said. "At like two thirty, I will go over to that little bonsai garden thing next to the library and I'll bring two coffees, and if you want, just come out and take a break from studying; we can chat, drink our coffee. That's it."

"Maybe," she said. "Maybe I'll come out."

"And if you don't, no problem, that's all. I'll just go into the library and try to find some other woman to call while I'm here."

"I'm not going to laugh."

〰〰〰

When I came down from showering Haley told me that she had to work.

"On the Sunday of Labor Day weekend?"

"When it happens, it happens," she said. "Singapore is pissed."

When I'd left, she had been just stirring in the bed, making comments about the grossness of smoking cigarettes, but now she was awake and dressed, wearing her glasses, already set up with her laptop at Denny's desk in the office.

"I can't believe I slept so long," she said, twisting in the chair and glancing at me. "I'm like Rip van Winkle over here."

"Do you want to go around and see anything?" I asked. "In town?"

"Like what? I truly do have to do this bullshit," she said, looking back at her monitor. "It's either now or..." She trailed off. "No. It's now. Mom and Dad will probably get here tomorrow morning and I'm leaving with them, then we're in the car, then their house, then home."

"You're leaving with them? Tomorrow? I didn't know that."

"I'm flying out of Chicago," she said. "Tuesday morning. Didn't I tell you?"

"No."

"I wanted to catch up with them a little, so I made it so I could at least spend one night at their house." She glanced up. "You know how Mom is."

"Yeah."

I lingered there, looking at my sister after she'd returned to her work. I thought about how great the differences were between her and Lauren, both superficial and substantive. Lauren was frank in a way nobody in my family was capable of being — there was a lack of irony to her that I admired, steeped as I was in the great involute communication properties of my father, my mother, my sister. But at the same time there was also something that reminded me of my sister in Lauren, and vice versa. Some quality. I didn't quite know what. Some kind of tenacity that I lacked.

I wasted time around the house for a couple of hours, then told my sister I was going to run some errands and buy the food for the barbecue tomorrow. She barely looked up when I said good-bye.

〰〰〰

I couldn't tell you why the St. Helens public library, a cold brown modernist rectangle on the western shore of the river, had a bonsai garden next to it. Some administrator at some point had decided it was a good idea, though, and I was sitting among the little trees, sipping my coffee, when Lauren appeared beneath the awning that served as an entryway, gave a small wave in my direction, and walked toward me. I held up her coffee.

"I didn't know how you like it," I said. "I brought you the things, though."

"Oh, black is fine," she said. She took the coffee and sat down beside me.

"How's the GRE?"

"Good," she said. "I probably don't have to study as much as I'm studying. I mean, the MCAT was insane. But it's been a while since I did, like, factoring." She looked at me over the lid of her coffee and raised her eyebrows. "You know? FOIL."

She asked me how it was to have my sister in town and whether I was looking forward to seeing my parents. I told her it was good to see Haley and that it would be all right to see my mother and father, although things with them were more complicated. It looked for a moment that she was going to ask me what I meant by that, but she only nodded contemplatively. I tried to remember what I knew about her family, which was very little. Something had gone very wrong with her father, I remembered that much, and I knew her mother was here in town. But when it came down to it, I really didn't know. And I knew nothing about what had happened with her husband.

"So," she said. "On the phone."

"I'm sorry about that," I said. "I don't usually debate women into seeing me. I think my sister being in town is making me more verbal than I usually am."

"Why? Are you usually the silent type?"

"I guess I am. But not on purpose."

"Oh, don't apologize," she said. "Anyway. I was just giving you my normal thing." She looked over at the library and said, "I have not dated in quite some time." She said it in a grave voice, tone descending. She was embarrassed.

"I'm guessing I probably have you beat," I said. "Or at least had you beat. Until I went out with Theresa."

"Really?" she said. "How long had it been since you were on a date before that?"

"I would say . . . somewhere around . . . two years? That's the last time I had a girlfriend, anyway."

"Four years," she said.

"How is it possible you haven't been on a date in four years?"

"What do you mean?" she said in earnest. "How is it possible you haven't been on one in two years?"

Things went on like this.

~~~~~

"He won't tell," Haley was saying. "He's been walking around like he has no secrets and he won't say *anything*." She pointed her brat at me to punctuate the accusation.

"There's nothing to tell."

My mother, father, sister, and I all sat around the circular table on Denny's porch, eating chips and brats and listening to the Allman Brothers — Haley had demanded a CSNY break — on Denny's yellow outdoor boom box.

"I can tell there's something to tell," said my mother, smiling. "Even *I* can tell."

She looked good, and she was more relaxed here than I had seen her in a long time. Haley's blond hair had come from my father; my mother had a darker complexion that came from her grandmother's Italian side. She sat back in her chair with a smile on her face, her glasses hanging from around her neck by a thin chain. For a long time she'd dyed her hair the same near-black it had always been, but she'd let it go now, and let the streaks of gray come.

"There's a young lady in town who I've talked to," I said. "There's no more information." I looked at my father. "You get no names."

"Something tells me we might be able to figure it out, Ben," said my dad. "St. Helens isn't all that big."

"Please tell me it isn't Theresa," my mother said. "For God's sake."

"It isn't Theresa. What would be wrong with Theresa?"

"Ben."

"You can't figure it out," I said. "Don't try." I bit into my veggie burger.

"Are those things any good?" asked my dad. "I already know the answer, mind you. I know that they're horrible."

My father was in a good mood. I expected he'd be cranky while he was here and mad at me for not yet going up to the cabin, and he also just tended to get discombobulated when he was out in the world (away from Chicago), especially during those times when my mother wasn't there acting as his corrective. She'd been on the fence about coming because of what had happened to Denny here, but she'd powered through. I could only imagine what this visit would have been like without her. She tempered him and together they formed a kind of Voltron of suitable social interaction, my father taking pleasure in providing definitive statements and passing judgment on all matters of the world (about which he knew quite a lot, I admit), my mother supplying nuance and good cheer and doing the work of cleaning up whatever bad things happened around the dinner table with their friends. I don't mean to suggest that taken separately, they weren't fully formed people, both with their own intricate moods, both very good, in their ways, at steering themselves through the problems of the day-to-day world. What I mean is they had chosen this default tag-team way of being as a supplement to who they were as individuals. And what did I know? Maybe that's just what happens when you're married thirty-five years.

"Okay, okay," Haley said. "He's getting pissed. We'll leave you alone."

"I'm not pissed," I said. "I'm discreet."

"As always," said my father, and I could not decode what ironic meaning was underneath his words.

My mother asked what it was like, being back in St. Helens.

"It's nice, actually," I said. "Nicer than I thought it would be."

"What did you think it would be?"

"I thought it would be a combination of macabre, because of Wayne and Denny, and totally alien."

"Alien?" said my father. "How could it be alien? You grew up here."

"It was alien then," said Haley.

"But I've always thought of St. Helens as so fundamentally *normal*," said my father, not turning to look at Haley after the comment. "Sure, you'll get your neurotic people wherever you go, but at least here there's a good straightforwardness to the way life works."

"Oh, please, Jack," said my mother. "You've romanticized it beyond all recognition."

"I've done no such thing."

"I could list a dozen examples of people here or things that have happened here that completely undermine whatever sentimental notions you have about St. Helens. Once and for all. It's darker and stranger in small towns than almost anywhere."

"All right," said my father. "Let's have them then."

"What?"

"Your dozen examples."

"Are you truly serious?"

"Do bears bear? Do bees be?"

"That expression."

"Don't get distracted, sweetheart," he said. "The job falls to you. But I'll let you off the hook. Name ten and we'll call it even."

"Fine," she said, leaning forward and resting both palms flat on the table. "Ten." All four of us looked at her fingers, splayed out as markers.

"Maybe we can start with the sadomasochism murder by the renters on McCulloh Street?" she said. "In 1984." She looked at my father. "You remember, don't you? The people with the plastic bags over their heads? Accidentally?"

"That's a solid start," I said.

"And since we started on murder, let me fill examples two, three, four, and five with various homicides that come to mind. Off the top of my head. The hit-and-run in the Farm and Fleet parking lot; the awful holdup of the Burger King, which we could count as a rape, too, but we won't. The man who killed his boss at the fish store. Jenny Munro."

My father looked at her fingers, then slowly leaned back in his chair and took a drink from his beer. "You can't do all murders," he said. "It isn't fair."

"How about just plain bizarre?" said my mother. "How about the woman they found living in the basement of the elementary school?"

"That was bizarre, yes," said my father, who had now realized he was going to lose badly. "She was down there eating birdseed for six months."

"Which reminds me of course of the Burlington Coat Factory that was using dog pelts to make their coats, but I'm not allowed to use it because that was in Black Earth, wasn't it? Just an aside."

"Well," said Haley. "That's disgusting."

"That was a complicated story involving fur contamination overseas," said my father. "That's not fair. It had nothing to do with Black Earth."

"How about when people realized, after ten years, that the bus driver at St. John's was a pedophile? Or what about the airplane that crashed into the farm off Thirty-Two? Where am I? Benjamin?"

"Eight," I said.

"You can stop now."

"Nine can be when John Buehler burned down the Glickmans' house after he and Bill Glickman swapped wives. Halloween 1973."

"All right."

"And ten…" she said, looking up at the house. "Ten can be Wayne?"

"What about Wayne?"

She shrugged. "Everything about Wayne."

"It's amazing how skilled you are, sweetheart, at turning a game into a bath of raw sewage." He looked at me. "Don't you think she should have counted herself on that list, Ben? Huh?"

I just stared straight ahead. As did Haley.

"You told me I only had to go to ten," said my mom, apparently unmoved by what my father had said. "But if I were to *keep* going," she said, "I just would have counted your parents."

My father burst out laughing, and, eventually, my mother giggled, pleased with herself for her joke. I thought it would be appropriate right then for an ominous clap of thunder to roll down out of the sky, damning us all to hell. My sister started eating her pickle.

"I withdraw my pastoral fantasy," said my father, who stood and went to the cooler for another beer. "Okay. You win."

"But it's been good either way," I said. "I ran into Grant at Golden's. He's doing well. He has a little kid."

"Grant MacDowell?" said Haley.

"Yeah," I said. "That's right, you knew him. From the store."

"I did know him," she said. "I liked him."

"How is John, by the way?"

I glanced over at my mother, who was leaning back in her chair with her lemonade, looking at Haley. She'd asked it very casually, but you could hear all the other questions that rode alongside the one she'd said out loud. She seemed to know something.

"I haven't talked to him," said Haley, who had, for her part, responded right away and in a tone that suggested she had no intention of being either forthcoming or apologetic. "So far as I know, he's a bastard."

"Whoa, Nellie," said my dad, who was still standing by the cooler. He had been looking out at Denny's yard, but now he turned. "Hey, Benjy," he said over the tractor-beam stare going on between my mother and sister. "You been doing any work down in Denny's workshop?"

"I finished the table he was working on," I said.

"The table of death. Take me down and show me, will you?"

"Sure."

Downstairs, leaning against Denny's workbench, my father said, "What in the fuck is going on between John and your sister?"

"You really have to ask her."

"Did he cheat on her?"

"You should just ask her."

My father nodded his assent to this arrangement. Seeing that I wasn't going to say anything, he glanced around at the screws on the workbench. "My brother the carpenter," he said, picking up a screw. He looked over to his left, at the stairs. "He died crawling up those," he said, pointing with the screw. "Ridiculous. Imagine it."

I looked at the stairs.

"You know he knew that his heart was not working properly," said my dad. "Right after he died, I couldn't stop wondering what was going through his head once he figured out what was happening. It wasn't one of those drop-dead-like-a-bag-of-concrete things." He nodded at the stairs. "He made it halfway up."

"I barely ever think about it, oddly," I said. "But I do think about Wayne."

"Do you?" he said. "What about him?"

"I found some stuff of his," I said. "I figure Denny still wondered about it. Like what exactly happened up there. Why he was up there in the first place. That's really the question."

"Denny remained preoccupied with it, there's no doubt about that," said my dad. "And he never came out and said it, but it was obvious to anyone who was paying attention that Crystal ultimately just said to hell with this, to hell with your mourning. Six months, a year, you can understand anything. People do anything; you understand, you go with the flow. But Dennis would bring Wayne up five years after the fact, as though it had just happened the week before. It was intolerable. I can't imagine what it was like for her. You can't heal if you keep picking the scab. No one can."

"I know," I said. "I remember."

"That's right," he said, pointing at me with the screw one last time before setting it back down on the workbench. "I'm sure you do." He reclaimed his beer. "He was still talking about it when your mother and I were moving. Still! I remember your mother lamenting the fact that you couldn't divorce your brother-in-law."

"What do you think happened?"

"Happened?" he said, after a drink. "To Wayne?"

I nodded.

"You mean why he died, all of that? How he died?"

I nodded again.

"Don't tell me you're making this into *your* job now," he said.

"I'm just curious."

My father made a face, somewhere between inquiry and disgust, and said, "Well, that's exactly the thing. It's impossible, there's no information at all, and it's therefore impossible to know anything, which is exactly why my brother set up shop there in the first place."

"What do you mean?"

"Having no idea what happened to him was its own perpetual-motion machine, which Dennis knew perfectly well because he talked to me about it. So he starts asking questions about his kid: Why did he go up in the dead of winter? Why didn't he just go inside? Was he nuts? Was he killing himself? Drugs? Accident? On and on and on, but the whole thing — and it's hard to describe now, but you could really feel it then, I mean *really* feel it — the whole thing was entirely inscrutable, Ben. Inscrutable. Which was perfect. So long as there weren't any real answers, it was perfect. The perfectly unsolvable puzzle to work on forever. In order to avoid living."

"But you must have an opinion about which option it was. Which answer."

"Me? I do. Of course I do. Wayne was up there doing exactly what my brother used to do, which was exactly why Denny built that place to begin with. He was up there taking LSD. He got disoriented somehow, thought for whatever reason it was a good idea to sit down in the snow and turn into a block of ice, do something fucking mystical, I don't know. It was an accident that Denny was at least partially responsible for, which he knew deep down, he knew it. And that is why he could not stop obsessing over it. Because it was his fault."

"Denny used to trip a lot?"

"Oh, I don't know," said my dad. "Would you call two or three hundred times a lot? Let me describe the first five years of my brother's life after he came home from Vietnam, okay? Marry Crystal, impregnate her, flip out, become a madman, buy land, go up north to work on a cabin all the time, away from your pregnant wife, drop acid, go up north to work on cabin, drop acid, repeat, repeat, repeat. Repeat."

"It's not like Denny was going up there tripping with Wayne, though."

"No," said my dad, "but I know for a fact he bragged about it sometimes, or at least told stories about it. Wayne knew what that cabin was for. And once he got a car, he was going up there doing the same thing. He was just the same as his dad. They two were identical, it was uncanny. And do you know what Denny said to me when I asked him if he thought it was a bright idea to let his kid keep doing it? This is beautiful too."

"What?"

"'It's good for him,'" said my dad. "'It's good for him, let him figure it all out. It's good for him, at least it's *safe* up there. No cops, no other people. He's figuring it out, like I did.' *That's* what he said! My brother, who never figured out a thing."

This was not a part of Denny's history that I'd ever heard my father speak about, and looking at him — looking at how angry and self-righteous he had become during his monologue, even though he was trying to act like he was amused — I could guess why. Denny's version of parenting sounded like the exact opposite of his own. And yet I had turned out more like Denny and Wayne than like my own father. Add to that what Theresa had told me, and I could see why he was acting this way.

But the story made sense, as did my father's guess about what had happened to my cousin. Hearing my father say it in this way, it seemed like there were no other possibilities.

"I tripped with Wayne once," I said. "When I went to visit him in Madison."

"What, when you were a teenager?" he said. "Are you kidding me?"

I shook my head. "Although actually, it seemed like he was maybe doing a lot of coke. Also."

"You too?"

"No. Just the mushrooms."

"Wonderful." My dad sighed then, but I watched him look around his brother's workbench and slowly swallow the anger instead of launching into a new tirade. Neither of us wanted a whole referendum on my past. We'd done that.

My dad tossed the screw back onto the counter. "Well," he said. "There you go. Case closed."

~~~~~

He wasn't angry with me. Nor was my mother in an apocalyptic mood when we went back upstairs, even though I assumed Haley had informed her of some of the more sordid details of her troubles with John. She and Haley had apparently gotten through whatever discussion they'd had and were now cleaning up the kitchen.

"Don't, don't," I said. "Let me clean when you guys leave."

"Too late," said my mother. "It's done."

"What time is it?" asked my dad. "Should we get going?" He looked at me. "What time does Denny's ghost usually start crawling up and down the stairs? Does he moan?"

"Jack," said my mom, looking over at him. "Don't. He's been dead two months. Don't unleash your sense of humor quite yet."

"I know that," he said. "I'm aware of that."

He and my mother had some kind of stare-off, something not too happy, and my father, hands in pockets, finally disengaged and walked into the living room.

We all ended up there. Haley made coffee as the afternoon wore on, and my parents (and even I, although I can't explain it) found excuses for them to stick around. My dad pointed to the canister of Denny's ashes and asked me when I planned to take it up north. I assured him I'd do it soon. He accepted this, behaved as though he trusted me. It had been five years, nearly, since the four of us had been alone together at all, let alone for this much time. Say what you will about the details, and no, it never lasts, but it feels good to be with your family. At times. The warmth of it caught me off guard. So much so that when my mother turned to me and asked what I was going to do when the house sold, I said, "I don't know," and didn't brace myself with the same defensive tension I usually did. Then: "But that reminds me. I need some ruthless advice."

"I can think of no more ruthless counsel," said my father, "than your sister, mother, and myself."

"Yes, we will kill someone for you," said Haley.

"It's not at that point," I said. "But it might be at the point of lawyers."

"This is suddenly very exciting," said Haley. "What could it be?"

As best I could, I explained to them the situation with Jeremy and the game. I told them about those first few months after Jeremy had returned and formed his company, and I told them about the informal way we'd collaborated on the puzzles, the suggestions I made from time to time about this or that part of the idea. We would talk about it when we played chess, but after maybe a half dozen conversations, Jeremy had said to me, "You know that you're good at this, right?"

"What?" I'd said. "Chess?"

"You're good at chess, too, but no," he'd said. "The puzzle part. The content side. Our brains sort of work alike, but only in some ways."

"Yours isn't nearly so clogged with THC."

"Look, I'm good at solving puzzles and riddles and those sorts of things. And that's fine, that's why I want to build the game. I want to play it. But you can actually *make* puzzles. Like write them. I can't do that at all. I wouldn't know where to start."

I squinted at him. "Why do you think I can write them?" I asked.

"Partly that I've heard the way you tell stories. How you do stuff like withhold the right detail for the end, tell the story in a certain order for a reason. You realize that most people don't do that."

"I do like a good yarn."

"And I have a matrix on my computer calling for three hundred and fifty puzzles, riddles, and yarns for the game. Real ones. That advance the story," he said. "Good ones. That are new."

"Are you serious?" I said. "You want me to write your game?"

"Yes," he said. "I am totally serious."

"And so let me get this straight," said my father after I had told him the rest of the story. "He then stole Allie away from you, you burned down his office, then you went to jail, *then* you wrote the game for him?"

"It was informal."

"Informal how?" Haley asked.

"Well," I said, "I would write one of the puzzles on a piece of notebook paper, test it out on some of the other inmates, fix it up, then mail it to Jeremy. To both of them."

"To Allie too?" Haley asked.

I nodded.

"So you were just doing that?" my dad said. "Without him asking?"

"We'd had the conversation before," I said. "Over chess. So I just followed through."

"Passive-aggressive, Ben," said my mom.

"I had free time," I said. "It made me popular."

"You were making a point about loyalty," said my dad. "I understand. It makes a lot of sense."

"I was fucking with Jeremy," I said. "But he *used* them, is the point. He used all of them, pretty much. The central story of the whole thing comes from one of them. They're in the game."

"You've played the game?" asked my sister. "How? He let you?"

"I stole his computer on my way to Wisconsin."

When all of them stared back, I added, "They don't lock their doors. They're like Eloi, the two of them. It was barely breaking in. I was going to piss on their bed. Or something. I don't know."

"This is quite interesting, Ben," said my dad. "*After* you got out of prison? For destroying his property? You immediately broke the law again? Wonderful. Wonderful!"

"This makes you a Morlock," said my mother.

"It doesn't matter," I said. "He doesn't care. I sent it back to him. It was just a — it was just a stupid thing."

"When did you talk to him?" Haley asked. "To Jeremy?"

"We G-chatted," I said.

"Show me the chat."

"What's G-chatting?" my mother asked nervously. Haley and I went into the office. "What does that mean?"

I logged into my account and showed Haley the conversation. "It's like speaking in tongues," I called out to my mother.

"He's joking, sweetheart," I heard my dad say.

"Can I e-mail this to myself?" Haley asked me, her eyes scrolling through the chat I'd had with Jeremy on my first day here.

"Why?"

"Because he admits it right here," she said, pointing at the screen so enthusiastically one of her nails tapped up against it. "That matters."

"Matters for what?"

"You're really this confused about the world, aren't you?"

I shrugged. "Go ahead."

I went back out into the living room and stuffed my hands into my pockets. My parents, both of them on the couch, watched me.

"What?" I said. "It's a friendship breakdown. Or whatever."

My dad laughed. My mom raised her eyebrows, sighed, and got up. "I'm going to the bathroom before the drive." She smiled at me on the way by. "Maybe this will turn out good for you."

I looked at my dad. "Please explain?"

"As the official velociraptor of this family, Ben, let me put it to you simply."

"Okay."

"We are going to sue the living shit out of your old friend Jeremy."

From the office, I heard Haley start clapping.

"What if I don't want to?"

"That's fine," said my dad as he got to his feet. "But let me give you some irrefutable, deeply accurate, exceptionally reliable advice about our world." He put both hands on my shoulders. "First you sue," he said. "Then you decide whether to sue."

〰〰

That night, I didn't spend much time thinking about Jeremy and Allie or that game, even though my family's enthusiasm for litigation seemed to present the situation in a whole new light. I couldn't get interested. I didn't know what would happen; maybe something good would come of it. In truth, though, to me,

Jeremy and Allie were both beginning to feel like the distant past, and the idea of the game ever actually *being* something — well, that all felt like an illusion, whether or not the file was sitting on the drive. I didn't care. I had written the puzzles in jail to occupy myself and entertain my fellow inmates more than anything else, and I also felt proud Jeremy had actually used them and figured out, with Allie's help, such a beautiful way to do the thing we had talked about doing so long ago. He had built something. And Allie had been a part of it too. I could tell that Allie had done the art at virtually every turn of the game's story. In a very strange way, the three of us had created the game, a triangle that could be placed right on top of our romantic triangle. The three fused into one. I honestly didn't feel much anger. More than anything, it felt like a kind of closure.

What I was thinking about, as I made tea and went back into Denny's office, was what my father had said about Wayne.

It made sense, what he'd said — so much so that when I checked my e-mail and found that I'd finally received a response from Ellen Barnum, the poet Wayne had taken classes with, I was tempted to tell her that I had been mistaken and that there was no need for me to meet her after all. This is what she wrote:

From: ebarnum@wisc.edu
To: hansonben3@gmail.com
Date: 9/1/2008
Subject: Re: Inquiry Regarding Your Former Student Wayne Hanson

Dear Benjamin Hanson,

Apologies for taking as long as I have to get back to you about this — it's a very busy time of year. I do remember your cousin, yes, and I'd be happy to talk with you about him. You could come to my office hours whenever you wanted. Are you in Madison? Tuesdays and Thursdays, 11:00–12:00, Helen C. White.

I'm happy to help in whatever way I can.

Yours,
Ellen

Tempted.

From: hansonben3@gmail.com
To: ebarnum@wisc.edu
Date: 9/1/2008
Subject: Re: Inquiry Regarding Your Former Student Wayne Hanson

Dear Ellen,

Thanks much. I'll come on Thursday.

Ben

Not convinced.

8

Just As I'm Making Some Progress with the Wayne Situation and the Me Situation and the Lauren Situation, I Encounter an Entirely Different Kind of Situation

On Tuesday morning — the morning of my test-dye leaf, but who is keeping track of such things? — I went into town. It was early, and I walked the streets for a while, looking at the storefronts and the quaint shops, amazed again at how thoroughly so many luxury items — wines, gourmet cheeses — had infiltrated the economics of my town. There had always been some old money in St. Helens, in part because of Astronautics, but also because of its proximity to both Milwaukee and Kettle Moraine. In the 1800s, St. Helens was the site of summer homes for wealthy industrialists. Most of those houses were along the eastern shore of the river, four or five blocks south of Main, and I wandered down toward that neighborhood, looking at the bright colors of the old structures. My old neighborhood, the planned development, was on the other side of the river and north. I still hadn't been over there. There was no reason to go.

When it was after nine o'clock and no longer seemed too early, I went back north, crossed Main, cut over to Third Street, passed a music store and the police station, and I got to the storefront office of Dr. Hendrix. The door chimed when I went inside, and I was greeted by the smell of all veterinarian offices: fur + shampoo.

Lauren was not behind the desk. A man with bushy white eyebrows and an octagonal head looked up from what he was doing.

"Can I help you?" he asked. His voice was around the register of a tuba.

"Yes," I said. "I'm looking for Lauren."

He looked back, his expression unchanged. "And who are you?"

"A friend. Ben Hanson."

"She's not here."

"Any idea where she is?" I was not trying to be pushy. I still didn't have her phone number, nor did I know where she lived. I could have hunted down her address somehow, maybe gotten it from Grant. But this seemed easier.

"Do you often go to where people work and request their personal information?"

"No," I said.

"Then go," he said, nodding toward the door. "I can't help you."

"How about you take my name?"

He was looking past me, out the front window. I'd said it like an asshole might say it. I turned. Across the street, Lauren was parking her truck.

"Or I'll just talk to her," I said. "Thanks."

He mumbled something. I didn't bother to say anything else.

I went outside and waved in her direction, and I was happy to see that she smiled. She didn't hate me yet, at least. "Hey," Lauren said, climbing down out of the truck. She wore jeans and a dirty sweatshirt. There was a streak of mud on her forehead.

"You look like you just played tackle football," I said.

Her hand went up to her forehead, and she smiled and rubbed at it. "I was just out on one of the farms," she said. "A llama ran me over."

"All creatures great and small."

"You have no idea," she said. She smiled again, having successfully cleaned her head with her sweatshirt. "So. What can I do for you?"

"I wanted to let you know that my parents' visit didn't kill me."

"That's good news," she said. "Parents are dangerous."

I put my hands in my pockets and looked over my shoulder at the office, then twisted back to her. "So listen," I said. "I don't want to be too forward or presumptuous at all, but I have to go to Madison on Thursday to talk to somebody."

Her smile had gone. She looked at me with her statue stare, the one I'd first seen at the art opening.

But I had learned that, with her, you sometimes just had to keep on. Eventually you'd get somewhere warmer.

"I thought if you had people at the vet school to talk to or something, or if you just wanted to see what the vibe was like..."

"Oh," she said. "Oh." She was blushing now.

"I know you probably have to work."

She looked at the window past me. "I don't, actually," she said. "Dick's feeling better lately."

I turned to look with her. "That's your boss, I take it? That kind man in there?"

"It is."

"Dick Hendrix is protective."

"What? Was he rude to you?"

"Just protective."

"He can get like that."

"It's fine if you can't make it," I said. "I thought it would be convenient."

"No, no," she said, apparently in the throes of an argument with herself. It seemed like she was saying no to her own reasons.

"We'd probably get back by late afternoon. Just the morning, really."

"Okay," she said, nodding. "Okay. Yes. I'll come."

"Yeah?" I said.

"Yeah."

"Great. So Thursday morning. Like nine thirty?"

"Okay."

"I'll pick you up."

"Okay," she said. "I live right there." She pointed to a three-story building on the corner of Third and Naismith, not two hundred feet away.

~~~~~

Theresa called when I was back at Denny's, sitting on a couch in the living room and reading the end of another Muir book, this one called *Journeys in the Wilderness*. She said there hadn't been a whole lot of interest after the listing. She wanted to have the open house over the weekend before dropping the price.

"So I can't be here?" I asked.

"It works better that way," she said. "You can sleep there. But it'll probably be best if you make yourself scarce for a few hours both days." She sighed. "Against my better judgment and years of experience telling me not to do it, the open house is going to be during the Badger game on Saturday *and* the Packer game on Sunday."

I looked across the room to Denny's canister, which was still on the side table where my father had left it.

"That's fine," I said. "Open house. I have a weekend trip. I have to go up to Denny's cabin to do something annoying."

"Oh," she said. "I meant to tell you that your father called and asked me to try to sell that property too."

"Did he?"

"I was going to see whether I could find an agent who knew the area and split it. Or maybe attach it to the house and sell everything together. I'm going to print up flyers, at least. What do you have to do?"

"Clean something up."

I told her I would make sure the cabin was in good shape and that I'd give her a call when I got back. It was actually good — this way I'd have something to do up there to get my mind off of Denny and Wayne.

"Okay, Ben," she said, all business. "Have fun on your trip."

〰〰

Lauren was waiting on the corner at 9:20 when I came to pick her up. She had a bag over her shoulder and was wearing a light vest. It had gotten cold all of the sudden. Overnight, the temperature had dipped down to forty-two degrees. The first week of September. I was feeling less sentimental about the seasons.

Lauren had two coffees in her hands, so I leaned over and opened the door for her once I'd pulled up to the sidewalk.

"Thanks," she said. She handed me a coffee. "Coffee karma debt."

"It's winter," I said.

"Not quite," she said. "Not yet."

As we made our way out of St. Helens, I thought of the long drive awaiting me over the weekend. It would be chillier up north, as my father had warned, but I doubted there would be any frost. There was a chance it would be pretty.

"What are you doing in Madison again?" Lauren asked. "Meeting with somebody?"

"A professor."

"One of your old ones?"

"No," I said. "An English professor. A poet named Ellen Barnum."

"How come?"

I asked her what she knew about Wayne. She said she knew the basics, partly because most people in St. Helens did, but also because Denny and her mother had been out enough times for her to have heard the story that way. I told her about the poem, and about my father's theory. She seemed interested, so I kept talking and told her about the strange way my whole family had dropped the open question of what he'd been doing up there.

When I asked her if Denny had talked to her mother about Wayne, she shook her head and said, "Not that I know of."

"Why didn't it work out with them?" I asked. "Do you know?"

"He just called her one day after a month or two and thanked her and broke up with her. My mom said he was polite about it," she said. "He just told her he didn't think it was a good match, the two of them. Which I'm sure was totally true. My mom has some problems with the general idea of men. So it's difficult for her to be matched with any man. All men. She does not like men. Perhaps you understand what I am saying."

"Oh yeah?" I said.

"She's not awful about it," Lauren said. "She's not aggressive. She just..." Lauren looked out the window for a moment. "I feel like she might have given up."

"My uncle put your mom out of commission?"

"No, no. She went out again after that. A few times. I think the last straw was a really, really boring guy, actually. A boring divorcé from Lake Geneva. Who also announced that he was very needy. He actually said that on the date. 'I'm needy.'"

"What could be boring about a man like that?"

We got to Madison at a quarter past ten. The semester had only recently started, and signs that it was in its infancy were everywhere, especially once we'd gotten past the capitol building. There were U-Haul trucks parked along the streets and what seemed like thousands of young people tending to property, moving along the sidewalks on either side of us like lines of carpenter ants. We parked in one of the ramps off State Street, and after we'd made our way down the stairs, we walked to the end of the blind street, passed through a line of black vertical posts put up to keep the cars out, and emerged onto State Street itself. We were right beside State Street Brats.

"My God," I said, looking at the sign. "I can't tell you how many times I threw up here."

She glanced at the sign for a moment, then turned and looked up State Street, toward the capitol, the dome of which we could see above the roofs of the nearby buildings. She turned again to look back in the direction of campus.

"There are so many people," she said.

I felt something brush against my hand. I looked down and saw Lauren's hand lingering next to it. She gave me an embarrassed look, then moved it away.

"Do we need to go . . . that way?" She nodded toward campus.

"We do."

We walked for about a block.

"So you're going to think that I'm a huge dork," she said. "But here's something about me: whenever I go to a new place, I try to memorize the map."

"That's sensible."

"I mean *actually* memorize. All of it. All the street names, everything. I'm just — well, I guess that's how neurotic I am, if I'm being honest and not trying to, like, hide it from you. I just don't like the feeling of being somewhere and everything around you is just an unknown *blank*. A complete unknown. Do you know? Do you know this feeling? Like, no context. I freaked out when I first got to college in Ann Arbor. I was calling my mom and crying every night; my roommate thought I was psycho, but being in a place so unfamiliar was just...too much."

"I know that feeling."

"You do? Are you just saying that?"

"My first two weeks in Denver were maybe the worst two weeks of my life," I said. "And actually, now that I think about it, I had to call my mother from Madison more than once. I kept going back my first semester. Like every weekend."

"I couldn't go back, though. So then my mom one night just said, 'Do you have a map? You need a map.' I said okay and went out and got one and laid it out on my bed and just...just looked for a long time. And it was — I don't know. It did feel better. Even though I know it's not a big deal."

" 'You, who are on the road, must have a code.' "

"What's that?"

"You don't know that song?"

"I don't think so?"

"I'll pretend you didn't say that."

I could feel her looking at the side of my face.

"What?" I said. "It's Crosby, Stills, and Nash. What?"

"No, not that," she said. "It's your neck. Are you all right?"

We stopped.

"There are many red splotches down the side of your neck, Ben."

I reached up to cover my neck. "What?"

She brushed my hand away and leaned in close to my neck, squinting. She was close enough for me to feel her breath wash over my skin, and each warm little gust sent a wave of something else up over the top of my scalp.

"It looks like hives," Lauren said. "What's happening here?"

"It's fine, it's fine," I said, turning and taking a few more steps. "It's nothing. I'm just having a reaction. This happens to me."

"You get hives?"

"I sometimes have reactions."

She frowned. "To Madison?"

I looked at her.

"No," I said. "To emotions."

"I'm sorry," she said. "You're allergic to emotions?"

"I'm saying I have reactions sometimes."

"What's the emotion? Right now? That you're reacting to?"

I said nothing.

"To *me?*" she said. She looked down at her hand, then held up her fingers, splayed. "Are you allergic to me?"

"I'm embarrassed," I said. "And this is unfair."

"Do you want to walk on separate sides of the street?"

"Hilarious."

"I could wait in the car?"

"You're enjoying this."

She made a brief fake frown, which I had learned was a kind of playful Lauren apology, then said, "I shouldn't make fun of you." She patted me on the back like she was my big brother. "That's okay, Ben. Don't worry about your splotches."

We started walking again.

She said: "You don't have botulism, do you?"

"Memorial Library," I said, very loudly, when we came to Memorial Library.

"I know." She pointed. "That's Humanities. Down there."

"No one would ever guess you were such a gifted comedian," I said. "After the first impression."

"Why. What kind of first impression do I give?"

"I don't know." We were strolling now by the food carts, which were parked haphazardly around Library Mall. "Inscrutable. Unknowable. We should meet back here for lunch." I looked at the Thai cart, which I could swear was being run by the same man who'd run it years ago, in my time. "All this stuff is great."

"I'm not unknowable."

"Not at all," I said. "Of course not. I meant on the first impression. I mean, on my second first impression. After I got back." She didn't move, so I took a step toward her. "I actually have a strange sense of knowing you. I mean, I felt like I knew you before I knew you. When I was first back. It was — it felt like you were already there." I shrugged. "Sorry I said you were unknowable."

"We did have the project. The seed."

"That wasn't anything."

"I'm guarded."

"So am I."

"No, you're not. You're allergic to feelings."

"Sometimes."

"Let's test."

She leaned toward me.

"How is this?"

~~~~~

Ripples. Small waves of something warm and fall-back-on-able moving outward from the center of my spine and up to my shoulders and down to my hips. I felt her after she'd walked away and kept feeling her as I passed the fountain and passed the union. In the elevator of Helen C. White, I found myself alone, staring at the circular buttons after the doors had closed, waiting for the box to take me somewhere without my telling it what I needed.

I had to sit and wait outside of Ellen Barnum's office until 11:15 — from inside, I could hear a male student explaining the meaning of the 490-haiku cycle he had written over the summer after completing his first novel in four days, rolling on ecstasy.

Professor Barnum asked only the occasional question between the gaps in the monologue. One that I recall clearly: "Why would a tapeworm make people feel that way?" He gave an unconvincing answer.

"Ben, I presume," she said to me from within the office after the student had walked out and started down the hall. "Ben Hanson?"

I stood, poked my head inside. "Hi, yes."

"Come in."

She looked like she was in her fifties. She had short, silver hair and wore a pair of thick glasses. Around her neck was a bright beaded necklace. She stood and said hello then held out a hand to shake. "So nice to meet you," she said. "Your e-mail was such a delightful surprise, packed in as it was between about a hundred from students champing at the bit to get going."

"Thanks for letting me come," I said as we both sat down. "I know it's a busy time."

She waved a hand. "Ah," she said. "Office hours. I'd rather talk to you than them."

"So you do remember Wayne?" I said. "A little, at least?"

She nodded and smiled. "I do," she said. "Some of them slip

right out of your head. You never think of them again. But I had him more than once, I believe."

"Twice," I said.

"And of course I found out about what happened to him that winter. He wasn't an English major, so almost none of the other students I had knew him, but it was all over the papers. So sad. He was...interesting. And talkative. That's what I remember."

"I remember him that way." I added: "He may have also had a slight cocaine problem."

"Is that so?"

"He might have just liked talking," I said. "I can't tell."

"And did you say in your e-mail that you went here for school too?"

"I did. I studied philosophy. Kind of."

She shrugged. "People hit their strides at different times, I've always found." She leaned back in her chair, then said, "Now. What was interesting about your cousin, I thought, was that he was in the sciences, but he came into our workshop and seemed at ease. I do know that he liked poetry. Very much. He liked Elizabeth Bishop."

"Do you remember the semester you flunked him?"

"I remember that I had to fail him, yes, and that he'd done better before. But I also remember because I so rarely have actually given Fs to students. Almost never."

I reached into my back pocket and withdrew the folded-up paper on which Wayne's nonsense poem was written, unfolded it, and showed it to her. "I'm guessing this didn't help his grade."

"Ah yes," she said, leaning forward and studying the paper. "That. Nonsense. Now I remember."

She nodded to herself as she read. "I was so, so furious with him for this. All semester he handed in these lovely, concise odd little poems that were truly intelligent, truly witty. I thought they were wonderful. They were light verse, very human, and almost none of the students felt comfortable in that everyday mode, that style of not even bothering to aim for profundity, just communicating. And then at the end of the term comes the time to hand in a full portfolio, all each student had done for almost four months, everything revised after workshops, and this is what he handed in. This is *all* he handed in. I gave him a chance to redo it," she said, setting down the paper. "I told him he could hand in all the other poems and he'd get an A. But he insisted that this was the summation of his semester of work. He had burned all of the other poems anyway. That's what he told me! He called them false."

"False?"

"Yes," she said. "That's all he kept saying. False. Words are false."

I slid the paper to my side of the desk and looked at the words upside down. "Does it mean anything at all?" I said.

"I don't think so," she said. "He told me it was all for the prosody. That poetry was only prosody."

"What's that?"

"The meter," she said. "The sounds. The euphony."

"Just divorced from meaning?"

"Yes."

"Is it something, though? Some form?"

She shook her head, pulling the paper toward herself again. "I mean, there are snippets. There are iambs, there's an anapest, it scans a little here and there. But nothing coherent." She tapped at it. "The end. Right here. It makes me think it means 'Perhaps nothing.' But who knows?"

"I was looking at it for a while and I thought maybe it was just a scrambling of a poem that exists that he liked. Maybe the length of the words are all retained, but he scrambled them? Like an anagram?"

"I don't understand why anyone would do that?"

"I guess I don't either."

"He admitted to me it was incoherent, actually. Now that I think of it. He actually told me that it meant nothing."

"What did he say?"

"He said that that was the point."

"I bet you hear that from students, though," I said. "Trying to be surreal. Or whatever."

"Well, yes and no. There are students who will say that because they're embarrassed about what they've done, they don't know how to do what they want to do, they haven't put enough time into it, and they disguise their deficiencies by retreating into a mediocre and abstract celebration of absurdity. Fine. That's old, that's boring. I didn't think that was what Wayne was trying to say, though, even though the end result was the same. He was very much in earnest with this. There was nothing funny about it at all to him. Which I think is an important point. It was utterly serious. I kept waiting for him to burst out laughing, but the more I pressed him about it, the angrier he got with me, the more frustrated."

I nodded, took the paper back, then folded it and put it in my pocket.

"I'm sorry if that's not helpful to you," she said. "And I'm sorry about your cousin. You look disappointed."

"No, no," I said. "In a way, it is helpful. That it means nothing does mean something. In its way."

"Ah," she said, smiling. "So you did study philosophy."

~~~~

There was no reason for me to come to Madison with Ben, even though I did truly want to meet the people at the vet school. I thought it might help me imagine myself there, imagine what it might be like to live there, be in school, be away from my mother and back, in a sense, in the world. Had I been out of it? Had these last years... It was not as though I had disappeared completely or that St. Helens had swallowed me. But sitting on the bench outside the building where they'd given me a hasty tour, then raised their eyebrows at the strangeness of my situation and nodded their heads — yes, please do apply — I felt the warm concrete through my jeans and the firmness of the cement under my feet and thought: I should. I am going to do this. This is moving forward.

I thought of Ben, wondered which building he was in, who he was talking to, what they were discussing. His cousin, I knew that, but the few times I'd asked him about what he was looking for, or why he was looking, or — I didn't say this, but maybe implied it here and there — how it could possibly matter, so many years past, he became evasive, uncomfortable. I knew he didn't know what he was doing or why he was doing it. But I liked to be around somebody like that, as it was so different than my way of being. I could not be comfortable not knowing. He was more at ease among open questions, it seemed. In fact, he maybe even liked them.

I thought of our parting down near the food courts. I did not know how to do any of these things, these normal things. I was embarrassed. I'd tried to joke. And I was almost thirty-two years old. But, unlike how such thoughts usually made me feel, there was no self-consciousness or self-pity attached to this. More like: I saw I was uncomfortable; I saw what I did to handle it. Now I thought: I am so exhausted by the weight of my own self-pity. I have been for years. I am tired of it. I am sick of myself.

This thought was not like me at all. Out loud, or in conversation with my mother, for example (My mother is my only friend! I thought then, but I ignored this and its implications, as it was too depressing), I would not even have admitted the *existence* of self-pity, let alone talked about how it might be too much to bear. Or that *anything* that could happen to a person would ever be too much to bear. Because this was how I'd always thought about the world, growing up. And yet now, here, I was admitting it to myself. What had happened had been too much to bear.

I felt like crying, thinking that. Just that feeling when you're inside of yourself, going, and you surprise a nest of bats.

I stood up and took a deep breath through my nose. I wasn't supposed to meet Ben until 12:30 or 12:45, so I followed the path away from Park Street and the carts and Library Mall (I knew this because of the new map in my head) and went in the direction of the student dorms along the lake. I remembered, as I walked, that there would be another path along the lakeshore that led back to where I needed to go. I decided to take it.

When I reached the dorms I found students trudging to and fro, into and out of the squat stone buildings scattered beside the lake. Freshmen. Their first weeks. I thought of how I'd been to my mother when I was that age, in Ann Arbor, so glad, finally, to be putting distance between her and myself. I was cruel to her that afternoon: I barely talked as we drove and said almost nothing to her when she hugged me for so long at the entrance to my dorm; she was trying to keep herself from breaking down, and there I was looking over her shoulder, embarrassed we were blocking the way for some fat father with a green pillow in his arms. Why had

I been so cold to her? And this was *before* Will. And she never brought it up, even when I called her every night those first weeks, no longer either brave or haughty. It took me all of one night away from her, listening to the soft whistling air moving through the snot of my roommate's nostrils, to completely crumble.

I found the lakeshore path and began to walk back in the direction of where I was supposed to meet Ben. I would feel old if I came here for school, I knew. Not that I would be taking walks past the freshman dorms and seeing the youth in the faces of the doe-eyed eighteen-year-old girls every day. But I had done all of this already; I would be old even for the vet school. And how much school, really, could one human being attend? There was only so much. A stream of joggers ran by. It was getting warmer. Don't worry so much, I thought, looking at the lake. And surprisingly, at least then, in the sun, the light shimmering on the surface of the water, it worked to think it.

I walked the rest of the way along the path until I got to the student union, thinking again of kissing Ben in the center of the scattered food carts. I thought: Don't worry so much. It had been a small kiss, almost nothing, and it was a joke more than anything. But it seemed now almost a matter of course that there would be a real one, or that…Despite our talks and the way that I felt peaceful around him, easy — safe, even — I didn't know him. I didn't know what crime he had committed, I didn't know why he didn't drink. I didn't know anything that had happened to him since I'd seen him at our high school graduation. This was all — I knew that this was a mistake.

Or not. I didn't know. I took another deep breath and held the strap of my bag as I walked down Park Street. This, though, was the fundamentally me too: I could stand to be happy for all of five minutes. Then the alarm would sound, and I would start discovering why it couldn't be true.

I was early, and I strolled from cart to cart, looking at all the different kinds of food, smelling the rich, mixed smells of Asia, then India. Hungry people lined up at the various carts; nearby, and on the grass in the open field to my left, others mingled or sat quietly and ate. I smiled when I saw the green of the Ethiopian flag printed on the side of the last cart. I wondered how much I would have to cajole Ben to try some if he hadn't ever had it. What kind of food did Ben Hanson *like*, even? Did he *eat*? It was another indication that I had no idea at —

"Lauren."

The voice came from off to the right and I knew — my whole body knew — before I turned.

It was happening. Now.

It was going to happen here.

I turned; I looked.

And there he was.

Standing not five feet from me, a dopey smile on his face and his arms open, as if this were all a great surprise. There was clammy sweat on my hands right away. It was him. And he should not have been here. It was him and it was as though thinking of him had summoned him.

"Get away from me," I said, backing up, looking over my shoulder.

He took a step.

"What are you doing here?" I said. I kept moving backward, feeling behind myself with my hands. "Why are you here, Will? What the *fuck?*"

"Whoa, whoa, whoa, Lauren. Hold on, hold on."

"Get away, Will."

I could hear the fear in my voice; Will could hear the fear in my voice. I hoped other people around were noticing, but I wasn't stopping. I could have run. I should have then, but I couldn't bear to turn my back to him.

He dropped his arms and looked hurt by my reaction. He kept following me. His broad face was pale, and he was unshaven, which was strange for Will. Even at the camp, he had been meticulous about shaving. At twenty-five I'd found that mysterious. What an idiot I had been.

"Why would I get away from you?"

I bumped up against somebody and Will made short work of the few yards between us and put both hands on my shoulders.

"Lauren, Jesus. I haven't seen you in years. This is an amazing coincidence. That's all. Calm down."

I said, "It's not a fucking coincidence."

I took a step back, hugging my chest, and Will let his hands drop from my shoulders.

He put one hand over his heart. "Completely, utterly serious. I'm here for a conference at the medical school. Really." He reached into his pocket and produced an ID badge on a lanyard. "Really," he said. "Look, I'm just here for work. I'm here for my job. What are *you* doing here?"

"You're lying," I said.

"I'm not."

"Did you follow us? From St. Helens?"

Now Will looked irritated. "Who am I, Charles Manson? Jesus, Lauren. Hi. Nice to see you." He shook his head. "Look. Okay. I saw you over there when you came up the street and I went back and forth about it for a while, yes. But you and I both know we have to talk. How we left things. Everything, you know? So yeah, I admit that this is a strange situation, but it's come about because of a coincidence."

There was a ring of white around the circumference of my

vision now, and the feeling of sickness had deepened and become adrenaline. The impulse to run was stronger, more possible. But again I imagined him just running me down from behind. So instead I stared at him, my breathing building up to hyperventilation. I tried to think whether or not it was possible, what he was saying. I tried to think if it could be true. He looked like he believed it.

"Lauren," he said, stepping toward me with a look of concern on his face. He put a hand on my shoulder again and said, "You gotta calm down."

I pulled away from him, but this time he kept his grip on my shirt.

"Don't," he said.

"I'm going to scream, Will. I'm going to scream if you don't —"

ᗺᗺᗺᗺ

I wandered up State Street after I left Professor Barnum's office, for the first time in a month feeling a good sense of peace about Wayne and the cabin and the way he had died. My father's version just had the ring of truth to it, especially when taken alongside Wayne's bat-shit crazy poem. Sometimes things just ring true, I guess. And sometimes puzzles help you pass the time.

I went as far as Nick's, then turned around and headed back toward Library Mall. I was happy about Lauren seeming so free before we'd parted, but a new feeling had taken root in my gut since she'd pecked me on the cheek; there had been something different, something quick and strange that had passed over her eyes as we stood there smiling at each other. A flash of her, for the first time, unguarded? And she was not the same, that way? There was another person inside of her? It hadn't lasted long, and besides, I had been distracted by my own desperation to pull her closer. We had gotten that close. And it had been close enough to see the flicker, whatever it was. Something. Something I hadn't seen. When I'd thought of her — the opposite of the blankness, whatever about her that was impenetrable. I didn't know what it was. The underside of something. Or just her. Not another but the actual. Finally.

Then again, maybe it wasn't something new, and this was just me, afraid. Me putting my own fear into her face.

When I got to the food carts, she hadn't arrived. I kept strolling, down to the Humanities building, a giant light brown concrete structure that I'd always thought looked like some kind of extraterrestrial rally point. Near that building, in the center of a plaza that was itself the final edge of Library Mall, a small crowd had gathered. There was a jagged concrete platform there that was a combination of sculpture and public pedestal; the speaker had to climb up a few stairs to get to the platform itself, which was maybe eight feet off the ground. There was a man in a black suit at the top, preaching. Around the platform, bemused students watched him and jeered now and then, depending on the degree of bigotry expressed.

"What the world has lost," the man said, "and what people are responsible for losing, is access to the tools of morality." The man was relatively young, and he looked like he could have arrived here from his job as a midlevel executive. When I found Lauren I would have to bring her back here to take in a little lunchtime insanity.

"It's people like you, the haughty, young, privileged liberals, who've helped to lose the map," he said, glaring at the circle around him. "And that comes from the common fears. Fears of the nigger, fear of the Jew. Fear of the Oriental."

Someone said, "You're not supposed to use the word *Oriental* anymore."

"But the causes are not what I'm here to talk about today," said the suited man. "I'm here to talk about the tools. The tools in that lost box. And the most essential tool, as always, is the tool that is most simple and profound, the hammer."

He paused. Someone in the crowd made a long, wet farting noise.

"The hammer of justice," said the man, "is what has been lost."

I turned away and headed back to the food carts. It's amazing, I thought, how similar crazy people sound once they get an audience.

I saw Lauren then, on the far side of the courtyard, standing with her arms crossed. At first I thought she was just staring off into space, but something was wrong with the way she was holding herself.

Then I saw the guy.

He was big. That's the first thing I noticed. He was dressed simply — just jeans and a white T-shirt. He was gesturing a lot. And when I got a little closer, walking faster, it became pretty clear that whoever he was, Lauren was terrified.

I was about ten feet from them when he grabbed her, and she started backing away, pulling at where he had her by the shoulder. I started to trot.

I heard her say "No" three times, and just as she said it a fourth time I got to her and I cracked the guy in the head.

It was a good one. There is an art to a nice punch; in my limited fighting experience, I'd landed only one that felt particularly excellent. It was at Chestik during a softball game. The man I hit was a financial analyst named Steve Davorkian, and despite what the guards and the other players saw on the field, which was something to do with baserunning, the punch had been brewing for about a month, since I had learned that he had stolen one of my favorite sweatshirts. In some cases I would have been able to let that go, especially if I liked the person, but in the case of Davorkian, who had buckteeth and never stopped talking about the general moral superiority of American foreign policy, I was unable to. And the punch, when it happened, was glorious. For some reason, Davorkian believed it was his right to take me out *after* I had already tagged him on his way to third, and he ran at me with the ire of a child, aiming for something of a push-shove, which I avoided easily. I stepped back, cocked my arm, and delivered a very wonderful jab to the center of Davorkian's face, knowing, as it happened, that my form was amazing. Davorkian went down. "That was for my sweatshirt," I said to him as he lay at my feet. Then they hauled my ass away.

This punch was more of a wild haymaker. Still: effective. Kind of. But without the elegance of the Davorkian punch. Something of a mess.

The guy grunted and went down to one knee, using his right hand to keep himself upright, fist pressed into the grass.

Lauren looked at me, still terrified, just then realizing it was me beside her.

Only a few people had seen any of it. And everything had happened so fast, I couldn't really explain how I had gotten to where I was or why I had done what I did, other than that I had had some general flash of instinct, some sense that she needed my help. It had not been a decision. My hand was throbbing. I looked down at it, then back at him.

"Are you okay?" I asked Lauren.

The guy started getting up.

Lauren and I took a couple steps back as he rose to his feet, slowly, and dabbed at his ear.

He looked at his fingertips, which had blood on them. He shook his head.

"That was a little much," he said, looking at me, and I saw the danger in him.

"Are you okay?" I again said to Lauren, over my shoulder. Had she not been —

"You're Batman, right?" The guy was pointing at me now. "Is this dude Batman, Lauren?" He chuckled.

"Let's just go," she said. She took my arm and tugged at it. "Come on."

"You can't punch people," he said. "Who are you though, really? Are you just a stranger?"

"Just fuck off," I said.

"I'm in town for a conference," he said. "I don't really want to fuck off. Lauren. Tell him."

"Come on, Ben," Lauren said once more, tugging at me again. "Come on."

"Ben, is it? Okay. Good. You know what? Don't worry about it. I'm okay; a simple misunderstanding. We don't need the cops, we don't need to make a big deal out of it. No need at all. Assault, yeah, but let's not make a big thing. No mind."

Lauren gave one last pull, and I turned and we started across the field, toward the union. After we'd gone about fifty feet, I looked back and saw him ambling up State Street, holding his ear, moving in a different direction.

"Is it him?" I called to her back, because it had only now occurred to me and I knew it was right. It had to be. "Is that your husband?"

Of course it was. But she was already well ahead of me, walking fast, and she didn't turn to respond.

〜〜〜

We were twenty minutes outside of Madison before she finally said something.

She'd been staring out the window, turned away from me since we got in the car. But finally she looked over and said: "I'm going to be sick."

I pulled over to the side of the road and turned off the car, and she unclasped her seat belt and opened the door and leaned out. She puked, and after she was done, she sat up straight and wiped her mouth with the cuff of her sweatshirt. She stared ahead, down the road.

"Tell me," I said. "It's fine. You can tell me."

She closed her eyes.

"I don't think you want to get involved."

"Too late."

"I mean more."

I looked out at the highway. "I probably shouldn't have hit him. Maybe I should have slapped him?"

She pulled back her hair and held it in a ponytail behind her head. "No, he was grabbing me. I mean, you should have hit him. That's when — that's when people should be hit. So far as I know."

"I don't really know."

"Is your hand okay?"

"It's fine."

"Let me see."

"No."

"Give it."

I held it out to her.

"Make a fist," she said.

My whole hand hurt, still. I'd never actually punched someone in the skull. Kidney? Yes. Center of face? See above. Skull was not really a great approach, I had learned, but it didn't seem like anything was broken. I could make the fist fine.

All I could think was that she looked fragile, sitting there with my hand in her hands. The color hadn't come back to her face. She was like drywall.

"How was the vet school?" I said. "By the way."

She laughed a little through her nose.

"It was really nice," she said. "Really nice facilities."

She wiped at her eyes with the cuff that wasn't covered in barf. She seemed a little better. I was about to start the car, but when I looked over she was crying again — really crying now, her head down near her knees and both hands up against her face. I put my hand on her back and she squirmed away from me. So I just sat there.

This went on for some time.

"What's wrong?" I said once.

She didn't want to say.

I finally started the car, and we drove the rest of the way to St. Helens without saying much more.

~~~~

Because what could Ben have done to help me? *Actually* help me? And what help did I even need? How can anyone help anyone, especially when a person doesn't know whether it's needed? Not during an encounter on a street but true help, real help. We were so new to each other. He knew nothing about my life, which had *so much* history in it, and so did his, obviously, and I could just tell that he didn't want to be a part of any of it, at least not in a way that would put him in situations like this again. Where he could get hurt? If he knew more, he would have no interest in me at all. And I wasn't going to make him know. I wasn't going to force information on a person and tell a long sob story that wasn't even that bad, that was a lot better than lots of people's stories. It was better than Zara's. He had his own problems and his own past too. Everyone had a past.

That's what I was thinking when he dropped me off, and I thought it even though he wouldn't stop asking me if I wanted him to come in or if I wanted to go to my mother's house or if I thought it would just be best to call the police. Or come to his house? Come to my house, he kept saying. Because what if he has your address? He's not going to have my address. He kept saying it and he seemed so frustrated. It took ten minutes of us sitting in the car at the curb, engine idling, before I convinced him to let it be, for the night, at least. I would be fine. Did he care or was he just responding to something all men think they have to respond to, some be-a-good-man opportunity that flashes in the obvious times but never causes anyone to stay around? (This part I didn't say.) I thanked him for his help in punching my ex-husband. Thank you, Ben. Yes. He left feeling very brave, I'm sure. He said I sounded unbelievably sarcastic and he didn't understand why I was being like this or why I was sounding like my ex-husband *hadn't* attacked me on the street now and sounding almost like I was apologizing on his behalf for the inconvenience of it all and I apologized and said I actually was grateful for his help, because it was true, and because — unlike what I had told him before — I wasn't sure what would have happened had I been alone. Will had looked sick. That's what I'd been thinking. That's what had made me feel so sick in Ben's car. Will had looked — I had never seen Will in that state before. I had seen Will in many ways and I had never seen Will like that. (Or at least, never seen him like that and been able to remember it.) But I told Ben that he just couldn't understand but that I was okay and safe and everything was okay and that I would call him.

Upstairs, doors locked, I called my father. I told him what had happened.

"Was it a coincidence? Or was he there looking for you?"

"I don't know. It doesn't seem possible."

"It matters."

"I'm not sure."

"What do you think?"

"I don't know."

He said, "Do you have your gun?"

I said, "Somewhere."

"Get it. Load it. Right now."

"I don't even —"

"Don't argue with me."

I looked at the closet. He'd gotten it for me and made me register it when he'd come to visit Bobby and me a couple of years before. The last time we'd seen him. Bobby didn't know about the gun, but of course that's because Bobby didn't know about anything. Neither did my mother. My dad was the only one who knew. Some, anyway. Just some. And some unspoken. But he knew what I hadn't said to him by the way I'd said everything else. So what is that?

"I wish I could come," he said. "Goddamn this. Fuck him to fucking hell, that man."

I guessed he was looking at his own trembling hand. My father couldn't get around well now.

"Do you want to come here? Stay for a week? Why don't you just get out of there?"

"No," I said. "I shouldn't. I can't."

"Sweetheart, do me a favor," he said. "Carry the gun. Until you figure this out."

"What do you want me to do?" I said. "Wear it on a holster?"

"Just put it in your purse."

"That's illegal."

"It doesn't matter."

After we got off the phone, I went to the closet and dug out the black case and opened it. It was a .38. I had fired it only once, at the range in Libertyville, where my father and I had stopped after buying it. But that had been almost three years ago; the gun had been in the back of my closet ever since.

I closed the case and stuffed it into my backpack, then I watched the corner from the window for a few minutes. The street was dead. It was dusk now. My truck was all by itself, parked on the corner. I went down.

I drove out to the Kellman farm, which was truly in the middle of nowhere, about thirty miles south of town. They owned woods too — a lot of woods, maybe a thousand acres. I knew where the fire lane was that cut toward the middle of their property, but from the other end, from their driveway and at least two miles from their house. It was dark by the time I got to the unmarked road and turned into the woods. There was strong moonlight, and it was a clear night, so I didn't have any trouble finding it. I drove about a thousand yards into the trees until things opened up on the right. There was a meadow there. I stopped the truck.

I got the gun from my bag, loaded it, and sat watching the rear-view mirror for a good ten minutes.

I felt weak.

I sat in the truck for another ten minutes.

I reversed the truck a little, pointing the lights out into the meadow, then got out and dug around in my truck bed, looking for something I could shoot.

〰〰〰

When the doorbell rings I am down in the basement, stacking my uncle's boxes of Wayne's things, putting them where I found them the month before.

The first thing I did when I got home was sit down at the

kitchen table, set my cell phone in front of me, and stare at it for five minutes. Then I scrolled through and found Allie's number and texted her. I didn't think about it. I just said:

I'M SORRY.

I doubted she would have anything to say to that, but I wanted to say it. I never really had. It could have applied to any number of things, but what I could not understand was that it had never even occurred to me to say it. Why this day, why right now…I didn't know. I could guess. Texted, so shitty in that way, but still: better than nothing. Maybe one day I would call her. Maybe one day we could talk about it.

I went down to clean up Wayne's things.

For a reason I did not want to understand, I didn't put the poem back into the folders and instead found an empty frame in Denny's office closet and framed the thing. I figured it was the perfect symbol for him. And truth be told, there was something I found a little funny about the stern red F in the lower right-hand corner.

Down there in the basement, I looked around for a few minutes, imagining Denny having his heart attack. I looked over at the stairs. I imagined him crawling up.

I am doing this, now.

The doorbell is ringing.

I go up.

When I open the door, she is standing on the front stoop.

I say: "Hey."

She has changed clothes and she looks more together. She's wearing a vest and has a backpack slung over her shoulder.

"Hey."

I step back, and she comes in.

She sets down the backpack in the corner.

I close the door.

"I couldn't stay at my apartment. I tried. You were right." She shrugs. "So."

"That's fine," I say. "Stay here."

"It seems like an imposition."

"It's not an imposition."

"Or inconvenient."

"It's not inconvenient."

She looks at the screwdriver I am holding. "Doing some work around the home?"

"Yes," I say, glancing at it too. I look up. "I was about to do some major furnace repairs."

She crosses her arms, then uncrosses them.

"I don't know what I'm trying to say," she says.

She shakes her head then; it looks like she is going to cry, and whatever it *is* is right on the surface, so I go over to her, and as I do, her arms come out. She pulls me to her, and instead of us hugging or just standing there, which is what I expect is going to happen, she kisses me, and her head bumps back against the door, and I think: This is happening. She tilts her head and breathes in through her nose, and it's as though with the intake of breath she melts something old and frozen within herself, because she opens her mouth wider and brings her hands up to my face then, and I squeeze her hip and realize that I still have the screwdriver in my other hand and I drop it on the floor and I pull her vest off her and let it drop down to the floor too.

"I was trying," she says, her eyes closed, my hand now back behind her thigh, her lips right up against my ear, our faces smashed together, "to say something."

"I know."

Soon we are on the floor, and soon there are far fewer clothes. Soon she is crying out and I am holding her in the darkness of the living room.

~~~~~

After I asked her to come up north with me, after she said she'd think about it, after she took a shower, after I made some food, after we drifted off in Denny's bed, after we had sex another time, this time a bit more comfortably, this time including smiles, I woke and looked at her sleeping face, lit now by gray moonlight. A tiny thread, I thought. A trickle of different water.

I got out of bed and went downstairs.

I washed my face at the kitchen sink, then went to the living room and watched Beau Pointe through the window. It was deserted at this hour.

Her backpack was over by the door, and I went to it and picked it up to put it on the chair, but it felt heavy, and I opened it and looked inside.

I've tried not to be overbearing, tried not to be too irritating as I tell all of this, perhaps not with complete success, I know, because I arrived with my problems as well, but this is what I felt right then, seeing her gun: All you can do is make course corrections. Taps and small adjustments. Do you know? And though that may sound insignificant, one or two degrees, given time and enough open water, those one or two degrees will put you on a different continent. It will take all of your energy, every day, to turn the wheel, as though down below the rudder is stuck in drying cement, and you're being pulled back to your lower self, the worst person you have within you, because you have that person in you and each person you see down there is closer to evil than you are comfortable with, and if you let go — I mean truly let go — the wheel you've been holding all that time will spin back to where it was, maybe worse than where it was before, that's the danger, and thinking these things, I realized that I did not know this woman at all. And yet this place I was — this night, this whole first month. Here. Knowing her. Knowing nothing. Starting from the real start. I wanted to know everything. I felt the unmooring strength of that desire and wanted to know anyway.

I wanted to know Lauren.

It felt good.

But I don't know.

You always have to also hear the nightmares.

BONUS LEVEL

The Tuesdays

4/16/2007

My Incarcerated Friends,

I am posting this document in my own absence (paradox!) as I will not be able to host Tuesday game night due to unexpected circumstances having to do with my ass. (I got food poisoning from the fucking chicken.) However, I have happened upon something intriguing and I hope the included mysteries will occupy you while I'm unavailable. I've talked to security/warden/etc. and they say it's okay to post, despite the somewhat dangerous content, as all agree most of it is the ravings of a madman anyway.

A few weeks ago I was doing research in the library and came across some prints of paintings by an American named James Stell, whose work I admire. I decided to read about the guy and looked him up and found out that he'd written an autobiography. Not long after I started reading it, I realized he was the son of an architect, a man named Walter Stell, and that this was a big coincidence. You know this man even though you don't know him. I could not believe what I was reading, but I swear to Christ, Walter Stell, it turns out, was the architect of this prison, Chestik. This! He designed it in 1963 and died ten years later.

Now, this would have been just a coincidence, nothing more, but as I kept reading I realized I was onto something important.

James Stell's autobiography contained a lengthy discussion of his father's descent into madness late in life, and it told the story of a letter his father left for him describing a "burning religious vision" he had had just before designing Chestik, and how a "voice" had told him to build the prison based on this vision and to include its secrets in the design. Walter Stell told his son that his madness had begun at that point, that he had been trying to hold it at bay since then. But he'd listened to the voice and had integrated parts of his vision into the design at Chestik.

The vision itself is vague. This is apparently what happened to Walter Stell, or at least what he told his son: One night in 1962, his car broke down in Clatsop State Forest, and while trying to hike out, he became lost and disoriented. Hungry, thirsty, nearly hypothermic, he wandered into a grove, and in this grove, he related, there was a river unlike any river he'd ever seen. His hunger and his thirst vanished just looking at it. "It glowed," he said. "The river glowed." He tried to get downstream but couldn't make it through the marsh. He told his son that he then walked upstream for some time and determined that this river had seven tributaries, small creeks.

He spent one month there, attempting to draw a map of those tributaries so he might find them again once he got home, so he could bring people back to this place.

One morning, walking toward the meeting of the tributaries, Walter lost his way again and ended up, to his dismay, out by the highway, not far from his abandoned vehicle.

A police officer was stopped behind it and he asked Walter whether the vehicle was his. Walter said it was. Walter, believing he'd been in the forest for a month, attempted to explain what had happened. As he spoke, he reached up to his face and found no beard there. He looked down at his clothes and found them clean, not shredded. The police officer listened, then informed him of the date. It was the same day it had been when Walter had left the road.

Needless to say, Walter never figured out how to get back to the river. That shit never works.

He became obsessed with his drawings. His imagination was overwhelmed by them, he told his son, and he was overwhelmed by the desire to return and understand what the river was. Commissioned to design Chestik not long afterward, he begrudgingly accepted the work and decided to embed what he believed to be the secret of the rivers into the prison itself in order to make the map permanent.

He did not explain to his son what this meant exactly, but in his autobiography, James hypothesizes that Walter built a secret tunnel leading out of Chestik, and that understanding the seven drawings of the tributaries would "lead a man to freedom—all kinds of freedom."

(Walter also told his son some very weird shit about fathering seven children by women he'd met who were all, each in her own way, "spirits of the tributaries," but James seemed less into telling that part of the story.)

James included the seven drawings of the seven tributaries in his autobiography, which I re-create here for you:

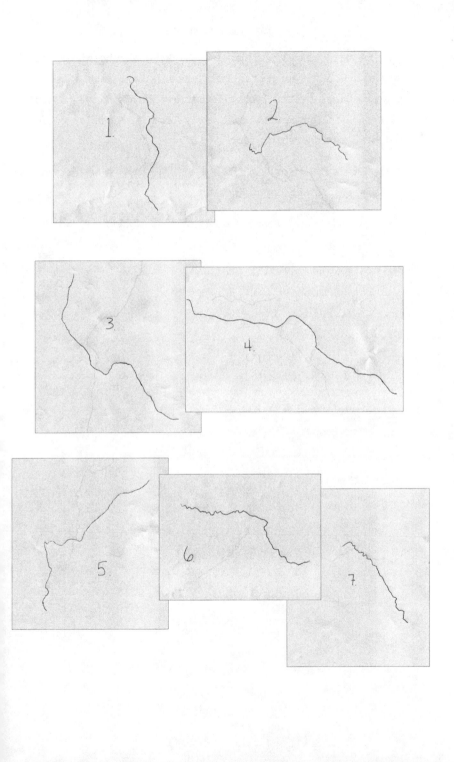

I'll be back next week and I'm thinking Parcheesi, as it was such a hit last time. I'll leave you all with a small passage James quoted from a letter his father wrote to him late in life, after he'd completely lost it. Maybe it could help you to understand too:

"Froe edmis eol, vyouf sref thon el, veosh. Testh. Rnety to letlt het rtuh who neyu. Know ohw."

Peace from Your Friendly Puzzle Master,

Ben

III

THE NIGHTMARES

"I give up. You are evil and wicked. I cannot go on any longer."

—Bartolomé de Las Casas,
A Brief Account of the Destruction of the Indies

9

Told to Ben As We Drove First through Milwaukee, Then North — Stopping for Lunch at an Arby's in Sheboygan — Because He Insisted I Come with Him Instead of Staying in St. Helens for the Weekend and I Finally Said Okay After He Asked Me for the Seventh Time, and at Some Point We Started Talking about Dreams, and Love, and Nightmares, and After That I Just Kept Going

I had this dream for the first time only six days after coming back home, actually.

(I'd been in Switzerland. Before that, Africa. Before that, Ann Arbor. Before that, St. Helens, yada yada. Before that, other places, no longer important. Already discussed. You know.)

It was tempestuous, this dream, that's a word I connected to it when I woke up and when I would have it in the coming months and years — it was stormy and, in a way, just more intense emotionally than anything I'd felt before, awake or asleep. Because in the dream, down in it, the first time and every time afterward — it was true — it felt like fear focused by sleep, Ben, somehow like a magnifying glass held over me and I'm an ant, normal fear but stripped of the world, gravity free, a hot laser beam of *feel this*, you know? Burning me.

And totally different too. More than I *could* feel awake; it went beyond that in the way dreams do, and when I had the dream it was as though I was on, like, a gurney with electrodes glued to my head and they sent pure evil into my brain. Totally pure evil. Do you know? Do you know this feeling? Probably not, I know, I know.

So the dream took place in a seaside shack somewhere in Alaska. Lauren, me, I'm the girl in the dream but also not, was trapped in a room of the cabin and could see, through cracks in the walls, monsters in the other room, hairy creatures, mammalian, and yet all of them also in possession of octopus beaks and fish eyes and tentacles and scales and more unidentifiable accoutrements of the ocean. Phallic, too, many of the extra appendages. The story of the dream was that the creatures were having a meeting. They were together to discuss a plan, some plot to kill humans, and this Lauren/me was unfortunate enough to be overhearing them. So it was a matter of circumstance. The first mood of the dream was that she didn't know how she got here even. In the dream she wore an old cotton nightie, dirty and white, too short, torn, and she was crouching, looking through the cracks. There was something about sex to it all, in the same way horror movies are at root about sex. She was turned on, looking at them, is what I'm saying. Which is embarrassing but whatever. She was terrified. Then one of the beaked monsters looked over and pointed at her through the crack, its tiny avian eye wide, looking right at her. "There," this monster usually said. In a soft, sad voice. "This one." Next its yellow beak would slowly close, the two hard bills clicking as they came together. "She's there." So they can see me. Right? And that moment is the moment when the fear is unbearable, and so that's why I always think it's a dream about being seen. Or maybe this, which is different: about being noticed for the first time by the eye of bad intentions.

That night I woke up with a sleepy and gulped yell and sat up in bed, first only sweating and breathing. I looked up at the ceiling and remembered where I was. Outside, soft rain. I started to cry, sitting in the dark, because of course by then I was remembering. I was back. I stared for a long time at the gray wall. To wake up and not feel Will nearby was unusual, and I hadn't adjusted to where I lived. None of it. The terror from the dream followed me too, and it was still there as I was awake, but after a few minutes I was able to sit still and breathe and tell myself, again and again, that dreams are dreams. Dreams are dreams. Lauren; dreams are dreams.

I turned on the light.

Sitting there, I thought of the shape of a neuron and considered the human subconscious. I quizzed myself on the brain. What is a ganglion? Remember, Lauren, at the end of the axons are terminal buttons. Polysynaptic membrane. Periaqueductal gray matter *is* neural circuitry, I thought. This trick of listing is what I used to do in medical school when I felt anxious, and it's also what I used to do when I prepared for spelling bees long ago, in grade school. Another kind of map, I think. You know? Go through the lists, know the material well. Memorize, and you won't be surprised. Know things. Know as much as you can. When you're tired, go through it again, then sleep, then wake, do more. The body, medical school — it was also a series of spelling bees. So in this case, remembering the very first thing we always forget, that we're physical, that it was physical — and that therefore dreams are physical things too, they really are, they're made by the brain, which is physical — put me at peace. Fear goes away when you remember it's produced by a machine. That you are a machine. That we are machines. The body and life are all physical; therefore horror can always be managed.

〰〰

And so the fear eventually slipped out of my chest in a vapor ribbon and I was able to go to the bathroom and get a glass of water.

〰〰

But after I finished at Michigan I was in Chad for six months, only half my original UniMed commitment, but I think not finishing was forgivable, as there was an evacuation. I didn't quit. I never moved forward, I never did a residency, so after that I stopped, yeah. But I didn't *quit.* I just never finished. I should have just gone straight to St. Louis after med school, they were offering me a spot. But I felt I needed to do something different, and to see something else. To see something far away and the opposite of what I knew.

Because before that, before Chad, there was only one thing: school. And I knew that I wasn't a genius, that whole thing was gone by then. That was wrong. I was motivated and focused, yes. I wasn't gifted. The harder work near the end of high school, the 4s instead of 5s on the AP tests, my trouble making any sense — *any sense at all* — of differential equations...I wasn't blind. I was not good Will Hunting. I was disciplined, driven, organized. I had limits and I knew where they were. I knew what I had to do to get to where I needed to be. I had few friends. I had one boyfriend my freshman year of college, then no more. Boyfriend if he could be called that — a graduate student named David from

Professor Ishagara's neurobiology seminar, which I'd talked my way into. He liked to walk with me after class and use the word *asinine* to describe the drunken undergraduates — this when I was an undergraduate — who ran rampant through Ann Arbor on the weekends. We had sex twice when I was eighteen. Both times were painful and horrible. Hot garbage breath.

I moved forward. I stayed still. I did well. I agreed to the UM offer to stay and enter their med school. Life was better then, to a degree, and I listened to my father's advice — I had opened up to the idea of a "phone relationship" with my father, BTW, sometime during junior year in college, upon his request — but slowed down and refused the accelerated path when they offered it to me. "You'll burn out," my father said on the phone from Montreal (again), living in what was probably squalor, his having been unemployed for some time in this era, but I never went to see him there and didn't know. "You'll burn the fuck out, kid," he said. "Slow down, genius," he said another time, and I rolled my eyes and shook my head at his ridiculous point of view.

I dissected my cadaver and spent hours — weeks — studying the human eyeball.

I made plans.

I dated no one.

I finished medical school.

I went to Chad.

~~~~~

This day is horrible, though. But okay.

The morning after that first nightmare, right when I'm back in St. Helens, is a Sunday, and I get up at 10:45 to find the house empty.

I wander downstairs to the kitchen in my pajamas, looking for coffee, and I find the Bunn pot warm and full. My mother has left it for me.

I stare at the brown liquid, still worried about the dream, still feeling all of those feelings. I know what it was. Basically. What it actually was, not what it meant. I think what I know now is that it's going to be a part of me, and that it has to be. I'm stuck. I'm a new person and I'm stuck with it.

My mother is at church, probably, or brunch. There's no note. So far I haven't gotten any pressure to attend either social or spiritual events (does attending the Unitarian Church count as a spiritual event, ha-ha? I'm sorry), but I worry about it whenever I imagine my mother sitting in a pew smiling while the congregants talk about their disillusionment with Halliburton. Or whatever. Talk about Darfur like they care. What are we doing about it? What *will* we do about it? Fist in palm!

I know it won't be long before I'm invited to attend too, and maybe even "relate my experiences" to the congregation. The people will lap it up with liberal-doggy obsequiousness, as though doing so with great enthusiasm connects them to me and therefore connects them to "being good."

Even though they are all exceptionalists with no intention of ever taking a risk or sacrificing a thing in order to improve the lives of other people.

Even though they don't care.

Even though they love their wealth as much as anyone else does.

Even though they would never, ever, ever give it up. Not for anything.

So.

I make a bowl of Cheerios.

I pour myself a cup of coffee.

I go into the living room.

I sit down and turn on the TV.

I watch *E! Entertainment News* for forty-five minutes.

I'm satisfied by it.

My mother doesn't know anything, I reason in the shower.

That's a problem and it will make this living situation unsustainable. This. Here. This won't work. Being back. It's not her fault, and I have to admit, my mom has let me be, so far hasn't pushed too much for details. Which is good, because she probably couldn't deal with it. And there are more complicated questions to be addressed too; for example: Did any of it happen? Any of it? Or is it all like that nightmare I've just woken up from, but a longer nightmare with different nightmares inside of it, and I am still in it but it's not real? And soon I'll get that amazing feeling of relief you get when you wake up from a nightmare and realize there aren't any consequences that have ruined your life?

No.

No, though.

It is real.

That's what I think, shampooing.

No, though.

How nice that would be to be the kind of person who pretends things don't happen. Or the kind of person who knows it's a lie and keeps going anyway.

I towel myself off and I think: Of course it happened. I saw it happen.

I let it.

Do you know this?

There is, in the world, one truth.

There is a sole sequence of events.

There is one true history made up of many, so large it can never quite be seen.

Do you know this?

There is one big river, Ben, and in that sense, yes, each moment in time exists and will continue to exist.

But we don't get to swim in that. It's too big and we would drown. You know? Instead, we swim in our own eddies. The little flows. Just parts. Little labyrinths of water.

That's why it's all so confusing.

And — at least what I thought that day, that morning, there in the bathroom, the first time I realized it, and to be clear, I don't think this anymore — life being like this is totally unsolvable and therefore totally unacceptable.

〰〰〰

Later, I went back to the kitchen in my mother's plush white robe and white slippers and poured another cup of coffee. I went to the front door, opened it, and looked down at the *Sunday New York Times*, wrapped in its blue sheath. I was surprised this could be delivered in St. Helens, but then again, it wasn't as though we were in a hidden backwater. Milwaukee was right there. I looked up toward Milwaukee.

Everything the rest of the country had was also here now, even though that was not how I remembered the town. I remembered waiting forever for video rentals. I remembered the movie theater sucking. I closed the door and wandered back to the living room. On the coffee table, I saw my copy of *Clarissa* and nearly burst out laughing.

It was the Penguin edition, black-spined and intimidating. Its size had caused me to pull it from the shelf in the English Classics section of the airport bookstore as I waited for the flight from Zurich to Chicago; I'd wandered in looking for a celebrity gossip magazine, as these had begun to draw my eye in the airport, totally numb as I was on that particular day, as they suddenly seemed so bright, so colorful, so warm, so rich with something that I wanted, so unlike Zurich, which had been so gray, so incredibly gray, but I saw the shelves of books and drifted toward it, thinking there was something wrong with my buying *Us Weekly*, it was something that other people bought. There was that feeling, but there was the deeper feeling when I saw the other shelf too: excitement about literature. Real books. How good they can be. How special they are; how nothing can be like them. You know? I had forgotten. It was the same kind of excitement I remembered from a long time ago, even before high school, when I would read the Baby-Sitters Club books for hours beneath the tree in the backyard, indifferent to my surroundings or to the comings and goings of my family. Actually indifferent. You went somewhere. This, maybe, before I was known as gifted? I can't remember. These were the new thoughts. In the bookstore, that version of me who is standing there, remembering that older version of Lauren — pig-tailed, wearing a pair of overalls, sitting in the dirt, sipping at a red box of Hi-C, so innocent, so good, so unreasonably happy as I wait for Mary Anne's story lines to come back but I go along with the other stories too because okay — all at once and from nowhere she seemed to come alive and take control, seemed to urge me toward the books, seemed to tell me, *Lauren, go to those*, in her little-girl adolescent voice. So I drifted, thumbs hooked to the straps of backpack, to the bookshelf and I looked for the most substantial and daunting book I could find: *Clarissa*. Samuel Richardson. I read the back. That sounded right. That sounded right if you wanted to look the thing in the eye.

A little later, I found my keys and soon was walking down my mother's street. I took the pills then. Hampton Street. There were birds. Two cars went by, courteously prowling, front bumpers almost smiling (right?) at me as they skimmed low to the concrete. Both were electric cars, and they sailed by with nearly no noise. I was in white shorts and a yellow tank top and I found myself walking (wandering) with my hands behind my back, linked loosely, one around the wrist and the other holding the book, feeling nothing. I was trying to look like a person who was enjoying looking at houses in the neighborhood. I was here on vacation, visiting my mother. Pretty soon I'd be heading to Kyrgyzstan or somewhere. I was a superhero, after all. I had more lives to save. Hands behind my back... it was an unusual way for me to walk — it was possible I had never in my life walked this way. I hoped it was an aristocratic stroll; I wanted to be the most casual and indifferent person on the street. The dry desert heat had been replaced by this soup of humid ninety-degree afternoons. Nothing was happening. The thin sheen of sweat that coated my face and neck was illogically heavy and for that reason offensive — how many grams could my total sweat weigh? If I had a way to pour it all into a bucket? Sweat: it reminded me of softball and beer. That's what America is, I thought. I looked at the sky. There would be thunderstorms tonight. Lightning would flash through the white curtains in my bedroom and the curtains would be expanding and contracting like a breathing bladder built into the side of the house. Would it be the world breathing or the house breathing? The bed was too far from the window. I asked my mother if I could move it. No. I passed a father playing catch with a toddler, one hand in his pocket. I said, "Hi," to the father, who smiled and seemed to be reinvigorated by the exchange, as though there had been a reshuffling of happiness, as though seeing me had reminded him of something he liked. He went back to his game. I unlinked my hands and ran one through my hair and made a sloppy ponytail that I held in place. My hair — I hated it. Always too dry and too thin. *Brown.* What? What seemed to matter now more was the way the African men had responded, the way they had accused me (fondly, faux nativism, *We are all so stupid here, we are savage*) of divinity because of beauty. I had no rubber bands. My mother's cat liked to eat them. George. And there was something comforting about the regimentation of life here — I had never thought of America as a regimented place before — but then again, the safety of this stroll was embarrassing. St. Helens was the most grotesquely safe place in the fucking universe and that was the one good thing about it.

How can I explain? I can't.

I passed a young couple, two boys walking with them. *You two are in love,* I thought. *You help me, I help you.*

Or: *You save me, I save you.*

Except there is no such thing as love, I thought.

But then, in response to this thought, I told myself to be fair. *Be fair, now.*

I heard it in my mother's voice in my own head. All this was extrapolation and when it came down to it, despite having lain in a hammock with him naked and despite knowing the intricacies of his lower back and the shape and feel of his ass in my hands and his smell and his everything else, I didn't know him well enough then to know, actually — hadn't he told me once that he didn't believe in the subconscious? "Existentialists don't believe in it." A declarative sentence — had that really been what he said? *Really?* And I'd actually been taken in by it? Like it meant he was someone I would want to know and get close to? I found myself at the coffee shop.

Hillary's, it was called, really the only one in town. It's still there. So simple, so small, so quiet. I had been here four times in my first week back in St. Helens, initially as a way to facilitate reading. Because I was doing a lot of reading. Now I'd fallen in love with the coffee shop. Both things seemed to be good things. (What *is* good, even? Not to get distracted. I remember thinking it right then, when I was in the bathroom, when I put my finger down my throat and I was puking in the bathroom and I saw what I thought was most of them come up and float harmlessly. I marveled at the question when it went through my head, as it was so simple and I really didn't know and had never thought about it.) I did not buy a coffee.

Outside on the sidewalk, I looked back in through the front window. I'd guessed, already, that Hillary was the woman who worked most often and seemed to pay most attention to the customers. I hadn't asked. There was something about the place. Something yellow and good. There were often fresh flowers in vases on all the tables. There wasn't a chalkboard with the typical excruciating pastel handwritten lists either. I imagined Hillary had transcended this aesthetic. Had thought: I recognize the custom and the comfort of it but I am tired of these pastel boards with writing on them. I will not do that with my place. Instead, there were three white panels hanging on the wall behind the counter, and the coffees and sandwiches were listed in a typewriter font. I looked at the few people who were in the shop. A girl by herself. An older man reading a newspaper. The possible-Hillary was behind the counter, cleaning something. Maybe, I thought, I would have a sandwich. Maybe, I thought, I might also — I realized that a mental room, a theater with no one in it, was still thinking about Will, and remembering, of all things, what it was like when his cock was in my mouth, how there had been something about him that redefined the act for me, how I didn't remember the strained nose-breathing or the pursuit of right place to hold for leverage, balls or ass or thigh; I remembered nothing in particular about his penis, it wasn't that; it was something about *him*, something good and rich and kind I always thought I saw, or did see, something in him that had made me more willing and less preoccupied with it, and in fact, not wanting to deal with the idea of sex at all. Since concluding my theories on the messy act of procreation so many years before, back in Ann Arbor. Its dispensability. With Will, there was a better tenderness there, more about the body, and reciprocal, of course. It had nothing to do with power or even pleasure. Just hot Africa and our hut homes and the sense of that life despite the feeling of it all when it was nighttime, when we were out there in the night, exposed to and overwhelmed by so much ongoing vicarious terror. Exposed to the idea that had started as a worm but had bored into me in only a few months: no matter how much help the West tried to give, it would not be enough. Because the West did not want it to be enough. Like all the people in the pews. It worked better this way. It was not going to change.

Not only that, but that the attempt itself was laughable, possibly condescending, unsolvable, corrupt. A kind of production. A play. A farce. The amount of healing in the world would always be less, exponentially less, than the amount of pain. Because of, in part, this really simple thing: it's too easy to destroy. It always is.

All true. Indisputable. So the formula was set. And right in the middle of it, Will. He had been an amazing lover right in the middle of *that*, and I found out that sex could be an incredible thing right in the middle of *that*, and of course he had known it all along.

I left Hillary's window and kept moving toward the park. A day like this, even though it was a little too hot, there would be plenty of people. I crossed Fourth and the hot lanes of growling, stopped cars, thinking about love now as a possible creator, not the biology of love but love on its own, love as a possible answer, and I escaped into the park. I walked along the third-base line of an empty soft-ball diamond until I was well into left field, then cut across to the grass. I hoped there would be no games today. Every time I'd tried to sit here to read for any length of time, a group inevitably showed up and wanted to do batting practice. Empty now, though. I was crying, very thirsty. I wiped at my face with the back of my hand. This was a very, very annoying thing. This would require a thera-pist. Perhaps I could find a therapist, begin doing some good work, then introduce him (or her!) to my mother and the two of them could date. This right here is some kind of episode, I thought. Right now. Where would I find a good therapist? Milwaukee or Madison? Or was there someone good here? They had WiFi now in St. Helens and so maybe they had psychotherapy? I went deep into center field, so far I was only thirty feet from the concrete path and the hot-dog stand. I liked it out here — alone in a field of green. I sat cross-legged in the grass and began to read. I was at the end of the ninth letter of *Clarissa* even though I had already read the first seventeen. But now I was back. I read the last page, which I had marked on the airplane, which ended with:

That no man should be allowed to marry another woman without his *then* wife's consent, till she were brought-to-bed, and he had defrayed all incident charges; and till it was agreed upon between them whether the child should be *his*, *hers*, or the *public's*. The women in this case, to have what I call the *coercive option:* for I would not have it in the man's power to be a dog neither.

I looked up. Two guys — high school, maybe? — were playing Frisbee out in right field, yelling and laughing, and I watched the green disk as it traced its silent path back and forth against the blue background of the sky. I looked to the left. On the path, a mother and father walking with a double stroller, and I squinted to make out the shapes of the two white faces. Both infants wore sunhats. It was quiet for a park, for so many people around. And the parents laughed to each other. Babies. Babies were always going to be a problem. I looked right. I felt like I could faint, maybe, just very quietly keel over in the grass. Maybe even die right there, right then. Or spontaneously combust. Wouldn't that be amazing? A girl sitting in the middle of a field with a book, but on fire, not moving? They did that in Vietnam. Zara. When it was through I would smolder, collapse, and it would look like someone taking a nap in the park. Or I could not die. I didn't want to. I knew that. A nap, and I would wake up and no one would know. I got up. I found someone — I thought I remembered finding someone. But I didn't remember much more because I actually then did lie down and almost die.

〰〰〰

Back more, the deeper nightmare in the nightmare: The day things collapsed in Africa, though, began with me in Will's arms at dawn, sweat soaked and claustrophobic. He stank in his sleep, he was apey and musty. I woke before him and lifted his arm and sat up and wanted to get back to my room before people began to move about and the camp came alive, before the women lined up, before the new arrivals came with their swollen feet and infected blisters, or worse. At this point it didn't matter much who saw me leaving Will's little hut, it wasn't that — people always saw, the UNICEF workers knew and treated us as husband and wife, pretty much, and most of the other doctors from UniMed — doctors who knew us better, knew more about our lives back home, knew that Will was supposedly engaged — had at the very least seen us laughing together here or sharing a moment there and had assumed quite accurately that we were lovers. Did it matter here? Hardly. No. What was sex in the face of what we did? That Will had a fiancée at home didn't bother anyone and in fact wasn't relevant, if you can possibly understand. Not even relevant to me. He would talk about her with me there beside him, we would have conversations about her, he would tell me why he loved her as though his fingers had not hours before been inside of me as he kissed down my neck and I'd looked at the thatch ceiling with wide eyes, teeth pressed together, his other hand at my breasts, his fingers scraping at my neck. My feelings on the subject — well, I just did my best to seem not to care when he talked about her, because it wouldn't make a difference and because I wanted him to think of me as that kind of person, as somehow bigger and more complicated than others. Bigger and more complicated than I actually was. Somehow so stabilized by science and the Hippocratic oath and what we were doing there and why we were there that marriage or commitments back in America, the land of the safe, were political things to be cast off in order to better understand the twenty thousand people, their lives upside down, who were living and often dying in squalor just down the road. I knew something was wrong with it, yes; you can't be unethical just when you're away from home, as though ethics stay in your house like furniture.

And didn't Will see the marriages that remained intact even there, in the camp? Yes, he did. Didn't he see the husbands and the wives who walked fifty miles together, with death almost literally at their backs, with nothing left but a few possessions and perhaps a child or two? Didn't he see them starving together and arriving with smiles on their faces, obviously in love? Didn't that mean something to him? It did, and it did to me too. Maybe that's what happened to him. That place — that place had not turned out to be the completion of the puzzle that was my perfect education. In fact, at this time, this place had begun to tear me open. Because of dehydrated children dying in my arms, yes, but because of love too. More because of love. Simple love. Here was Will talking about his fiancée back home and also professing to me that he didn't believe in love, not really, and I often nodded and added my two cents on the subject and my heart said: You love him already, Lauren. This is what it is. I had fantasies that went beyond an affair with him here, in Iriba, but each time they began to quicken a little in my head, I turned away and told my heart to shut *the fuck up* and thought of a spelling bee or the makeup of the human inner ear, that thing again, and that was that. I had things balanced for a time.

"Come back," Will said to me from the bed, eyes still closed.

I was on the other side of the room, brushing ants from my shoes and my pants. I looked up at him and smiled and saw that his arms were out in a comic-size hug, as though I would run back to him and leap into bed.

"I have Zara," I said. "I gotta go."

"It's five in the morning."

"She comes early."

"It's five in the morning."

"You can't sleep anymore anyway. Don't you have antibiotics to hunt down?"

"I grow antibiotics in my hydroponic setup," he said, "beside my wicked kind bud." He let his arms drop down, then opened his eyes. Something, but no smile. I pulled up my jeans, found my shirt, wiped it off as well. At first I thought there was a grease stain but then I remembered the night before, Will coming on my stomach after he pulled out, and exactly at the moment I just lay on my back, hypnotized by the initial squirt of semen, and I thought: We actually are machines, my God. I lay there listening to his grunts, just thinking that, but then I remembered that my shirt was on and I said, "No!" and pulled it up and let the rest of it land in my belly button.

"Loser," I'd said to him. "Just come inside me next time. I'm still on the pill."

"I got caught up."

I poured water on the stain now and rubbed at it. I passed my thumb along the whitish crust. Dried semen reminded me of Bill Clinton. I used to wonder (in the '90s) how exactly he'd accidentally ejaculated onto the dress. The specific details. The exact look on his face when he sees what he did. I wondered, too, whether it had occurred to him that he should clean it himself before he left. Because DNA! It wasn't so big yet, but he knew, he was the one so crazy about the Human Genome Project, so you have to wonder.

I could tell people it was toothpaste. Like it mattered.

I pulled the shirt down over my head, feeling dirty and tired. My hair was greasy, and I pulled it back into a ponytail. I needed to bathe. So easy to forget, and even with the sex it didn't matter. He liked it to be dirty, he didn't care, and in the last month I'd been surprised to find that I, too, liked to be dirty and sweaty and still smelling of the day's work when I came here and we drank and he made love to me. Everything was so human. This place. Now. This morning I was feeling queasy. I would have time for a shower, but only a quick one, standing beneath the drizzle of the cold water back in the shower house.

"I'm glad you stayed," Will said. "I hate it when you don't stay. I feel like a whore."

He was sitting up now, watching me dress from the bed, his hair sticking out in all directions. So charming, so insouciant. I'd seen Will save many lives, more lives than I could count. Here he was racking them up as though this were a video game. His score kept adding up in the right-hand corner. And what if it were someone else in his place? Someone slightly less talented, slightly less calm in the face of an appendectomy or a ruptured spleen or a mystery pain in a child's head? What if that somebody else saved 89 percent of the Sudanese Will had saved? That made him a god. Was he not an angel, here, at least? Was it not entirely justified that he did (and he *did*) anything he wanted? Ignored the Chadians, walked right past them with their guns, had no time for the UNICEF helpers, bitched out the French Legionnaires whenever he could? Was he not allowed to do whatever he liked?

For this reason, and other reasons, I had fallen in love with him.

He had a hairy chest but he was fit; I liked how the muscles beneath had shape. I once joked about waxing him, told him that I wanted to see him hairless. He'd said, "We don't do that where I'm from," with a smile, and I'd said, "You come from California. You do do that where you're from," and he laughed his hearty laugh and that was that, no Nair. He was such a man. When I thought of Will I thought of power. He was such an adult man, so different than the man to whom I'd lost my virginity. David. The boy. So different than my brother and my father, even, who were men, but weaker.

"Truly," he added. "You never stay anymore."

"Maybe that's because I don't want to be the camp whore," I said. "Which I am already anyway."

"I just said I'm the one who feels like the camp whore," he said.

"You're a man," I said. "That's a point of pride."

"It's not like you're not allowed to care about me beyond sex," he said. "Right?"

"I do care about you beyond sex," I said. "Have you not been listening to me?"

"I have."

"Have I not told you a thousand times I've had sex with one other person in my life? That this isn't something I do?"

"You have told me that a thousand times, yes," Will said. "You don't have to keep saying it. I get it. But you're sitting on another continent. Maybe you should admit you're already a little different than you were when you got here."

"How do I respond to that?"

"I promise you, you are not the camp whore," Will continued. "I met the camp whore. I treat the camp whore every other day for whatever STD she's got. Then I treat all the men who say they caught it from a witch doctor who touched their penises in the night when they were sleeping."

"You're talking about Africans," I said. "I'm talking about aid workers."

"What's the difference?"

"You know the difference."

"Your reputation will not be following you home. Only the glory of helping people and this aura of..." He waved his hands around above his face. "I don't know. *Good.*"

"Don't be a dick," I said.

"I'm reminding you that no one cares we're together," he said, softer now. "Serious. I like you. It's not the sex. I like you."

With that, he twisted and put both feet down on the floor and sat up. He was naked. He slept naked. His dick was hard and he was staring at it as though it were the newspaper. I rolled my eyes and looked for my socks. I never slept naked, even though he tried, every night, as we were drifting off, to get me out of my pajamas. I didn't know why I resisted it so strongly. What would happen? I would wake up to him fucking me? That happened anyway. No. No, it was something beyond that, some admission of intimacy I didn't want to make. I am naked with you and you are naked with me and there are no barriers between us. Awake, we had two walls of consciousness to protect us from such closeness. Asleep, no. Awake, three drinks at the end of a day, lonely-shoulders sore, needing to be touched by him, I could admit it then. And in fact I could say even more: I could admit that I had been yearning to be touched like he touched me, and to be picked up by the hips and turned and just fucked sometimes, for years. For the years I had been a woman, not a girl, and couldn't find anyone, or wouldn't let myself be found. All that anger, all that energy put into focus. Almost as though each test that came back perfect for the last decade had been paid for with a loss of physical intimacy. I'm yours, I thought, or this new voice in my head thought, after the three drinks and the day in the sun amid dying, lonely-shoulders sore. Even though this is wrong, even though this is not me, even though you have a life at home, even though I am from a small place far away from here, even though I want a husband who is a nice man, and you are not a nice man, I can see that, not by a long shot, and you may have something off. In the head. There have been moments. Even though all these things, please, yes, Will, do what you have been doing. More of that. All that when awake, okay. But still in sleep, I had to protect myself. It was almost as if I knew he had danger in him. It was almost as if I knew.

"How's Zara doing?" Will asked, feet still down on the floor.

"You know."

"This is the Zara with the scar? Under her eye? The pretty one? With HIV?"

"She's fine," I said, now sitting on the floor to put on my shoes. "She's thirty-four weeks. She might be the only person in this place who trusts I'm going to get her baby out safe. Every time she comes in she has a story about her sisters thinking I'm trying to use her child for an experiment."

"And the husband?" Will asked, still looking down. "Still a problem?"

"Not really," I said. "We talked. We have an understanding."

"Which is?"

"He leaves me alone and I give him condoms and I don't talk to Zara about it when he goes."

"Is he also positive?" Will asked, squinting.

"No. Somehow."

Will raised an eyebrow. "A gentlemen's agreement, then," he said. "I bet your idealism didn't run such things by you when you were living in the Michigan dorms."

"I never lived in the dorms," I said. "Not the real dorms. I was stuck in overflow housing."

"You didn't live in the dorms?" he said. "In the Big Ten? You missed everything, baby, didn't you?"

He stood, and I got to my feet. He was a big man, well over six feet, and broad. Again, I looked at him, saw what I always saw in him, felt all those things, ignored what I always ignored. I saw strength. I believed (hoped?) he had a heart. He did what he could to pretend there was not one there, but it had been only three months.

"You enjoy making me sound naive," I said. "Don't you?"

"I do not."

"You do. Do you not realize how much you get off on that?"

He smiled, shook his head, frowned at the floor, and started looking around for his underwear. I pointed with my eyes to the corner of the room and he went to it and brushed it off, examined it both inside and out. As he pulled the black shorts on he looked up at me and said, "You're not naive. I think you get off on thinking I get off on it because you wish you were naive. I'm not a sadist."

"I know I'm some kind of object to you," I said.

"What?"

"Why would I wish that, by the way? Why would I wish that you were turned on by thinking I was naive?"

Will shrugged, went past me to the sink. He squirted some toothpaste onto his brush, then carefully replaced the cap. "We really don't have to talk about this," he said.

"Wait," I said. "You're not joking?"

"I am joking," he said. "I'm joking. I'm sorry." He looked at me, brush poised in front of his mouth, and tilted his head to the side, gave me a smile. "I'm *joking*," he insisted.

"Is your implication that I'm masochistic?"

"No. What? No. It wasn't supposed to be."

"That's where you ended up."

"I have seen what turns you on."

"You do have something weird about me," I said. "Why do I always feel like a symbol when I'm in here in the morning? Like I have meaning? And I'm not Lauren?"

He started brushing his teeth then, and I watched him for a few seconds. I did want to know the answer. I had not been able to articulate this point until now, but once I'd said it, it felt true, it was a real concern. I prided myself on shedding my romanticism. He had taught me that, maybe.

He worked his front teeth, then the molars on the left, then right, then spat. After he spat he looked at me and said, "I love how smart you are. Do you realize how stupid most people who come through here are? I mean, do you have any idea?"

"Symbol," I said. "Go back. Symbol."

"What symbol do you think you are to me, Lauren?" He poured some water on his brush from his bottle, then brushed at his teeth again for a moment. When I didn't answer, he took the brush from his mouth and raised his eyebrows and said, "I know you have some theory. So what is it? Spit."

"I think you like the idea of deflowering me," I said. "Again and again. That I'm your virgin. Or at least was."

"You weren't a virgin," he said. "You told me about the TA."

"We had sex twice. You and I have had sex maybe a hundred times. And he wasn't my TA. He was just a grad student."

"Well," he said. "I don't like your theory."

"Not the virgin, not the whore," I said. "Maybe the virgin you converted into a whore? Is that the fantasy?"

"Jesus, what happened to you in the middle of the night?" he asked loudly, turning one palm up. He held the toothbrush at the corner of his mouth, hooked there on his lip. I was surprised, too, to hear myself say something like that. His eyes widened a bit and I recognized the pre-coffee impatience within the words. And yet his bedside manner was incredible. He could sit beside a woman after amputating her leg and talk to her about what it would mean and how she'd be able to adjust and what she could expect about the pain and the phantom pulses and let nothing condescending, not an *iota* of anything but compassion, get through. He could smoke out front with the husband and tell him more, even though he hated smoking, and he could pull long and casual drags from the cigarette — Russian tobacco, even — as though he'd done it all his life. "Seriously," he said, turning back to his mirror. "Did you have some dream or something?"

"No."

A few other things I could have said went through my mind.

I could have told him that I wanted to know him beneath the armor of Iriba, but that would be . . . he would laugh at me for that. I could have said something about stress and he would laugh at that as well. He was right, though. Something, this morning, was different. Last night? Could it have been last night? It had seemed normal, it had felt like every night. But maybe there had been a word here or an exchange there, more violence in the way that he held me, and while I slept it worked in my mind and turned into a new wariness. Maybe there was a new problem and it would come to me later. I remember thinking that. I really remember thinking: Maybe. Maybe maybe. And that I would think about the night some more. Away from him, as I worked, I would think about the night and find it, because he was right, something was wrong, I was angry with him. I didn't know why. And I wish I had had the time to think it through more. I did not.

"So what, then?" he asked, compassionate again as he opened the spigot above the sink and began to fill it. "Are you homesick? Is it your dad?"

"My dad's sitting in a bar," I said. "It's not my dad."

The sink was full. Why am I still standing here? I thought. Soon he'd be ready, soon we'd be walking out of the house together and into the morning and there would be no disguise at all. I'd have to eat with him; this would have to go on for hours. Just walk out, I told myself. You need to be alone. You need to be away from him or he'll suck you into his thing. He is better than you at it.

"Look, okay," he said. "You've been here for almost three months. This has happened to people, I saw it happen to your predecessor. All the shock wears off and then you go a few months and you start to think, Hey, I can handle this, it's fucked here but it's normal, I can do this. And you settle in." He made a cup with his hands and dipped it into the sink, then splashed water on his face. "Then a few more months go by and you're not even in culture shock anymore and you know people and you even think they're your friends. Like your Zara."

I waited. I didn't like the subtext of the speech, how it made me into just another doctor in the string of them he'd been watching come through for years. But I wanted to hear the end. About where I was now.

"So then you usually dip again," he said. "Everyone does. I did. You get used to it and right when you're used to it, brain comes up and says, Don't even start to think that where you are now isn't the center of the universe and all these people are gonna die anyway and you're not doing any good at all."

"I don't feel that way," I said. "Not at all."

"Okay," he said. "It's just one theory. What's yours? And don't say it's about deflowering you, please. It makes me feel like a predator and I'm not. Be careful with your words. They mean things."

"It's something else," I said, looking at the door. "It's not you. I have to —"

And suddenly he was there, shirtless, in only his black shorts, face still a little wet, now smelling of deodorant. He had me in his arms and despite myself I was glad — glad again, about the power, the protection — and he hugged me and said, "Just do the work. Let's talk tonight. Okay? I have other theories."

"Do you?"

"Sister, I know things," he said kindly. "Just remember where you are and what you see before you get too down on yourself, okay? Genius child? You've still got a heart and it's still a living hell three hundred feet out that door for all those people. You serve the residents of the living hell. I don't know if that means we work for the devil, but it's bound to crack you open a little bit. All right, kid? You're *way* out of your comfort zone."

"Is that from *Casablanca*?"

"No."

"Your speeches make me feel like I'm twelve."

But I didn't say it with malice. Just to be able to do this — to be able to be in somebody's arms and talk, this close, to have someone, not a narrator in a book, tell me earnest and complicated things. I would not have been able to do this before I came here, before him. No matter how much I wanted to escape him and see him for what he was — the alcoholic, narcissistic head of medicine at a refugee camp in the desert who banged all the incoming female doctors until they left or moved on or until he found a new one — my heart asked me to stay where I was in his arms, and I listened.

〰〰

The next year was better in terms of mental-breakdown recovery and being sane — my brother Bobby finished art school in Cleveland and moved back to town, in part to be near me and make sure I didn't actually kill myself, and so I had a friend. It was fantastic.

And soon Bobby's friends, in St. Helens and in Milwaukee — he was better at that kind of thing than me — became my friends. He set up a studio for himself on the first floor of a house just a mile away and made the top floor into his apartment. Occasionally he would have parties; I once kissed his friend from New York on the balcony, drunkenly, but later, when he tried to kiss me again, this time alone in the kitchen and this time both of us much drunker, I put my hand on his chest and said I had to go to the bathroom and left the party and walked home alone without my jacket, furious.

I was furious again. All of those same old feelings.

The house was paid for by our father, who lived in Montreal and rarely visited, but he had money again now and he was generous with it when he had it. Every Christmas he bought three of Bobby's paintings for more than Bobby was asking and once, maybe as a show of gratitude for all the generosity, Bobby and I flew to Montreal to visit him and to meet his new wife, a French-Canadian woman named Margaret who served us bread and ten different jellies.

I started working at Hillary's, the coffee shop. I got a job there. For meaning. The place where I had barfed.

Hillary turned out to be far from the ideal, maternal presence I'd imagined her to be those first times I went and drank coffee and read. Less maternal than my own mother, in fact. She was more like one of the wound-up lunch ladies I remembered from elementary school.

I often thought of Will during this time.

〜〜〜

Somehow — and I can't really even remember the specifics of the conversation, and I have only a memory of him standing with his hands on my shoulders talking to me for what felt like forty minutes, an endless monologue explaining himself and explaining the situation and explaining that he did in fact love me as well, and that he'd told his fiancée, and that I should not go back, and that he was not going to go back, that we didn't ever have to go back to America, and that there was a place we could go together to make a life, and that whatever I thought had happened on the day the guerrillas rode into camp was some kind of illusion brought about by the trauma, or the chaos, and he wasn't saying that to be condescending, it just made no sense what I was saying, and that he was sorry that Zara and the baby were dead, and he was sorry for what the husband had done, but that more than anything I needed sleep, I needed to rest. Zara was dead but that didn't mean it was my fault. I remember saying, "I don't think that it's my fault at all. It's her husband's fault." "That's not what I mean," he said, shaking his head. More important was to concentrate on what we had found together in our months there. Something real, better. He had a place we could go. I felt so confused. Had I ever been to Zurich? We didn't have to go back at all. It was a bad assumption, you see? He had a plan. There was a job, and he could find me a job as well. We didn't have to get on the plane. There was no reason for either of us to go back because we were going to be married and be here, together.

〰〰

I eventually moved out of my mother's house and into a small apartment after everybody was consulted and we all talked for a long time and decided I was much improved. It was an isolated incident, that thing that had happened. PTSD. Solved. I hadn't followed through. And more important than that: I went to the St. Helens veterinarian, Dr. Hendrix, and asked if I could work for him. This truly was something good.

"Just so we're all clear," Dr. Hendrix had said to me. "I do animals."

"I know," I said. "I know what you're saying."

"Formal arrangements about this sort of thing can get very difficult," he said. "You can imagine why. Imagine if I went to the hospital and asked them if I could work on a couple people?"

"I'm not a veterinarian. I only want to intern."

"The last intern I had was a fifteen-year-old cheerleader who could barely answer the phones. I caught the previous intern stealing the horse tranquilizers."

"So I'll be a step up."

I knew Dr. Hendrix was aware of my history as a crazy person — he, like everyone in St. Helens, regarded me with curiosity and kindness both. The town had welcomed me back without asking too many questions; no one talked about what happened in the park. Occasionally, I felt eyes turn toward me when I walked into a store or went to a St. Helens High basketball game, people looking at me as though I were a washed-up and disgraced celebrity, something like that, but still someone to be regarded, despite my fall. I sensed that my reputation was solid and that I received, probably unfairly, a fair share of the goodwill the people in town had for my mother, beloved librarian, but I also knew that people thought of me as someone who had once had a total mental collapse and therefore, even after more than two years of my serving them coffee with increasingly complicated smiles, I was someone to be feared.

But Dr. Hendrix snatched up the opportunity to have a trained physician working for him — one he could pay nearly nothing, and one who was happy to do the work at that rate. They called me an administrative assistant. I had delivered children on tarps, conducted surgeries, and had a good bedside manner too, so I understood how to calm the worried owners of pets; I could do whatever math needed to be done and understood how to calculate dosage based on size and weight. More important, I was a sponge, and throughout that first spring I absorbed everything Dr. Hendrix told me. I took to learning on my own too: I asked for books, studied medical histories, went with him to the farms and watched him deliver calves and treat blackleg, listened to him as he talked to farmers about their herds, paid attention as he drove us around the county and explained the history of the different plots of land and told me about the families, the people. He had been in the same place for almost thirty years and knew everybody, and I saw how people throughout the county responded to him, how everyone seemed to like him, how Dr. Hendrix knew how to treat the owners of his patients with the perfect, respectful light touch. One day, riding in that truck, looking out the window, I thought this: *It is possible to find the bucolic even after you've done away with the romantic, seen hell, died, come back. You can find it again — it is this. It has something to do with this.*

He was professional at first, then became avuncular as he began to trust me. That's why he was so protective, like you saw.

One night, late in that first summer, he asked me whether I ever considered going back to school to study as a veterinarian. He said that if I would consider it, he would be happy to hire me on and eventually turn the practice over to me.

I said yes. In theory. I'd been thinking about it; he was right. But I didn't know. I told him that I still had to think.

"School is…" I started. Then I said, "I don't know if I want to ever go back to school."

"That's understandable," said Dr. Hendrix. "You did so much. Although you wouldn't have a problem, I don't think. You've probably taught yourself enough by now to coast through at either Madison or Milwaukee."

"Thank you for saying that," I said. "I think."

"Of course," he said. "It's true." Dr. Hendrix was in his early sixties; that day he wore a checkered short-sleeved button-down tucked into his slacks. We were in the office, he behind his desk. I was standing in front in my scrubs, hair tied back in a ponytail. (I loved vet scrubs, by the way — they were much better than the MD version. They had patterns, like colorful doggy footprints near the neck.)

"I'll start looking at some of the programs," I said. "Maybe I'll look this fall."

"Do what you want," he said, nodding. "Of course, it's entirely up to you and you have plenty of time. I'm not retiring. But I am a little ashamed that I can't give you the position you deserve. Betsy recently asked me how long I plan to continue running a sweatshop."

"It's fine," I said, smiling at the thought of Dr. Hendrix's wife saying that to him. "I have the coffee shop; my dad helps. My mom helps. It costs nothing to live here anyway. I'm not exactly saving up for anything."

"Okay," he said, nodding once more, looking down at his hands, which were placed side by side on the desk. "I am going home then. Betsy and I are going to the movies."

"What are you seeing?"

"Something called *Becoming Jane*."

"That's the Jane Austen movie."

"It is," he said. "I'm concerned."

"I heard it's good," I said. "Where is it?"

"New Berlin, I believe," he said, sliding his chair away from the desk.

At the moment, there were no animals in residence in the back, and so once Dr. Hendrix left, I had the place to myself.

I made some tea. It was quiet; the smell here was always the same, and I liked it. It was four thirty and I would lock up at six, then go home, shower, eat, and go to Hillary's, where I would work until closing. This was my life.

I went to the computer.

I had this e-mail:

From: Besco, Will
To: Sheehan, Lauren
Date: 9/23/07
Subject: Long Overdue

Dear Lauren,

There are many, many things we should discuss. I miss you. But I know that won't get through now, so let me tell you some thoughts I've been having.

First, Zara. That accusation has haunted me most since our final argument because it is, out of your many wildly misguided accusations against me, somehow (insanely) the most plausible, the most likely to have *actually* happened if we're just looking at the facts. So I'll speak to it first. I did not sleep with Zara, Lauren. And if he thought it was my baby, he made it up. Why would you believe him? Truly, think about it. Did he have an ounce of credibility? Had he not been visiting the brothel every night for months? Was he not raving at that point, psychotic and delusional? Not ten minutes later they were all dead—he killed her, the baby got hit, he killed himself. You can't listen to a man about to do that. I did not ever have sexual contact with Zara. Nor did I ever, ever have any form of sexual contact with any of my patients or any of the refugees. I don't know how to defend myself against a charge like that other than to state the truth and trust that you know, in your heart, that no matter how crass I may have sometimes been and no matter what happened between you and I, my responsibilities as a physician and my responsibilities to all those under my care would have made it, in a word, impossible. I would not do that. Are you sure of what she said earlier? Of how she said it? It's not true. She had reason to make it up as well, you know that. And still I'm sitting here thinking that I should say I'm sorry. I'm sorry that you've spent all this time believing that about me and sorry for whatever untruths came to pass that led you to believe it. I'm sorry that five pickup trucks and fifty men came to the camp and started shooting that day. All I can say is that day was a clusterfuck, through and through, and somehow the wires must have gotten crossed. Whoever told you what you heard must have been confused. Zara must have been confused. Joseph was confused. And armed. It's simply not true!

I would have begun with a more direct apology to you for whatever confusion happened in Zurich, but this issue of Zara—this issue of what you think happened between Zara and me—has been the exact thing that's made me feel unable to make contact for the last years, and to tell you the truth, I also believe that it's *because* you always believed this thing about Zara that you *later* reenacted it between the two of us. My therapist has brought this up more than once. You and I both know that I did nothing to you. I did nothing to you, Lauren. I did not hurt you. I was your husband. You drank a profound amount of alcohol. I should have stopped you, I know. I hope that you can understand and try to see it from my point of view, allowing yourself to believe, for an instant, that I might be telling the truth, and what it might then feel like to an innocent person who loves you to hear you say what you said. You made yourself clear that day, and for all this time, I've not been able to imagine a way to say a thing to you that would not have sounded monstrous. (You seeing me as a monster, as you said.) But things have happened here to make me rethink that assumption. (I am in California; I am married now.) And enough time has passed. I need to talk. I need to see you.

Your blood test has haunted me as well, as that is an actual fact, at least. There are a multitude of explanations, unfortunately, perhaps the worst being that someone else at the bar spiked the drink, not realizing that you were there with your husband, in which case I thank God you were with me and I could at least protect you. Also, another theory: those tests are simply not reliable, Lauren. I'm sorry. But you know that.

I am so desperately, unbearably, wretchedly in love with you! That doesn't go away. And in fact, it's worse—it's worse than it's ever been, now that I don't see you, now that we don't talk. I'm coming apart, Lauren. You have to communicate with me.

I loved you then. We never talked about it and I don't think I understood what it meant. Lord knows how dangerous such things can be. Anywhere and under any circumstances. But especially those.

I want to talk. I need to. Can we please talk? We had so much. Please look into your heart and ask yourself if this punishment is fair when there's no evidence, when I did nothing but love you. Please. I'm begging you.

Yours,
Will

My response:

To: Besco, Will
From: Sheehan, Lauren
Date: 9/23/2007
Subject: RE: Long Overdue

Don't ever contact me again.

10

Continued from Above, Told to (a Now Quieter) Ben by Me North of Sheboygan and in Green Bay at a TCBY and Also in the Hotel Room, Getting Sleepy, But at This Point I'm Not Going to Stop, Because I Can't, Because I Have to Finish

There's still a part.

I've left a large gap.

Can I?

~~~~~

Instead of going home and running away from him when I had the opportunity to do it, I married him. It makes no sense.

We moved to Zurich.

It makes no sense.

I was twenty-seven when I arrived and I stayed there with him for eleven months. I left alone. That's when I went home to my mother.

There was a nervous breakdown.

Going with him there makes no sense.

But Will. Will worked mostly in the ER of University Hospital. He could speak German well, as he had spent some time in

Switzerland when he was younger, imagine that, and this made our lives much easier, certainly. But it also — I soon discovered — often put me in a position of needing him and in a position of relying on him. Most people in Zurich spoke English and I could make do with that and the little German I remembered from high school, but it's impossible to feel at peace, completely at peace, when you live somewhere where the lingua franca means nothing to you. Will liked this. I didn't understand it then, how much it mattered, and it was only after I'd been home in St. Helens for at least a year, when the many disparate and fractured details of our lives together, and of Will's personality itself, began to drift together in my mind to form a true image, a real map of where I'd been, that I understood this. And what I realized was scary. Not having been able to see it then becomes more shocking to me as time goes on, but at the same time, if I consider the person I was, someone who knew virtually everything about the human body and yet nothing whatsoever about people, or was only just then learning, it makes perfect sense. Will was the only man I'd ever been with — ever been naked beside, ever made love to (not counting the unfortunate incident with what's-his-name, okay), ever been in a relationship with, ever loved. I was happy in his orbit. It felt safe. He knew everything and didn't seem to be afraid of anything. He hardly drank, he saved people's lives, and he called me his queen. I was therefore a queen. But even through all of this, I can remember moments of doubt, I can remember that I knew. I knew. I *knew*. In the hut that morning, arguing with him. I knew. Later, in Barcelona, not a day after I'd seen Joseph kill his wife and seen what happened to the baby happen and seen Joseph kill himself as well, I knew. I *knew*. I knew it was true. For a moment I could see that it was absolutely true. But then it faded. Then he consoled me and it faded.

Will was able to get me the postdoctoral fellowship, and although there was an academic element to it, the job was very simple: I worked at a free clinic near Langstrasse and I treated prostitutes and sometimes assisted with abortions. After the first weeks, when I realized this was what I would be doing for the next year of my life, and possibly longer, I had a few days' worth of doubts. But it was all very abstract. To be honest, I immediately loved the women, who were utterly unself-conscious about their bodies and who discussed things like genital warts with the detached and systematic professionalism of bankers.

Banks are the language of Zurich — banks, right angles, and cleanliness. People there — the women at the clinic, my supervisors, even Will from time to time — took it as a given that Zurich was boring. I found it beautiful. There is no place quite like a refugee camp to make you appreciate truly clean surroundings, and there is no place quite like Switzerland to ease your newfound compulsiveness. My work was interesting; living a normal life with Will, my husband, and imagining our shared future made me feel strong, as though I'd finally become, after so many years of confusion, a real woman; but the deepest passion between Will and me, the feeling, early in our affair, the feeling of starvation if I hadn't seen him in three hours, cooled a bit. The hottest parts of Will and me stayed in Africa. Our love turned comfortable, Will worked a lot, and my new affair was with the empty streets of Zurich.

So I walked. I've always loved to walk. As was my way, I memorized what I could of the map (seven-thousand-year-old European cities tend to look a bit more complicated from above than the county-drawn straight lines and rectangles of Wisconsin) and wandered the different sectors with my time.

Sometimes I thought about Zara and the camp.

But that faded.

~~~~~

Here is something.

(As Ben is so fond of saying.)

I've never been a big cleaner. And Will didn't care that I was messier than him; we both worked so much that we really only slept at our apartment, and we never had people over. Every few weeks, though, I would come home and find the entire apartment immaculate and know that Will had reached his entropy-tolerance limit and spent three hours *adding energy* to the chaos.

One day, I was home alone looking at my pile of laundry, reflecting on my slobbery, and I decided that for once, I would be the energy adder. And so I got to work. I piled up the laundry, his things and mine, and took it all down to the basement and started a load. I sprayed the glass table and wiped it down. I vacuumed. I organized the junk drawer. I dusted the bookshelf. I scrubbed the toilet. I cleaned the stove. I threw away bad lettuce. I went through all the junk mail. I mopped.

After this, I went back downstairs to change the laundry. I moved the wet clothes to the dryer, dumped new clothes into the washer. A pen fell out of one of Will's pockets, and so I went through the other pockets.

And really it was nothing, especially then, but I remember it. In the back pocket of his Carhartt pants I found a folded-up to-do list reminding him to get the keys copied, pay the rent, and stop spending so much valuable time thinking about the past.

〰〰

We had been in Zurich for almost six months when Will came home one night and, after dancing around it while we drank wine and ate the mediocre Thai food I'd made, said he'd been thinking about having a baby.

"Men can't get pregnant," I said. "No matter how good a doctor you are."

He ignored me and said, "I know it would be a serious sea change for us."

"Wait," I said. "You're not joking?"

"Why would I be joking?"

I looked at him, waiting — sometimes he was so deadpan that I couldn't read him at all. Now, though, he just continued looking back, and I thought: There would be no reason to joke.

"Sea change?"

"Sure, whatever," he said. "More than a sea change. A major paradigm shift."

"I have just not even come close," I said finally, "to thinking about that."

"You must have. You must have in your life."

"Of course I've thought about it in my *life*," I said, taking his plate and standing up. I took the dishes over to the sink, then came back for my wine. "I just —" He looked at me, over his shoulder, waiting for me to arrive at the rest of the sentence. I was surprised, truly — all that time I had spent imagining Will and I together, it had been only the two of us someplace. That was the core of my fantasy. I had assumed that after the camp, after seeing what we'd seen, Will thought about children like I thought about children: You're taking a risk, because putting a person in the world will send that person somewhere you don't determine, down a road you don't design and can't know. The audacity and the death and the pain we'd seen — not just death and pain, but the death and pain of children — made intentional procreation seem almost cruel.

That's what I thought about it, anyway.

"It's just not even on my radar," I said.

Will, still looking at me over his shoulder, reached his arm up awkwardly and took my hand. "I know," he said. "Me neither. Not really. I mean, put it this way: It's coming as a surprise to me too. To be thinking about it. But I keep thinking about it. I don't know."

"Did something prompt it?"

He tilted his head. "Yes and no," he said. "We had a woman come in with a stillborn last week. I've been thinking about her."

"How did it happen?"

He shrugged, let go of my hand. "She tried to deliver at home, way out in the sticks." He waved his arm.

"But how many babies did you see die in Chad?" I said. "Why would that —"

"It's not the reason," he said. "I said yes and no. It's just been on my mind, that's all, and a woman handing me an infant's corpse and asking if he was well and saying that she wanted to name him Gustaf, after her father, didn't *immediately* evaporate out of my mind."

"Jesus."

"Yeah, well," he said, shrugging again. I cleaned up the rest of the table and Will poured himself more wine.

"It's not as though the impulse comes from entirely negative reasons. I don't want it to seem like that."

"No, I know," I said, sitting down. "It's just crazy to imagine all the changes it would mean. Will I ever be able to do a residency and practice? And where would we live? California?"

"I haven't thought about any of that," he said. "What would be wrong with here?"

He leaned forward and took my hand. "Just start thinking about it, okay?" he said. "It's just that we're so stable. And it could be amazing."

~~~~~

I thought about it. I didn't want to have a baby.

What I told Will was: "Okay. Yes. I want to have a baby."

This made him incredibly happy, and for a month it was all back, everything, just as it had been in Africa, when the affair was illicit and untoward, when it simply was not right. It was illegal again. I have sometimes wondered if Will didn't know that this would happen, whether he sensed something new and erotic to be found in the idea of coming in me without protection or (worse) he felt the changes between us as the death of the relationship, not a shift toward comfort. Whether the excitement was not so much about having a baby, let alone raising a baby, as it was about dominating my body in *every* conceivable manner before he did away with me. And what is the ultimate domination if not this: man deposits one-half ounce of semen into hole, woman's body fundamentally changes, transforms, and expands, woman then loses psychological autonomy forever, woman's body expels approximate replica of man?

It all turned him on.

We fucked like we had fucked when it first started. For weeks I went to bed drunk on dopamine. And we played. Once he asked me to be one of the women from my clinic. He told me how the story should be: that I needed his medical advice regarding the safety of different positions.

"Are you serious?" I said, laughing, the first time he told me about the fantasy. "You're crazy."

"I'm embarrassed," he said. "But it's fun, right?"

"I guess it might be," I said. "But you know I'm not a good actor."

〜〜〜〜

There was all that sex. For months. But I didn't get pregnant.

Will was casual about this and shrugged it off, but I was worried enough to talk to one of the physicians at the clinic, who sent me to a fertility doctor she knew. I did all this without telling Will. It was the first time, really, I had done anything without telling him, and it's another thing that I wonder about when I look back on my time with him in Zurich. It would not be right to call not telling him a conscious choice, not exactly. And I wish I had a friend who was there who could help me remember, or that I had been writing my mother with updates and questions or meticulously sketching charts of my ovulation cycle — anything that could be a record of the past, because I don't know, I truly don't know, and it feels as though actually understanding, and having more certainty, would change the way things are now and help me make peace with the past. I remember being in school in Montreal, in geography class, and being shown a Victorian map of Africa, clouded in the center, and seeing that the title at the top of the page was "Africa: The Dark Continent." But I had been there. Europe is the real Dark Continent. And America. Wisconsin. No maps were possible. My memory of Africa is crystalline, I can recall so much. There was horror there and I was outside of it. The memories are bright, hot and dry. The memories from Zurich, though, feel at least twice removed, maybe more. They are drowned and sea soaked. They are eroded. They are memories of dreamed memories.

It took me three weeks, after I knew, to work up the courage to tell

Will what the fertility doctor had told me. I wasn't pregnant. I couldn't get pregnant, and I'd never be pregnant. My body did not work.

~~~~~

One night in the inky black center. (This part is not my own blindness. That is important, still.)

It was the end of July.

First I will say exactly what I remember. I have to do this as though I am a phenomenologist, because Will's version, from his later explanations, is fused so well with my own narrative that I think my brain — or part of my brain, at least, the part that searches so frantically for narrative that it will soak up information with no regard for the source — lapped up his story with its information-parched neurons and began, that very next day, doing the work of encoding it as the truth and depositing it forthwith into my long-term memory without my consent. This is how our minds betray us — this is the way in which they act against our greater interests, and this is what fascinates me about human beings (even though, in this case, the object of my fascination led to pain): There are moments when we learn that our minds and our selves are not the same creatures. Often they act in concert; what's important is that we seem to be our own masters and commanders. But the truth is much worse than that the mind and the self are separate, and I feel as though women know it better than men. The truth is awful in a way that eclipses pain. The truth is that despite how it may seem, despite that sense you have, walking down the road, that you are free, that you can do what you want... I'm sorry, but none of it's true. All people are made into credulous idiots by what we think of as consciousness. *Your* consciousness. *You*, Ben. It is not acting in your best interest. It will convince you that it is. *You*, what you are, are underneath it. *You* are trapped down there. We do not get to decide a thing.

Here is what I remember:

1. Will was — if I am being honest — amazing when I told him about the infertility.
2. He was everything — a part of him became concerned physician, inquiring about the details, consulting the ob-gyn, looking into second opinions, reading up on treatments, moving through implications. There was no sign of rage.
3. He was kind. I want to remember that.
4. He tried to hide his sadness, but I could see.
5. I felt a great need to apologize, which I found myself doing all the time.
6. Each time, he told me that I didn't need to apologize.
7. Why would somebody apologize for circumstances out of her control?
8. It was around this time that we started to drink a lot.
9. We drank as a couple, which is worse than drinking alone, because in this way we could turn every night into our party.
10. In celebration of what, I don't know.
11. Will had met another American doctor whom he liked very much, and so one night — July 25, 2004 — we went out to dinner with him and his wife at one of the better restaurants in Zurich.
12. I remember thinking that the wife, a writer from Atlanta, had amazing breasts.
13. And she was also warm and lovely.
14. I remember that the husband was funny.
15. And loud, but not in an annoying way.
16. Will told a long joke I had never heard him tell, something about a farmer trying to protect his daughter's virginity.
17. I remember laughing so hard at the punch line that I nearly

threw up on the table and the wife had to hold my arm and pat my back as I laughed.

18. I remember the bathroom.
19. I remember that this bathroom was amazing.
20. The thought, I mean. I remember having that thought.
21. Aqua tiles that weren't just on the floor.
22. On the walls and the ceiling too.
23. As though every night, after the bar closed, a man came in with a hose and sprayed everything.
24. Everything.
25. I remember talking about karaoke.
26. I remember the husband liking this idea.
27. I remember her saying: "Do you know what nightmares are? Actually? Nightmares are just by far like the most efficient way of processing everything that's horrible and getting on with it. One nightmare is good for like two weeks of bad feelings."
28. I remember looking through a binder.
29. With him.
30. I remember an amazing duo of gay Swiss businessmen singing the Michael Jackson/Paul McCartney duet.
31. I remember Will at the bar.
32. I remember myself at the bar.
33. I remember a failed attempt at Kanye West.
34. Things get very hazy.
35. I remember a small and cold pool of gin on the tabletop.
36. I remember staring at a light.
37. That is all I remember.
38.

Here is a perfect memory:

The desert. My mother, her boyfriend (who was my former therapist), Bobby, and me. All of us tucked into the four corners of his Cadillac. All I have been wanting to do lately is go to SeaWorld. Now we are going. I have learned about sea lions. I have learned about orca whales. I have learned that it's unfair to call orcas killer whales, and I have imagined, a million times, seeing one burst up out of the water, arc through a soft parabola, audience silent, and slip back down into the pool. I have learned that whales, when they squeal to each other underwater, don't say things directly, they don't say, "There is food here," or, "There is danger here." Instead they transmit their feelings. Instead of saying, "There is food here," they say, "I am hungry right now, although I am *also* happy," and the other whale has to figure out what that means, what the whale is actually doing. I have imagined them all figuring it out. I have imagined myself cheering afterward. My mother's boyfriend, the therapist, thinking we need a fun weekend, has convinced her that we should to take a trip to San Diego (on my recommendation) so I can see the orcas.

Bobby, next to me, is asleep.

I am looking out the window at the mountains in the distance. The Cadillac has air-conditioning and I'm drinking a rectangular box of Hi-C. The doctor is talking to my mother about Gram Parsons, a name I don't know but will remember because I like the way it sounds. We're listening to Gram Parsons on the radio.

We come to some rocky crags that are close to the road. And I see, up at the top, a rock that looks exactly like Shamu.

〰〰〰

And this memory could be made of rock as well: My brother and I are sitting at the Olive Garden in Ann Arbor. He is nineteen and I am twenty-one. We are both undergraduates at Michigan. We're waiting for our father to arrive; he's gotten in touch and he wants to see us.

In solidarity, we're both sitting on the same side of the booth. We both have Cokes.

We see our father come through the door.

He's twenty minutes late.

He anxiously scans the room.

To me, it's amazing how scared he looks. He's so human.

"My God," Bobby says. "Dad looks like Pat Sajak."

~~~~~~

I woke up facedown in bed the day after the karaoke. The room was bright; I was by myself. It was past noon. I had an awful headache, and when I rolled onto my side, I realized I had to throw up. I made it to the bathroom, barely, then stayed there at the toilet for at least five minutes after I'd flushed it, eyes closed, hands on hair, breathing through my nose. I wanted to die.

I was still nauseated when I stood and scraped through the medicine cabinet for the bottle of ibuprofen, knowing that my stomach probably wouldn't be able to handle it but wanting to get at least a percentage of a pill, at least *some* milligrams, into my body. I closed the cabinet and frowned at my reflection. My face was smeared with eye shadow, more than I recalled putting on.

I was leaning forward, wiping it off with cotton balls, when I started thinking about coming home. I could not actually remember coming home.

I remembered the couple and the restaurant.

I remembered ordering a second drink before the food. Will saying: "Are you sure you want that?" Matt telling him to share it with me. Him saying, "Anything for the lady."

I drank some water from the tap, nearly threw up again.

I took a shower.

In the kitchen, I found a vase of flowers on the table and a note that read:

LOVE YOU.

I went to the phone and called Will's cell, not expecting him to answer. Instead of his voice mail, though, he picked up and said, drolly, "Good morning, sunshine."

"Oh my God."

"Is it bad?"

"Oh. My. God." I sighed and lowered myself onto a chair at the kitchen table. "We need a new word."

"Bad enough for me to bring an IV home for you?"

I put my forehead down on the table. "Can you bring it now?"

He laughed a little and said, "I can't, actually. There's a car accident on the way."

"I'm a car accident."

"You were in rare form last night."

"I can't remember anything from after the restaurant."

"Anything?"

"Nothing."

"Jesus, Lauren," he said. "That's not good."

"How much did I even drink?"

"Hm. Well, two before we ate, which was probably the first problem. Then I think two glasses of wine with the food. And then at the karaoke bar you told me you were going to stop, but when you were singing with Robin you magically had a vodka tonic in your hand. Maybe she gave it to you."

"Jesus. What did we sing?"

"You covered a . . . wide range? Of eras and genres?"

"These people will never be our friends now, will they?"

"No, no," he said. "It was a great time. You weren't embarrassing. It was fun. I've never seen you let loose that much before."

I looked at the flowers.

"Did we have sex?"

"Uh, yes?"

"Why do you say it like that?" I said. But I knew why he was saying it like that. I was sore all over.

"Because you got a little crazy about it."

"I am so embarrassed right now."

"Why? Don't be. I'm your husband. We had fun."

I burped a little bit, away from the phone. The burp was vomit. I tried to swallow it back.

"I have to ask," I said. "Did we have anal?"

"We tried. For a second. Then you said it hurt too much."

"It feels like I slept with a shampoo bottle up my ass, Will."

"We *barely*, barely did it. Not all the way in. Not even once."

"Was I disgusting? Am I completely disgusting?"

"Not at *all*. You're beautiful. You were beautiful. It was…hot. Hot, I guess."

"I can't move. I can't imagine even getting back to the bedroom right now."

"Eat something greasy. Try to cook something. You'll get better. You don't have to do anything today, right?"

"No."

"You're fine. You were just…letting off steam. It's okay to do that sometimes."

"I am still disgusting. Thanks for the flowers."

"Stop saying that."

"That's how I feel right now."

"But you're joking. Right?"

"Maybe. I guess."

"Okay, they're coming in. I gotta go," he said. "I'll see you around nine, I hope."

"Bring the IV," I said. "Really."

"Okay. Love you." And he was gone.

~~~~

I said before that the brain betrays the mind, and I do believe this, but it's never quite so simple.

The opposite is also true. Anterograde amnesia is the betrayal. But it doesn't have to limit logic. Or the feeling that something is wrong.

Like how I'd felt that morning in Chad. How I felt in Barcelona.

I slept for another hour, had a dream about penguins living in our apartment. Then a second, stranger dream, and even though I felt physically better when I woke up, I couldn't shake the sense of dread. The second dream was a kind of variation on the seaside dream. In this one there was no me, not in the same way. There was just my point of view. The scene didn't take place near the sea, but rather somewhere in the woods. There weren't multiple monsters. Just one. And I never saw it. I didn't know exactly where it was. Just that it was somewhere, and that I was hiding again.

I ate some bread in the kitchen, made some tea, and sat on the couch for an hour reading a copy of the *New Yorker* Will had brought home from the airport the week before.

I was back in the bedroom, making the bed, when I looked at the bedside table and noticed the lamp wasn't there.

It was an odd little black lamp that I'd found at a shop in Niederdorf. Tall and simple, the shape of a lava lamp but opaque. To turn it on, you pressed the top, and a small clear cylinder with a lightbulb in it would rise up out of the center. I remember standing at the kiosk holding it, looking at it. Thinking: I find this so efficient. And also: This reminds me of a penguin.

Anyway, the lamp wasn't there.

I walked around the bed and found it down in the corner, lying on its side, broken.

I sat on the bed and picked it up. You could still press the cylinder of light back down into the base, but the bulb had cracked. I closed it, then opened it again, then closed it. I set it on the table.

And sitting there looking at it, I saw my own fingers reaching for it. And not being able to reach it.

A wraith. A wraith of a memory of that.

And with the memory, a cold, cold feeling — the dread, but more distinct — billowed up.

And I knew.

I knew all of it. I knew about Zara. About Joseph. About Will. About me, even. That I was one of those.

I don't know how I knew. I don't know why. This has always been a part I don't understand. All the moments from the past tumbling together into the right pattern. Or maybe just something simpler; maybe just a sliver I truly could remember. No images, no sounds. A memory of a feeling.

And so me, an hour later: I am dressed and on the train.

∿∿∿

Here's a nightmare:

I get to the clinic a little past five and swipe my key card at the door.

My supervisor is an old man named Dagan Gohl, and he comes out of one of the conference rooms with another doctor as I make my way to the rear of the clinic, where my tiny office is. He likes to practice his English on me. When he sees me he smiles and says, "Ah! But it's your day off, no?"

I smile and tell him I need to pick up some paperwork.

"Very bad, Dr. Sheehan," he admonishes.

The other doctor just looks confused.

I draw my own blood in my office, door locked.

I watch my red blood fill the syringe.

I am emotionless, looking at it. I am. I have done this hundreds of times before, for all manner of tests, and it is a strange, cool comfort to be both patient and doctor simultaneously. The two have always been so distinct. On the one hand, the story of suffering. On the other, the story of healing.

But it's not that way now, and in fact it's never been that way. And it wasn't that way in Africa. Neither story is ever quite true. I am a foolish girl.

I put the test tube in an envelope, label it with the made-up name, slide it into Pia's mailbox with a note asking her to run the test.

A *new girl*, I write in the note. *She just came in today.*

I lift myself up, stare down at my own writing.

I imagine the new girl.

I lean down and write: *Rohypnol?*

〰〰〰

Ben and I we were in a hotel room just off the highway north of Green Bay, both of us on the bed, uncomfortable, I think, with the finality and darkness of my story there with us. It may as well have been sitting on the cheap table across the room staring at us. I had taken it out of myself.

"And?"

"What do you mean, and?" I said.

"The test. What did the test say?"

"What do you think it said?"

We weren't yet far from civilization; the hotel was a Marriott tucked away amid a cluster of other hotels and franchise restaurants of this stopover, one of Wisconsin's many villages of brightly colored lights, parking lots, and signage.

He didn't respond.

I was so tired. It was awful to hear it that way, condensed and in a straight line from my own lips. This. Then this. Then this. Because it hadn't felt like anything as it happened — that is most frightening — I don't quite know how to explain. I had been happy and in love for almost all of it, and now, looking at it, it was a nightmare. How could one thing become the other? How can you not know you're living through a nightmare? Will and I were a love story until I realized that we weren't. That is not fair.

"So that's him," Ben said finally. "And he's fucking crazy."

"That's him," I said. "He's something."

"And now he's back."

"He came to Madison," I said, "but maybe it was a coincidence."

"That was the first time you've seen him?" Ben asked. "In Madison?"

"The first time."

Ben leaned back against the headboard. "Jesus," he said. "Jesus."

"It felt good to see you punch him. I downplayed that."

"I'll bet," he said, looking at me. He turned back and looked at the ceiling. He held up his hand then, which I took. The knuckles were bruised, but I'd looked at it already. Nothing was broken.

"He has a fucking hard head," Ben added.

I thought: I don't know Ben. Not really.

We were quiet then, both looking at the TV, which was turned off. Ben seemed lost in thought and I began to worry that I shouldn't have told him anything. But I was exhausted. Not in the moment, but with the years. I'd wanted to. We hadn't slept much the night before, at his uncle's house, and even though it was only nine thirty now, I could feel sleep pulling at me. I twisted, put my hand on his chest.

"This has been a very intense forty-eight hours," I said. "We're both in the vortex right now."

"What vortex?"

"I don't know. The vortex of hearing about somebody."

"I'm sorry all of that happened to you," he said.

He turned his head. "Really."

"When you say it like that, it's like I got struck by lightning," I said.

He turned his head a little more. "Well, yeah. It's awful. It's an awful story. I'm sorry. That's all I'm saying."

I didn't say anything.

"You can't think any of that was your own fault," he said. "Right? That's not what you mean."

"It was more than just circumstance," I said. "It wasn't random."

I sat up, got out of the bed. Ben watched me quietly as I went to my bag to get my pajamas. Now I felt furious again. And furious with myself for being furious.

"I shouldn't have told you."

"What?"

Kneeling down, looking at the string tied to the zipper on my bag, I said, "I was somehow open to him. That's the whole point. Or to someone like him, at least." I opened the bag. "I'm credulous. I used to be way too open. That's my point."

"I didn't realize you had a thesis statement."

"What does *that* mean?"

"Maybe you were a little vulnerable to a certain kind of man."

I felt another pulse of anger run through my chest when he said this, but as I dug through my bag, I thought: Don't. It isn't him.

Keep this. Keep what's real.

11

Wayne's Nightmare

When she fell asleep I slid out of the bed, got my key card from the top of the dresser, and left.

I took the elevator down and went past the kid at the desk and through the sliding doors, then I stood for a while under the lights of the Marriott entranceway looking down at my shoes and the red rug. The parking lot was full. There were plenty of other travelers on their way up north too, looking to get one last weekend out of the season. The T.G.I. Friday's where we'd eaten dinner was only a few hundred yards away. I started to walk in that direction.

Her eyes in Madison the previous morning — maybe now I knew. Not much more than caverns of pain carved out well and left behind, empty, to be filled by God knew what. And again last night, at Denny's house, in the bed. I reasoned: Think about what love actually is. Past a certain point, you can't go back. There's a threshold at which you can stop, but if you cross it, you can't go back, and that means you're stuck to somebody else.

I thought all of these things.

This is not safe, I thought.

I was standing in a parking lot.

Maybe it was her smell. Or something else very simple, something that had nothing to do with hearing her talk. That had been a good feeling, it really had. She had been a wall and there suddenly was no wall. Everything.

Which reminded me of something.

The T.G.I. Friday's was crowded. It had been calmer when Lauren and I ate. We sat in the booth. Now I asked for the same booth again and ordered a Sprite.

On a napkin, I wrote out the versions of him I had known and the versions of him I remembered and had been remembering. I felt something new and far off that I knew was prompted by hearing all of her story in that way, packed together like that, hearing it all pour out of her — something to do with a deeper sense, what she was talking about when she was looking at the lamp, a sense that each of us has and one that has nothing to do with the others. I knew that what I felt that night had something to do with him as well. The whole time she'd talked, I'd not been able to stop thinking of Wayne.

I wrote:

Wayne
1. Tree house → Riddler
2. Escarpment → Pothead philosopher weirdo
3. Las Casas → Evil obsession, plus family
4. Poem → Nonsense (. . . Chaos?)
5. Cabin → ?

And I said to myself: *Look at it, Ben.*
Just look.
Shut up.
Listen.
For once, look right at the thing.

〰〰〰

Two men sit in a booth at a bar.

They're talking.

One's a little older than the other.

The older one says: "Have you ever heard of a man named Bartolomé de Las Casas?"

The other says: "I don't think so."

"Dominican monk named Bartolomé de Las Casas, writing in the sixteenth century, Bartolomé de Las Casas. Okay. No. He was Spanish. He came over to see the New World. And he was totally and immediately fucking horrified by what he saw the soldiers and the conquistadores doing and so he just went right to the notebook and tried to record as many of the atrocities as he could? Just knee-jerk: This is what I can do. Someone needs to remember this. Someone needs to see it and remember it and bear witness. And his reaction was completely against the standard ideology of the time, *completely*, with like a contemporary universal-human-rights human-dignity point-of-view thing. And this is a *monk* in like 1550. A monk, Benjy, this bookish dude on an island in the West Indies that's stacked with a few thousand meatheads, just like a complete army of human monsters, and he's there saying, 'No.' So dignified. 'No.' I mean, he can't stop anything, and he's way out of his element and not advocating a very popular point of view, so there's no way he should have seen things the way he did, but he knew what he knew and he was all about just recording it. A mirror, I guess. Or not a mirror, because no one cared then, but a record. I mean, with him it was all bound up with God, but whatever. He recorded the atrocities and slaughters that he saw. That's what I'm trying to say. Sort of in real time, as they were happening. And so he eventually put them in this book called A *Brief Account of the Destruction of the Indies*, right? He has more, but that's what I'm talking about, that's what I read. You haven't heard of it? No? Seriously? I mean right, sure, St. Helens Fucking High is not exactly gonna be pushing A *Brief Account of the Destruction of the Indies* on sophomores, I guess, I don't know what I'm saying. But not for the reason you're thinking, right, not because it's too subversive to them or will rile up your seven Ho-Chunks for a couple of weeks. Not that reason. Mostly because the shit is X-rated levels of violence, like way way *way* worse than anything on TV or in movies, way way worse than anything that really *happens* to people anymore, much worse than those *Faces of Death* things you were talking about before, I'll tell you that much. And it makes those horror movies like *Friday the Thirteenth* or whatever seem like they're made by a bunch of children with ketchup packets and pitchforks? Like there's a guy, some lone psycho hunter out there and he's hunting down people? As though evil is one man who has lost his mind and is hunting you down? He's coming to get you for what you did? Or didn't do? I mean, I just laugh at those movies now. The banality of the illusion. The try *behind* the banality of the illusion. And those movies used to make me so scared I couldn't sleep, Ben, I used to go and wake up my mother when I was like *fifteen* because they scared me so bad. But not anymore. That's not real horror, dude, and I can think of two reasons right off the bat to support that thesis, okay? Totally accurate, good reasons. Dispute them if they're wrong or something, I mean, maybe there are holes, but I don't know what you can do with these. First, one: Las Casas is *more* gory. *More* gory. Than Hollywood. For starters, every page of the thing there's some poor fucking Caribbean Indian tied up to a gibbet — you know what a gibbet is? — tied up to a gibbet and some Spanish soldier is down there stoking a fire by his feet and everybody's laughing it up. Not the worst thing you've ever heard, right? But hold on, okay? It's not like *Oh, we're going to burn the bottoms of your feet for a little bit and make you uncomfortable.* No. I mean that's how they *killed* the dude. Yes. Get it? Slow. They cooked people. But they kept the flame little so they wouldn't die. Thirty minutes, an hour of this. I don't know. They got the fire going and cooked his feet forever until the *bottoms* of his feet *melt* off and the bone cracks up and fractures and the *bone marrow* drains out of the guy, and I'm saying this is what's in this book, this Las Casas book. You know? And that's just — that's just like the default death in the book, Ben, Las Casas is just throwing those in every other line to remind you. It's like filler. 'Gibbet.' 'Gibbet.' 'Oh, another gibbet.' 'Then they brought out the gibbet.' 'He sent for the gibbet.' But the gibbets are like the punctuation marks of the real slaughters in there. I mean, I don't know. What are some examples? Lemme think. There are like a million. Okay, off the top of my head, Indian gets away somehow, runs, but he gets caught. Soldiers drag him back and they lay him out in the dirt in front of his family and saw off his legs and leave him there. Saw them off. Set them by his head so he can look at them while he dies. Or, okay, yes, this: Soldiers hanging around with nothing to do, just free time, they're stuck posted in a village, and they decide to have a contest, they wager on who can do the cleanest, slickest job *cutting a dude in half from his skull down to his groin in one hit.* In one huge sword swing, I mean! So like they bring out a dude, tell him to stand there, position him, everyone's hanging around watching, probably feeling the exact same feeling you feel when Jacke's running up to the tee to kick off and start a game for the Pack, and Juan, amid this anticipation, comes up to bat, sizes it up, and then Juan *fucking bifurcates* a human being with one swing, and all of his friends just start laughing and going *crazy,* and Juan's doing his little soldier jig, using his sword like a cane or whatever, just dancing around and truly elated because he just won a gold ingot from his pal and he's done something super-impressive. This is *leisure* time, Benjy, this is downtime on Hispaniola in 1510. Okay? And right over there is the captain, and all the authorities, all the men in charge, the *moral scions,* and they're hanging out and chuckling and clapping about the game. Dude's wife is screaming right there. Whatever. Her soul's been crushed. Whatever. Everything she cares about on Earth has been converted into amusement and it's entirely arbitrary and there aren't going to be any consequences and there sure as fuck isn't going to be any justice around any of this. So she's screaming. And Carlos, who's irritable already because he hates Juan and now Juan's all popular, goes over, grabs her hair, gets her in a headlock, and cuts off her nose with his dagger — his thumb's the anchor, like when you're cutting off a piece of banana — lops it off, chucks it, looks at her, kicks her down, and then rapes her so she *really* learns her lesson about screaming about the death of her husband, and of course now all the dudes start to laugh at that. Hey! Whoa, check *that* out. Carlos has a new game. Cut off the noses and then rape them *immediately.* Everyone starts running around looking for a woman. Natives run, scatter. They all get caught *because they don't have horses.* They're brought back. Again with the legs. Back to that. So on and so forth. Do you see what I'm saying? And I mean, this is a sampling. It's grotesque on almost every page, yes, I apologize, but it's kinda the point, and yet you get the sense that Las Casas is even skipping stuff and just doing a *light dusting* with it. And gore's not even my good reason why *this* is real horror and those movies are just child's play. Right? I'm going on forever but I said there were two reasons, I think. You with me, cousin? You doing okay? I'm noticing that you don't look so good. Is it the subject matter? The shrooms? Which? You're nodding. Combo? You're saying combo, okay. I'll stop talking about this in a sec. Did you puke down in the bathroom, by the way? Did you actually puke or just gag a little?"

"I'm okay. But yeah. Puke."

"Did you see your shrooms in the puke?"

"I don't think so."

"Probably digested by now. That's *totally* normal. You're good. Do not feel embarrassed. I am not a hard-ass about this stuff. I can't stand it when people get all hard-ass. I mean, it's about this, it's just about talking, you know? It's about exactly this. So many kids at this school are into some kind of complex drug porn thing that really misses the point."

"It's fine."

"You're feeling okay then?"

"Better."

"Because I'll be honest with you, and this is the only reason I'm sticking on this point, but you're green right now. You're literally green. I mean, we're sitting in a bar and one of us is a seventeen-year-old green person drunk and high and about to start tripping so long as he digested those shrooms before he puked. You don't even need to trip right now, actually. Just tell me you're okay, all right? Thumbs-up or something. I'll stop with the mother hen."

"I'm fine."

"Okay. The other reason. Boom. Two. Why is *this* real horror and Jason not real horror? Simple, Ben. I'm glad you asked. This is real horror because this *is* fucking real, Ben. This is how it went down. This is the origin story of Europeans in this hemisphere. Your roots. My roots. Really. I really mean that. That's us. The sound track of life here in America is those screams. Always. These guys,

Christians, exact same Bible as the one you can look at wherever you go today, right on the heels of Columbus, almost right away, these guys just poured over into these gorgeous, peaceful, bucolic, pristine islands — this is heaven, is what I'm saying, Ben, I'm making an argument that Europeans, all of them Christians, entirely against all expectations about reality, metaphors, everything, actually *located* the heaven of their own religion *on Earth*, they located it, it was just *over there*, and the people who already lived there were like *Hey, sure, come on. It's amazing to swim in this really blue water.* These people didn't have any real weapons; these people could not *conceive* of the scope of brutality that was the everyday status quo just across the pond, and I mean they were not dumb, Ben, I'm not saying it was because they were dumb that they were so vulnerable, I'm saying they were *nice*, Ben, the culture of these islands was built around being *nice*, and I mean they lived it, they didn't espouse it, they lived it, they couldn't even stop themselves from slapping together one big outrageous fruit basket after another and running out to *greet murderous, insane soldiers* whenever they saw a galleon floating up; for years and years they would do this, it's all in the Las Casas, and for years and years Spanish soldiers were just like falling over themselves, they couldn't believe it, just completely climbing over one another, trying to get out of their boats and get to their swords fast enough to get a quick, easy lead-off beheading of a holy tribal king without even thinking that *maybe* it *might* violate, oh, I don't know, the entire Christian moral code or, that whole thing aside, that it might go against just obvious, timeless, and basic human *good-versus-evil* restraint, you know, something like that was around even with cavemen, the totally simple idea that maybe needlessly causing excruciating, savage, horrifying, life-ending pain to another being, to a brother, to somebody like yourself, might not be the thing you should do. They found their heaven and they turned it into a hell. On purpose. *Intentionally*, Ben. That's the legacy. That's your legacy. That's what we are. That's what *we* believe in. We believe in *making hell*. We are male descendants of Europeans, which means we are monsters, Ben. Think about that. I'm not just saying this. I mean, it's real. We are monsters. I'm not saying it satirically. We are. It's like a let-sleeping-dogs-lie situation, but the dog is so brutal and huge that if we *did* wake it up, it would just ravage everything, so we just *can't*. That's where we're stuck. That's the boat we arrived on. An army from hell, we're like, like, like, like *terraforming* the rest of the Earth, Ben, making it hell too, and that's what we're *still* doing. We! You and I, Benjy... because we're Euros, we're members of that army still and we can't help it. Us. That is reality. So if you take that to the next step of thinking, then none of it — nothing really actually mat —"

"We're not Spanish. We're from now."

"You're missing the point."

"Why did you read this book, did you say?"

"I had to read it for this class I took. And I'm sorry I keep jumping scopes on you here, but this is just the Las Casas, this is just the first fifty years. I can't remember how many they killed. Fifty million, I think. I mean, with smallpox, all of that, which was worse numbers wise than the actual murdering. But that's the first few decades, and that's just the islands. There's a whole continent here, you know? That's just the Spanish. Are you feeling something? You look like you're starting to feel something. Sit there, feel it. Lemme get a pitcher. We just may as well get a pitcher. Let me give you something to think about while you're here by yourself, okay? Just muse on this question I've been musing on, because I'm interested to know what you think. Simple question. We can get away from the conquistadores for now because I know that's disturbing and I'm not meaning to be glib about that, there's a bigger point to it, but it's gross shit. I know. So here's a classic. What is the value of family?"

"..."

"What've you got for me? Are you good with your beer? Here. No. You've barely had any. That's probably for the best. Have the water. I found us three cigarettes but there is no lighter. What did you come up with about family?"

"You said the value of family?"

"Yeah."

"I dunno. People to help you."

"I think that's probably a lot more profound an answer than you even know, Benjy, and I also think that it's gentlemanly of you to actually hold the lighter out for me and do it that way, as though I'm your lady, thank you. But you're totally right, and that's totally profound. Families are ostensibly valuable units of organization because the world's a tough place, I mean, a tough fucking place, right — Las Casas, for example, right? Hello? It can be bad out there, and so if you want to stay safe, if there's a group of you and you want to stay safe — and I know that look in your eye, Benjy, you're over there thinking there's this big biological element to this conversation, aren't you, big evolutionary behavioral stuff and how it makes sense to help out the fam because the fam's got your same stuff and you've got the fam's stuff and you're all trying to just keep it doing well, you're *totally* big-timing me with the biology angle, but you're so right, and you can cover that, you can hit that, I just have a simpler point that's more about numbers — so if you want to stay safe, what you should do in this little group is just be sure you *all value one another more than you value anything or anyone else in the world,* right? And if everybody agrees to that guiding principle and does that, then chances are you'll all do well because, first off, you'll never be working at cross-purposes with the people near you, you'll never be crossing the streams with someone else in your little pod and be in conflict with them because that would fuck up the basic code, right, the very basic code, and you wouldn't be valuing each other like you should be. But it's also effective because you've all got one another's back in a family, right? So that means someone from the outside world comes in and tries to hurt somebody, everyone else is all over it because they're all tuned in and watching one another and the hurt doesn't happen, it gets averted, it gets blocked. *Then* there's the whole other thing about revenge. Like if someone does get hurt in the fam, in the pod, and it's over and done with, do you go out and get revenge? Sort of on principle?"

"Are you asking?"

"Yeah. I'm asking. What do you think of revenge? In principle. As a principle for guiding behavior, I mean."

"You mean — so you mean what do I think of revenge when it's your family?"

"Yeah, sure. Or if it's easier to think about it, for just you. Somebody wrongs you, hurts you, but the danger's gone. It's not physical anymore. Do you go out anyway and hurt the person back just because? Just to get something — I don't know, something in the universe — back to even?"

"It doesn't even have to be some big thing out there in the universe, though. Some abstract thing. It can just be because it feels good."

"What do you mean by that?"

"I just mean — I mean, okay. This. So a few years ago, when we were fourteen, this kid and I were riding —"

"What's his name?"

"Andy."

"Sorry for interrupting. Continue."

306

"This kid Andy and I were riding our bikes over to this other kid's house way on the east side, and this car drives by, some T-Bird or whatever, guys in it not even from town, and it slows down and comes up alongside us, and the guy in shotgun is laughing, and he pulls out like a Gatorade bottle or whatever and sprays the Gatorade around and it gets all over both of us, and they laugh super-hard and then drive off. Andy's in front of me and he stops and I stop and he goes, 'That was piss,' and he's totally right, I can smell it now too, and it's all over my face and my neck."

"Disgusting, Ben."

"So then a year goes by, and I was out at County playing golf by myself one morning, and —"

"Hold on one second, Ben. Playing golf one morning? You golf?"

"Yeah. What? What's wrong with golf?"

"Just a total environmental rape, but also I'm just pointing this out to you out of cousinly concern for your image, totally cousinly concern for your image, but golf's kinda thought of as a rich man's sport and you're kind of a member of the ruling elite because of your mom's family and everything, so I'm just —"

"You don't think I should golf?"

"I'm taking it back. I take all of that back, totally judgmental and shitty of me. Totally derailed you. Totally a fucking baby-boomer-hippie-sixties-cliché-argument-trope-barf-topic thing anyway, it's not even *true* in Wisconsin, I'm wrong about that, it's not a class thing at all. I just completely said something my dad would say. I think I actually like golf. Go, though. Your story. I'm an asshole. I'm shutting up. Go."

"So the point is I finished and was on my bike and leaving and riding through the parking lot and I see the car. The T-Bird."

"You're sure it's the car."

"I'm sure it's the car because it's got the same fat tailpipe things, you know those things? That makes me think it's the car. But then I go around to the window and look in and it's the same seat covers, which I saw really close up when the guy was spraying the piss around."

"Okay. So you're there, it's the car. You're thinking revenge and you piss on the hood."

"No. I smashed all the windows with my three iron and then rode away. It was just this huge parking lot and there was nobody anywhere."

"Get out. Get *out*, Ben. You busted up that whole thing?"

"They sprayed piss on our faces."

"And so you're saying it felt good."

"What?"

"Revenge. Getting revenge. You didn't do it to right a wrong, you did it because you were angry about something that happened and it felt good to destroy something that had caused it."

"Yeah. I guess. Yeah. It felt awesome."

"That's because it is awesome."

"I see two birds sitting on your shoulders right now."

"Do you?"

"I do. They're there."

"Bear with me for one more topic here though, okay? One more point to hit, because I'm sure to you it seems like your crazy cousin talks way too much and darts all around wanting to cover all these abstract things when you're sitting here just trying to have a good time with some birds and chill and talk about that girl in that booth over there who I swear to Christ has been staring at you for the last ten minutes. Do you see her? She's looking at you. Right now. She just did again. You're seeing her, right? Okay. Noted for in a second. But one more thing for you. The anger-revenge answer thing was great, by the way. The illustrative story? Are you gonna do philosophy when you get here? My man? Smart-test man? Anyway. So do you think actually our own family, the Hansons, and so I guess I'm talking about the St. Helens crew, which would be you four and us three . . . do you consider our family good or evil?"

"What?"

"As a unit, you know? As an entity."

"We're good."

"You see."

"What?"

"I mean, it's an impossible question. If you were really gonna answer we'd have to go through a whole thing where we figured out what good was and what evil was and pretty soon we'd have fucking *Phaedo* on our hands, Wayne and Ben do *Phaedo*. I'll cut to the chase, though, about a couple of things, as your eyelids are not doing well over there, and you said the bird thing, and we should do some good walking now because they're starting to hit me over here a little too, but just to finish this up, Ben, to let you know where I'm coming from here. I'm — I've been pretty deep down in some sorta tough things in the last year or so, um, some of it totally personal, some of it more, uh, intellectual, all this stuff we're talking about, just trying clarify a couple of big things for myself and sort through the big ones and just feel like I'm walking outta this place next year with, like, with a real education, you know? Just walking out of here at twenty-two with my good old geology degree in my back pocket and a good sense of what I'm gonna do next, but also a feeling that I actually *know* some things, know like a handful of good, totally true, totally reliable ideas. That I can use to decide about action. Living. But kinda *mine*, you know. To have a few that are mine. And not because I want to own thoughts or anything stupid, you know what I mean.

Know the road *to* the idea, not just the idea. Or at least that really weird thing about old clichés being meaningless when you hear them *as* the cliché, but then one day you've gotten all thoughtful and you're thinking really hard and then you're writing down a few things in your notebook, just sorta realizing, and you stumble upon it and you didn't even know you were going toward it, you *get there* in your original way, I'm saying, to the idea, and suddenly you're like 'Holy fuck! Roommate! Yes! The golden fucking rule that they taught me in kindergarten is actually a totally amazing ethical principle! *I just also came up with the golden rule!*' But you can't go and take credit for it. People would think you were crazy, and really actually creepily delusional, if you went up to someone and made that claim. But now that you *got there* in your way, maybe the idea now actually means something to you because someone hasn't forced it on you. It's a private thing. Look, wander. Make really fundamentally true things — because there are a couple out there, and I don't mean what they do in science, because scientists, Ben, lemme tell you, as far as I can tell, most scientists just can't *think* richly, can't be flexible and imaginative and daring, but that's a totally different conversation, I'm talking about the wandering. You go wandering, idea wise. Pretending you have no goal, no specific goal. But you sorta gotta trick yourself when you're doing that wandering though, don't you, because really, you *are* looking, but you don't want to admit it because you might spook it if it knows you're looking for it, like the idea's like a fucking deer out there or something, so you pretend there's no destination or goal, or more than pretend, you kinda trick yourself about it, but you're out there fucking *wandering*, right, *you're there*, so you probably are looking after all because otherwise you wouldn't be wandering, you'd be on your couch. Am I right?"

"Totally."

"I'm really trying to wrap this up for you, buddy. Stay with me. I don't even know where I was trying to — oh. Okay. Yes. So the family. That good-and-evil thing is a huge problem right now for me. The Hansons, we're talking about. Us. Because I'll spare you the treatise on each one, I mean, we could do that if you wanted but it *really* makes me feel bad about myself, because I'll also just get it out of the way and say I fucking love every single one of us, just absolutely love your dad and your mom and your sister and you and my mom and my dad. Just love everyone. So much. Individually, as a group, whatever. But that's lately really hitting up against this other issue in my head, this other voice I'm listening to that's pretty clearly telling me that the upper tier, the four adults up there, are collectively a pretty fantastically evil group of human beings. And those four are our leaders. And I'm seeing by the expression on your face right now that that's *way* too heavy of a statement to lay on you and I see also that it's last call, so I'm skipping right over that, we're just zipping right over it, pretend you didn't hear that, I do totally see the birds in my peripheral vision also, just so you know that we're both seeing them, they're just sitting on my shoulders, that is amazing, but we just zipped right past that thing I just said that doesn't even matter, *zip, zip, zip,* that's cool too, *zip,* try that, *zip,* see that? Yeah. Exactly. Okay. It's bar time. I am really talking a lot here. Jump in any time. Really. I'm all about conversing. You're a great companion, you're a great listener. I really feel like you're here with me, you're processing in there, you got this way, I can really see you processing. Last thing. *Last* thing, I swear to God, and then we're going to walk the shit out of this town, we're going to do some serious walking. And this isn't even one of those big questions, this isn't one of those big topical things. This is actually just me telling you something that I think. Um. Yeah. I'll just tell you. I know you're younger, I know she's out there at Yale now, I know this might be a hard piece of advice to actually implement, but I really, really think you need to really watch out for your sister."

"Haley?"

"Yeah."

"Why?"

"Because...because...because she — she's a certain combination of qualities in a person that's rare and makes her really rare, and by *rare* I mean *really* rare, I mean, not like diamonds but like orbicular granite, if that possibly means anything to you. You're looking at me like I'm nuts. I'll stop bullshitting around. You remember when she came out here to visit? Exactly like what you're doing right now. She stayed with me? It was a few years ago, I was just a freshman, it was Halloween?"

"No."

"Do you remember this Halloween? Few years ago. You were probably busy getting sprayed in the face with some guy's piss. I'm pretty sure your parents were out of town."

"Oh. Yeah. I stayed at my friend's. She stayed at her friend's."

"Well, no, she didn't. And she obviously didn't tell you about it, which means I probably shouldn't be telling you about it, but you're cool, you're not gonna say anything, it's ancient history anyway, so I'll tell you. She didn't stay at her friend's that Halloween. She, ah, borrowed your dad's Jaguar and drove out here and stayed with me in the dorms, spare bed and everything, because the Eritrean roommate was out of town, which was a nice relief, and so she happened to call up out of the blue and she told me she'd heard all this stuff about Halloween at Madison, da da da, and I said yeah, but take the bus, or I'll come get you, it's right there, and she said no, no, it's fine, I'm a super-good driver, it's fine. So I said fine. I dressed up like fucking Groucho Marx with the whole deal, all of it, I even had the shtick, I had the jokes, I found us a party to go to, I was all set, and I'd told her she should be Harpo 'cause she's blond and it'd be great and funny, and she'd told me yeah, she liked the idea, and then she gets here and I give her the room to change and I come back in, and she's not Harpo. Take a guess what she is."

"Karl?"

"That's hilarious, but no. No. She's a slutty hot cheerleader."

"But she was a cheerleader. Actually, I mean."

"And what I'm telling you, Ben, is that she had procured for herself a cheerleader outfit that would not have been permissible in some *strip clubs* I've been to, okay? And I took one look at her standing there in the middle of my room, fists on her hips with that kinda tilted pose, big goofy smile on her face, I took one look at her and thought: I'm dead. I'm fucking dead. Somehow this is going to kill me tonight. And of course right then she did some cheer, she jumped and landed in the big X thing, and I was like: She actually knows how to be a cheerleader on top of it. I thought, Wayne, if you let this girl out there dressed like this — because I know she's your sister and you probably don't want to hear it, and cousins can be a little more objective about this kind of thing, and this is all even more delicate because she was about *sixteen years old* at the time, Ben, *sixteen*, but all that said — I know we gotta go, I know, just two more minutes for this story, I'm sorry, we're going — if you let her out there amid those animals — she looked about twenty *then*, especially with all the makeup, and I'm telling you that there was a real good chance that in the eyes of most dudes, dudes into cheerleaders or not or whatever, but in the eyes of most of the twenty thousand or so dudes on this campus, maybe more because it was Halloween, she was the hottest girl in the entire city. If we built some kind of hot matrix for what your typical twenty-year-old frat guy, college guy, whatever young guy thought of as hot, and we made that machine, what I'm saying is that the machine would have broken when we scanned her. Smoke, the *doing-oing* spring noises. Then the machine would have packed itself up into its own crate and checked itself back into the warehouse. And so usually I'd be like, hey, great for Haley, there's my little cousin whom I haven't seen in about four months, who's definitely had a growth spurt or something, who happens to be very attractive, who happens to have sort of shocking Brigitte Bardot–like measurements, actually, all of the sudden, and is also really comfortable in her own skin too, but she's a real person, she's the opposite of vapid, she's also great and very smart. Great job, cousin. But this was *Halloween*, Ben. Halloween. I didn't even know what it was gonna be like. I was totally in the — okay, yeah. Yeah. We'll go. Yup. Paid. Come on. We'll just — excuse me. You know? I mean, you'll see if you come here. You can guess. It's nuts. In the fun way, but also in that mob way, that pagan Dionysus way, like everyone might think, secretly, that there just aren't any rules for this one night, Spanish-soldier style even, but *probably* no one's going to act on that. Excuse us. You'll see. Okay. Uh, okay. One cigarette left, sir, which we can share right now, and I don't even know — okay. Come this way. We'll go up the hill first. We'll check out Lincoln. God. Perfect. That guy. Perfect night. Amazing. Right? And you're not even sick anymore, huh? You have color."

"What happened?"

"The birds?"

"Halloween."

"Yeah. You know what, man? I really didn't intend to tell you this whole story. I didn't intend to get here, telling you this. Haley's tough, she can take care of herself wherever she's at. I mean also, she's at Yale. She does crew. She's safe and sound. She's got…triceps."

"Why would you start the story by telling me I had to look out for her, though?"

"You're listening! You're always listening to things, and I hit a pretty serious new plateau with the alcohol right before we got onto that topic, and I just — okay, I'll admit it, I always kinda wanted a little sister and I think I was just like playing that out by putting it on you like it was advice. Here is Library Mall. Here's the library. Here's this creepy brown building. What is a mall, technically? Did you ever wonder that? We're gonna go straight, cross, then walk up the hill there. That's Bascom Hill."

"Just tell it."

"It's actually nothing. Really. I mean, me freaking out was really the story. That moment."

"So you went to the party?"

"Yeah, yeah. We went. It was over on, uh, Langdon. Over there somewhere. A frat. Typical huge big house party, they let us skip the line because I was looking really attractive. And so we got our cups, drank some beer. She danced a lot, dudes definitely talked her up. It was a fun night. It was a good night. Yeah."

"Right."

"The *only* thing. The *only* thing that was kinda not good — because okay, I see that you can see that I'm sort of bullshitting around this now because I didn't want to tell this story, but okay, here's sort of that nugget of badness that you're sensing. So at one point pretty late, hours later, I'm up in the kitchen talking to this Nancy Cartwright girl who's actually in Rollerblades, and I thought Haley was there too, but I look around and I don't see her, so I go around looking for her. And it's not like she's locked up in one of the bazillion bedrooms or anything, it's nothing bad. She was just downstairs in the basement, back around this little corner by the washing machines, and she was making out with this dude, this kind of big, beefy dude dressed up as George Washington. And it's like totally a consensual situation and everything, that's obvious, I'm standing right there and I can see that it's consensual, but then I'm like *What the fuck am I doing?* and I go over there and grab her by the shoulder and tell her that we gotta go. She's super-pissed, George Washington is super-pissed, he starts getting all up in my face, telling me to let her do what she wants to do, chill, and I said, 'I know you were a really, really great leader for this country and we needed you at the time, but she's sixteen, George. She's sixteen years old.' So he just kinda looks over at her, then looks back at me, and I go, 'You look at least twenty-three or twenty-four. No lying now, right, George? Right? *Can't.* So. You know. Easy mistake, probably shouldn't make a big deal about it.' And he goes, 'Well, she was the one who came up to me,' and the guy sounded so dumb and so drunk I just suddenly imagined that this is what a triceratops would sound like if it could talk, you know? And at this point Haley is cutting through the crowd, all stompy, and I just left him there and went after her and I caught her right outside. She sort of stormed her way halfway back toward the dorms and I was right behind her, but then she didn't know which way to turn, and it was raining a little now, and she calmed down, and I gave her my Groucho jacket and she put it over her head. And then we went back. So it was sorta just like — I don't know. Just the combination. Jesus Christ, my lungs don't work. But here. Okay. Check it out. Abe."

"What combination?"

"Oh fuck, Ben, come on, man. Let me off the hook with this, okay? She's very attractive. She's very bold. She's obstinate. She seems to like to do things that she knows will piss *other* people off, you know? Like doing this to A will drive B crazy. She's all that shit. But on top of that, she's just actually naive, I think. She's a little naive."

"About what?"

"About what? Are you kidding me? Oh, good Christ, I think I need to go to bed, maybe. Even. Lie down. Check out this grass. Just lie down and feel it. Yes. This is good. About what. About what. About family. About that Spanish soldier. The one I made up. The second one. What'd I name him? José? Juan?"

"Carlos."

"There he is, always listening. About Carlos. She's naive about Carlos. So I thought: Hey, tell Ben to keep an eye out. Big deal. But then I thought about it while I was talking and I realized it was just patronizing, it was just more of the same shit about men owning women, it sounded too much like dudes telling women to not dress up sexy because that invites monsters to pursue you. Fuck all that. Your sister is gonna land on her feet wherever she is. I'm the fucking one who needs a guardian angel, Ben. Who am I? Jesus. Where's my huge, muscular, dangerous, snarling, protective older dyke sister when I need her? Someone to steer me right. Punch me. No, dude. We can't pass out here. We should not pass out here. I'm fading."

"The stars."

"Carlos, though, man. He's the motherfucker. That's my true thing. Because Juans are usually fine, you can see them coming from a mile away. Just showboaters, whatever. It's the *second* guy. You know? Ben? You there? Yea? Nay? You're done? I'm talking to myself here? Ah. No worries, yeah. You're a good kid. Fucking Carlos. Sneaky, petty. Dumb and drunk dinosaurs. You, man. I'm looking at you. You're the devil. You come in second. You think that means you gotta be better. And you end up being way worse."

12

We Both Begin to Feel Again

I heard the door close behind Ben when he left — I was half asleep, dropping down into the dream again, and so I lay still for some time, feeling the first waves of fear that came with it. They were so familiar to me. That seaside shack. Where would Ben have gone? I wondered. But the squid people were there too, and I didn't want to linger. There was one answer: he went somewhere to get away from me because I was now toxic.

I sat up and looked over toward my phone, which was charging on the desk, then got out of bed.

I held the phone in my hand and thought about calling him to ask him where he was. Exactly what my mother would have done. Probably he was just outside. Probably he was looking for a vending machine.

I set down the phone.

I put on my sweatshirt and my shoes.

Cheetos, I thought.

I want some Cheetos.

~~~~~

There were plenty of reasons to think it, with or without my cousin's behavior that night. Enough reasons for me to sit at the table for the next hour, staring at the window, remembering as much as I could.

When I couldn't anymore I looked instead at one of the big TVs and pretended to listen to talking heads make predictions about the NFL season. I drank Sprite.

Eventually, feeling a light buzzing all over my body, I asked the waitress for the check, and when she got it for me I gave her the money. While I waited for the change to come back, I thought about how many times in the history of the Earth a man had sat alone but within reaching distance of a woman he cared about. Or the other way around.

The change came.

I made a pile for the tip, then got up to go.

I paused halfway up, looking down.

There was a single beneath the pile of change I'd made.

I brushed the coins aside.

I stared.

I stared, and I knew that it was true. All of it.

George Washington stared back, implacable.

~~~~~

I've always liked to wander down the hallways of hotels at night. I think it comes from the flight from my father. (How much of what is me comes from the flight from my father?) We drove all night the first night, but we stopped in Nebraska the next afternoon. We stopped at a Holiday Inn in Omaha, Nebraska. Bobby and I played tag in the hallways. I remember a man pulling open his door and yelling at us to be quiet. He was in boxer shorts and wore glasses. I remember thinking, as we ran: You will never be able to catch us, old person.

I got Cheetos at the vending machine and then I went down to the first floor to see if Ben was in the lobby or right outside.

He was not in the lobby.

He was not right outside.

I used the internet in the hotel's BUSINESS CENTER, which, for some reason, seemed hilarious.

I looked to see if there was a medical conference in Madison.

There was.

There was, but it was all a lie. By this time Will was north of Madison.

Walking back to the elevator, I saw the sign for the pool and an ← and I smiled.

I turned and asked the man behind the counter what time the pool closed.

"Usually ten o'clock," he said.

He was really more of a boy.

He smiled. "But for you, eleven."

It was sweet. He was young and it didn't sound convincing.

"Are you going in?" he asked. "Otherwise I was gonna lock it up."

I ate a Cheeto.

"I do have my suit," I said.

~~~~~~

I sat on the bed for a long time before I saw her note, and in that time, I considered the possibility that she had left and gone back to St. Helens. Don't ask me how. Her things were still there; it wasn't that. It was just that I thought it was possible.

I stared at the dark TV.

I thought back to the space station.

Before I could get too sentimental, though, I saw the note sitting on the little table by the window. The pencil was still beside it.

It said:

Dear Ben,
I've written you a riddle. Here. Try to solve it: I am upside down
and can't breathe. Where am I? I love all hotels. Find me!

xoxo
Lauren

I waded in the shallows before I dunked my head. At first I only
wanted to get wet, to smell the chlorine smell and bob around on
top, but the pool was clean, cold, and perfect. It didn't feel like a
bath, and I was alone in the big tiled room. I started to swim.

I went from wall to wall, all the way under, and came up for air
each length.

I did this for another five minutes and then I came up and saw
a pair of shoes at the edge of the pool.

I jerked back across the water, then looked up and saw Ben
looking down at me, hands in his pockets.

"Oh," I said. "Hello."

"Hi."

"Where did you go?"

"Back to the place."

I squinted at him.

"Thank Goddamn It's Friday's."

"Were you drinking?"

"No. Just Sprite."

"Oh. Okay."

"Just thinking."

"About what?"

"Things."

"And where did you think I went?"

"What?"

"When you came in and I wasn't there. What did you think? Where did you think I was? In that first moment you realized I wasn't there."

"I don't know."

"That's an interesting moment."

"I guess?"

"You didn't think, Uh-oh, where's Lauren?"

"I saw your note," he said. "So I knew you were here."

"You're saying you solved the riddle before you even knew I wasn't there."

"I did solve it, yes. It was hard, but I did. No time paradox, though."

I twisted, turned, and pushed off with my feet, looking at him upside down as I floated back toward him.

"How's the water?"

"It's nice," I said. "You should come in. Jump in right now."

"I don't have my suit."

"You don't need it. No one's around at all. You could jump right in wearing all of your clothes. Go."

"Isn't it closed?"

"The boy said it was okay."

"Maybe I will. Maybe I'll just cannonball right there."

He pointed.

Silence.

Then me: "What made you leave?"

"What? The room? Before?"

"Yes."

"I don't know."

"You don't know?"

"Your story made me think of a story I remembered. Then I

thought of something completely different. I had to think. I like to be alone sometimes. To think."

I looked at him.

"That's the actual sequence of events."

"You wanted to get away from me. Tell the truth."

"Not at all."

"What then?"

"I know — I think I know — why my cousin was up at the cabin."

"You do?"

"I think so."

I just floated.

"Why?"

"Why what? What was he doing there or why did I think of it?"

"Both."

He wouldn't say.

"That's good, right?" I said finally. "That's your quest?"

"What?"

"That's your quest? Of your triumphant return home?"

"What do you mean by that?"

"Aren't you on a quest?"

"No."

"Oh. Are you sure?"

"Can I ask you a question, Lauren? And it's not, *Are you fucking with me right now?* Because I honestly can't tell sometimes with you."

"Okay."

"It's an abstract question."

"Okay."

"When you think... What comes into your head if I ask you what evil is?"

"Evil?"

"Yeah," he said. "Like you said before. About your squid-monster dream. Like actual evil. The thing. What it is. Because nobody is *actually* evil, right? Or at least, no one thinks they are. No army ever invades in the name of evil."

"I don't know," I said. "Something having to do with doing harm, I guess. Harm on purpose. Why?"

I thought he was going to say something, and he opened his mouth like he was about to add to what I'd said, but then he stopped himself.

"What?"

"It just seems like," he said, "it can be on both sides."

"What do you mean?"

"Of the spectrum."

"What spectrum?"

"It can be all the way to the side of principle, just like purely principled behavior that's so … principled that you don't even know what you're doing anymore. You're just a big walking principle."

He cleared his throat — he looked like he was struggling to understand what he was saying. I definitely was. This was Ben thinking, though. I liked it.

"Or," he continued, "there's this other side." He pointed to this other side, which right now was by the hot tub. "When you've just completely let go." He looked at me. "You either care too much or not at all. Both of those." He did a flapping thing.

"What did your cousin do, Ben? What do you mean?"

"I'm not even sure I wanted to know."

I didn't believe him, but I didn't say it.

"How are you doing?" he said. Now it was like he was here, in the room. Finally.

"The pool is super-warm. It's like lava in here. I'm dying."

"I mean how are you *doing* doing?"

I was moving away from him again.

"Please don't ask it in that way, though," I said.

"What way?"

"I can hear it. I'm so tired of talking about myself." Because I knew what he was going to say. Something sensitive and sympathetic. I couldn't bear it.

Then he said it: "I'm glad you told me what you told me, if that's what you mean."

"You did say it."

"What?"

"You're welcome?" I said.

"I'm serious. I'm trying to thank you for trusting me."

"I don't think it's quite trust," I said. "I puked that at you."

"Well, whatever it is."

"I trusted you to catch my puke."

"Don't do that."

"It's like I've been waiting for someone to puke on. You just happened to be there at the right time."

"Don't."

"I had to tell somebody. At this point. What if I turn up dead somewhere, Ben? Who would know? My father knows only some. Who would find my body?"

"Oh, pardon me. It's a matter of being practical. In case he finds you and kills you."

I thought about this. I thought about Will. I thought: Yes, actually. Will *is* capable of that.

"There are actual practical things to consider. It's not like they're not real."

"That's an incredibly fucked-up thing to say to me. Considering."

"Considering what?"

"Last night. Everything. Today."

I didn't think so.

I had reached the other side again, but instead of turning on my back, I let my feet drop down until I was upright. I wanted to fight him. I didn't know why, but I wanted to fight him.

It was shallow enough to stand, but I let my toes scrape against the bottom and sank down until the water was at my chin.

"I don't think so," I said.

"I do."

"I'm being honest. You should try it, Ben. It feels good. Maybe it would make you less allergic to being human. Maybe you should stop mumbling through the world. Or complaining about privilege. I feel like you may not quite understand how unbearable a trait that is."

"I sense a little sarcasm."

"Can I ask you something?"

"You asked me if you can ask me something."

"So I can, then?"

"Yes."

"I told you my things. So tell me. Something. You know? There's too much me now. In between us." I showed him with my hands. "Tell me. I feel like you haven't told me anything. Anything at all. Even though we keep talking. Forever. There's an imbalance of invitations right now. I'm starting to resent you."

"Tell you what?"

"Something that feels real."

"I don't know how you could have gone so long," he said, "just not *talking* to someone. I mean, you really talked to nobody all this time?"

"You're avoiding telling me something."

"I didn't think we were done talking about you. How could you have gone so long?"

"No," I said. "I didn't *not* not. I tried to get as close as I could to telling my father without actually telling him. That was enough for him to always understand enough. But not the details."

"Maybe this is why you have nightmare problems."

"You think? Do you think that, Carl Jung?"

"You're still being hostile."

"Because I'm pissed. About so many things. I am so fucking pissed, Ben. At almost everything."

"I know that."

"I don't think you understand."

"You can't —" he started. "People can't do that," he said. "You have to talk."

"Listen to you."

"He should go to jail. I mean, he should die, probably, but he should go to jail. So you have to talk. And what is he — is he practicing medicine somewhere? He's a doctor still, I assume? This is just like a guy out in the world? Just some crazy motherfucker?"

"In Sacramento."

"That's why you talk. To create consequences, for one thing."

"Why else?"

"Why else?"

"Yes. Why else should people talk, Ben?"

"So this is me talking now? You're going to interview me?"

"You're apparently too stupid to understand any other way of me saying this to you. So answer me."

"So they can not be as angry? I don't know."

"Why else?"

"So they can know one another?"

"Why else?"

"So they can figure things out? Talk through problems?"

"Why else?"

"Because secrets are poison?"

"Why else."

"You're treating me like I'm in fourth grade."

"Why, Ben? *Why?* For real? Why?" I yelled it.

He was quiet.

He mumbled something.

I said, "You're mumbling."

"So they're not numb," he said.

He was just another man, in the end. I could stop this. I could. In any number of ways. But when it came down to it, when it actually came down to it, I just didn't want to. I wanted to keep going. I liked him and I wanted to be with him so I could talk to him whenever and so we had to do this. I liked the way he stood at the edge of the pool, hands in his pockets, looking down at me, answering the questions. I liked his nice voice. I liked his eyes and his heart. What else do you look for? In a person? I felt like I could ask him one hundred million questions and he would continue answering them, only slightly irritated, like he was right now. He would do that infinitely for me, no matter how angry I got. He would do that forever. That made me want to cry, thinking it.

"Or frozen," he added.

"Tell me about that," I said. "*That's* all I'm asking, Ben. Okay? Open." Now I did the flipper thing, but in reverse. Opening.

"Tell you what?"

"*Anything.*"

He squatted down at the side of the pool, his hands on top of his shoes. He licked his lips, then looked past me, at the wall.

"I've just always felt like that."

"Why, do you think?"

"I have no idea."

He shrugged.

"Here's something. I was in that restaurant drinking my Sprite just now because I'd started thinking — worrying — that once you weren't a good person, that was it. You know? Like, what if it's not fluid, what if it's not that redemption version of it. It's more like — it's more like ripping that little tab off an old VHS tape so you could never record anything on it again. Do you remember? It was for good if you did that. No turning back. So, what if you can't come back, because it doesn't work that way? You either remain good from the start, from baby, or go bad. Once you go, you go. You go off. And that's it. No going back. No returning later being good. That's the kind of thing that makes me completely lock up and feel like I am not capable of living."

"You could put Scotch tape over it."

"What?"

"Where you ripped off the tab," I said. "You could put Scotch tape over it and it would record again."

"You're missing the point. Stop fucking with my metaphor."

"Am I?"

"I'm just saying it's what I started to think about," he said. "But don't you think that's just as arbitrary as the redemption version? I mean, who knows? About what's good and not good?" He turned his hands up and smiled a little bit. "What? Why are you looking at me like that? This is me telling you something. Here is Ben. This is what I worry about. I'm trying here."

"I don't get why you think that anything is that rigid?"

"I don't actually think it."

"You just told me you were worrying about it."

"But you didn't choose," he said. "Anyway. What happened to you. That whole story. The rape. Someone did that."

I shrugged. "I played a role."

"Are you fucking kidding me?"

"No," I said. "I'm not. I mean, it's years later. I can say that. It

329

doesn't make it less awful, but I can say it. That's what makes *me* feel like I can't deal with the world. That kind of thought. But you can't tell me what I can or can't say about it."

"A *role?* Whatever it is, it's not that."

"No," I said. "I know. It's not. But what you're saying is too simple. Even if it feels like that. It's complicated and simple at the same time. We must admit. You know that it's that way. Everything. Or it should be, anyway. If you're telling the truth, that's how it sounds. That's the ring of truth. You know when they say that? It's that. When you can feel how complicated and how simple it is at once. Both of them. Together."

"I've been trying," he said, "to think more about what I say."

"I'm just so mad at myself, I think."

"I feel like I wasted everything I was given."

"It's okay. All of this is okay."

"You did nothing wrong."

"Come here," I said. "Just come into the water. God."

He looked down at the water for a moment, then back at me.

"Come in."

"Is this a test now?"

"No, shut up, just come, really," I said, pulling at the water. I was crying a little. "Let's stop talking. Can we? I would like you to swim. Stop joking."

He looked.

"Just come."

I put out my arms.

He planted his palms at the edge.

He let himself down into the pool, because now it felt as though he could.

It made a wave and a splash, but he didn't go under, and he walked toward me through the water, arms doing the wading motion.

I was crying but I laughed as he did it and my laugh echoed around the room.

When he got to me I said, "I didn't mean with all your clothes on," but I think that is what I'd meant. I'd wanted him to do it.

I put my arms around him, then started digging in his pockets.

"Here. Your phone is in here," I said, pulling it out and holding it up. "It's dead. Look. Take these things out. You'll ruin them. What are you doing, Ben?"

I think I was whispering. I kissed his ear with my poolwaterwet lips.

"I don't know," he said.

"You do. I know you do."

We put his phone and his wallet and his Swiss army knife and his keys at the side of the pool.

We floated back out to the middle.

"What am I doing?" he said.

"Be quiet. Listen to how quiet it is in here."

I took his hand.

We listened.

"What am I doing?"

He looked at me and smiled. We were floating on the top. The pool was warm like a hot spring.

"Why am I in this pool right now?"

"I don't know," I said. "You're the one who listened."

～～～

We left early the next day. Ben said a part of him didn't even want to go anymore, that his father's phone was probably dead too, that the whole thing with the ashes was totally stupid, that he was stupid, that his entire life was idiotic, that he was going to do many things now, that the Wayne thing was a placeholder, and that since we'd been in Madison and he'd spoken to the teacher, he didn't care so much what had happened to his cousin, it didn't matter in the same way that it had. The ashes, sure, but big deal, he said. Yeah, maybe I do have some new thoughts. I'm probably actually wrong, now that I think about it after sleeping on it. Now that it's the light of day. Maybe I know now, but it's so old, it was so many years ago. None of that matters now. He'd gotten obsessed, he said, but he thought that a lot of that might have had to do with just missing his cousin, who'd been smart, who would have been a good person to have around. Or maybe it was that he'd started to believe that there was a single true thing you could believe, and once you figured it out, life would be better. The *City Slickers* model, he called it. Just get it and you're good. I told him I'd hated *City Slickers*. He said he thought it might have to do with coming home, too, or avoiding wanting to deal with the future, or avoiding the past. He said he had this whole thing with his old girlfriend and his old BFF that he hadn't even told me about. He said everything with his cousin had been some kind of illusion. He said that actually, there really was no reason to go up. He said he was going to turn around. Okay?

I told him he was being stupid and that it sounded like he wasn't telling the truth anyway. Again.

I said, "Tell me what it is if it's no big deal."

"There's no actual need," he said. "We should get back."

"We're already almost up there," I said. "We're already here. It's fall. I want to see the leaves and build a fire, at least. I want to be Jack London one time. I don't want to be home."

"You enjoy fires, do you?"

"Who doesn't like fires?"

"I don't know," he said. "Some ladies."

But it didn't take all that much to convince him. I didn't believe him when he said he didn't care. He cared.

We drove north on Highway 41 and soon passed under an arch, like a miniature version of the arch in St. Louis, with a sign that said GATEWAY TO THE NORTH.

When I told him it reminded me of St. Louis, Ben said, "Ah, exciting St. Louis," like it was a joke.

I asked him what it meant.

He hesitated.

"What?" I said.

He told me he had a long story about his sister and her husband — if I wanted to hear it.

Did I want to hear it?

I said I did.

So he told it.

~~~~~

Long ago, Denny drew the map to his place with a Sharpie on a blank sheet of notebook paper and Xeroxed it to help any guests he had up, and once we were at Norway, where we bought some groceries and got gas, I pulled it out and handed it to Lauren and tasked her with directing me the rest of the way. We drove for about ten minutes on smaller and smaller roads until we came to what seemed like nothing more than a dirt path, even though it was named too. There wasn't any snow yet. The road looked swampy. The map said that after about a minute we should look for the smaller road on the right that would lead up into my uncle's land. The map warned that there would be a chain hanging across the entrance, locked in place with a big Master Lock. I had the combination, along with the keys to the cabin.

And so we drove slowly and we watched the thick wall of trees trickle by on the right, passing a couple of likely smaller-road candidates, moving on after a moment's investigation of each.

There were few neighbors out here — the cabins were spread far out, and you could spend a whole season living in one of them without ever hearing a noise from another.

We came to a new gap and Lauren said, "There it is."

She pointed at the little wooden sign at the side of the entrance. It was a brown rectangle that rose up alongside one of the posts. Carved and painted yellow, the sign read simply: HANSON.

"Home sweet home," she said.

I got out of the Nissan to unlock the lock and remove the chain, but then I saw that it wasn't there. I stood for a moment looking up the darker driveway, which seemed to rise unexpectedly into the woods then turn jaggedly to the left, out of sight.

The only sound was the engine, and I felt a cold feeling, looking up the road.

The real place. Not the idea of the place. And in the map of the world in my mind, this place, here, was the epicenter of so much that scared me.

I hadn't been here in twenty years. It was lonely already at this time of year, but in the dead of winter, I couldn't imagine. The evergreens would be coated in snow, and the road itself would be a white line leading to the north — who knew whether it got plowed. Denny's private road wouldn't have been. Where I was right now would be the place to stop for a moment and look around and realize the extremity of the weather, realize how exposed you were, how there was probably not a single person nearby to come and help if you needed help. Even just turning the car around might have been difficult, depending on the snow. To arrive here in the middle of the night, the temperature below zero, wind blowing — well, it seemed crazy. That's what it was.

The private road continued to curve up for three or four hundred feet, then straightened out when it reached a crest.

We went slow.

What we found at the end of the road was a place I didn't really remember.

Lauren was quiet.

I looked at the side of the cabin through the window, thinking we were at the wrong property, despite the sign — the color didn't seem to be the same, the shape of the building didn't seem to be the same, the roof seemed different, the porch seemed different. Hanson. But I didn't recognize it.

Perched on the edge of the ravine, the small parallelogram of a cabin faced west and overlooked fifteen slowly descending acres of dense forest. A cantilevered porch extended horizontally from the face of the cabin, supported seemingly by magic, and you could sit there and watch the sun go down. From where we were, you could see nothing man-made. Literally nothing, except for the cabin itself. It was as though here, in this patch of woods, Denny had found a point where one could look out on a sea of forest, the Bright River snaking through it, and that was all.

The cabin was in disrepair. Weeds had grown up along the foundation and around back; half the dark brown shingles on the exterior wall had fallen off, mostly due to rot. There was an overturned trash can ten feet from the northern wall. A few ripped shreds of plastic and empty bottles on the ground.

We walked around the cabin — I righted the trash can as we went by — and ended up at the west wall, just beneath the cantilevered porch, looking down at the easy grade of the ravine, which led to the Bright.

The boathouse was right there.

"Maybe we can take a ride," I said. "In the canoe." I looked at her.

She smiled.

"To be Jack London."

"That would be nice."

I looked west, first high and at the horizon. Then I let my eyes drop and I started to scan the trees nearby, to the north, wondering under which specific tree Wayne had died.

~~~~~

When he said it, I looked at the slope that led down to the river, where there was a small dock and a boathouse at the end of a straight path. The hill was covered in long grass and dotted with boulders, but it was open, and I could see a stretch of the riverbank and the water flowing from left to right.

All of it was pretty.

"Where did your cousin die?" I asked.

Because Ben was looking at the woods. I guessed he was thinking it.

He pointed to a tree at the side of the slope about fifty feet down.

"There, I think," he said. "That birch. See the little cross? Or whatever that is?"

It was more of an X, nailed into the birch.

"It's sad," I said. "It's not a very good marker. It seems like he should get a better one."

"I know," Ben said, taking out his keys and going to the door of the cabin. "Sad and weird."

We both turned. He started to walk. I followed him up to the door.

Inside was a mausoleum of insects; ladybug carcasses covered the floor, making a black and red carpet. The mass of them shooed away the cabin's lingering wisps of utopia. There were dead things everywhere. The smell of the place, air sealed in for years, began to wash over me. There was a stink to it that went alongside the stale.

There was a small couch, a potbellied stove, an enormous wooden table Ben said his uncle had made using four stumps he'd pulled out of the ground on the land for its legs, and a tiny kitchenette. Up above the kitchenette there was a loft and a bed. To the right, there was a small supply room. A back door too.

"Would that not be crazy?" he said. "To just live up here? Like this?"

"Yes," I said. "It would."

"Can you imagine that kind of life? Instead of all the stuff?"

"What stuff?"

"I don't know," he said. "Technology. Airports. Fast food. All of that."

I smiled. "Maybe we should try it," I said. "Maybe we should do a month. Maybe it would be really nice. And easy."

"Maybe that would be nice," he said. "We'll see how you're feeling after the canoe."

We went outside again and wandered down the path that led to Wayne's tree.

I looked up at the treetops and listened to the sound of leaves — dry and crispy leaves, leaves at the edge of fall — *shhh-shhh*ing against one another.

It was fall here. Not down south yet, but here.

At the birch, Ben put one palm on the zebra trunk. He glanced up at the wooden X nailed to the tree, touched it.

The wood was clean.

"I guess this is it," he said. "And yeah. It seems like Denny would have made something nicer."

"It looks more like a marker," I said, "than a memorial."

Ben looked up at the cabin, then down to the boathouse.

"Yeah."

I looked at the ground. Imagined Wayne dying.

"I'm going to go down there to grab the phone, actually," Ben said. "And see if the barbecue stuff is locked up in the boathouse too. I think that's where Denny kept it all." He smiled. "If it's not there, we might be trying to cook on an open fire. We didn't get charcoal, did we?"

"No. We got Twizzlers."

"Oh, well. Fire then."

"Then I hope you find nothing," I said. "I like fire. I'll sweep up all those ladybugs, how about?"

"Okay," he said. "I'll be up soon."

He leaned forward, then, and gave me a kiss.

I walked back up the hill.

I found a broom in the closet and swept bugs for a minute or two, but I got distracted by the pictures along the mantel above the potbelly. There were seven or eight framed family photos in a row. Most of them were pictures of people who I assumed were Ben's aunt, uncle, and cousin — a happy-looking and attractive couple, and a boy with an eager and broad smile. But I found one with all seven of them too — Ben, his sister, and Wayne all lined up in front of four adults, all of them in swimsuits, all of them ankle deep in the shore waters of some lake. Ben's sister looked fourteen or fifteen, just on the cusp of womanhood, holding one hand on one hip and pointing at the camera in a mock accusation but with her father's hand on her shoulder too, his smile revealing what I thought might be his last attempt at keeping her a child. Wayne had stuck his head forward and was smiling with his teeth. Since he was already taller than both his mother and his father, it was disharmonious for him to be in the front line, with the children; his parents had to lean out a bit to be seen behind his shoulders. And Ben, on the other side of his sister, both arms hanging down. Funny look on his face. Not a smile. His father's other hand was on Ben's left shoulder; his mother's was on his right.

I picked up the photograph and wandered to the door to see if Ben was coming back up, thinking of how much time I had spent in my own childhood wishing, more than anything else, that this, or something like this, was what my family looked like. Safe. Normal. Big. Solid. Together. Lasting. A castle. An institution. I used to dream about replacing my mother and my brother with better versions. I used to put myself among a group of people who were much stronger in all ways, a group that wouldn't have so many open flanks and vulnerabilities. A place that could not be invaded by any of the versions of evil Ben had talked about by the pool. Whichever. Family didn't care about the definition of *evil*. That was what made it strong.

Ben's sister, Haley, in the picture, was a queen; on either side of her, a young man who would rather die than let somebody harm her, and behind, older, stronger, and wiser men who would also rather die than let something happen to her. The mothers, coy and watchful, aware of the unity they had created by many years of work and sacrifice, content to see the made thing, now with its own life, move forward in time.

Haley seemed to know, too, what it meant to be where she was, that she was invulnerable.

On my way out of the cabin, I glanced over at the sink, which was really nothing more than a repository for water that dripped down into it through a tube from a container you could place above.

Beside the sink, I saw, there was a cell phone.

I picked it up.

Ben had told me that his dad left it up here. But hadn't he said it would be down by the river?

I tried to turn it on.

The battery was dead.

I stepped off the low porch and into the grass near the foot of the path and looked down the hill.

I saw that the door to the boathouse was hanging open, but I couldn't see Ben.

I heard the faint flow of the river mixed with the light wind moving through the trees. The *shhhhhhhhshhhhhhhhhhhhhhh-shhhshhhhhh* again.

Something felt different.

I saw the car where we had parked it.

I saw the birch.

I imagined Wayne again.

I looked back down by the water.

I lowered the picture to my thigh, waiting for him to come out of the boathouse.

I waited.

I put the phone in my pocket.

I waited.

I called out to him.

"Ben?" I called.

He didn't come out.

I took another step.

"Ben?" I called again.

One more time.

And a fist, then, a fist from the left. It hit my cheek and nose with so much force that my feet came up off the ground.

And so:

I am in the air. Then —

— on my back, no wind, my vision dimmed at the edges, bright wedge of light clawing for grip at the back of my eyes.

First I am looking up at the sky.

Will is above me.

I see him.

Will is here.

Not the story of Will but Will.

He is standing with his feet on both sides of my torso, looking down, finally here, finally here after all my years of waiting for exactly this, for him to hunt me down and finish me, and he has a fistful of my hair in his fingers, and he is here to finish me.

He leans, looks into my eyes.

We stare at each other.

He is here.

No, I try to say, but nothing comes out.

The taste of blood, and his enormous face, hovering, examining me.

"What did you do?" I manage to say. But I already know. And it is awful.

"He's dead," Will says. "I'm sorry. I killed your boyfriend."

He looks down at the river.

"He's down there."

He lets go of my hair, and my head drops back and hits the hard dirt.

I see clouds.

13

Will's Nightmare

It was always there, a quiet river in the background that only sometimes overflowed, flooded over, say, every four or five years, when the rains were heavy or the snowfall in some other county, or country, or season led from this to that.

The river became swollen. Now and then, it happened. Always the threat of a real flood, something dangerous, but always a recession, never quite like this. There comes a point when everything is speculation.

Imagine, for example, racquetball in Sacramento.

Two men, both respectable physicians, playing a heated match. They're friends. They're on their third game and they've split the first two. Being physicians, both men are competitive. And imagine yourself on the other side of the Plexiglas barrier, say you've just come past to get a drink at the bubbler. The sounds of the game — echoing squeaks, grunts, the impact of the rackets on the blue ball and the almost immediate thump of its impact on the wall, the higher tones as it ricochets off the sidewalls with depleted velocity, other sound waves exploding out and around and bouncing and reconvening, muting one another, canceling. Moments of calm and muttered, echoing scores spat from the sweaty mouths of men. What you know for sure is that both men want to win.

One of these two men is named William Besco.

This is a few weeks ago.

If you stay long enough, you'll see him lose.

~~~~

Will stayed in Zurich for another year after Lauren left, engaged in what he came to think of as consolation. His friends and colleagues were sad to hear that his (lovely, somewhat immature) wife, Lauren, had returned home to America and hired a Swiss lawyer to handle the divorce; sad to hear that their good friend Will, after so many months of fighting for the marriage and trying to make it work — you heard about the argument they had about her drinking, right? She didn't seem to settle in very well here, she seemed to be at sea, Will thinks something may have happened to her in Africa that he didn't know about, she may have been traumatized, there's more to the story — was resigned to signing the papers and moving on.

"Fight *more* for her," the wife of a colleague said to him one evening at dinner, an evening when everyone at the table could see that Will wasn't himself. "That's what women want," she added knowingly. "To see that you won't stop fighting."

Will thanked her for the advice and said, smiling wanly, "I think we're past the point of chivalry. Although it would be nice to live in that world. The truth is that she doesn't love me anymore. I have to accept it."

Everyone nodded with great sympathy.

~~~~

Also, another confusing thing for someone like me: Will Besco grew up in Sacramento with no self-esteem problems to speak of and only a few odd instances of instability. He played basketball in high school and was an early bloomer, which led his coaches to put him at center his freshman year and move him to the four, his more natural position, only when the other boys began to sprout up around him, and his ball skills began to blossom. He played all four years and perhaps could have walked on at Stanford, but he declined the offered tryout and chose instead to concentrate on his studies. He wanted to be a doctor because doctors were respected.

~~~~~

Say you're the janitor at the Sacramento Racquet Club.

Labor Day weekend is coming; you're looking forward to the start of the football season.

Put yourself in the Sacramento Racquet Club locker room — you are wiping down lockers, actually, one at a time, inside and out, just as you do every day, because that's what this club is like. You and your fellow janitors are ubiquitous, even though you probably wouldn't use that word; there is always someone cleaning, so much so that the staff tends to go unnoticed. Especially in this large locker room with its many nooks and aisles.

You see a member seated on a bench in front of an empty locker, still sweaty, not yet showered, straddling the bench, staring at either his racket or the floor, you can't tell which. He looks both furious and stunned. Mad at himself, lost in concentration as he replays key points of the match in his mind. Or so you guess. As though he's a professional racquetball player. As though any of this matters. As though wealthy people here have any real sense of the troubles of most people. You look down. You see this kind of thing all the time, guys angry about matches, and, just as always happens, when you look up again, the man has snapped himself out of it and is standing up in front of his locker.

Nearby there's a half-open locker, and around the corner, someone's taking a shower. Steam wafts out.

Everything's pretty normal.

You watch as the man, now shirtless, regards the steam. He goes then to the other locker as though it's his. (*This*, you think, *is not so normal.*) As though the pants hanging from the hook inside are his. As though the wallet he removes from the back pocket is his. As though the ID he slides from the wallet's window is his.

Curious, you watch as the man puts the ID into a side pocket of his gym bag.

But this job is good, so in the end you look away. Who are you going to tell?

~~~~~

Speculation.

Will worked that week — he had a twenty-four-hour shift on Labor Day, which turned out to be something of a bloodbath, as a good half of the local charter of the Banes, a motorcycle club, came in with gunshot wounds from a barbecue gone bad. But that week he also registered for the conference in Madison. He had seen the e-mail blast six months before. Usually he had no interest in such things, but he had noticed the location and spent a few afternoons daydreaming about the possibilities. But that was right at the time when he and his wife, Valerie, whom he'd married the year before, found out that she was pregnant. So the fantasies ceased as Will attended to that joy. The water receded for a time.

But here was the problem with the existence of Lauren Sheehan, and here was the cause of the eventual return, months later, of the same half-sketched daydreams — or fantasies, I guess they are; kinds of dreams — the same thing that had caused him to write to her so many times, the same as all the rest: it had always been there, this feeling, even before Lauren, and once in a while there were floods and overflows — four times, maybe — but each of the previous incidents had had its own organic resolution, as it were, each had played out with the neatness of a perfect surgery, with the closing of wounds using material that would over time degrade until the sutures were not there. Boston. London. Chad. So, three. Each was different but the point was the same: resolution. With Lauren, though...Lauren had just left. She wouldn't communicate. After that night, he'd never seen her again. She had undercut the timeline. She had not given him the space he needed to convince her in order to get to his resolution.

At the very least, talking to her was important. Before his baby was born, talking to her would be important. He just needed to do it before his baby was born, because that felt like an important marker. Then everyone could move on. This all could be over. For good. Once his baby was born, it could end.

He had to pay for late registration at the conference, which was irritating and unfair.

〰〰〰

Your name's Bob. You're on an airplane. You're going to see your kid before the start of his semester because you feel guilty as fuck for what happened at Christmas and you've never actually gotten around to seeing him "in his element," a phrase he's picked up in the last year or so as he's gotten more sophisticated with his goddamned guilt trips, a nightmare you were sure you'd woken up from forever when you finally, wisely, divorced his mother. Apparently you'll have the pleasure of navigating the same sea of bullshit until you die. She passed it down to him. Perfect.

You're drunk right now, here, on the plane. But you're aware that it's a problem, like a problem with the rules, and so because of that awareness you've got it completely under control, it's not like this will be some incident, some *terrorist* incident, hilarious, no drunk white man has ever been accused of colluding with al-Qaeda. What are you? A member of the Taliban over here? You're shaking your head. You'll be sober when you land.

You will have one drink, as you have an extra hour in Chicago.

Flights. You think about flying. Everyone's a nightmare when flying. The human comedy at its worst. You do think of yourself as an amateur philosopher.

And you *definitely* should not have ended up stuffed into this sardine can next to this asshole with big shoulders, this guy who right now is staring at the tray in front of his eyes as though it's his mother's tit.

Just when you think this thought, the guy turns and looks right at you.

Creepy stuff.

〰〰

Will's mother was a professor of classics at UC-Davis. Her sole book, a redundant study of Aeschylus, sold 237 copies after an optimistic print run of 2,000. It was nominated for nothing and seems not to have been reviewed at all. Anywhere.

His father was a meteorologist.

〰〰

Say you're him.

In Madison, you land, rent a car, and check into a hotel. You call your wife to tell her you are safe. You tell her that the conference starts today, even though it doesn't start until Thursday, and then you boot up your laptop and look at the map, remembering how Lauren always was with maps. That neurotic string. Something hot about that. There is a small (digital) red pin sticking out of Lauren's address in St. Helens, Wisconsin.

It was not hard to find Lauren's address in St. Helens, internet being what it is.

You've had Lauren's address for a year.

You've thought about it.

You press another button and the red line appears on the map telling you how to get to her apartment. It's basically a straight line to the east.

The internet is amazing.

You try to watch television.

You wonder if you should write to Lauren.

Write her a long letter. A letter explaining everything in great detail and also serving as an apology.

That could close the circle.

You begin, but you then remember that you already did something like this. It would be suspicious to do it again, now. You think.

〜〜〜

You leave for her backwater hillbilly town at dawn. You can't sleep anyway — not well, at least. When you have managed to sleep, you've only dreamed of fire. You're in some kind of new place, past where you've been before. You are afraid, but curious.

The town is exactly what you expect it to be, so much so that you start laughing as your car stealthily finds its way to the downtown area, and the first thing you see is a store that calls itself an apothecary and that has a Harley-Davidson parked in front of it. You wonder who this Saint Helen was, what she could have done or how she could have been killed to draw the attention of the people of this place. These people. Midwesterners. Good God. They may as well blow it all up, you think.

You park on Lauren's road, near her building, and as you wait in the car, drowsy now, you continue the thought: First of all, Helen probably got hung upside down for a long time. Probably impaled by many, many arrows after about six hours of hanging there, all the blood pooled in her brain and her chest. You imagine Helen popping like a water balloon full of blood when the arrows start to hit, and in this fantasy you are actually one of the people shooting the arrows, which is confusing until you realize she's dreaming, and by that you mean you are dreaming.

You wish you had some coffee. But you don't want to leave and miss her.

Which is a wise choice. Wise.

She comes out just past nine.

You are stymied, hit hard by love for a moment, leaning forward, holding the steering wheel with both hands as you watch her, forgetting that this is an undercover operation. You imagine yourself with a whole bag of peanuts in your lap, which is something a stakeout professional would have had along. Lauren is angelic; that's the word that goes through your mind. You feel a deep ache for having let the relationship crumble in the way that it did. For giving in. For hurting her. How could this have happened? How could you have been this foolish, so blind as to not see that when it came down to the nitty-gritty numbers, the statistics of it all, you were not going to find, ever, the same exquisite combination of the exact kind of beauty you respond to along with intelligence and submission in another human being? You simply were not. And she could make you laugh. Sometimes.

You should be hiding, though. You slink down. She is walking by on the other side of the road with a backpack on her back. You slink way down.

When she has passed, you consider your options. It's clear that it will not do to follow her in the car, as this would lead to a kind of slow prowling that would be noticeable, and so you get out of the car when she turns the corner, and, with your hands in your pocket and your heart pounding in your chest, you begin to walk down the street behind her. Will you talk to her now? But what possible explanation could there be for your presence in her town? There isn't one. There is one for Madison, not here. You have to be smart, now. Be smart.

You watch from far away as she enters a coffee shop. You mind your own business and wish you had coffee as well. But Lauren is in the coffee shop.

Then she's moving again, and you are slinking and undulating and minding your own business.

She goes toward the river.

She walks over the bridge to get over the river.

So do you.

She goes into the library.

You think for a long, long, long time, staring out across the street.

◇◇◇

But are you actually screaming during the drive back to Madison? Are you screaming? If you actually *are*, you stop yourself, then start scrabbling at the radio in search of NPR.

Who in the *fuck* was she talking to? There? Really? Who in the *fuck* would she sit with for that long, and talk to — for *that* long.

She is your wife.

~~~~

You call the person who is technically your wife from the hotel room. You've eaten dinner somewhere, at some restaurant. You have been reasonable throughout every conversation and you ate in an extremely civilized manner and you paid properly and even saved the receipt because you will be expensing everything on this trip. You appear normal. But there is a great anger now. And it is rising.

~~~~

But you are restless. The thought of another man, Lauren with another man — somehow this contingency never occurred to you, as though in order to put that phase of your life to rest you necessarily have had to think of Lauren as not here, not continuing forward in time without you, but dead.

You have been imagining her as dead.

But now you're seeing she is not.

You consider a pay-per-view movie and scroll through the options, but you can find nothing appealing.

You decide to go out.

Riding the elevator, you laugh to yourself as you remember that you're here for a conference and realize that you've forgotten what it's about. But you only chuckle, actually. You're in control of this situation.

You find what looks like a crowded street that soon becomes more crowded. It reminds you of Telegraph in Berkeley, how you'd always been jealous, when you went there to see friends, how you wished you'd chosen Berkeley instead. More exciting. More free. No matter.

You pick a bar, one that contains literally hundreds of drunken idiot students. They are spilling out of the door, even out of some open windows. They are an infestation. Inside, there are no lights but the colored lights of signs on the walls and the dimmed spotlights above the bar itself, each casting a yellow cone down onto the five or six moving, tattooed young people serving the hordes around them, wordlessly converting their extended wads of cash into sloppy drinks in plastic cups. What is the music? It is so loud that you experiment with speaking in your normal voice as you wait in the crowds at the bar, holding your money at the ready but calm about it, as you're older, you've become quite mature, as you don't need to lean and yell and plead with anyone at this point in your life, and you find actually that your hypothesis is correct: you can't hear your own voice. You remain accurate. True sound doesn't even get to your ears. You smile, wonder at the strange physics. Someone in front of you leaves with drinks and you step forward. You look right and down and see that there is a girl beside you, looking at you and laughing. Her eyes are enormous and her cheeks have turned bright red with the heat of the crowd. She has a mass of half-formed brown dreadlocks piled atop her head and she is wearing a black tank top. You realize, after a moment, that she's seen you talking to yourself, and that's why she's laughing. You smile back at her and lean down and say, very loudly, using the wells of testosterone at your disposal to project it, "I can't believe how loud it is in here! What do you want? I'll get it for you."

She has turned her head obligingly to listen, which can only be a good thing, and after you ask she says she wants a vodka and cranberry juice and you nod and hold up a finger — pause — and decide that it's time to be assertive, as you are, after all, surrounded by children, and you push forward through a crack and you are enormous and looming, you see yourself in the mirror behind the bar, you see the size of your shoulders and the tininess of the boys around you, and your voice is booming and magnanimous as you order three double vodka cranberries, you don't know why you choose three, and you slap the cash down and give the girl an enormous tip, it was a fifty you put down, because that's the man you are, and you gather the drinks and turn and take them back to the girl, who is waiting for you nearby and who laughs when she sees your bounty. "Do you have a friend here?" she yells, taking one of the drinks, and you shrug, it's actually unbelievable how casual you are about everything, and you say, "I thought it would just be easier to share this one instead of going back! When we're finished!"

She likes you, it's obvious, and she's plainly already intoxicated, and by the time you're sharing the third drink you are standing so close to her that you could probably lower your chin and rest it on her head as though it's a tabletop and you are a dog.

You talk about everything and it's all very interesting. You go back for more drinks. She's waiting for you again. She says something and you begin to laugh hysterically because you're certain it was a joke even though you have no idea what she said. Her response to your laughter indicates that you've guessed right. After you finally catch your breath she says, "Come outside with me so I can have a cigarette. Come on. Who *are* you?" She takes your hand as she leads you through the bar and you see her exchange a long glance with another girl standing against a post, and the girl looks at you and gives you what seems like a lurid smile and you sense that something positive has been communicated. She has signed off with her guardian friend. That's it.

She does smoke, but the two of you walk, no waiting around — first down the crowded street and then a side street, then a darker side street. At the door, as she fits the key in the lock, she says, "So lucky. My roommate is completely in Eau Claire right now," and you are stymied for a moment by the concept of "completely" being anywhere, how this implies that incomplete presence is possible, and you know she is just speaking in idiom and what have you but you think she might be onto something profound.

Soon you're completely fucking her in her bed, and she insists on being on top, which you realize is what she thinks of as domination, very cute, the way she's pressing your elbow against the pillow with no real strength whatsoever. She has all along only ever been fucked by boys, the same castrati man-children you saw trying to order drinks at the bar, but you sense that she's someone who might be bigger than that, have some broader intuition about it all. Maybe it's the dreadlocks. But for the moment you lean back and close your eyes and reach up and hold her tits and ribs and enjoy the sound of her moans, which are inconceivably loud, given what you're doing, but you open your eyes and see that she has indeed gone off to that other place where women go, her eyes half closed and head tilted, ass bouncing in good time, hands down on the center of your chest now, and you think: I hope I do not have a daughter. Do *not* let the baby be a girl.

You lick your thumb and reach behind to her ass and press it up against her anus, which certainly improves her posture and makes her big cat eyes pop open for a moment, and you say, "Okay?" and she nods, nothing to say, she is cool about your thumb up her ass, sure, man, so you let her thrusts slowly do the work, each thrust allowing the thumb a little farther in, and the pitch of her moans goes incrementally up as they become more like gasps. Then she says, "Take it out, take it out, your fingernail is super-long," and — like a coward — you remove it as you feel her cunt tighten its grip with a series of stutters and she comes, comes pretty gloriously, dreads now hanging down beside her cheeks like she's Predator, hands on her bed next to your ears, and with her ass in the air from the shift you push up and feel yourself coming too. As you do, she lowers her mouth onto yours, and you hear yourself moaning as well, but moaning into her skull, which creates a slight echo that's fairly surprising.

Perhaps you could go away with her.

Again you dream of fire. This time it's the burning of the camp in Chad; it's a specific fire. You see a pitch-black man on a pitch-black horse swinging a machete, and it all makes you think of the Apocalypse, the same as you felt when it happened. You are pulled from sleep when you see a refugee infant, perhaps Zara's unborn daughter, your daughter, engulfed in flames, lying in the dirt, get run over by a pickup truck, and when this happens you immediately reach over and find the girl's warm, sleeping body and turn it on its side and you push your cock into her and lever her up until she is on her knees on the bed, only waking now, coming to with her forehead pushed down into the pillows and your enormous hard dick in her, and instead of talking she greets consciousness by moaning again, acknowledging what is happening to her and agreeing to it by placing both palms down on the mattress's edges and gripping the corners, the moans muffled a little this time by the pillow as she straightens her posture, and her hips and ass rise up higher. From this angle and the way that you've got her bent, you can drive downward, far deeper than last time, and you can soon feel yourself so far inside of her taut, immaculate, immediately wet pussy that you pull back on her hip bones like they're handles and you wonder for a moment if you will damage organs doing this, pushing as hard as you're pushing, not necessarily strong thrusts but sustained force with each cycle, slowly pushing farther in. You find yourself wishing that your cock was in her ass instead, but trying to do that, who knows how things could go wrong, who knows whether you'd be able to get it anywhere near as deep as it is now or how long it would take just to convince her, and so you close your eyes and imagine it instead, then tell her that you're imagining it, and she says nothing, which you take to mean a refusal to actually let you do it and she simply continues holding on to the corners of the bed and you increase the speed of your thrusts, and her deeper moans go to higher-pitched calls or cries or something, bursts each time, and when you come this time you find that you've lowered a little and are holding her quadriceps now, not her hips, and her feet are down alongside your knees. This time, you let yourself make a lot of noise. This time you fall asleep and there are no dreams at all.

Then it is hours later, and you are moving in the shadows and the darkness, collecting your things, trying to remember where you are, wondering if you should attempt to fuck her a third time. You step on a cat. You distinctly hear someone say, "See you later, random fuck king," but then again, you are standing in the lobby of your hotel, and the sleeve of your shirt is on fire, and you're waving it wildly, trying to put it out, until the elevator swallows you and water, a relief, splashes down on you from above.

You wake up in your hotel bed. It's 6:00.

You sit up.

You have to go to St. Helens.

~~~~~

It turns out you are lucky you got up and got moving when you did because you have not been parked on her street for more than ten minutes after your frantic drive to the backwater town when Lauren comes out and stands on the corner and he, the man, pulls up in a car, a Nissan — of course — and she gets in and the two of them drive off together. Just as you are with everything else, you are skilled about the way you signal and pull away from the curb and remain three cars behind them as you follow them out of town. Where is it that they could be going? She had a bag over her shoulder, which makes you furious, the more you think about it, because going away with somebody and leaving a town for another town is an intimate thing. Extremely intimate.

They are getting on the highway. They are going back the way you came.

Who is this fucking guy? You wonder again, yes, you're mad, and then you realize — see through the anger, see better — that there needn't be a big mystery about any of it, actually, and that a good PI or FBI agent or spook or whatever it is you've become would simply run the numbers, whip out the pad and run the numbers, take down the numbers and run them through the system, and so you accelerate a bit and get closer and you do it, you read the license plate out loud, you say, "R-N-J-two-three-eight," out loud, which is the first step, but then you look around and you have no notepad and you decide that this means you will not be able to take down the numbers. Expertly, you drift back through the light traffic and let them get away from you, all the while saying, "R-N-J-two-three-eight, R-N-J-two-three-eight, R-N-J-two-three-eight." But don't be tricked. You'll need to remember the numbers for later, but also remember that it's an *Illinois* plate. You saw. No, man, you did not fool me. There's a trick to this. But you won't forget.

They drive to Madison. You follow them to Madison. It's too good to be true, because of course you realize what this means, don't you, you realize that it will have to be today, that you'll have to have the conversation with her today, now, because it's here, now, when your cover is most credible, because you are supposed to be here, you're actually registered for the conference, and now they are here, and she is here. For a moment you attribute it to good fortune, but as you watch them enter a parking ramp and choose not to follow them in and to instead park on the street, where there is a spot right there, you see it for what it is, for the first time in your life you catch sight of the larger matrix, the matrix you did not know you did not know was there, you see it for what it is, the embodied code that lies beyond the subjective, which is the nonlinear landscape that is out of time and perception.

You sense the great importance of the insight, even though it also seems a little crazy, but you follow the thought: they have come back here *because* this is where you'll be able to most naturally approach her, and you received the e-mail advertising the conference *because* she would be here on this exact day, and the idea of coming lingered in your mind *because* this was what would make it work, and what has happened thus far has happened thus far *because* what happens has always has happened, and the feeling you get when you make a choice to do something is only a type of blindness, *because* it's already decided, it's not an accurate assumption, and whether or not you push in one direction or another for however many years it simply *does not matter in the least*, because reality is shaped like a homeostatic landscape of rolling hills and people are tantamount to large ball bearings and they inevitably are going to collect in certain pockets together because *that is the shape of reality already.*

You put your hand on the wheel. Could this be true?

You consider running out into the street and telling whomever you can find, but you know — a cool and collected part of you knows — that this will ultimately hurt your credibility, that raving about something hurts anyone's credibility, that being "crazy guy" hurts your credibility, that despite the balls rolling through the hills, the *small things still matter*, but in their way, in a different and important way.

Because there is a deep natural trend toward harmony, a trend but not a law, and you turn and start going through the papers in the backseat, looking for that goddamned ID badge you know you have here somewhere.

∿∿∿

Yes, you are going to kill him.

After you walked away, you found a coffee shop and, in the bathroom, you dabbed at the blood with a paper towel.

It wasn't much of a blow, really — the surprise of it was what put you down onto one knee. But you're proud of yourself for how you handled the situation, all things considered. In the end, you were the reasonable one. He lost his temper.

And after all, what use is anger anymore? Anger is an emotion of the blind. You know — you truly know — that you will never feel anger again. You'll be killing him for different reasons entirely. Essentially intellectual. It's hard to see how you could possibly have a reasonable conversation with Lauren when a person like this is around.

You drive back to St. Helens. This time you're not following them, there's no need to rush, you know that the landscape will pour you into the proper place together, so long as you follow the pathways and do not bother pushing hard against the energies in the air, which will carry you on their own. You spend a peaceful half hour in the park, talking to a statue of a wizard using only your brain.

You spend dusk looking at the river.

Once it's dark, you walk back in the direction of Lauren's

home, wondering if now will be the proper time, but when you get there, her truck isn't anywhere on the street, and all the lights in the building are dim. You look up at her window for quite some time and try to smell her. She's not here, you think. If she were I would be able to smell her. She would not be here. She would be with him.

What had she called him? You touch your forehead delicately, soothingly. It will come. The name will come.

And you are right.

It comes.

The name is Ben.

Peaceful with the flow, because you know the next part as well, you continue stroking your forehead. Information. You have it. What were the letters and numbers on the license plate? You are calm about it. Those will come too.

Well? What were they?

Do you remember?

Can you go back?

There is no need.

So you'll use the internet next, of course, that's how this will go. Where is your laptop? Back at the hotel in Madison.

It wouldn't be right to go all the way back there. And so there will have to be another way. Where is the internet?

You nod now. There will be a *library*, and they'll have the internet at the *library*.

Someone honks at you, and you see that you're standing in the middle of the road, nodding.

You get out of the way.

You wave at the man who honked.

The man looks pleased and waves back.

~~~~~

It takes you all of thirty minutes to find the address. Another sign that you're simply doing your job, which is to follow the energies.

It's not so simple as just entering the license number and taking out your credit card and paying the site. The same gaudy OnlineSnooper site, in fact, that you used to find Lauren's address last year. There are steps. There is sleuthing to do on your end, there is a right way. For example: They tell you you need a library card if you want to use the computers at the library, and you nod obligingly, take out your wallet, and hand over, very casually, Eric's driver's license, which of course you stole last week for this very reason, despite not knowing then that this would be the reason. And later, when you find that the car is registered to a Benjamin Hanson but that his address is near Chicago, in a land called Peregrine Park, you don't panic, you don't immediately stand up, convinced that you have to now drive there, because probably, probably, he lives here in town — otherwise he would not have picked her up *in the morning* for their journey to Madison. And so next you pay for another background check on *him*. And surprise, surprise. He is a felon.

According to the report, this man lives in Portland, Oregon. But that's not right either.

For a few minutes, you're entirely stumped by the puzzle, but you're not concerned.

Life will give it to you. Even as an announcement comes over the PA telling you that the library will be closing in ten minutes, you're not concerned.

It will come.

And it does. Again.

It's very simple.

You type "Benjamin Hanson" AND "St. Helens" into the search field on the browser.

The top result is from the news.

Two months old. An obituary. Dennis Hanson. He is survived by so-and-so and so-and-so and his nephew Benjamin. The address for the wake, Dennis Hanson's home, is printed at the very end.

You highlight the address and click Copy.

You put it into MapQuest.

You print the map.

~~~~~

Now you are in the catbird seat, now there is no hurry — nobody is going anywhere. And the landscape will push you at the proper moment. And so you'll do a little walking. You'll get pulled toward the river and look down at the dark water for a long time, because rivers, you sense, are extraordinarily important. You'll cross the bridge and follow the river walk for almost a mile, until it becomes a dirt path and you are on the outskirts of town. Not pretty here. You look up and see a bridge and imagine jumping off it.

What you should do, really, is find an emergency room and walk into it. You are not well. You know this. You do know this.

The river is a gorgeous thing, though. What is it called, do you think?

You go into it and swim.

The water shows you the future. It shows you what will happen later. It comes in a fantasy, too, involving a complicated apology to a number of different women, because you will eventually come to see, while in the bed, in the place, convalescing, that perhaps, well, that there could have been other ways to let it come over you, that it hadn't had to — that it was possible that what you did to the different women served as more of a *hindrance* to the process because it relieved an important pressure and had you just resisted and remembered that — well. You will think about apologies. You will. And you will think that you will perhaps one day compose one for each of them. Not Zara, because you can't. You will have to write something for Lauren. An apology, real this time.

But you will wonder: Did you fail or succeed? Ultimately? The answer will elude you and it eludes you now, swimming here in the center of the river, looking up at the buildings. Succeeded in that you will have properly unshackled yourself and stepped onto the appropriate plane, but failed in that you were plagued, from time to time, by uncomfortable moods and states that caused you agitation that you will believe are related to the issue of apology and perhaps that you are doing something deeply wrong. No one will listen to you. You will understand. You will wait patiently, too, for the day when either Valerie or Lauren — you will hope it won't happen on the same day, of course, because it would be painful for both of them — come to you to discuss their regrets from *their* side of things. There will be a right way to let Valerie down and a right way to let Lauren down, but the speeches will both amount to the same message: We traveled together for a brief time, like two leaves fallen into a river, floating side by side, but the inevitable and inscrutable factors at play, such as wind, mass, saturation, and water temperature, have made us drift apart. Misery arises from the denial of the routes the natural order has already chosen for us. We can't resist the grooves. Pain comes from attempts at change. Please, both of you. I loved you both. It's time for us to part.

Choice.

~~~~~

You've made some kind of error, perhaps, as it's now day and you've woken up in a soft bed of mud beneath an old iron railroad bridge. You are filthy.

There's mud in your hair and caked beneath your fingernails and when you stand, you see that you're surrounded by waves of lines, claw marks in the mud. You don't remember exactly why it seemed to be the thing to do, but you realize you should go. This is exactly the kind of behavior that might raise some eyebrows.

(However, you're very careful about it — you're sure to check for your keys and your wallet.)

Now is the time, you think, walking through the brush along the river, trying to find the trail.

You don't know where the fuck you are.

You know where the valley dips.

~~~~~

You look at the red Honda for a long time as you stand beside the mailbox — the mailbox that is decorated with a colorful string of triangular flags and which serves, you shrewdly observe, as the anchor for three yellow balloons. The Nissan isn't here.

Nothing really makes sense until you take a few more steps, move past the pine trees, and see the white sign planted in the yard.

The white sign says:

OPEN HOUSE

You get it. You cross the driveway, cross the yard. Once again, objective reality has provided you with a cover and a reason to be here. Okay. It's all downhill. Everything is downhill. Remember the slope and just go with it. You gather yourself at the doorstep, wondering how it will unfold. Because you as a part of mankind are still linked to the subjective experience of it all. Does it matter that you have no weapon? No. You'll kill him with your hands, which are so glowing and powerful that, you realize, they have always been meant to strangle somebody like Benjamin Hanson. Right around the neck. Air, not blood. And then you see it again: not somebody *like* Benjamin Hanson. This Benjamin Hanson.

You should go to the emergency room.

You should not go into this house.

Go to the ER, Will.

You raise a fist.

You knock.

But the latch isn't fastened, and the door drifts open.

You don't like it.

You expected to see a few people milling about, looking at the built-ins (very nice) and glancing at papers. You expected a table of cookies.

Instead, you've found an empty house and a door that is ajar. When is a door not a door? You smile. But you remember that this is serious.

One hand goes to your pocket.

"Anyone home?"

Nothing.

You wait; listen. You look at the living room. The light is good.

You look at the stairs.

You do not like how this feels.

Here is when you find the woman.

You've gone through a door. She is sitting on the bed, legs crossed, looking through a large binder. You have been silent on your way up the stairs, and she only now realizes that you're here. When she sees you, she gasps and jumps a bit, her hand goes to her chest. But then she smiles. "Are you here for the open house? I'm sorry. I left the door open, didn't I?"

"Yes."

"It's actually not until tomorrow."

This is a test. This is new. This has to be a test.

The answer is obvious.

You nod nicely, go down the stairs, and go into the kitchen. Where? Under the sink. No, that's not correct, but then you go through a few drawers and there you have it. There are also kitchen knives, and you take one of those. You have the things. And it's just as you've fully outfitted yourself that she comes down the stairs, sees you there, sees what you have, and starts to scream and turn.

You get to the door as she does and you slam it closed, hand on the wood over her head, just as she tries to pull it open. She is a small person. It is not hard to get her down. You set the knife aside as you tape her hands together, then tape her feet together. Then you tape her mouth, because she is making too much noise, but you realize as you do that you'll need to talk to her. But at least she's silent as you carry her back up the stairs and dump her on the bed.

You've always had a good bedside manner.

You remember the knife and go back and get it, then return to the room.

You kneel beside her.

You remove the tape.

She starts to scream.

"Calm down, calm down," you say.

This doesn't help at all. She keeps screaming. You explain to her, over the screams, that you need to ask her some questions, but if she doesn't quiet down, you're going to put the tape over her face again and cut her. You're perfectly happy to wait her out.

She quiets down.

You add that you have no interest in raping her or hurting her, actually, because you don't, you don't do that sort of thing, you were just trying to get her to quiet down.

"Well, what, then?" she says. "What? Who *are* you?"

"I'm looking for someone named Benjamin Hanson," you say. "He may have been with a woman named Lauren."

"Jesus Christ, what did Ben *do* out there?" she says.

"I don't follow," you say.

"You're not from the West Coast?"

"No. Well, yes. Yes."

"Who are you?"

"Do you know where Ben Hanson is?"

You stare at each other for a long time.

"I will eat your foot in front of you while you think about it, if you'd like," you say, pointing.

She closes her eyes; revulsion. Fear. Only a tactic, you think. Means to an end.

"I have a kid," she says. "Please."

"It's up to you," you say.

She opens her eyes.

"Downstairs in my bag," she says, "there's a folder with copies of the specs of a property. A cabin. It's up north, in the UP. The address is there. There's a map."

She is sorry but she has no choice. You see this and are sympathetic.

"What's the UP?" you ask.

"The Upper Peninsula," she says. You keep staring. "Of Michigan," she adds.

"And that's where they went?"

"Yes."

"They're there now."

"I think so."

"How long does it take to get there?"

"I don't know. Six hours."

Of course. Because it is perfect.

"When did they leave?"

"They were leaving when I got here," she says. "Two hours ago, maybe."

You look at the floor, think it through.

"When is the open house?" you ask.

"What?"

"When does the open house begin?" you ask. "You said tomorrow. What time?"

"At noon."

"I'm going to have to leave you tied up here until then," you say. "I apologize. I need the time."

"Are you — what is wrong with you? Are you actually — are you completely fucking insane?"

"I'm sorry?"

But she just breathes and stares, this woman.

You use the duct tape to secure her feet to the bed itself, then finish the roll up at her hands, making sure her fingers are encased in the lump as well. You get her a glass of water and help her drink. You find the map and the papers. You sense she was telling the truth. You go back into the other bedroom and say to the woman, "I'll leave the tape off your mouth. No one can hear you screaming outside anyway. The neighbors are too far. You've done the specs. You know."

"Why are you going up there?" she says. "What are you doing?"

You consider this.

"You'll have to pee in your dress," you say. "I'm sorry."

"Look," she says, and now her voice is nice, kind, warm. "You don't have to go up there. What's — what's your name? You don't have to hurt anyone."

You leave her there like that, even though you like the sound of what she said. But that's just subjectivity again. Susceptibility to flattery. Human things.

She is a spark plug, it's true.

Predictably, because it's needed, you also found a gun in her bag.

〜〜〜

There is no *time* (per se) as you drive north, through Wisconsin. You have never been here and you sense the many changes in the strata of the state as you cut directly up through its middle, bifurcating, as though you are performing surgery on the place, a straight line starting at the bottom, slowly drifting east after a city called Tomahawk. You inhabit each part of the journey simultaneously. There are faces in the windows of the cars you pass and the cars that pass you, each a portrait in a trapezoidal frame — taken together and out of time, they amount to a mausoleum of humankind through which you slowly stroll as you amass information on the relevant questions and topics: sadness, boredom, anticipation, heated conversation, chats, talks, silences, histories, pasts, loves, wanderings, helps, warnings, wanings, undisclosed reasons for daylong, weeklong, monthlong journeys to anywhere. Here are semitrucks braking hard at unexpected curves; here are pickups with the carcasses of dead deer visible beneath flapping tarps.

Your trip, this journey, this pilgrimage, whatever it may be, both begins and ends in a circle. But you are, you know, an expert in the field of concealing your new knowledge; when you wait for the gasoline to pump at a station, for example, nobody can tell how many times you attempt to swipe your new library card through the machine in order to pay before you realize what you're doing. What would your father say to all of this? The man was too small to comprehend where you are now. He'd say something about cumulous clouds, probably, but in that way he would be begging to offer a kind of unmentionable admiration for your transcendence. At least it will all soon be over.

A woman at another pump looks at you and you nod and you consider saying to her: *Please help me.*

It's during the nighttime portion of the spectrum when the first two fires begin to light the sides of the road on your behalf. You believe at first they are impossible — what fire jumps trees at 70 mph, and in perfect harmony with a driver? A particular driver? They seem to peter out in your rearview mirror and burn strong only in your peripheral vision. They light the road and make the darker parts of the trip more manageable. Evidence of this presents itself with the unfolding of earthly events: you don't make a wrong turn because you can't.

You reach a small town called Norway.

It's night, but the grocery store is open.

You tell the man you're looking for hard plastic ties. And no, not the colored ones you twist. The plastic kind that lock.

~~~~~

It makes perfect sense that they haven't yet arrived. You work it out — you know. You've passed them along the way because of your spectral efficiency. The paper has the combination to the lock.

You drive the car up the driveway, then past the cabin, farther into the woods. You drive it into the trees, as though you and it are one great and ancient metal door. So they won't see you.

You are in Michigan.

You wait the night.

You wonder what sorts of spirits once inhabited these woods.

You wonder what's become of them.

~~~~~

You find yourself standing in the woods, then, pointing the gun at his head.

You're wondering if you have good enough aim to hit somebody like this, considering you don't know what you're doing. You've never shot a gun and he is moving.

What is the reason for this again? You slow down for a second. You wonder it as he makes his way down the path and you remember as he approaches the wooden boathouse. You breathe deep, gather yourself. He would certainly otherwise interrupt the conversation you have to have with her. You remember how he hit you the last time you tried. Which is fine. Everything has its place. You're not angry.

And then the world — *again* — demonstrates for you that all of this has already happened, and that once you have inertia on your side, being what you are is no more difficult than running down a mountain. Or floating in the current of a river.

He is having trouble with the door, pulling at it, first with sharp tugs and then with a sustained backward lean.

You have stepped out of the woods and you're watching him do this over the orange dot at the end of the gun's barrel, captivated by his struggle with the door. He changes his stance and pulls with both hands. He changes his stance again. He mutters to himself, squats, studies the handle of the door. He is solving a problem.

He stands, takes a deep stance far from the door, his back to the river now, and tries again, straining so hard that you see the tendons in the side of his neck bulging.

The door comes unstuck with a sharp and quick moan.

This is a problem for him.

Off balance, your enemy Benjamin Hanson backpedals wildly, and you see his heel catch a good-size rock at the edge of the little ridge.

You now watch, fascinated, as he flips over backward.

You hear both the thud of impact and then a splash.

Amazed, you walk through the high grass and look down at the river.

And there he is, facedown in the water, silently drifting downstream.

You point the gun at him, but you realize there is no need to fire as the river has already killed him.

And what's more, if you do shoot, she'll hear.

You lower the gun and watch him drift, impressed by the power of the moment.

He's now thirty yards away. The river has done its work.

This is what it had been trying to tell you during your earlier conversation when you yourself went into the river in the other place. This was the message.

You plunge back into the woods.

〰〰〰

Later, you regret that you've broken her nose. You regret it when she comes to, raises her head from the table, looks at you with a face smeared with so much blood that she may as well be wearing war paint. It's in her hair, too, matting everything. It's disgusting, actually, and you don't know how you're supposed to talk to her like this. And yet this is what you wanted. Here she is. You can say it. What is it? She is breathing through her mouth, her lids half closed. Soon she discovers that her wrists are bound to the leg of the massive table, hands together down underneath, and so she'll have to sit in her chair and hug the corner and finally give you the attention she should have given you long ago. Before she left. She'll listen to you for as long as it takes you to explain yourself. You sit.

"Something something something," you try.

"Something something," she says. "Something."

"Something."

"Something."

What a very long, difficult, tedious conversation it becomes! But you *do* have her attention; this is working.

You keep talking.

"Something."

"Something."

"Something."

"Something."

You stand in frustration, brandishing the gun, telling her.

This goes on for what feels like hours.

You're not sure.

She doesn't seem to be afraid anymore, though, which makes this all easier.

You're not sure.

You sit down. Another reason you love her.

"I am not sick," you find yourself saying indignantly, and she watches you closely, realizing that she can see the frustration on your face.

"You are," she says. "You can't tell, Will. You have to trust me."

"No. I don't have to."

"You have to trust me."

You look out the window so she can't see your face.

And then it's clear. Finally. There's the last thing.

You go to the door, step out into the high grass, stare down at the river and the shack.

You turn back to her.

"Do you see it?" you ask Lauren. "Can you see it? Try telling me that I'm sick. Look."

You turn again and point down to it.

You feel much relief. You want her to see all the fire, because it validates this, so you go back inside, glad that she'll finally now be able to understand what you've been trying to say this whole time.

What you've been trying to say is that it's too much. You're not strong enough.

No one is.

IV

THE DELTAS

*When we try to pick out anything by itself, we find
it hitched to everything else in the universe.*

—John Muir

14

Alive!

An upward spin and a rise into the world you only learn about halfway up. It's the world you left, and at the moment you get the basics, the idea that you are you and you are living, you're confused again by the senses coming back — you see the sky but don't know what the sky is, you hear sounds but don't know words have meanings or that you might be the one making the gulping noises.

Coming to.

This is terrifying because you can witness the world as it is.

This is hell for a moment — having no self, for an instant, and seeing what the world is without the protection of a self.

This is a glimpse of hell.

When you get knocked out, you see it. Then you come back.

And in this case, in the river, now, floating facedown, my first thought: *I am not breathing.*

Or rather: I am breathing water. Which doesn't work.

I roll, I am cold.

I'm coughing. I am floating.

I know I almost died.

I am Ben.

Eyes open.

~~~~~

I watch the trees slide down my field of vision, foregrounding the white sky.

It's pretty.

I cough more.

I am up north.

I know. I know, too, that my head hurts.

I concentrate on the pain. I struggled with the door...

I roll again.

I swim over to the shore, lips already blue.

~~~~~

Here is something.

Wayne and I, here on the shore of the Bright River, and Wayne leads me through the woods one hundred yards in the other direction. Eventually we come to a tree that hangs over the river, and he looks at me and nods. He has a backpack. I ask him what we are doing.

"Do you not think," he asks, taking the pack from his back, "that this tree is literally just asking us to make a rope swing?"

Now I can see the rope swing. Down there.

I'm there.

~~~~~

I get up on the shore and stand for a moment, wobbly on my feet, and then turn and look back upriver, where I came from.

I'm not sure where I came from.

I can't see the open patch of my uncle's property, can't see the boathouse. I floated all the way around a big bend, a good deal of it facedown.

I'm a ways away.

I'm not sure how or why I was in the river.

My eyes aren't working yet.

I look at my hand, then at the water. My vision is blurred, and I lean forward and put both hands on my knees and start coughing hard.

I puke a bucket of river.

～～～

Here is something.

It is January, and Lauren Sheehan has just left my house. I am sitting at a table, looking at the problems on the problem set, still smelling the lingering smell of her perfume, or her deodorant, or whatever it was. There is no more salsa left. My mother is in the other room talking on the telephone. I am looking at the problems but I am thinking about Lauren and wondering to myself why I have never really noticed her before. I am thinking to myself that she is uptight but that I like her.

My mother comes into the room.

"Well," she says. "That was your father. Apparently he has to go to Atlanta for a meeting."

"Tonight?" I say.

"Yes," she says. "Right now."

"Oh."

"I guess it's just the two of us," she says.

～～～

There is no path back along the bank. I start to pick my way up the hill through the trees, dense enough to provide good handholds. I have to go up instead of over.

I am slightly better.

What is Lauren thinking right now? I wonder. *Does she even know*

I'm not still down there hunting for my father's phone? And also: How long was I actually floating? How far was I? Or worse: What would she have thought if I'd just never come back? I would have been another Wayne. She would have had no idea. It would have just been a totally —

I am at the top of the hill. In the woods. And for some reason, I find it strange that I am standing in front of a tree.

There is something about the tree.

It's a white pine. It doesn't look right.

It looks too young.

It's too thin.

I look at it for a second, then turn toward the cabin. I'm at the top of the ridge now and I should be only a thousand yards away. I walk with my hand on the back of my head, looking right in front of my feet, breathing through my mouth.

I'm almost to the second car before I realize that it's there.

〰〰

Here is something.

It's yesterday morning, and Lauren and I are lying in bed. We're drinking coffee.

I say to her: "So. Listen."

"Listening."

"I feel like everything is fine," I say. "With the guy. I mean, I know. Scary. But I feel like you're fine."

"I don't think you get it."

"I mean, I know I don't know. But I'm just saying. I doubt he's coming back, I doubt there's any risk at all. But I have to go up north to do this thing with the ashes anyway. You should just come with me." I shrug. "Like two nights."

"The thing is, Ben," she says, "I'm credulous. I'm a credulous person."

"You keep saying that."

"Yeah," she says. "Because it's true."

"We'll go up north, we'll see some trees," I say. "It doesn't have to be about anything."

"I know," she says. "But it always is."

"Are you asking if I'm going to hurt you?"

"Yes," she says. "That's what I'm asking."

"No," I say. "I would not hurt you."

It's a blue Ford Focus with Rhode Island plates, and it looks new — brand-new.

I put my hand on top of the hood and look right. I can see the side of the cabin through an alleyway of trees. A few hundred yards away. The alley is wide enough to drive through. You could come up the dirt road, drive behind the cabin, and enter the woods. You could have . . .

I look toward the cabin again, then back and through the windows of the vehicle. In the passenger seat there is a pile of what looks like thirty or forty beef-jerky wrappers.

On the floor I see some papers with the Hertz logo. I see the open-house flyer Theresa e-mailed to me.

I know, looking at these things, that it's him.

I know that it's Will.

That she was right to be afraid.

That I was wrong.

That he's here, whoever he is, and that all of Lauren's stories are true and that Wayne's nightmare was true and that we are suddenly here, in it, inside of some other thing Will has made. This is not what's normal. This is waking up to flames, feet still up on Jeremy's desk. Or the time when there is no more perseverating and there is nothing left but what's raw and real. A naked bath of what's raw and real. What's more, there is no time to adjust.

He is still here.

And I go. I run toward the cabin in a low crouch and press myself against the back wall under one of the windows. The top of my head is pulsing now, and when I touch the egg, my fingers come back bloody. At the woodpile I swivel and get onto my knees, then rise up and look in through the window. I'm at the back — there's a second door here and a small room that houses the generator, camping gear, and a pile of old coats and hats. Through the open doorway I can see the main room and part of the table.

I see Lauren at the chair, arms wrapped around a stump table leg like she's tied up.

Alive, at least.

I can't see Will but I can see his hands moving everywhere with wild gestures and I can hear his emphatic voice.

He is talking about flames.

I hear him say, "I have been looking for the fire."

I can see he has his own gun.

I think: this man is insane and has come here to kill her.

I sit back down against the wall, not noticing the cold anymore.

Her gun. Where is her gun?

The gun. Or is the gun he has her gun?

If that is true, then there's no solution. But maybe it's not true.

Not in the car. It's in her bag. I think: You saw her bring the bag inside.

But it's now in there with them, which means I need something else. I need some weapon, at least.

All I have in my pocket is my Swiss army knife, which I take out and open. The big blade looks pathetic. I need a real weapon. Anything.

Or, I think, closing the knife, a way to get him outside. Away from her.

I look at the stack of logs that I'm up against and see the smear of blood my hair left behind where I'd been pressed against the wood. But this makes me think of the boathouse again.

Then I am running hard toward the Ford Focus and tearing back down the hill, through the woods, using the tree trunks to keep control.

~~~~~

I crash through leaves and make too much noise, but the cabin doors are closed and the sound of the river will be enough to cover it a little. Near the bottom of the hill I veer left toward the boathouse and creep around it on the outside, keeping it between the cabin and myself. You can see down to the boathouse if you walk out of the back door or out onto the cantilevered porch, so I stop for a moment, looking at the water, my back to the west wall. I will have to risk him seeing me. It will be two, three seconds. The door is open.

The boathouse is big enough to enter, so I'll be visible for only a few seconds as I come around the side and slip in.

I put my arm out and take the handle of the open door in my left hand, still protected from view. I see the rock my heel caught when I fell backward.

I take another few breaths, then go.

It's quick — quick enough, I think. I use the handle on the door as a pivot and swing around and into the dark, musty boathouse, pulling the door closed behind me as I get inside, careful not to slam it. There's a window, and enough light is coming in. I start scouring the place for a weapon. Anything.

Denny's old aluminum canoe takes up most of the space,

and on the other side of it there's a stack of paddles and a pile of old and rotten life preservers. In another corner I see the grill, a few half-empty bags of charcoal…I keep sifting…some cans of paint, paint thinner, fishing poles…up above on the shelves extra shingles, a cooler, some rope…an old weed whacker and a can of gas…there aren't any usable weapons, not really. Maybe a paddle? I think. But that would —

Consider the problem, though.

I think: Consider the actual problem, Ben.

Her gun is inside; she is tied to the table. I need to get him outside, out the front door. I don't need to go in armed, not if I can get him outside.

Get him to come down here. While I go up there.

Once he's out, go up and in.

Get the gun.

Maybe.

So the question: What will get him to come out?

I look again at what is here.

I think.

There is that.

I start dumping charcoal.

Then the gas.

I'm running back up the hill, through the woods, my hands so cold now I can't feel them anymore, just hoping that the boat-house won't go up completely before I have time to get inside the cabin. It will be only a few seconds. But there are more questions. Will he even go outside? Where is the bag, exactly, relative to either door? What will I do with a gun in my hands? I don't know how to use a gun, not really. She probably knows better. I am the Space Marine from *Doom*. But as I think these things through I also feel a certainty about it: I am not going to die here.

And then I can see, as I run from his car to the cabin for a second time, the black line of smoke against the sky.

And I can see, through the window, Lauren watching him in silence as he walks out the front door.

And I am inside.

Eyes wide and frantic, I'm saying to the back of her head in a hoarse whisper, "*Where is your gun? Where is your bag?*"

I see, and ignore, the smear of blood on her face when she turns to me. It breaks my heart but I ignore it.

I see her bag. In the corner.

I move.

I go past her.

I see my own hands fumbling with the zipper, then grabbing at the gun.

I see my hands trying to slide bullets into the holes, fingers shaking.

I hear Lauren, her own hoarse whisper: "He's coming."

"I don't know how to do this," I say, fumbling now with the last bullet.

"Lock it back," she says, looking at what I'm doing. "Lock it back. Flip it."

I lock the chamber — it clicks into place.

"Now *cock it*," she says. "Pull the hammer down."

I cock it and pull the hammer down.

I look at her.

I look at the door.

I am sitting in the corner with the gun and the bag, and immediately, I mean at exactly the moment I raise the barrel, he walks back through the door saying, "There's a beautiful —" and he sees me.

I shoot. Just as he's trying to lift his own gun.

He shoots. Just as he's falling to his knees.

Lauren, beside me, screaming louder than I have ever heard somebody scream.

I see the red coming outward from the dark new hole in his stomach, the stain a growing circle in his shirt.

He shoots before I shoot.

The bullet hits me somewhere on the wrist, then comes through the other side and I feel it in my ribs.

The gun is no longer in my hands, I see.

I slump back, see Will ten feet away, see him over my extended legs and my shoes, see him seated in a similar way, as though I am looking in a mirror.

He is holding his stomach, looking at me with great alarm in his eyes.

I am dying.

His gun is no longer raised.

I'm struggling to breathe.

He leans sideways, tips, and collapses.

But I'm also dying.

I think he is dead. But then he starts dragging himself out the door. There's elegance to the way his legs incrementally disappear. His legs are dead, I think. That's why. Look at how he's dragging himself.

And then he's gone.

I let my eyes close for a moment.

"Ben."

I open my eyes.

Lauren. Lauren is here and at the table, I remember. I am here.

"Listen to me," she's saying. She is calm. It's as though I am the dog. What was the name? She is calm and serious and stoic. I can't believe such a stern and authoritative voice can be coming from a face that bloody. It's beautiful underneath, something I might say to her. Her hair is as wet as if she were the one who had gone into the river. It's her blood. And there in the river, in the water, in the river that was the swimming pool, we found ways to be there, to be together underneath as well as on the top, both sides of it, what came before and what came after and the present in the middle, but also what is on the surface and what is underneath, face and story, name and nightmare.

He must have hit her in the head too, I think.

"Do not pass out, Ben. You cannot pass out."

And what else could I do?

"Do you hear me? Are you hearing me? I need you to respond, Ben. I know it feels like you don't want to, but you can. You have to listen."

It's odd. Yes, I do hear you, her. I think that. I breathe through my mouth, which leads to a gargle of blood at the back of my throat and the feeling that someone is pressing a sword through the right half of my rib cage and I think: Oh yeah. What is this text but a log of information, ordered, leading up to my own death? What has all this been but that?

"You have to cut me free, Ben."

Which is my uncle. Pain in the chest. First Wayne, then him. I open my eyes again. I had not realized I closed them.

"Ben, listen to me."

I nod.

I can.

"Okay," I say. "I'm listening."

"You have to cut me free. If you pass out, you're going to die. I can't help you like this."

Perhaps she's not calm after all, I think. I roll my head and try to keep focused on her. She's leaning so hard that she's not on the chair anymore. She's on her knees, hands stuck back over her own shoulder at the tree-trunk leg of the table. I can't imagine Denny building it. Can you imagine? I watch her pull against it. The table isn't moving at all. It's a motherfucker of a table. Trees. I mean, trees. I mean, you can't move it. She is trying to move it.

I am dying. I realize that I am dying. This is my death.

"It's okay," I say.

I flap my arm in her direction. This is when I see that I'm shot another place too. There on the left.

"It's fine," I say to her.

"You have to cut me free, Ben!"

It is so loud I have to close my eyes for a moment.

What I see is the thing. What could have been, what might have been. I remember Pierre the Jesuit on the hill. What was it that he'd whispered to me? I know that he was talking about my sister.

My eyes open.

"You have to cut me free so I can help you!"

I don't respond much, and she twists down and turns and starts kicking the leg of the table.

"It's not going to break," I say. "It's a tree."

I start to move. Kind of. I roll down onto my shoulder, at least.

"Just don't pass out," she says, looking over her shoulder at me. "Don't." Seeing that I'm moving now, a little calm comes back into her eyes.

"That's good," she says, smiling. "That's good. Stay awake so you can cut me out. Come closer. Come on."

I don't know what it is. Three feet, maybe. She's no more than three feet away from me. It's funny what life can come down to. Because now I think: This is not my death? And so strange what people can do if you give them time — do you remember what I said about the taps, the small adjustments? — a whole lifetime, to work at something. Or give them a minute; either way. What if I said to you: You. Person. Move three feet in your life. You'd think you could probably do it, right? Go around the world, drop a bomb on a stranger in a jungle, build a city, devise the chemical that goes in that bomb, cut somebody in half, hurt somebody, push somebody against a wall at the bottom of the stairs because you're angry, look at her, poison someone, behead a man for greeting you, hike a hundred miles over a mountain in a day. Develop a philosophy. Or: Go to the office and sit for a very long time, thinking about very little, imagining. Smoking a cigarette. Looking over. Looking at the garbage can, imagining, thinking: What would *that* be like? Not just that, then. Don't just imagine. Live it. You know? Do you know what I mean? Living out that fantasy?

I am resigned to die, I mean.

I think about Wayne, and how both of us will die at the same place, how unlikely that is. Haley had talked about the quadrants.

Haley.

"Do not pass out," Lauren says, talking now, not shrieking. "Listen to me."

I try not to, because now I am too tired.

"Don't stop."

And a little while later I am scraping at the knife in my pocket, because I am close enough, it seems, which is a miracle.

Another impossible task, once it is out: opening the scissors. Because now I am starting to believe her.

Reach up and fit the blades around the plastic tie.

Cut.

Hands come free.

Fall down, eyes close.

15

Trees

Lauren could do only so much. The other reason I didn't die on the floor of the cabin was Grant. He had been the one to find Theresa back at Denny's house, still with her hands and feet taped together, still on the bed, just as Will had left her. Grant came for the open house at noon, wearing a suit and tie, having no intention of actually making an offer on the property, coming just to talk to Theresa and, God willing, so long as bravery was with him, ask her out. Find some way to ask her out. Because to Grant she'd always seemed like an interesting woman, he'd told me that, and she was a mom, so she could be a mom, which made so many things so much easier. He'd talked to her a few times at the league and it had gone okay, but he'd never made it very far. He'd hung around, watching. Grant's crush saved me.

He came fifteen minutes before anyone else got there, which was also tremendously helpful for Theresa, as it meant she didn't have to be found tied up and dehydrated by someone who actually intended to make an offer.

Grant called the police, and soon Theresa was frantically explaining to them Will's destination. They tried to call me, but nothing — my phone had zonked out in the pool. The sheriff called another sheriff up north, who sent two squad cars to Denny's cabin. On their way to finding Lauren holding a blood-soaked towel over the hole in my stomach, they found Will down at the bottom of the hill.

〜〜〜

The first hospital was in Marinette. Later that same day — still Saturday — a helicopter brought me to Green Bay, where a surgeon dug around in me. It was there that Lauren says I finally stabilized, as there was some concern, up in Marinette, that I would go into cardiac arrest.

I missed all of this.

I have one memory of being in the helicopter, looking up, and seeing Lauren nearby, white tape across her nose, big headphones on her head.

She didn't know I'd woken up and that I was lying still, looking at her. She was looking out the window and down into the darkness.

By the time the surgeries were over and I was able to stay awake for any length of time, both my parents, Lauren's mother, and Lauren's brother, Bobby, had arrived. I have the oddest collection of memories from the next days, when everybody was nearby: my mother in the room with me, knitting in the corner; Haley, laptop in lap, or under arm, or in a bag with the strap slung across her shoulder, joking with me that the family always knew that I would be the one to get shot first; my father, more serious than I'd ever seen him, sitting with a crossed leg, absently working the crossword between long monologues regarding the board at Hedley and his various business transactions. He was so forthcoming about business, in fact, that on the third or fourth day after my surgery, I asked him if there had been some kind of big change in his attitude about life because of what had happened to me. Whether he was going to start recruiting me to work for him again. A half joke. But it sure seemed like something was different.

He laughed. "I think a felony history might create some road-blocks," he said.

"Reduced charges," I said. "Besides, it wasn't on purpose, and besides, I saved someone too. It's a wash."

"Oh yes. Excuse me."

"You know what I thought, though," I said. "The thing with Denny's house."

"What?"

"I thought you were going to try to get me to work for you," I said. "Eventually. So long as I didn't somehow fuck up."

"Your mother would have probably liked that."

"That didn't go through your mind?"

"No," he said. "Are you actually interested?" He tilted his head the other way. "I've assumed — perhaps since that's what you told me — that you have no interest in what I do."

"That's not totally true," I said. It wasn't, but I understood what he meant, and I understood the assumption. My father made top-tier decisions for a corporation I'd seen throughout my twenties as contributing to the miseries of millions of people.

But then again, this was the fundamentalist view, this was why it was so easy to be single-minded about right and wrong. I had never said to my father: What you do for a living hurts people, let's discuss it. What you do for a living, and the degree to which you are compensated for it, is shameful. To him — and not just because of his need to be argumentative but because he truly did believe it, and my perspective wouldn't make sense to him — better instruments in an airplane was a necessarily good thing, and chemical products very obviously *reduced* pain and saved lives, ultimately.

"No?" he said. "Not totally?"

"Not totally," I said. "I know it's complicated."

"It is," he said.

"Yes," I said, looking at him. "It is. Isn't it?"

He did not know what I meant.

~~~~

Lauren was around the whole time.

Her nose was broken, and she had two black eyes to go along with the white horizontal stripe of tape across the bridge of her nose.

"You look like a raccoon," I said to her one day.

"I know."

She was staying in a nearby hotel; her mother and brother had already come and gone. I watched her as she took the chart from the foot of my bed and read my reports. She was eating a carrot. A full-size carrot, Bugs Bunny style.

"How am I?" I said.

"You're doing well," she said, distracted. "Reasonably well."

She took a loud bite of the carrot.

"How are you?"

Her eyes ticked up.

I meant everything, of course. But I could tell: She'd gone back to the turtle in the shell.

I thought of saying more, but I didn't know what.

"How's the hotel?"

"It's fine."

She returned to the chart.

We hadn't talked about it — not enough, anyway. She'd spent at least a half hour in the room with Will, tied to the table, and I still didn't know what he'd said to her. Or what she had said to him. Or what Will had come up there to ultimately do to her. Maybe he told her. I didn't feel right about asking. Not yet, at least.

There was also the uncomfortable fact that I had killed someone she'd once loved.

That.

"My dad is saying he wants to come down," she said. "I don't really know what to tell him."

"Tell him to come down," I said.

"I'm not sure," she said. "We'll see."

She returned my chart to its caddy and said, "That reminds me. Do you want to stay here or move down to Milwaukee? You need another week, but we can take you closer to home, if you want."

"No," I said. "Here's fine."

She went to the other side of the room, where her purse was on a chair, and withdrew a small white box from it. "I got you the charger," she said. "BTW."

～～～～

What made it so hard to think about, for so long, was that I thought it was just one question. I thought it was: What happened to Wayne? But I shouldn't have thought about it like that. There were too many distinct questions packed into the one question, like a braided rope. You had to answer each in turn before you could answer one alone.

First, a question with its own branches: Why was Wayne up north that night?

And second, a question with many others: What happened to Wayne when he was up north?

Totally different things.

~~~~

For now, here's something:

My cousin Wayne sits in the cabin, eating dinner.

Maybe he's listening to the wind-up radio. Maybe he winds it.

He's in here.

It's cold outside.

Much, much colder than it was supposed to be. Wayne had heard the weather report before coming up and knew it would be warm early, then, the predictions said, it would be in the teens, probably not much snow. And that was the case when he arrived a few days before. Warm first. Then a little colder.

He had no trouble getting his car up the driveway and to the cabin. And he had a day or two of good weather. He did some things around the property.

He decided to stay a little longer.

Then the storm came, which on its own wasn't the worst thing in the world.

Nine inches of snow.

And it's gorgeous, worth it when he wakes up the next morning — pristine and perfect white all the way down the hill to the river, frozen over.

But the beauty makes him stay another day. And that is a day too long. The beauty of the snow and ice, out here, with almost no one else around. It's become dangerous.

It's a pretty time up here, he thinks, looking out, knowing that he made a mistake.

It's gotten cold.

Very cold.

My cousin Wayne can feel it rush in if he opens the door just for a second, as though outside the little tiny cabin, heated by just one small stove, an army of a million arctic ghosts stands waiting in the dark, each soldier silent. Whenever he opens the door, as many of them who can fit come rushing into the cabin in order to save themselves, and they bring their cold with them. If he steps all the way out, onto the frozen snowfall, solid enough now to hold his weight, he can feel it even more — he can feel his body crying to go back inside and feel how the exposed flesh on his neck doesn't register what it feels as *cold* anymore, how there is an illusion to the impression. The neck sends confused signals of heat and pain. Fucking awesome.

The power of this place is awesome, my cousin thinks.

It's dangerous to be here, there isn't any doubt. Real danger. But it's also interesting, this degree of isolation. No one could get to him if he needed someone. He's here, this is it. He's in it. You can feel what it might have been like for the people who inhabited these woods as their home, the Menominee, better wonder at the awesome and overwhelming power of the natural world. Wayne is no coward. Wayne wants to feel it. He especially wants to feel it now. That's why he's still here. Fuck it. He doesn't care about the world that's back down there. He doesn't care about jobs, about school, about people. About what his life might turn out to be. About meeting people. Knowing things. He doesn't care.

He probably shouldn't be here.

What, Wayne thinks, *have I done?*

Standing on the porch, feeling this feeling of his neck and considering all these things, my cousin Wayne looks over at his car, parked at the top of the drive. After the snow fell, he scraped it off, so it is not now encased in ice, at least. This is good, because if it stays this cold for too many days — and the radio is saying that it will, and that tonight it will reach forty below in Marinette, so who even knows about here? — his battery will be shot. And that will be a real problem, because that will mean hiking out, which is doable, but dicey. Very dicey. Another storm, another cold snap. Well, he knows the stories. People get lost a lot faster than it seems like they should. So the battery: he has to take it out of the car and bring it inside and keep it by the fire. Tonight. Now. He doesn't want to do it, but he doesn't have any choice. Not unless he wants to freeze up here.

He goes back inside, warms up. He smokes a joint.

He'll need a wrench. Maybe pliers.

He starts looking for his father's tools.

He avoids looking at the brown jacket hanging on the hook.

My cousin Wayne looks for the tools.

He looks at the jacket again, gets irritated by it, and in a flurry of movement stuffs it wholly into the stove, where it eventually catches.

He liked it.

It starts to smoke up the place. Stupid, but he doesn't care. He slams closed the iron door.

He thinks of the tools.

Soon, he's got it. He remembers his last visit here: the fall, his father. The last time they were up together. They'd worked on the boathouse and dock that weekend. October. Denny had left early. My cousin Wayne had stayed an extra day. On his way out, Denny reminded his son to bring up the tools.

Said: "Hey, chucklehead. Bring those up before you go, okay?"

"You got it."

Wayne, standing near the stove, smelling the burning jacket, is sure of it. He forgot. The tools are still down in the boathouse.

Which is a huge bitch right now.

Wayne puts on his hat, gloves, and jacket, and gets his

keys — on his ring there's a key for the lock on the boathouse door, which he hopes is not completely frozen. The thing sticks as it is.

He trudges down the hill through the snow.

He cannot believe how goddamned cold it is.

He thinks back to the conversation.

He's worried about it, but he finds, after some scrabbling, that the lock's not frozen. The metal inside is cold as fuck and swollen, but it's new from the fall and still lubricated well. He hears it click open, holds the keys in his left fist, tugs at the door.

It's stuck.

The door is always stuck. Why didn't they replace the door instead? Here's a piece of advice: replace the door that's always stuck. Wayne shakes his head.

Person: Have you ever watched someone attempt to solve a minor problem? I would wager you this: if you presented a hundred people with a sticking door, you'd get the same chain of behavior from each of them.

The door is stuck.

Open it.

Okay, you say.

First you yank. You give a couple yanks. When that doesn't work, you move on to sustained force. You try a few more yanks after that. You think: Okay. I got you, door. I know your thing. I will push in, then pull.

You try it.

That doesn't work.

You're getting frustrated. Eventually, maybe because of the mild frustration, you back up, widen your stance, and lean back so you can use all of your weight.

Which was what I did and which must have been what Wayne did too. And he went ass over teakettle too. Only now, back here in 1994, it's the dead of winter, the coldest night in twenty-five years, it's the underworld up here, he's alone, and Wayne catches his heel on the same rock I caught and plunges backward over the bank and disappears through the ice and into the freezing black water.

Shoop. Vanished.

The clock starts as his life begins to drain from him. The Bright is taking it away from him.

The whole place — river, woods, cabin, hill — is silent while he's under.

Wayne struggles underwater, then bursts up, gasping.

He cries out, his voice echoes across the property. Water freezes on his face the instant it touches the air. Legs cramped, body shutting down. The Bright's taking away his life.

And my cousin Wayne, trying to tread water, his torso now numb, knows that there's a good chance he's going to die here, which is an amazing, new, alien feeling suddenly there in his chest, something nowhere near any other feeling he's ever felt. Truly foreign. It may already be over. His mind goes up to the cabin, to the previous night, to the previous day. He thinks: What have I left unfinished? He goes through it, treading water like that. He thinks of his father. He thinks: Everything is finished, either way. He thinks: The jacket was the last thing. I should not have waited so goddamned long for that. He thinks: I should not have said a thing to him. He thinks: I should not have done it.

He's getting closer to the edge.

He thinks: I don't want to die.

The cabin is there. He can *see* it up at the top of the hill. It's warm. It's not far. It's *right there.* Some people deserve to die. Not him. This is not karma right now, this is not justice. This is not *that* happening to him, because that is not how it works.

My cousin Wayne, terrified now, struggles at the edge, clawing at the breaking chunks of ice with hands he can't feel, having to assume his legs are churning, working to drive him up and to shore but unable to feel them. He makes progress, but slowly. It takes too long. His body is cooperating, but it's using everything he has down here, in the water. He leaves too much behind.

My cousin Wayne does get to the shore. Eventually.

But here, out of the water, down on hands and knees, he has no energy. He looks up. It's right there. But fuck it all if you can't even move when you're in this state. The third stage of hypothermia — his skin no longer even bothering to heat itself, it's just a suit of soggy leather, body conserving what little heat it has left for his brain, for his heart. Wayne probably feels like going to sleep down here — they say that's true. It can only be speculation. He knows what that means but he feels it. Some part of him sees the illusion. It's right there, though.

He can't stand up.

He wants to. He should be able to. Goddamn it, he *should* be able to.

He should be able to go three feet.

He tries again.

He can't.

So he crawls.

He makes it halfway up the hill. And he's not actually sitting up in his last moments with his back against the tree. That had never been right. I invented that. He's facedown. His face is in the snow.

I think of him looking up the hill one last time, using everything he has to look, looking at the cabin his father built. I think of that being what he sees before his eyes close.

His face goes down.

~~~~~

I was at the hospital in Green Bay for three weeks — I'd decided that it didn't matter what hospital I stayed in. And I thought of this image — this image of my cousin's face, his eyes closing just like that — again and again. I dreamed it, I ran it through in my head, I played it back, I ran it through again. It was simple, but there was more. I knew that there was more.

I read a lot.

I read one e-mail over and over again.

There was only one that really mattered. The one my father sent himself the night before he'd gone up with Billingsworth's ashes.

~~~~~

October had come, as had a new chill in the air (or so I heard), and I watched a leaf outside my window lose its green. I watched the Packers on my room's little TV. I surfed. It's amazing what's on the internet. You would never think: college newspapers. All college newspapers, their archives going back deep, going back decades.

Sometimes I set the laptop aside.

I was staring at a tree when I heard a knock on my door, turned, and saw Jeremy standing there, one hand in his pocket. He had something under the other arm.

"Whoa," I said.

"Yeah," he said.

He looked good. His hair was a little longer than he used to keep it. More important, his skin looked like it had for once seen a little sun. More Hawaii, I thought. Like the picture.

"Can I come in?"

"Of course."

He entered the room and held up the box he'd been carrying. It was a cheap chess set, the kind that came in a board-game-size box. He shook it a little and rattled the pieces.

"Found it out in the lobby," he said.

"And you want to play a game to see who gets to have Allie."

He smiled at that, raised his eyebrows. He held up his left hand, and I saw the ring.

"I see," I said. "Too late. Congratulations."

"You have amazing timing with your texts, by the way," he said, setting down the game and sitting in the corner beside my bed. "You apologized to her while she was at her bachelorette party. Which was the night before the wedding."

"That's a coincidence."

"Yeah."

"It was a real apology. For what it's worth."

"No, I know. She thought so too."

"Although maybe a text doesn't count for a full-on real apology," I said. "Yet."

"It's the world. It is what it is. Communication." He smiled. "Give it until about 2015, right? Then texts will have the same authenticity value as every other kind of communication. Still lagging. Slightly."

"Well," I said. "You still sound like a robot."

"So obviously," he said, "we heard about what happened. We were both worried. Obviously."

"Obviously."

"I had a meeting in Chicago this week so I called your parents to find out how you were. They told me you were still up here."

"Here I am."

He nodded again.

"Um, Ben?" he said. "What the hell happened?"

"It's a long, long, very boring story."

"I bet."

"Do you want the short version?"

"If that's what you're offering."

"He was chasing after the girl I was with. I didn't know him."

"No, I know," he said. "The paper had a little."

When I didn't respond, he pointed at the chessboard. "You wanna play? Actually? We don't have to talk. I get it."

"Not really."

I had nothing against him anymore, I really didn't. But I don't know. Not all friendships have to go on forever. Love dies. We can be content with this. I guess the residue of hating somebody with too much energy can never really be flushed from your pipes either.

"Listen," I said. "I'm sorry. About the office. About all of that shit. I wasn't myself."

"It's okay," he said. "I appreciate that, but it's okay. There were . . . unspoken problems. Maybe you were just surfacing them."

"Good God, don't use *surface* like that."

"You know what I mean."

"I was angry. Not even about Allie."

"I know."

There was probably a whole speech folded up inside of me that I could have unfolded right there for him, but I knew he knew what I meant. I knew I didn't have to do it. I could have. But I didn't have to.

"I'll get to it," he said. "Why I'm here. I came to offer you your buyout."

I looked at him, thinking. "When does the game come out?"

"The first of January."

"And how much of this has to do with my parents' lawyers?"

"It's not a competition, Ben. No one has to win or lose. We can both win, if we do it right."

"Is the game even that good?" I asked. "What can a stupid game about puzzles really be worth? It's not like we invented Jenga."

"First of all," he said, "it's not stupid. Second of all, it's not about puzzles. It uses puzzles. But it's more than that. It's about art too. It's about the story. It's an experience. It's about the way it's all put together. People pay for that — for the recombinations. That's what drives the economy now. The *how*, not the what. People pay for that. And the world is changing. They're looking for it in different forms. Novels are boring."

I looked back at my tree.

"Do you see that?" I said, nodding at it.

Jeremy looked.

"Horse chestnut," I said. "Pretty."

"Ben."

"The story's pretty lame, you have to admit," I said. "In the game. The crazy dude and his rivers. I can't believe you guys used that."

"Whatever you say. We liked it."

"I'm not just saying it," I said. "You used the rivers but you used the story it took me five minutes to write. You didn't actually use the puzzle."

"I know," he said. "We couldn't figure it out." He laughed. "We both thought the story was better than the puzzle for that one anyway."

"That's because I forgot to send you the other part."

"What part was that?"

I looked back at him. "I tacked that letter up on the bulletin board," I said. "And there was a number written on the back of a business card I posted next to it. I didn't explain to anyone what it was. Just a number. But you needed it to solve everything. A key that was off the frame."

"What was the number?"

"Do you get it?"

"Do I get what?"

"That the whole puzzle was off the page anyway," I said. "The puzzle was that the puzzle was not where it claimed to be. So it's a lateral puzzle. You know."

"So why didn't you send us the number?" he said. "If it was the actual key to everything?"

"I totally forgot about it."

"Ah."

"Slight error."

"What's the magic number then?"

"Now I forgot that too," I said. "I don't know it."

"Well," he said, shrugging. "It doesn't really matter. We liked the story about the crazy architect and the rivers. So we used it. Either way, it's the same. We used it for the story. Games need stories. Everything needs stories."

"You realize that the only reason I wrote all those," I said, "and sent all of them to her in the mail…you realize I was fucking with you, right? And wasting time? And entertaining people there? And dreaming that I was out of prison and we were back in our little white house, fucking and living?"

"I think you liked making them," he said, "and still wanted to follow through on what we started. Despite yourself."

"I have terrible follow-through."

"And yet you did anyway," he said.

He got up and went toward the door. He had something new to him — not just the tan and the hair. I had been foolish to concentrate on those things. The way he walked was different. The way he talked. He didn't seem so fucking scared of everything anymore. He was a real person. I guess.

"We have a sense of what it's worth already. A lot of smart people have put a lot of resources into it. I mean, we could go a different way — you could sue us for what you think is the right ownership stake, we could spend a few years in court. I'm not intimidated by your family's money and lawyers, if you think that. For every vicious genius there's another vicious genius. You can hire as many as you need. There are people behind us. This is really just the first project for the company."

"All right, Bill Gates," I said. "What's the offer?"

He looked past my bed and at the wall. "It's in the box," he said. "The check. I just wrote it. Fuck it. You know? You have until the first of January to cash it. I'll cancel it after that and assume you're going to litigate. Or do nothing. Feel free to take nothing too."

I looked at the box.

"Can I ask you a question?" I said. "Unrelated."

"Sure."

"Will you look at something for me? I don't even know — hold on." I was digging around my bedside drawer. "I don't even know what it is. Really. And I'm embarrassed to say that I can't figure it out."

He looked at me cautiously. "Okay?" he said.

"This is not me fucking with you."

"Okay."

"I need your help."

"I said okay."

"I think I'm actually blocking it out," I said, "because I don't want to know what it is. It seems like it should be easy. I know what it is and I don't."

I pulled out my notebook and my father's phone and rewrote the text of the e-mail for Jeremy, then twisted the pad and let him see it:

Bw/C⏎
(241d,120p)bx.e⏎
(37d,250p)o⏎
(250d,350p)HUGE w.p.⏎
(200d,120p)w.p.

"Context?" he said, staring at the pad.
"An e-mail a person sent to himself."
Jeremy glanced up. "That's all?"
I nodded.
"Who?"
"It doesn't matter."
"When?"
"When did he send it to himself?"
"As in, under what circumstances?"
"Before he was going somewhere."
"Where?"
I looked at him. "A cabin," I said. "Up north."
Jeremy looked at me for quite some time, then finally scratched his ear and looked back down.
"Did I tell you that Allie and I got a boat?"
"No."
"We have the GPS nav on there and everything, but lately I've just been feeling a little overwhelmed by all the gizmos and tech stuff, and so I've been orienteering instead, which is when you've

got the map and the compass and you're almost pretending like the modern world doesn't even exist, and those things are all you have?"

"Okay."

"So it's a pain in the ass to find the little degree symbol," he said, "when you're texting somebody, using a keyboard, whatever." He shrugged. "So I always just put a *d* there. Like those *d*'s. They're all under three hundred and sixty."

"What do you mean?"

"They could be compass notes," he said. "If you were e-mailing them to yourself. Would you know the degree symbol writing an e-mail? Would you bother finding it? And so instead of a map, though, I'm betting the letters are a stand-in for — I don't know. Buoys, I guess. You know. Markers."

He tapped a finger on the *Bw/C*.

"If that's what it is, it shouldn't even matter what the other letters are. You just need to know whatever Bw/C is. And that's your starting point."

"What about the *p*'s?"

"Distance. How about paces?"

I closed my eyes.

"Paces."

"Sure," he said. "You've got direction, then you need distance. So that's on foot. Find whatever Bw/C is, get a compass, and follow these directions to wherever they lead."

Now I was staring at the pad, thinking.

"Do you know what Bw/C is?" he asked.

I nodded.

"Yeah," I said. "Birch with cross."

16

Truth

Looking across the table on Christmas Eve and seeing my mother and Ben chatting to each other felt like watching Fred Flintstone talk to Jane Jetson: Almost unbearable disharmony, and yet also a forced admonition that, yes, the people you know, and the people you love, don't all live in their own hyperbaric chambers. They can interact. And Ben seemed happy that night, even though he'd spent the afternoon complaining that we had to wake up on Christmas morning, get in the car, and drive to Peregrine Park. When Ben complains it's sometimes hard to understand his comments as complaints, especially if you don't know him well. And for all that had happened between us, and despite the urgency I felt whenever we weren't together — a need to stop whatever I was doing and find him — I didn't know Ben. Not really. I knew that. Not in the way that two people who've known each other for a decade, or five decades, know the expressions that the other person has the ability to make or the meaning of a comment like "Christmas is about wearing a robe until at least noon, so fuck this," before that person goes outside to shovel snow for an hour.

"Shoveling is not what you should be doing," I said to him from the door. "Your body is still broken."

He looked up. I saw that he had his earbuds in his ears. "Huh?"
I motioned for him to pull them out of his ears.

"I said you shouldn't be shoveling. What are you listening to?"

"Yanni."

"What are you listening to?"

"*What Color Is Your Parachute?* audiobook."

"Why are you being like this?"

"It's okay," he said. "I'm okay." He leaned the shovel against the car and waved his arms up and down. "See?" he said. "I work. It all works. I'm healed."

He was like that all day. But by the time we went to my mother's house, he seemed to have relaxed about it, and I watched him talking to Bobby from the other side of the table and felt glad that we were here.

Later, when I was in the kitchen with my mother, she said, "You two seem to be doing well."

As I did know my mother, I understood what this meant.

"We are," I said. "It's good."

I still had my apartment, but she knew that I had been staying with Ben at Denny's house every night. How could I be away from him? I hadn't tried to hide it from her, even though the violence of it all had only made her more wary of him, of me being with him. I would point out that Ben saved me from dying; she'd point out that I never would have been up there in the first place, up at some god-awful cabin that the uncle had tried to get *her* to go to a few times, if it weren't for Ben; I would point out that Will would then have found me in St. Helens, maybe while I was alone.

"And tomorrow, then?" she asked. "His family?"

"We're leaving at eight."

"I did like Dennis," she said, tossing a dish towel onto the counter. "I'm not saying that. But I'll tell you what: I never did like the other one. Ben's father." She crossed her arms.

"Why's that?"

She made a sour face of confirmation. "Just a sense," she said. "I never got a good *sense* of him. He's an opaque man. And Dennis did not like him at all. That I know." She closed her eyes, recalling something.

"Why not."

"He said he was arrogant," my mother said, opening her eyes. "He just always came off as... condescending. He thought he was too good for this place. Superior. Especially toward women. I once was behind him in line at the RadioShack and listened to him just absolutely... *take apart* the poor girl behind the counter, who'd said something to him that he didn't like." She shrugged. "I don't know," she said. "Anyway. Just a sense."

"But you can see that Ben's not like that at all," I said. "Right?"

"I can, actually," she said. "Ben's like Denny. That might be even more worrisome."

"How come?"

She said, "Because Dennis loved women more than anything else in the world. Those ones come with their own problems."

~~~~~

I was worried about Christmas at my parents' house, fine, yes, I will admit it, but I hadn't told Lauren what was actually bothering me and had been bothering me for three months.

Maybe *bothering* isn't quite the right word. Maybe *tearing me apart from the inside out* is a better way to put it.

I hadn't told anyone and had no idea, as we drove south on the barren highway toward Illinois, whether I was even going to say a thing. Or if I did, who I was going to say it *to*. There comes a point when you have to ask: When is it time to stop? Whatever the answer, I knew the time was close.

Windswept snow like dust danced out on the road; Lauren, beside me, was reading a book, something I had never been able to do in a car. These are the small things you learn about a person.

Peregrine Park is at the southwest corner of Chicago-land's glob. *Wealthy* isn't the word — I'll spare you the sociology. To get there, you exit 290 onto 17 and drift for about a half mile through the suburbs' gateway of commerce, places like Home Depot and Target. Ikea. Soon you're deeper in. At the east end of Peregrine Park are the more modest homes. To the west, the mansions. The big mansions.

And then there was my parents' home.

"Well," Lauren said, looking at it from her seat in the parked car. "It's big."

"I know."

"But you never lived here?"

"Not really. I do have a room." They'd moved here when I left for school, and I'd rarely come to stay with my parents.

"Are we allowed to stay in it together?" she asked. "One room?"

"We're in our thirties, Lauren."

"You've met my mom?"

I looked back at the house. "I think it will be okay."

We were out of the car and getting our things when I looked up and saw my sister at the door beside the garage. She was holding her youngest child in her arms. The baby. I'd never met her.

"We can't come out," she said, smiling. She waved. "No boots."

We went to them and I gave Haley a hug, then backed away. "Who's this?" I said. I pinched her toe. But I knew. Her name was Pearl.

Behind Haley, in the house, John was helping their son with his mittens.

We said hello.

~~~~~

We were going to eat dinner early, at 5:00, but it was a few hours before that when I found the right time to ask my mother if I could talk to her.

"What kind of talk?" she said. "Gossip?" She was looking through the cupboards for paprika. At the stove, a woman I didn't know — the new personal chef, whose name, according to my father, was "Misereldina, or something similar to those sounds" — was prepping hens.

"Up in your office, maybe," I said. "Just a few minutes. Some money stuff."

She gave me a slightly concerned look, then took off her apron. She was in here assisting, even though Misereldina seemed to have everything well in hand.

"It's nothing bad," I added. And I thought: What a strange thing for me to say.

"All right," she said. "Let me just get my *eggnog*." Sung.

We climbed the stairs to the second floor, where my mother had her own office. Just like the cooking, there was a redundancy to it all — somewhere there was a team of a dozen financial managers spending hours and hours of their weeks minding my parents' money. They had survived the dot-com bust without so much as a scratch; they'd never been leveraged very aggressively toward technology. And even though the economy, for reasons that went way over my head, was apparently completely fucked up now, and would continue to be for a very long time, as we all now know, there was no doubt in my mind that for my parents, a lengthy recession would end up being at worst an inconvenience and at best an opportunity to make money in some other way. What was it to pause accumulation for a small amount of time? Nothing.

She sat down at her big old oak desk.

I sat at the other side.

"So," she said. "What kind of shady backroom deal are you interested in making?"

"I'm worried about so many Democrats coming into power lately. I'm worried that a communist imam is leading them."

"Oh, he's not so bad," she said. "Obama? At least he's handsome. I was tired of the cowboy routine. And you joke, Ben, but you'd be amazed how many times, at dinners, I've heard someone say the same thing you just said. *Educated* people!"

She mused privately on this for a moment, then said, "Did you vote?"

"No."

"Were you still at the hospital?"

"Mom."

"Oh," she said. "Oh, yes. I'm sorry."

We looked at each other for a few moments.

"You know I settled with Jeremy, right?"

"How could I forget? No need for a contract or anything *insane* like that, correct? No need for any unruly lawyers?"

I reached into my back pocket and took out the folded check. I slid it across the desk to her, and she unfolded it and looked at it where it lay.

"It's for Denny's house," I said. I'd made it out for what they were asking, which came to about a quarter of what Jeremy had given me.

My mother removed her glasses and looked at me. "Ben," she said. "Listen to me. We will *give* you the house if you want the house. That was the whole point. Don't tell me you didn't understand."

"I understood."

"This is unnecessary."

"Don't tear it up," I said. "Wait." Because she had picked it up and was holding it at the center with both thumbs and forefingers.

"It's for the trust too," I said. "The different times you guys paid for rehab. It's for the whole decade. That's just your vig on the decade."

"What's a vig?"

"Your points, Mom. Your compensation. I know it's not even close to what you guys have spent on me. But it's just an . . . I don't know. An acknowledgment."

"Well, then, it's acknowledged."

She again looked like she was going to rip it up, and I reached across and put my hand on her wrist.

"Really," I said. "Don't."

"What else do you think parents want to spend their money on, Benjamin?" she said. "This is exactly what money is *for*. This would be . . ." She shrugged, turning up her hand as she looked for the word. "This would be an arbitrary exchange. It's all the same pool."

"Then we'll shift a bucket of water from one side to the other."

She said nothing, so I went on: "I just need you guys to cash it. For my own peace of mind. You would be helping me."

"Okay. Fine."

She set the check on her desk.

I stood and went to the wall, where my mother had some of the same school photos Denny had on his mantel. My senior picture. Haley's senior picture, in which she was dressed in the Choate uniform. No Wayne.

"I'm proud of what you did," said my mom. "At the cabin. You saved that girl's life."

"She saved mine too."

"You could have run away," she said. "You could have run to the highway, flagged down a car, called the police. Anything."

"No one would have done that," I said, "in that situation."

"You don't think?"

"No." I looked back at the picture of Haley. "People want to help people."

"I'm not so sure," she said. "I think plenty of people would have run away." Then she added, "Running sometimes makes more sense. And I disagree with your statement. Most people are cowards."

"The situation changes it. When you're there."

"I guess I wouldn't know."

"I need to ask you something."

I turned, put a couple of fingers on the top of the desk, trying to think of how to say it. All the plans in my head and all the different versions I'd imagined each disassembled into a worthless little heap with her looking at me.

"You don't have to answer. But I need to ask. There's nothing else I can do but ask."

She continued to look.

"Okay," she said.

"So I'm asking you."

"All right," she said. "Ask."

"Why did Haley really go away to Choate?"

~~~~~

I talked to Ben's dad for a long time, the two of us sitting on the couches in front of the fireplace in what I gathered was the living room. It was a big room, and behind the couches, John and Haley had laid out a brightly colored blanket and scattered a whole toy store's worth of items for the entertainment of their youngest two. Vivian, the older girl, wanted nothing to do with her little brother and sister, and instead she sat in a comfortable-looking chair not far from the Christmas tree, conspicuously reading a book. Earlier I'd asked her what she was reading, and she'd held it up for me to see. *The Trumpet of the Swan*, by E. B. White.

She said, "I've read it before. This is my third time reading it."

"That's a lot of times," I said. "Sometimes I do that too."

"What book?"

"There was one called *Bridge to Terabithia*," I said.

"I'm not allowed to read that yet," she said. "My mom says I have to be eight to read that."

Haley, overhearing this, looked at me over her shoulder and said, "When she's nine we're going to give her *Fear of Flying*."

Here's what I thought as I talked to Ben's dad: This man is lovely. He asked me about myself, he listened when I spoke. He told a funny story. We talked about an article we'd both read in *Harper's* about Darfur. I told him a little about the camp I'd been at. He said a few pointed and intelligent things. So much of that camp was gone from my mind. It was so easy for it to be gone, me sitting here.

It made me wonder about what my mother had said the day before, her description of Ben's dad as unbearable. He was not. What he was was confident and at peace with himself. He was a man with self-possession. And it occurred to me just how blind my mother was, at least when it came to her sense of other people. Maybe just her sense of men. Her human radar was broken. She couldn't see them well; she misinterpreted parts of what they were, the meaning of things they said. Willfully or not. She was credulous at the wrong times and skeptical at the wrong times. She had to be if she had fallen in love with my father.

I thought of Will then. Talking in Barcelona. Talking me into Zurich.

I was like her. But I was different.

John, Haley's husband, sat down beside Jack on the couch and asked me whether I was still thinking about becoming a veterinarian.

I looked at him and smiled. I imagined him sitting in the car in St. Louis. "No," I said. "I gave that up, I think."

He asked me why and I said, "It was more than a whim, but it wasn't quite real either."

"You know, there's something smart about that," Jack said. "You need to drift a little in other directions. Some wandering. Just so you don't end up despising the path that ultimately feels right."

"Here's to the prodigal son then," John said, holding up his eggnog. "And daughter."

"Did you do that?" I asked Jack. "Drift?"

"Yes and no," he said. "Once we were married, I knew my fate was to one day work at her father's company. Corporations of that size are . . . they tend to act a little like black holes. It's only a matter of time before they pull you in." He looked at the fire. "But I did hold out for almost twenty years. Steering my dinghy around the edge of the vortex as long as I could."

"You mean staying in St. Helens?"

"That's right," he said. "Hometown holdout."

He seemed proud of it, even though I found his metaphor odd.

Ben came down after a half hour. He went straight to the fire and dropped a few sheets of paper into the flames, then came over and sat down beside me on the couch. "Hey."

"What was that?"

"My old report cards," he said. "I'm getting rid of anything you might find in this house that could humiliate me."

"You'll have to get rid of us then," said Jack. "Consider burning down the whole joint."

Ben looked at his father for a moment, and I thought I could see anger in his eyes.

He turned to John.

"What's up, John?" he said. "What's new at work?"

John turned to look at Ben, trying to understand what he meant, exactly. This was very complicated. Everyone knew. Brothers, sisters, husbands. Defense. Ben held his gaze. When he first said it, I had thought he was prodding John, trying to push his buttons. But when I looked at Ben again I realized he was actually just asking. Or at least seemed to be.

We were all there in the room together for the next half hour, talking and playing with Haley's children. Vivian put down her book and began rooting through a chest in the corner, pulling out the well-used cardboard boxes of board games, digging for the one she wanted. Eventually she sat up, holding a rectangular box above her head. It was Jenga. She turned to look at her mother. "Can we play?"

"Sure, honey," Haley said.

"And I am going to get things going on the grill," said Jack, slapping his thighs, then standing.

He turned to Ben's mom, who'd come quietly into the room.

"Is the timing right?"

She nodded. She looked like a ghost.

"I'll come out there with you," Ben said, also standing, not looking at his mother.

"But you're the reigning champion," Haley said. "You're the big kahuna. We want to take you down."

Ben nodded toward me. "She can play in my stead," he said. "She knows how to do surgery."

~~~~~

Here is something.

It's later that evening, after dinner, and Justin is in his pajamas but is refusing to go to bed. I am coming down the stairs and Haley is upstairs in one of the guest bedrooms, feeding Pearl, and I turn the corner, hand on the railing, and see Lauren and Justin at the bottom of the stairs, smiling up at me.

"Justin has a joke he'd like to show you," Lauren says.

Justin, hands behind his back, can hardly contain himself.

"Okay," I say. "Show me."

Giggling, Justin slowly reveals what he's hiding. He holds up an orange box of Uncle Ben's rice and begins laughing hysterically.

Hardly able to speak, doubling over as he tries to hold up the box, he says, "Uncle Ben! *You're* Uncle Ben!"

He cannot stop laughing.

Lauren says: "It's your rice. Get it?"

~~~~~

After all that, we'd forgotten to spread Denny's ashes. Okay, maybe not forgotten; I suppose there wasn't much of an opportunity the first time around, and what's more, I'd never really felt as though spreading ashes mattered one way or the other, as Denny was gone already and I find such things to be sentimental and meaningless. Not everyone in my family agreed with this dismissal, though, and so I went back up in the late spring, alone, at the end of May, when I was sure the weather would be nice and after Grant had already gone up once to clean what he could clean. Which was not too different, I told him, than how I'd first shown up at my uncle's house. A cleaner.

"Consider it your wedding present," he'd said.

This was one afternoon in February, my first winter back in more than a decade, and I was remembering just how bad it could get.

"I'll go up there when it gets a little warmer and clear some of that shit out. You don't want to see that place like you left it." We were at the bowling alley.

I said, "We're not married yet," standing near the ball return, waiting for my ball to roll out of the hole. My hand hovered there, fingers already in their claw shape. But I'd turned to him to say it, and right when I had, my ball had popped out and knocked against my knuckles.

"Fine," he said from the scorer's table. "You're gonna get married eventually, right? An advance, then. Say it however you want it."

"That's nice of you, thank you," I said. "I've been dreading that, actually."

"I clean up blood all the time. I immerse my hands in flesh for a living. Fuck it."

"There's probably not any flesh."

"No. But there's probably blood."

"If you go down to the boathouse, be careful," I said. "The door sticks."

"I thought you burned that down."

"Oh yeah," I said. "I did."

I turned and rolled a seven.

In May I drove north, this time neither pursued nor running, this time in the spring. I left early and didn't need to stop along the way. I got there at night and had a bonfire out back. First things first: I cut up the table with a chain saw and burned it.

Watching the flames, I felt some indignant streak in me resisting the idea that since this cabin was a place where bad things had happened, where pain had been felt, it was no longer a place I could love. That did not fit with my sense of the world, which had been coalescing for a long time. Maybe that was the single, simple thing. Maybe that could be the centerpiece to which all things connected. If anything, it meant that I should love it more. I suppose I had come to believe the opposite of what *moving on* implied: there is no actual flight from history, and trying to eliminate it does nothing but increase the speed at which it chases you. And this held true in all cases, always. This was a true thing, one of only a handful that I had. There were true things. Just not many. And we all should link ourselves to the few true things we find when we're alone. The alternative is a terrible mess.

I wanted the land and the cabin. I didn't want to sell it. And I did not want to pretend that the past was not the past. I wanted all of that.

My first time back, May of 2009, when I finally spread my uncle's ashes in the river, was two years ago.

The next morning, after the fire, I went and found the tree. Again. But this time by a different route.

I will tell you, though: I sometimes still think of myself as having died on the floor during our encounter with Will, Lauren straining against the plastic tie to help me. I also sometimes think of myself running away when I had the opportunity, stumbling headlong toward the highway in desperation, my mother's version; or floating down the river, facedown, knocked out too long to even help myself, let alone Lauren, just before knowing any of it. There are many versions. And those are just the versions that have to do with me.

Before that Christmas, after so long lying, thinking, guessing, there were versions in my head that went beyond nightmares but which now stay alive only because of their audacity. I admit that I spent some time wondering whether my sister and Wayne had let themselves fall in love with each other, let go for the amazing risk of it. That the transgression was their thing. Or maybe not love at all. Maybe simpler, with no romance to it whatsoever, some underbelly of lust most people don't explore but one that intrigued them both. Maybe, I thought, when my sister went to Madison to stay with Wayne, they got back from that party and fell into bed together, and it was platonic until it wasn't. These things — these things do happen. They happen and we don't know. They happen, sometimes we find out, the family starts the long process of trying to forget. That's what happens.

Darker, worse, this nightmare for a time worried me too: our parents. Wayne's mom with my father, perhaps, making Wayne and Haley half siblings. Denny and my mom with the same result, my father having signed off on the transaction. Or more, why not more? Denny and my mother giving in only later, after Haley and Wayne were both born, making me the odd one out, the half sibling to both.

None of these versions are true, is what I'm saying.

I considered them, and I did not think of them as impossible, but they're not true.

None of these versions would have brought Wayne up to the cabin in the absolute dead of winter. None of those would have made that make good sense. I had figured out the *what*. But what about the *why*?

That kept bugging me.

~~~~~

But say it's 1994.

Say it's January 1994. I'm a few months away from graduating high school. Haley's a sophomore at Yale, Wayne's about to finish at Madison. He's already sent off a few applications to grad school and is waiting to hear back. He's coasting through his final year.

It's a Thursday night. Wayne's sitting at a bar. Say it's Nick's.

Say it's Thursday, January 20.

Say a man walks into the bar.

He sits down at a booth with a girl. Say the man looks to be around twenty-five, too old to be an undergraduate. (Because he's not — he's a fourth-year grad student in chemistry named Michael Haverstead.) He's on a date. The girl is some undergrad who doesn't matter in the story — maybe she's not even there, and Michael Haverstead sits down at the bar alone. Maybe he even walks by the windows, and Wayne happens to be looking out. Or vice versa.

What matters is that Wayne recognizes him.

There's something about the way he holds himself — you can see it in his posture, in his frame, and somehow Wayne knows right away, there's something he recognizes, even though he starts looking for more evidence. (This is why I don't think Michael Haverstead walked by the window. I think Wayne probably heard his voice, and that was the real verification. But it's also possible that there wasn't a sole chance encounter late in Wayne's time at school and that he'd known since Halloween of freshman year who he was, found out right away, had known his name, had been planning and waiting almost since the moment it had happened. Planning with the patience of geologic time. On principle, and with the destructive patience of a glacier.)

Imagine that house party.

Halloween.

The way Wayne told the story, after becoming concerned for her, he went around from room to room until he found Haley down in the basement, dancing a little too close to a beefy George Washington, one red cup in her hand, arm around his waist with the other, cheerleader skirt so short that Wayne could see, when she twisted, her turquoise panties, the two of them making out some, and Wayne, relieved that he had found her, took her arm and led her upstairs.

They left the party, Haley so furious that she walked in front of him part of the way home and wouldn't speak to him until the next morning.

It had been easy to take such a story for what it was from my cousin. I was seventeen. Easy to acknowledge it, knowing how my sister was, and move on.

But I got to thinking about those parties, especially after I'd gone to many; I thought about how people are, how men are, where monsters have been imagined from, how everything is, and it occurred to me that it was just as likely that Michael Haverstead raped my sister.

Maybe it was probable.

Whatever the case, three years later, in the dead of winter, Michael Haverstead, fourth-year graduate student, son of Gregory and Susan and brother of Naomi, disappeared from the Madison campus.

Shoop. Vanished.

He wasn't heard from again.

That's because he was dead. He was dead, and his body was buried in Denny's woods. My cousin Wayne killed him and put him there. My cousin Wayne believed he'd raped my sister, and the belief was all that mattered, and my cousin Wayne decided that Michael Haverstead had to pay for what he'd done.

~~~~~

And so that evening, when Lauren and my family began playing Jenga and began stacking blocks, after I'd spoken to my mother, I followed my father out to the barbecue to discuss with him what I already knew was true. One last thing. And then I would have to make a decision.

"Son," he said when he saw that I was behind him at the door.

He propped the door open for me with his shoulder, as he was holding two cutting boards, one of them with the steaks and burgers. "Coming to learn from the master?"

I stepped out onto the layer of snow.

"No. I need to talk to you."

"Can I just quickly tell you beforehand," he said, putting down the cutting boards and scraping at the grill with the brush, "that that young woman is charming? Do you understand what you have on your hands there?"

"I need to talk to you about something serious."

"Oh? Are you finally joining the circus?"

He said it without looking up from the meat, which he was now laying fastidiously across the grill.

"I know," I said.

Then only the sounds of the steaks and the small burgers he was adding. They were for the kids.

"Dad."

"What's that?" he said, not turning. "What do you know?"

He took the tongs from their rack and lifted one steak for a moment, then finally turned to me.

"Wayne killed someone."

His face didn't change.

"His name was Michael Haverstead," I said. "I don't know if you ever actually knew it."

He was silent.

"I found your phone," I said. "I found the e-mail you sent to yourself. With the directions. To the body." He said nothing, so I continued. "That's what you did up there when you went, right? You could care less about the ashes. Deep down you think the same thing as me about that bullshit. Ashes. Whatever. You went up there to make sure that his hiding place was still safe. That no one would ever be able to see, no skulls sticking up out of the dirt. Because you wanted to see whether you could sell the land and be rid of it all and not put yourself at risk. You didn't want to own that land. Ever. But Denny's left it to you. So you're stuck. And you know what's on it. So you need to sell it. But selling is a risk."

He watched me as I said this, then turned back to the grill and looked down at the meat for a long time.

He started poking at the smaller burgers, causing a little flare-up from the grease.

"So what do you want?"

"For you to tell the truth," I said.

"You seem to know it."

"Some of it," I said. "I doubt all of it."

He closed the top of the grill, re-racked the tongs, turned, crossed his arms, and leaned back.

"Neither do I."

"You know a part."

"Why?"

"Why?"

"Yes. Why do you want to know? This part I know?"

"There's a body up there," I said, "Wayne put it up there. Why do you think I want to know? That kid has a family too. It was murder."

"Keep your voice down."

"Because it matters," I said. "And because I thought you'd like to know what happened to Wayne."

He frowned. "How could you know that?"

"I figured it out," I said. "When we were up there. Before Will."

"What happened to him?"

"You first," I said.

"I don't understand your argument. That it matters. Does it? Does it matter for you to know? Do you want to know what your problem has always been, Ben? Since you were a little boy? It's always been the same. You think you can control things once you understand them. You think that's all you have to do. Know something. Then it's as though it won't affect you. You're protected from it."

"Do you understand how insane it is," I said, "that you are giving me fatherly advice right now?"

"It's not. Because these things are obvious. Any adult knows these things. And I ask you again. I want to know why it does not occur to you, in this case, this very complicated situation, with your entire family right inside, why it does not occur to you to let some things alone. Let sleeping dogs lie."

"Because letting it alone doesn't work. Not in this case."

"Why not?"

"Really?"

"Yes, really."

"So I can decide what I'm going to do about the body," I said. "How's that?"

Another long time staring at each other, my father probably thinking through what this might mean.

But he knew. I think a part of him agreed. My father was many things, but he wasn't a criminal. He was a father. He knew, in his heart, what was right. Everyone does.

"Dennis showed up at my office six months ago, down here, early June, and told me that he needed to speak with me. He said he'd taken the train and explained that I needed to drive him back up to Wisconsin, but he wouldn't tell me what it was about before we started to drive. And the first thing he said to me once we were in the car was: 'This is a little tricky, Jack. I gotta ask you something that'll sound strange at first. But you can just say no. And that'll be the end of it. We can drive in silence.'"

(My father doing his amazing impression of my uncle for this story.)

"'Wonderful,' I said to him, because of course this was already irritating and very Denny, and I couldn't for the life of me imagine what he had on his mind. My brother, God rest his soul, had spent most of his life pushing my buttons, and this all felt like another instance of the same. And so I said, 'Ask away,' and he said, 'It's a general question. Say there was a situation,' he began, and he was looking out the window the entire time, he kept licking his lips, that's what I remember, 'a situation wherein someone you knew well — really well — had been hurt pretty bad. But whether or not you ever found out about it might not make a difference. On the surface. Say that that was out there, and you could choose whether or not you knew the details. I mean, before you knew. Would you want to know about it or not want to know about it?' 'What in the fuck does that mean, Denny?' I said to him. Because of course I thought he was talking about himself, I thought he had something he needed to tell me. But I couldn't stand how cryptic he was being. He didn't answer, and so I said, 'Of course I'd want to know. I'd want to know about it.'

"'Even if it had consequences to you,' he said. 'Knowing it. You'd still want to know?'"

"'Yes,' I said. 'I would. And now you can't go back anyway. Now that I know there's something, I have to know.'

"He nodded. He said: 'That's what I thought you'd say. Okay.'

"And so he told me the story in the time it took to drive back to St. Helens. The simple story. He told me that the week before he was found, Wayne had come to stay at the house unannounced and Denny had found him down in the kitchen eating cereal at about two in the morning. He asked him what was going on. Wayne told him everything. He told him that Haley had come to Madison for Halloween when your mother and I were out of town and that he lost her at a party, lost track of her, realized he didn't know where she was. And that he started searching through the house at this party, some big house, and when he couldn't find her he started opening up doors and bursting in on couples in the different bedrooms, and he finally came to the bedroom at the end of the hall and found your sister lying on a bed, unconscious, mostly naked, and found a young, obliterated man there with her, staring dumbly at him, at her...like some...And Wayne broke it up, and left with her, and he carried her over his shoulder all the way across Madison, Benjamin, back to his dorm room, and she came to only once to vomit down his back, and when she woke up the next morning, he asked her if she remembered anything about the night and she said she didn't. And he told her that she'd drunk too much and he'd had to carry her home."

My father let this sit for some time.

"And so a few years passed," he said then, "and Wayne told nobody about this incident involving your sister, until the day when he found him at a bar and became certain that it was him, it was the same kid. And he said that it had been building up in him the whole time, since that day, for years, and a part of him knew that this...that a kind of rage, he said, a kind of whirling, monstrous thing within him had come to life at that moment he opened that door and saw Haley on the bed, saw the man...a storm...and that the time would come eventually that he would have to let it out into the world. He knew all of this immediately. And he decided that the right thing to do was to kill the young man for what he'd done.

"And so Dennis said to him, at this point in the story, '*What did you do?*' And Wayne said, 'He's out in the trunk. I did it. Go look. It's done. He's fucking dead and fuck him.'

"Dennis told me it was the worst moment of his life, hearing his son say that, seeing the look on his face. Because he knew what he meant.

"And this is the tremendous part, Benjamin, this is the part — this is what I find most astounding. He told your uncle Denny, and Denny went and looked in the garage, where Wayne had parked his car. The car was running. Okay? Running. Denny realized what Wayne had done, opened the garage door, killed the engine, popped the trunk. Saw what was in the trunk. Closed the trunk, closed the garage because it was all over already. Wayne had killed him already. He went back in.

"He said he and Wayne screamed at each other in the house. They argued for a long time, Wayne being of the mind that he'd done the right thing, Denny being of the mind that he hadn't. Wayne probably won when he told him that it didn't matter anymore because it was done. He got up and said he was going to finish it. Dennis asked him why he'd even bothered to stop off. Wayne said he needed to get the keys to the cabin anyway, as he'd forgotten his in Madison. And then he walked out and got into the car and drove away. He said he'd be back in a few days.

"And so Denny and I are in my car as he's describing this all to me, and at this moment of the story, Benjamin — can you imagine hearing this story? For the first time? Out of nowhere? I mean, I suppose you are now, but you seemed to have an inkling. Can you imagine hearing it with no inkling? — I find that I'm just blinking over and over again, blinking at about ten times the rate you usually blink, feeling as though I might have a heart attack, truly, and so I pull over in the emergency lane and put on my hazards. I can't describe to you what I felt. Something horrible, something... I saw something, Benjamin. Some chaos that... I don't know. I can't describe it. The storm, this same storm. Just what Wayne had said. And here it was, in me. Only because of what I knew. All I know is that this was the worst moment of *my* life. Because there were two waves to it; there was... Haley" — the word choked out, horrible tears now, I want him to stop, I can't look away from him — "my *girl*, and then there was *what* Wayne had done."

Composure; breath.

"It was too much to take in. I tried. And I found myself ignoring, for the time being, the story about your sister and concentrating instead on the fact that there was a body on my brother's land, and that his son had taken it upon himself to exact revenge, that this whole grand thing had played itself out years ago, under my nose, and my brother had inexplicably done nothing about it all these years, and now I knew about it too. Now I knew. I could never not know. And I said, finally, very quietly, hands still on my steering wheel, 'You should have told me then. You should have told the police. You should have stopped him.' And he said, 'Maybe,' and I said, 'Not maybe.' 'But Jack,' he said, 'I know what you would have said. You would have said let it go. You would have said let sleeping dogs lie.' 'I absolutely would not have.' 'Are you so sure about that? And are you so sure Wayne shouldn't have done what he did?' 'So why tell me now?' 'Because I can't stop thinking about it. Still. And his parents. The kid's parents. Because karma, man. Karma. The same thing happened to Wayne *a couple days later*. I mean, *I* know what it's like to have a son disappear too, but how rough is the universe with *that* shit? And I still don't know what the hell happened to *him*, why he didn't come back. And it's killing me. I don't know what to do, Jack. I didn't know then and I don't know now.' 'What could you do?' 'Go up there. Dig him up.' 'You know where he is?' 'I do.' 'How?' 'Because Wayne did a shit job of burying him like he did a shit job of every task and I went up there and did a better job the next spring. I found him right away. It was easy. So I took him farther and I put a tree over him. I put a tree right on top of him.'

" 'Don't tell me where it is,' I said. 'I don't want to know.'

" 'Fine,' Denny said. 'I'll hold it.'

"I didn't say anything. This was another — it was just another one of those same waves. I didn't know what to think, what to feel. This was well, well, well beyond anything I understood. You can imagine. You know me. But I found myself saying, just before getting home to my house: 'We'll call the police and dig him up. Now.'

"Denny rolled his head back and forth, deliberating. 'I suppose so,' he said.

"But then, of course, Dennis died before we could do anything."

~~~~~

My father stood still, arms crossed, looking at me. He was looking for my surprise, but I wasn't surprised.

"And Wayne?"

"What about Wayne?"

"When did Denny realize he hadn't come back? That something was wrong? Back then?"

He looked down at his shoes, squinting as he calculated,

remembered. "I never asked him about that. About a week later," he said.

I imagined my uncle sitting at the kitchen table in his house, phone against his ear, suddenly beginning to wonder.

"And what do you think happened to him?"

"You said you knew what happened to him," my father said. "So you tell me."

I told him about the rock, about the door. About my guess about Wayne going into the river.

He listened patiently, once turning and opening the grill to mind the meat, then closing it and turning back around.

When I was through he said, "Maybe," nodding.

"What?"

He glanced up at the sky. "Not exactly the Occam's razor version," he said.

"What do you think then?"

"Something simpler than that."

"Like?"

"You realize your cousin was a pathologically depressed drunk, don't you?"

"I didn't know what that was then."

"Of course you didn't," said my father. "You were too young. You thought that youth was an excuse to destroy yourself, which is what our masochistic culture taught you to think. And on top of that, he was good at hiding it. Or better than most. He couldn't hide it from Dennis. My brother. He talked to me about it all the time." He shrugged. "He was drunk when he drove the young man to Denny's house, for Christ's sake. He was...not well. For all those years he was in Madison. There are plenty of stories."

"So what do you think?"

"I think it's simple," he said. "I think people destroy themselves when they hate themselves. That's always the explanation. I think he took him up there, started burying him, realized what he'd done, drank a whole bottle of bourbon, and passed out in the snow. That's it. Nothing more. I think it finally dawned on him that what he had done was demonstrably and obviously evil. And immediately upon understanding that, Wayne, who was fundamentally a good person, realized he could not live with himself."

My father turned again and opened the grill. He began to pick off the steaks and burgers one by one and place them onto the clean cutting board.

"You'll have to lie and tell them that you didn't know what it meant," I said.

"What what meant?"

"The directions. Through the trees. You can tell them that I was the one who figured it out. Just now. At Christmas."

My father stood motionless, holding the cutting board.

"Lie to whom?" he said finally.

"The police," I said. "And everyone else. We have to dig him up."

My father turned.

I said: "You know we have to dig him up."

~~~~

And that May, at the cabin, this conversation having played and played again and again in my mind throughout the drive, the consequences pondered, my father's point of view considered, the images of the different ways it could have happened flashing in with the flames as I stood and watched the bonfire the night before, the images continuing to do so as I lay on the cot inside, I, the next morning, pulled out my copy of my father's directions to himself, directions that had been willed to him by Denny, paced through the woods as they commanded (birch with cross, box elder, oak, HUGE white pine, white pine), followed the trees with my compass, and found myself at a twelve-foot-high young tree, not twenty years old, under which Michael Haverstead was supposedly buried.

I was holding a shovel. I hadn't said anything yet.

I sat down.

It was the same skinny tree I'd seen. The same one that had been out of place.

Imagine roots. Down below, roots running through a set of bones. And I thought to myself: You can always keep trying, Ben. I could dig up this tree right now and see. Or I could choose the other way after all. I could never say or do a thing, and whom would it hurt? For whom would it be easier? And regarding Wayne and what happened on the hill, in order to know more: I could search the woods for broken shards of the bourbon bottle, assuming that he'd finished it and thrown it into the woods before sitting down in the snow, because if my father's guess was true, where was the bottle? Or: I could search the bottom of the river for the keys he must have been trying to use on the door that night as he yanked, because wouldn't they have flown through the air when the door came unstuck? Landed on the ice? And then, after the ice melted, would they not have sunk down? If my version was true, were they not down there? I could do more.

But there comes a point when you don't know fully, but you know enough.

Lauren had found my father's phone inside the cabin, sitting on the countertop. It hadn't fallen out of his pocket; rather, he'd left it there. On purpose? To be found?

No, not quite that.

But there are mistakes, and there are mistakes.

That was a printout from the *Daily Cardinal* that I'd burned in the fire on Christmas, by the way — it was an article about how the police were looking for a grad student named Michael Haverstead who'd last been seen by his roommate at the McDonald's on Park Street. There was a photo of him staring stone-faced at the camera. Student ID. And not twenty feet away from me as it burned, there was Haley, victim of the disappeared man's failure as a human being. She was playing with her kids, kids she hoped to escort into adulthood in a way that would prevent them from ever being like, or falling prey to someone like, the man on the burning paper. She was a grown woman.

I hadn't shown the article to my mother in the end, nor had I said anything to her about what I thought Wayne had done to Michael, and why Wayne had been up north that week. I was not as convinced then as I was after hearing my father's story, and besides, the question I had asked her about Haley's choice to move away had noticeably shaken her. Enough for me to know that she knew *something*, which meant that Haley, contrary to what my father's version implied, also knew what had happened to her. Or suspected. Of course she did. It was our fantasy that she did not. The three of them — my mother, my father, and Haley — each knew different shards of the truth. Yet no one really knew the whole thing, which was squid-like and impossible to hold, impossible to see for more than a moment. And life had been balanced like this, like a boulder at the edge of a ravine, held in place by a single stone. Who was I to topple it?

After: They ate the overcooked meat; I made myself a veggie burger. My father told a story about my parents' most recent visit to Italy. But I saw him, now and then, glance in my direction. He hadn't reacted well to what I'd said about the body.

Digging it up.

Not that it mattered.

Later, while Lauren was getting ready for bed, I walked down the hall to one of the many guest bedrooms and knocked on Haley's door.

"Who is it?" Haley said.

"It's Ben," I said. "Can I come in?"

"Only if you're okay with a feeding fiesta," she said.

It took a moment to understand what she meant, but eventually I opened the door. The room was lit only by the moonlight coming in through the south window. Haley sat in the corner, in a rocking chair, holding a swaddled Pearl to her breast.

Her free hand was on a small laptop that was resting on the arm of the chair. Its glow lit her face and she looked up, smiling.

I thought it might make a painting.

"Hey," she said quietly. "Leave the light off. I'm playing your game."

I sat down on the edge of the bed.

"Having fun?"

"I am," she said. "It's pretty. And also: isn't this thing neat?" She held up her laptop. "John gave it to me for Christmas. Tiny, right?"

"Very small."

"How do you beat the waterfall part?"

I stood, leaned over, and looked at her screen, remembering the particular puzzle. Allie had converted it into a painting based on my terrible sketch from two years before. Looking at it like this, I didn't even care about the actual puzzle. Which had always been the goal.

"You have to turn off the flow of the water," I said. "Temporarily."

"How do I do that?"

(A few years later, when she isn't so mad at me anymore, and when she's finally patched things up with John and it has turned out she was right, to some extent, right that she could rebuild a new wigwam of a marriage and be happy within it, they visit St. Helens. Lauren is there, Grant is there — he has a new girlfriend who seems a little young, but nice. We are at the bowling alley. Grant's kid is being babysat along with Haley and John's, and we're just there, there is laughing. It's a life. This is a place. Snowing outside. I think: *There is no force that can destroy all things.*)

"Do you remember that huge rusty spigot thing? From closer to the bridge?"

"Yeah."

"Did you figure out how to turn it?"

"No."

"You have to go back there," I said. "You turn it there. And when you come back here, the water's off and you can get into the cave behind it."

"This is all a little tedious."

"You're the one playing it," I said. I sat back down on the bed. "I know."

"So what's up?" she said, pausing the game and looking up. "Are you having a good time?"

~~~~

It wasn't until that summer, about a year after Lauren and I had pulled into Denny's driveway and only days before they chainsawed down the little white pine and started to dig around the trunk, that Haley and I had the first real conversation. Not that night at Christmas. I couldn't do it then. But summer. In the summer, finally, face-to-face, I said everything and she said what she thought. And yes, it was hard. But nothing was elided. There is no need for that part to be told.

In that dark room I didn't say: *I know what happened to you.*

Or: *I'm sorry.*

Or: *I don't understand it.*

There is a kind of knowledge beyond language. The truth was too big for feelings or concerns, too much of a conversation for a quiet night alone in a quiet room with her and her baby after a day like that day. Despite what I'd said to my father, I didn't know what I was going to do. I didn't really decide until May, when I sat alone in front of the tree, the grave, sat there thinking just as my father had sat there thinking, imagining other parts of the story, like Denny, mourning, after losing his son, coming up to find the sloppy work he'd done and finishing it and living with *that* for almost fifteen years, on top of all the rest, of doing it right under the noses of the police investigating Wayne's death; or Denny, later, deciding that he couldn't hold the story on his own any longer, it had grown too heavy, too much to bear, he wasn't strong enough, and the relief he must have felt upon confessing to my father; or my father's relief upon telling me; or my mother's version of the same; or Haley's — though I know she wishes I hadn't ever dug this up, she has told me as much — and I'd seen the truth plainly, seen it for what it was. There is no answer. And it was as though all of us had been passing burdens to one another in the hope that there was.

Wayne murdered somebody, and the truth had to come out.

It did.

The white pine's roots came up. The bones were there below.

I saw them. That made them real.

I watched men with latex gloves lay them out, one by one, on top of a blue tarp. Until slowly, the shape of a skeleton came together. I saw it and it was real.

Soon after, newspapers.

The story.

The history.
The Haversteads.
The questions.
The discussions.
Everything.

~~~~~~

I left Haley there in the room that Christmas night, checked on Lauren, saw that she was asleep, and went downstairs, feeling the old feeling, knowing I wasn't going to be able to sleep so easily. I once more remembered Pierre Bettencourt and that first night in St. Helens. Six months and the world was different.

Dressed in my winter coat and hat, trudging through the cold down my parents' driveway, I knew this feeling would keep me awake. This restlessness — what was it in me? I had been tied up in a hundred knots and was still tied up in a hundred knots. How else would it be? But my cousin had not been right about his army, at least: I suppose that was a loosening. One more of the handful of true things you can know. Maybe more of a consolation: The past is not the future. There's always what's next.

And bourbon's not the only way to fall asleep either. I looked back at the house. Lauren's window was dark. I wanted to go to bed and lie down beside her. I couldn't think of anything better. Here was a person, here was a good stroke of fortune. Her light was out; she was there. But I knew it was too early. At the end of the driveway, I turned again and looked at the empty road. I would walk the insomnia out of me first. Leave it on the street. Think about the snow. Walk first, and then be done with it. That's what's usually better for the soul.

I picked a way and went.

July 16, 2012

I am at a really nice coffee shop in downtown Chicago.

I don't know its name.

Ben is at the top of a skyscraper.

It's ninety degrees.

I am waiting.

My mother brought Bobby and me to Chicago one summer — the summer we moved to St. Helens, before school started, when both he and I were complaining about the town and sulking about our new lives, friendless. She took us to the planetarium and then the aquarium. We loved both. Everything was better. Moms.

And so this morning at the hotel, when Ben was getting ready for his meeting, I thought of that feeling and I told him through the shower curtain that I was going to see outer space. I told him where he'd be able to find me when he was through — I'd done a long study of the downtown map and had located the ideal coffee-shop location.

"It's called Argo Tea."

"It's like our project," he said from the shower. "From high school."

"What?"

"The space. The outer space. Not Argo Tea."

"Oh, you're right," I said. "It's also space."

I took a cab to the lakeshore, paid my donation, and wandered through the dark tunnels of that place, looking at the cross-section models of planets and stars, learning fusion, trying to land a moon probe with a joystick while a pair of nine-year-olds watched and criticized.

~~~~

That winter and that spring after we'd returned to St. Helens, I went back and forth for a long time about what I was going to do. Ben was distracted in the spring and in the summer after he decided to talk to the police, and I was lonely, I will admit. There were many times when I came close to leaving him; there are stories for all of those moments; life has been life — because he and I both got to know each other, really, and that descent is a different kind of moon landing. It's not a manic weekend. It's not that feeling. It's a different feeling. Both are crucial, I guess. And it took almost a year before the haze of Madison, and Will, had finally lifted and I could look at him and say honestly that I knew Ben now and saw his flaws and loved him and wanted to be with him.

My nose healed; Ben healed; what happened stayed; old nightmares came back, as well as new nightmares, nightmares about Will in that cabin, about what he said to me, about what had happened in Africa, about later. And I was depressed, I think, for that whole first year. I thought of Will often. He was dead, and he had obviously had a psychotic break, I don't know, and no one who recounted the story ever thought about it in sympathetic terms. Clinical? Yes. Figurative? Yes. Just not sympathetic. Not even his family did — I know because they sought me out to apologize for him when Ben was in the hospital. We're sorry our son tried to kill you. We're sorry he wanted to burn you in a bonfire. Ben never talked about him. Nobody did. Nobody talked about how that was not him, not really. How something had fundamentally gone from his mind. How I didn't understand, when it came down to it, where that particular thing *goes* when it goes, and what is left behind, and *what* happened, how one person can become another, how the seeds are in us to be almost anything. Some of the seeds grow. What does that mean?

So I struggled; I didn't go to his funeral. Ben didn't want me to, I didn't want to. But it didn't make sense and I doubt it ever will.

I applied to the Madison vet school after all, despite what I'd told Ben's father at Christmas, and was accepted in the spring. I went back to work for Dr. Hendrix and started taking classes the next fall, and life went forward in spite of all the worries. It did what it does. I finished last month and am taking over the clinic in September. I am happy with this. I am happy with myself.

Ben does work around St. Helens when he can find it. He painted the Jankowitzes' house in May and he retiled Mrs. Kane's bathroom two weeks ago. He also convinced the *St. Helens Beacon* to let him write a column. He is known as "the Puzzler," absurdly, and every week he submits a new riddle that gets published on the back page. They are too hard and nobody ever solves them. Sometimes it seems as though Ben is most satisfied by thinking that they can't be solved. The editor hates him. People submit answers during the week. They pay him twenty dollars for his services and I imagine he'll be fired soon. And meanwhile, he seems indifferent when I point out to him this or that new success Jeremy has had with his company and how the success of the first game, the one Ben helped make, was nothing compared to the cheaper, smaller, simpler, not-beautiful, irritating games that came next, pollinating the feeds of my Facebook page every time I log on to check in with the forty-seven people I know. It's garbage now. Jeremy's company, Jypsum, is in the news all the time. He has become one of those internet people. Looking off into the distance. I believe he and Allie are still together.

Without Ben, the games' content is not good.

I point this out. I say: Look. Hint hint hint. Do something. Ben shrugs. They have not talked, I don't think, since Jeremy came to see him in his hospital room. And here we are, in our lives in St. Helens, having nearly run out of money after my years of school, after Ben's years of doing... well. I worry that he only drifts.

Three weeks ago, down in the basement, I found Wayne's poem and asked Ben why he'd framed it if he was never going to put it up. He told me he'd done it before he knew any of the story, which changed things for him, but as he said it he took the frame from my hands and looked down at the nonsense words for a long time.

I said, "Please, no."

He looked up at me and said, "What?"

"Please don't go down into some rabbit hole now," I said. "Again."

"I won't."

But he didn't put it back in the box.

Instead, he brought it upstairs, and for a few days I would find it out on the kitchen table or on the table in the living room, and beside it, I would find pages of Ben's notes and sketches and guesses about what the poem meant. The grids that he makes. I knew what Ben was thinking, even though I didn't understand the grids. Somewhere in there, somewhere behind those letters, beneath the jumbled mess of text, of disordered information, Wayne was still talking to him, offering an explanation for his actions, detailing his plan, saying what was on his mind, what vision of evil he had seen and couldn't shake. And that would be one more piece to make it all real, or a way for Ben to be haunted less. Of course I suppose it's possible, but I pointed out to Ben that codes didn't really sound like his cousin's way of doing anything. He wouldn't listen. For a week or so. And I started to get scared that Ben was not ever going to stop.

One time he said to me: "Do you think there's any difference between what my cousin did and what I did?" He meant Michael Haverstead and Will.

"Yes," I said. "I do."

He nodded and didn't respond.

What I thought — not that Ben asked — was simple. Just that Wayne was a smart person who was too smart for himself, and that he had the wrong vision of people.

Ben was something else.

Finally, though just last week, he stopped.

I found the poem, still in the frame, in the garbage.

I asked him why it was there.

He looked up from his book.

"It actually doesn't mean anything."

～～～

He is up at the top of the skyscraper talking to lawyers. His parents are up there too. Haley's lawyer is there, but Haley is not, as things between her and Ben are still not right. It's better with his parents now, but only lately. And there are new problems. They are doing the paperwork of death, the paperwork of the future, and they have continued to hold out hope that Ben will have a change of heart about his refusal to take their money as his own once they are both gone. They are in fine health, they say, everything is okay, but Ben's

father has been furious with him since he heard this pronounce-
ment, which Jack must also take as a condemnation. Of course.
After months of arguments between them, and between Ben and
his mother, Ben finally agreed to come to Chicago and to see it all
laid out and listen to what they have to say, at least. I have never in
my life heard of a person trying to hold out against the inheritance
of great wealth, and not just once but twice, and I've told Ben I think
he's in denial about who he is and where he comes from — that there
is something self-righteous and blind about it, something even more
privileged about saying no than saying yes — but yesterday, starting
when we woke up and continuing through the whole drive to Chicago, he kept saying what he's said all along: It's not about being self-
righteous, it's just that all that money would destroy us. That's what it
always does. We have a house, we have a place, we have each other.
Live a simple life; that's all I need. Isn't that what people need?

That's some of what people need, I said.

So I don't know what he will say to me when he comes to get
me here. I don't know what will have happened. Maybe he'll walk
in and say that he changed his mind. Maybe he'll walk in and say
that he didn't. Maybe there will be a third version.

We will be okay, whatever he decides. I can't tell him what
to do.

I don't want to.

~~~~

The easiest way to drive from St. Helens to Chicago is to go east
to Milwaukee and go south from there, but yesterday morning, we
were up early with nothing to do, and Ben suggested we take the
back roads down to Lake Geneva and have lunch by the lake, then
go on to Illinois. I had only been to Lake Geneva once. My mother

always suspected there was something snotty about it. When I told this to Ben, he laughed. "It's nice," he said. "You'll see."

On the drive we listened to the radio. WPR was doing a retrospective about Madison in the sixties — first the protests, then a piece on Sterling. I knew those stories, and Ben said something about the sandwich shop that one of the bombers had owned years later. We started to talk about it, and I asked him if the sandwiches were good, I'm not sure why, but the radio show took an unexpected turn then, and a new piece discussed a murder that had happened near Sterling a year before the bombings. Ben didn't answer me and instead turned up the radio.

We heard about a series of murders that went on all through the seventies. The Capital City Murders, the piece called them. There had been ten in all, all of them in and around Madison, all of the victims young women, stabbing victims. All of them unsolved. Nobody remembered them because the bombing had washed everything else away.

I looked out the window. We were passing a lumberyard, and I looked at the long triangles of lumber stacked up all in a row. The pyramids of the woods.

"What are you going to say to them?" I asked him. "When you're up there?"

"I don't know," he said. "What should I say? Do you know?"

"You should say what you think is the right thing to say."

"I don't know what that is," he said. "I guess I'll see what I say when I'm up there."

We crossed through Kettle Moraine on 12, not talking then, listening to the classical music WPR was playing, and connected to 67. We turned south toward Lake Geneva.

When we were fifteen miles away from it, Ben said, "Is it better to know everything or to know nothing?"

"About what? The past?"

"Yeah," he said. "Or whatever."

I could describe now the long debate, which we'd had before and which extended through the rest of the drive, through our time in Lake Geneva, and for the rest of the way to Chicago, but I think it's easier to just say that there are different ways of looking at it and that different moods push us this way or that way, so we see in different ways, and that the answer to the question, to me, is a moving thing that changes when you try to see it.

I remember a nice moment, though, near the shore of Lake Geneva, down the road from the pier and the strolling people, boats, children, noise. I was sitting on a patch of grass, and Ben was standing closer to the water, looking out, eating one of the saltine-and-peanut-butter sandwiches he had packed for our drive. The sun was out and the water looked inviting. Ben watched a sailboat with an orange and yellow flag.

I leaned back and put my palms in the grass. "So what are you going to do, sailor?" I said. I thought that it was a funny thing to say. And I don't even know what I meant by the question; it could have meant any number of things. I just remember feeling that the world seemed new in that moment, and for once I felt okay.

He put the last of his cracker sandwich into his mouth.

He chewed, looked back out at the water, swallowed, looked at me in the grass.

"I don't know," he said, and he wiped his hand on his shirt. "Something, though."

"What?"

He smiled at this. He thought something was funny. Then he reached to me.

"First let's swim."

Acknowledgments

Thanks kindly: Alexis Jaeger, Ben Warner, Mark Rader, Maggie Vandermeer, Sandor Weisz, Bill Jaeger, Zach Dodson, Ally Burque, Dean Bakopoulos, Reagan Arthur, Brettne Bloom, Tracy Roe, Mike Fowler, Scott Stealey, Daniel Talbot, Scott Robbin, Andrew Huff, Marlena Bittner, Tift Merritt, and Chris Deitch. Thanks (as always) to my family. And thanks much to the MacDowell Colony, where a good deal of this novel was written.

About the Author

PATRICK SOMERVILLE is the author of the story collection *Trouble*, the novel *The Cradle*, and the story collection *The Universe in Miniature in Miniature*. He lives with his wife and son in Chicago.